The Tapestry of Death

The Chronicles of Brother Hermitage

Volume the Third

The Tapestry of Death

Howard *of* Warwick

Published by
The Funny Book Company
Dalton House
60 Windsor Ave
London SW19 2RR
United Kingdom
www.funnybookcompany.com

A catalogue card for this book
is available from the British Library.

Kindle edition ASIN B00E1LP9NM
Paperback ISBN 978-0-9929393-5-9

Cover design by Double Dagger
Original artwork by Adam Fisher
www.fisherart.co.uk
Typeset by Lodestar Books

CONTENTS

Tie, Die

HE BODY OF BRISTON THE WEAVER WAS TIED UP. Definitively, comprehensively, and indubitably tied up. All over. From head to foot, he was bound in close fitting cord; apart from his boots, not a peep of his body was visible. Not that Brother Hermitage wanted any peeps of dead bodies.

Even though he didn't like to disturb the practical details of the world as they passed him by, he could see that someone had done this. It was not the sort of thing anyone could manage to do to themselves. In fact, there was more tying up than body, which raised interesting questions of nomenclature.

The fellow who had summoned him and Wat the Weaver to this gloomy place stood respectfully by the entrance of the canvas mausoleum. Perhaps out of respect for the dead, but more likely because Wat had said, "Move and you're dead" when they entered the tent.

'Not Briston.'

Wat's voice was intense as he looked down on the tied up body.

Hermitage gave his companion a few quiet moments for contemplation while he thought about this. Perhaps it shouldn't be tied up Briston at all. Maybe Bristoned tying up?

The dull light of an oil lamp hanging from the centre of the tent dropped slowly on to a sad scene, somehow made more poignant by being at this early hour of the night. Poor Briston's body had expired with the setting of the January sun, and his soul's journey faced the long darkness of a winter night. The lamp was old and the oil was cheap. The light was not comforting and seemed to press on Wat's drooping shoulders.

'We've been forced to look into two deaths now, Hermitage, and I couldn't have given a hoot about either of them. But Briston?'

Hermitage, still recovering from the rush to get here, didn't have the breath to chide his friend for thinking ill of the departed. Albeit that the particular departed they'd just dealt with had been an old monk due to die anyway, and a rather despicable Norman.*

He also didn't like to interrupt. For once. There was real emotion in the weaver's words. Hermitage relied on Wat as his rock. A firm, steady presence in the face of life's travails. Wat could always find some note of optimism, even when Hermitage's execution was being arranged, usually for the deaths he was actually investigating.

His lungs told him they hadn't been full since they set off at a run from Castle Grosmal, which was only round the corner really. He was still young, even a couple of years younger than Wat, but life had prepared him for mental rather than physical exertion. He saw his appointment as King's Investigator, first by Harold and now by William, as an opportunity for careful thought and analysis. If the job was going to involve a lot of running around, he might have to resign. He imagined resigning from a job King William gave him was quite straightforward. You died then you didn't have to do it anymore. If you weren't old enough for death, or just weren't keen on the idea, you simply carried on.

'We go so far back.' Wat was shaking his head and running his hands over his face. 'And, he was my age.' Wat seemed to find this fact particularly unbearable. 'At twenty-something, you think you'd have a good ten years left at least.'

On their journey, Hermitage had tried to get more information about the victim, about Wat's relationship with him, and about weaving in general. Wat always seemed reluctant to discuss his trade.

---

* The volume entitled The Garderobe of Death will reveal all…

'All will be revealed, Hermitage,' was all Wat would say. 'All,' he added, as if the Book of Revelation was going to be explained. But *that* needed no explanation as it was as clear as day to Hermitage.

'You,' Wat snapped, emerging from his reverie and striding across the tent to the man by the entrance, whom he grasped firmly by the throat. 'What do you know about this?'

Wat gestured to where Briston lay, like some awful caterpillar.

The ex-weaver's tent was the last thing standing from that day's Great Market of Baernodebi, a title so adrift from reality it had floated over the horizon. It may have been great once upon a time, but certainly not in living memory. The truly great markets of Lincoln or Nottingham with their bustling business, bubbling with the raucous energy of a hundred tradesmen, were magnificent places. Still further afield, markets in Norwich or the amazing London were simply dazzling. Exotic goods and people jostled with rich merchants, nobles, and the ordinary man. Even if you had nothing to buy you would go, simply to gawk at the marvels brought to your doorstep.

If you wanted to gawk, you could also go to Baernodebi. You'd want to gawk from a distance, preferably up a hill and most certainly up wind, and if you did gawk close up, it was essential you didn't touch anything. Quite apart from the risk of disease, the merchants were a jealous lot. The slightest hint of a sale would have the purse out of your breeches before you could say, 'Do you mind?'

Hermitage had noted the place was deserted when they arrived. Only Briston's tent remained standing in the small square field surrounded by hovels. If just three hovels can surround anything. True, everyone else had departed with the falling sun, but it had also been the case that Briston was the only trader who had a tent.

'What do you know?' Wat repeated slowly, having had no reply.

Hermitage gently touched his friend's arm and indicated that the man in Wat's grasp was being most effectively throttled and couldn't get a word out. Wat let the man go, but a glare kept him in his place.

'Nothing,' the fellow croaked. 'I just brought you the news. I found him after the market closed. Everyone else had gone, but his tent was still up. I thought he was probably doing business and obviously didn't want to get too close.'

Hermitage frowned at this piece of information. It sounded like some sort of contagion. It was only weaving. Perhaps Briston did business with nobles and well-to-do folk and so couldn't be interrupted. Hermitage remembered the market field and the hovels, and thought it highly unlikely a noble would come anywhere near the place. The Normans had been in the country for months now, ravaging, pillaging, and just plain stealing everything that wasn't nailed down. Even they hadn't touched Baernodebi market, and their standards were remarkably low.

'And, when you *did* get close?' Wat demanded.

'We found him. Like this. All weaved up.'

Hermitage thought this a fine description. It was indeed as if Briston had been woven to death. He squatted at the side of the body and examined the cord, except it wasn't cord or rope. It was tapestry thread, the thin delicate strand from which great beauty sprang. In this case, many strands had been wound to make a thicker binding and the only bits of Briston visible were his boots at the bottom and a clump of hair at the top. They certainly didn't look beautiful.

Most incongruously of all, the colour of the thread was flesh pink.

Hermitage acknowledged that whoever had done this had been very neat. Each pass of cord was precisely laid against the next, and the whole formed a rather agreeable pattern. This body-shaped tapestry was lying on its left side, its face pressed against the wall of the tent. Evenly laid bands ran round and round his legs and on to the torso, clamping the arms to the side. Indented towards the top was a most effective and well-ordered noose, which tightly grasped the man's throat. This continued on around the head until the whole ensemble finished in a masterful knot on top, leaving those few wisps of hair struggling out.

'Weaved up is right,' Wat breathed. 'So you came straight to us in Castle Grosmal?'

The man held out a crumpled piece of pale cream parchment, 'I found this.'

Wat took it while Hermitage looked in wonder. It appeared to be a fine piece of material, ill-used, no doubt, but the quality was visible. Clear writing could be seen, and in a good hand. Wat looked at the thing and handed it to Hermitage, keeping his attention on his captive. The monk reverently turned it over in his hands. It was indeed of high quality, or rather had been some time ago. It had weight and durability. Some of the edges were frayed, but that was to be expected. It had clearly been crumpled and thrust into this fellow's pocket. A thought that gave Hermitage the shivers. He looked at the paper and the writing upon it. This too was old, but completely legible. He read it to himself once and frowned deeply.

'Recipe for the sousing of herring gizzards?' he read out loud, wondering what on earth that had to do with the murder of a weaver.

'The other side,' the man bemoaned.

Hermitage turned the paper over and read more writing. This was in a far less learned hand, but the words were simple.

'If I die,' Hermitage squinted and read out slowly, 'he's misspelled "die", by the way.'

Wat simply glared.

'Sorry. If I die, pass this to Wat the Weaver. He is now at…' Hermitage held the paper some distance from his eyes. 'There's a lot of writing and crossing out. Looks like a list of some sort.'

'It is,' Wat said. 'Just read what's at the end. Not crossed out.'

'Erm,' Hermitage scanned down the document to find something he could make head or tail of. 'Castle Grosmal,' he read out in some wonder. 'How did he know you were there?' He looked further. 'Before that it says De'Ath's Dingle, crossed out. How did he know you were at the monastery?'†

'He was worried,' Wat explained. 'It's a death note. Look.'

Wat released his prisoner with a glare of warning and pulled another piece of parchment from a small pocket in the waistband of his breeches. This was neatly folded and in much better condition. He handed it to Hermitage.

Unfolding it the monk read, 'If I die, pass this to Briston the Weaver, he is currently at… then it's blank?'

'That's because I wasn't worried someone was going to kill me. Briston plainly was. It was an arrangement we had.'

'A rather risky one,' Hermitage observed. 'If the threat of death arrived, you'd hardly have time to find out where your friend was and then write it down.'

'We get threatened all the time,' Wat shrugged. 'You get to know when it's serious. That's when you start keeping tabs on one another. Pick up word from the markets, other travellers, that sort of thing.'

Hermitage shook his head. It was clearly an appalling way to live.

'Wouldn't it be more effective to have a help note?' Hermitage asked. 'One which said "someone is after me, come and help". That way you might not have to actually die before help arrived. Which is a bit extreme, and a bit late, if I may say so.'

'It's just a sort of will, Hermitage,' Wat explained. 'We weren't tending one another like lambs.'

Hermitage didn't find this satisfactory, but Wat clearly didn't want to go into the subject any further.

'Who would threaten you?' he asked instead. 'And what for? I

---

† You can find out why Wat was at the monastery by reading *The Heretics of De'Ath*

don't understand what you could possibly do in the way of weaving that would make someone want to kill you. And all these crossings out,' Hermitage reasoned, 'show that your friend had been under serious threat for some time.'

'He always was a chancer.'

'A chancer?' Hermitage hadn't heard the word before.

'One who takes chances, risks, always on the lookout for big fortune. Perhaps taking some money for something he hadn't done. Passing off work as his own when it might not be. That sort of thing.'

'Ah. Dishonesty, but not you.' Hermitage stated a fact.

'Cautious and steady, me. Always have a fall back.' Wat was reassuring, but he hadn't actually denied being dishonest.

'You've done very well for yourself.' Hermitage acknowledged the fine cut of Wat's clothes and the quality of his boots.

'I have. And when someone wants to kill me, my general approach is to avoid them. Briston's approach was usually to rob them some more.'

'How awful.' Hermitage gazed at the body as these revelations about life in the world were more shocking than those of Saint John at the end of it. 'Still,' he tried to sound positive, 'we've resolved issues such as this before. We've found killers. I'm sure we could do it again.'

'That's the easy bit,' Wat said, standing once more. 'I know who did it.' There was steel in his tone.

'Really?'

Hermitage was impressed. They'd only been in the tent for a few minutes and Wat had already identified the murderer. Hermitage looked around in some intellectual frustration. What clue had he missed? He checked the old parchment in his hand in case Briston had written the name of his killer on it. He held it loosely as he considered the processes required to make a note of a murderer's name while you're being murdered. He considered it unlikely.

'It's a guild execution,' Wat announced.

The man with them, who had been sidling towards the door since getting his throat back, now made a run for it, shouting, 'Assassins, assassins,' all the way back to his hovel where he bolted inside and threw a goatskin over the entrance.

'Let him go,' Wat said as Hermitage started to move after the man. 'He didn't have anything to do with it. I just thought he might have seen something.'

Hermitage returned to Wat's side and they looked down on Briston's woven resting place.

'It's called the Tapestry of Death,' Wat explained.

Hermitage thought this was a fine expression, but no explanation. He turned his head to his friend and raised eyebrows in question.

'It's the ritual of execution for those who breach the code of the guild.' Wat was sombre and serious. 'There's an awful lot of ritual in the guild. Books and books of the stuff, but this is the end of it all.'

Hermitage nodded sagely. Then he had some thoughts.

'Weavers?' he said, incredulity creeping into his voice.

'Yes,' Wat snapped back.

'The guild of weavers executes people?' The incredulity had gone up a notch and had been joined by an undertone of mocking.

'A significant body,' Wat insisted.

'Oh absolutely,' Hermitage agreed, not wanting to offend his friend. 'Maintain the standards of the craft. Ensure the proper training and appointment of apprentices. Let prospective customers know that their weaver is a man of quality. Perhaps even see off those of inferior workmanship, or expel people in extremis. But execution?' Hermitage found it hard to believe that the guild of weavers had an office of murderers. 'I mean,' he went on, 'it's a bit strict, isn't it?'

'Only in the most extreme cases, obviously.' Wat was rather defensive.

Hermitage was still on his train of thought, 'Guild of murderers I could understand, if there is one. Certain chivalric orders, perhaps? They might have to kill their own members. But for a bit of mucking people about and being a, what was it, chancer?'

'It's more than that,' Wat insisted. 'Much, much more than that.'

Hermitage thought hard, but couldn't imagine what more a weaver would have to do to justify execution.

'Did Briston kill someone in the guild?' he asked. It was the only thing he could think of.

'No, of course not,' Wat answered. 'Don't be ridiculous! We're weavers.'

'But you just said…' Hermitage began, puzzled that Wat had just described the self-same weavers as a desperate band of killers.

'It was Briston's subject matter.'

Hermitage struggled to get his head round this. 'You mean he was executed for what he created tapestries of?'

'Exactly.'

'Good heavens. Must be pretty unique for this to happen to you.'

'Believe me, it was. Even though I know it was the guild, there are still questions. Someone actually wove the Tapestry of Death on to poor Briston and there aren't many who can. I want him first.'

'Ah,' Hermitage didn't like the sound of that. Wat's tone wasn't of a man who wanted to resolve an intellectual puzzle. It was the tone of a man who wanted to hit things. If there was a *first*, there would probably be a *second*.

'Then there's the guild master who ordered it done. He's second on my list.'

Now there was a list.

'You have a list,' Hermitage tried to sound supportive, but it came out as a bit of a squeak.

15

'And there could be a third man.'

'Another one?' Hermitage was concerned that this list was quite long.

'It's possible someone asked the guild to do it.'

'Ah,' Hermitage was hoping the list would come to an end soon.

'Unless there was some sort of group,' Wat speculated. 'A number of the aggrieved getting together and deciding to take action.'

'Let's stick with two for now, shall we?' Hermitage offered.

Wat nodded a sombre acknowledgement, 'One at time,' he mused, 'one at a time.'

'That's the spirit.'

Hermitage knelt once more at Briston's side and laid a hand on the man's head in blessing. As he touched the large topknot, the body overbalanced and rolled on to its back.

Wat nodded as the whole structure was revealed, 'Definitely guild work.'

Hermitage looked at the head of Briston as the covered face was presented.

'Ah,' he said in some interest at what he saw. 'Erm,' he didn't like to ask the next question of Wat. He didn't know if it was going to be blindingly stupid or blindingly clever. Perhaps this was part of a standard weavers' guild assassination. 'Is he, erm, supposed to have blood all over him?'

Wat peered down at the forehead area, which had a large and intense red stain all over it. Whether the figure had been bound and then hit or hit and then bound was difficult to tell. It also didn't matter very much. Certainly not to Briston.

'Ah,' Wat said, rubbing his chin. 'Now that's not in the ritual. Death by tapestry. Not death by being hit on the head.'

'So, not the guild?'

'Still the guild. No one else can do this kind of tapestry work.'

'Are you sure?' Hermitage thought it a bit of an assumption to make.

Wat gestured at the complex woven structure, 'Who else would bother?' he asked.

'I suppose so.' Hermitage could see it would need a lot of training and practice to produce something like this. Not the sort of thing anyone would do as a pastime.

Wat was thoughtful, 'This only doubles the force of my promise.' He came to some sort of conclusion.

'Promise?'

Hermitage hadn't heard any promise. Wat had promised a couple of things to the peasant who brought them here, but Hermitage thought them inappropriate at the time. They were certainly not relevant now. What else could the weaver be talking about? He rubbed the death note between his fingers and thought. The old familiar sinking feeling descended on his stomach. 'These notes?' he asked with a slight tremor.

'They were promises,' Wat said. 'Promises that if either of us died and left the death note, the other would avenge.'

'Oh.' Hermitage didn't like the sound of that at all. He noticed Wat's fists were tightly clenched. Another alarming sign. Investigating he could do. Well, he could do it now. Well, he'd done it twice and neither time had actually resulted in his own execution. Although both came close. Avenging sounded much more dangerous.

'Avenge by bringing to justice, perhaps?' he offered in place of the image of avenging that had sprung into his mind. This involved running around with swords and getting in fights, all of which he lost.

'No,' Wat snarled, 'avenging by hunting down the men who did this. The guild master who invoked the ritual and ordered Briston's death and the paid killer who did it. I'll get them if it takes the last of my breath, and I will dispense the only justice possible.'

'Ah,' Hermitage said, 'hunting down a professional killer then. Marvellous.

17

Guild Goings-on

ITUAL. DARKNESS. FIRE.

There wasn't a move the figures in the stone chamber could make that was not governed by arcane ritual. This was beyond important. It was life itself. It was written, it was controlled, and it was a spiritual necessity. It was also a practical one, as the darkness meant that if you didn't follow the ritual, you would probably bump into something sharp. The fire was mostly for effect as it illuminated virtually nothing. Its effect was very good. It cast shadows that could scare the colour off a cockerel.

The chamber of the weaver's guild in Scunthorpe was vast. Or so it seemed to those standing in the darkness, frightened by the fire. The head of the long room was flanked by six sentinel stone columns. Aligned with a huge door was a dais that seemed born aloft by strategically placed torches. Upon the dais was a chair. Upon the chair upon the dais was a figure, dark and cowled. Its forearms dangled over the sides of the chair, which was more like a throne. They rested the way kings rest their arms on thrones. Like the chair should be grateful.

'Approach,' the figure growled.

The man at the end of the room took his first ritual steps in the darkness and was assailed by fire and voice. There was a count of three between each pace. When he came parallel with the first column, he stopped.

'The column of the sheep,' he intoned and bowed.

'Approach,' the figure on the dais growled again, this time it concluded with a short cough as some of the ritual smoke from the ritual fires got up its nose.

The man took more steps.

'The column of the shearing,' he intoned.

The ritual was repeated and he advanced three steps at a time.

The columns of the carding, the spinning, and the dyeing were passed. He dare not pass the column of weaving. He knew his place.

After a silence just long enough to make the man wonder if the figure had nodded off, it spoke.

'The ritual of weaving,' it rasped.

'The weaving is woven.'

The man bowed as he spoke the proscribed words. He made the necessary gestures with his arms, a loose interpretation of weaving, and cast a short length of pink thread between himself and the dais.

He almost jumped back as a shape detached itself from the back of the chair and came forward to whisper in the ear of the seated figure. Even in the dark it was clear this new arrival was ancient. It was bent double and shuffled across the floor, clearly unable to take actual steps. Whether it was man or woman was impossible to tell, and not very pleasant to speculate about. It wore only rags, but an awful lot of them, piled one layer on top of another. The whole ensemble melded with the long grey hair that hung from the head and almost made it to the floor.

'The Hoofhorn,' the man breathed to himself. 'What the hell is the keeper of ritual doing in this God-forsaken outpost?'

The man's muttering was alarmed, as if carefully prepared plans had been disturbed. Everyone knew what The Hoofhorn could do to you.

'Too far,' the cowl on the dais snapped, having listened to the definitively ragged whispering shape.

The man abandoned ritual for a moment and hopping forward, moved the thread a couple of feet back from where it had landed. Much closer to the required distance.

The figure took more advice. 'Better,' it snapped.

'Beg pardon, I'm sure,' the man grumbled under his breath as he stepped back, fear of the ritual being elbowed aside by a natural rebelliousness at apparently pointless instructions.

After a brief exchange between the occupier of the chair and the mysterious Hoofhorn, the coagulation of rags and hair skipped down from the dais with remarkable agility.

'The ritual calls for release,' The Hoofhorn announced in a voice sounding alarmingly like a bleat. It made releasing sorts of movements with its arms, raising its hands to the sky. The sleeves of the rags fell from the wrists, revealing the arms of The Hoofhorn in the flickering firelight.

The man gasped. The arms were woven. He shook his head in the gloom as he realised it was tattoos. Good tattoos, and coloured to look exactly like a woven arm. They must have been pretty impressive when The Hoofhorn was young, if The Hoofhorn ever was young. Impressive, and very painful to get done. Now though, the sagging flesh of the arms gave the tattoos a wrinkled and distorted appearance, which detracted rather from their effect.

> *The ritual of release*
> *From the cauldron of the boiling fleece,*

The Hoofhorn bleated a slightly sing-song rhyme. It was the sort of not-quite singing tone used by all bards when they're trying to convince an audience their awful rhymes are masterpieces.

> *As one who was of the guild*
> *Has been released from this world*
> *By the ritual of weaving,*
> *So a release of doves*
> *From the copper cauldron*
> *Of the boiling fleece must be proceeding.*

Even The Hoofhorn seemed to have doubts about this atrocious verse.

'Open the cauldron,' The Hoofhorn's command rang out.

The man looked confused.

'Well, do it then,' the voice from the dais was tetchy.

The man took the ritual step forward, shrugging at the order. The shrug was not part of the ritual. The Hoofhorn noticed this sacrilege and hopped over to smack the man on the head with the ritual sheep's bladder on a stick. The victim raised his eyebrows to the ceiling in a most disrespectful manner. He did flinch at having The Hoofhorn so close though. Fear of the ritual was ingrained in him. Fear of fleas was just natural.

The great copper cauldron of the boiling fleece was off to the right between the columns of dyeing and weaving. It stood on a three-legged iron stand and was big enough for the man to climb in and close the lid behind him. The edge of the cauldron was at head height and getting the lid off really needed a ladder. The whole thing was polished to a fearsome shine. Polished by someone who knew their ritual and did it properly.

The cauldron distorted and reflected the scene in the room. Rounded flames flickered back from its surface and dark shadows of the man and The Hoofhorn stuttered across the columns.

The man leaned forwards, stretched up over the sides of the cauldron, and grasped the lid.

'Not like that, not like that,' The Hoofhorn snapped. 'Like this,' the ragged creature demonstrated by skipping around the cauldron. He held one hand over the lid until he had circled it three times. He then mimed leaning forward, bowing, and lifting the lid, skipping smartly backwards once he had done so.

'You are joking,' the man of rapidly diminishing awe responded.

'The ritual,' The Hoofhorn screamed into the room with outrage.

21

'The ritual,' the figure on the dais repeated, insistent, but with less genuine enthusiasm.

The man sighed the sigh of all men who have been told that the perfectly satisfactory job they've just done wasn't good enough and will have to be done again. He held his hand over the lid and walked ploddingly round the cauldron.

'Skip, skip,' The Hoofhorn insisted, smacking the man's knees with the sheep bladder.

The man skipped, just the once. It was a skip of little commitment.

'We will have to consider your place in the guild once our night's ritual is complete,' The Hoofhorn threatened.

'Please,' the man muttered, 'see if you can find anyone else who'll do the sort of things you want done.'

The Hoofhorn did not seem to hear. He gestured with his bladder stick that the revolutions were complete and the man could remove the lid. The man did so. More in the manner of taking the lid off a pot of rancid stew than the ritual cauldron of the boiling fleece.

'Where are the doves?' the figure on the dais called out when nothing emerged from the open cauldron.

The Hoofhorn was dumbstruck. But not so dumbstruck that he couldn't make bleating noises. They were incoherent though. Unless perhaps you were a sheep. Or another Hoofhorn. It waved its bladder round and round in the air, as if trying to conjure the doves from the cauldron through mystical movement alone.

The un-awed man stepped forward, stood on tiptoe, and peered over the edge of the cauldron.

'Ah,' he said.

'What?' the figure on the dais asked.

'Erm, how long have these birds been in 'ere?' he asked with a wrinkling of his nose.

'The ritual period,' The Hoofhorn replied.

'I think you might want to check the ritual,' the man responded, reverently putting the lid back in place with a grimace.

'The ritual is complete,' the voice from the dais stated.

'But the doves,' The Hoofhorn complained.

'Let's take the doves as dead,' the dais instructed.

The Hoofhorn's head bowed in thought. 'We should invoke the thirty nights of naked cleansing.'

'Let's not.' The dais was very clear on this.

The Hoofhorn shrugged and wandered into the darkness mumbling about heretics and tradition.

'Now that's out of the way,' the dais was matter of fact, 'you were not disturbed in your task?'

'Nah.'

'And, the work in question?' A hand emerged from the sleeve that dangled over the arm of the throne upon the dais. It wanted something.

The man sucked his breath through his teeth in the confident manner of a tradesman who has his customer exactly where he wants them.

'Where is the work?' Each word was growled clearly. It was also illuminated with individual tones of threat.

'Safe,' the man assured.

'I think not. Safe would be in my hand in the next minute. Safe for the tapestry, safe for me, safe for you.' The threat stopped being illuminated; it was now in the room and ready for action.

'You wanted the work out of circulation and it is. That's safe for me. If I handed it to you, I might find *I* was suddenly in harm's way. You know, all trace of the tapestry and anyone who's seen it?' The man made a slicing movement across his throat, and accompanied it with a noise imitating someone having a slicing movement made across their throat with something sharp that made all the blood come out.

'My dear fellow,' the dais wheedled.

'Yes, I am, aren't I?' The fellow now held out *his* hand.

'I see we are at an impasse.'

'A what?'

'I have the rest of your money and you have my entire tapestry. I feel no urge to complete our trade when the goods have not been delivered.'

'Perhaps I could just complete the half of the transaction that results in me getting the money, in return for keeping the tapestry safe,' the man proposed as he drew a significant dagger from his belt. He took a profoundly un-ritualistic step towards the dais.

'Hoofhorn,' the dais called.

'Oh please,' the man scoffed.

He stopped scoffing when The Hoofhorn appeared.

'The ritual of the piercing,' The Hoofhorn bleated with glee as it emerged from the darkness hefting a pretty mighty looking sword. Hefting it with considerable alacrity and skill for an apparently ancient and decrepit loon. He whooped the thing around his head and stepped down from the dais.

The man turned to check his escape route.

'Right,' he said, pointing the finger people point at their enemy when they're about to run away, 'keep your money. I'll keep the tapestry.'

'No, you won't,' the cowl on the dais said with disturbing confidence. 'Hoofhorn, get the tapestry and kill the man.'

'Oh, by the way,' the man said as he backed quickly towards the door.

'What?'

'I lied. I wasn't disturbed, but a message got out. Help was sent for.'

'Who could help?' The dais laughed the traditional laugh of the evil doer in total control.

'Wat the Weaver,' the man announced as he turned and ran.

'Noooo.' The scream of anguish from the dais followed the man as he turned and ran from the room. Even the bleats of The Hoofhorn seemed raised to a new and unearthly pitch.

Caput III

Tapestries Revealed and Revealing

IDON'T SEE ANYTHING HERE that would justify execution.'

Hermitage gestured to the three sides of Briston's tent supporting some tapestries. It was a fairly large affair – well maintained and well assembled. It was tall enough for a large man to enter and stand without bending much at all and wide enough for Briston to entertain at least two full-size customers at the same time. It was furnished with two high-quality camp chairs, totally inappropriate for a place like Baernodebi.

Briston's final resting place was against the back wall. At his feet, leather cases and tubes were stacked, doubtless storage for the products of his craft. Most incongruously of all, the sides of the tent were hung with fine tapestry, as if they were the walls of a great manor. Except when Hermitage looked closely, they weren't really that fine. Some of the thread had pulled from the scenes and the colours were faded and bland. The edges were ragged, and two or three of them had started to curl up. Hermitage's nose wrinkled as he leaned close to one scene, overpowered by the reek of mildew.

'Just samples,' Wat explained as he saw Hermitage's disappointed expression. 'The good stuff will be in the boxes.' He gestured to the pile of packing stacked against one wall.

The works on display were all standard scenes. The first was that old familiar, some maidens lounging in a garden, apparently completely content that there was a small dragon nibbling the roses. The second would be for the male customer. A knight on horseback, the horse's face being the more intelligent of the two. Finally the scene of aspiration. A large figure off to one side, gazing out in command across a valley, which was probably his little kingdom. Hermitage peered more closely and could make out tiny figures in the valley carrying out their daily tasks – harvesting the corn, building a bonfire, putting the witch on top. Hermitage reviewed his judgement. These were good pieces. Or rather, they had been some time ago.

'All very normal.' Hermitage turned to Wat and shrugged.

The weaver looked his friend in the eye and took a deep breath. 'Hermitage,' he said.

'Yes?'

'It's time we had the talk.'

Hermitage loved to talk; he preferred it to listening, but he wasn't aware there was a single talk to be had.

Wat went over to the pile of cases and examined them, looking for one in particular. Spotting what he wanted, he moved several boxes out of the way until he revealed a nondescript wooden case about three feet long, one wide, and the same deep. This was well made and solid. He dragged it out into the middle of the tent. Placing it between the two chairs, he gestured Hermitage to sit. Dropping on the other chair, he leaned forward to the box. The thing had a large and complex catch, a decorated wide metal bar that clamped the lid shut and ended in a very expensive looking lock. Sophisticated machinery in a place such as this gave Hermitage pause. This was clearly a significant box. Wat pulled on the catch and it immediately sprang open.

'Should it do that?' Hermitage asked, thinking that it wasn't very secure.

'No, it shouldn't,' Wat replied, examining the lock closely and holding it up to show Hermitage where the wood behind the catch had been scraped by a hard object.

'Forced open,' Hermitage concluded.

'Yes. Could be we won't find anything. This was probably what they were after.'

Hermitage watched closely as Wat opened the box. Perhaps it contained poor Briston's life's earnings. That would explain a murder. Not why it was carried out by his own guild, of course. Unless they were plain greedy. His opinion of weavers thus far had been based on Wat. He'd assumed they were all intelligent, caring, helpful people, who simply weaved. A whole new world was opening up before his eyes now. He hated it when that happened. He forced himself to stop speculating as Wat examined the contents of the box.

'Seems to all be here,' he said, in some puzzlement. 'Perhaps they left it as a warning to others.'

'What is? Who did? What warning?' Hermitage asked.

If curiosity killed the cat, it had claimed sanctuary in Brother Hermitage's head. The opening of a book was a wonder, never mind a box full of secrets. He leaned in close.

'Now, Hermitage,' Wat produced a rolled up tapestry and pointed it at the monk.

'Yes?' young Hermitage bubbled.

'What I am about to show you will be a great shock.'

If it had been Wat's intention to get Hermitage even more excited, he was succeeding.

'Marvellous,' the brother breathed.

'It won't be marvellous,' Wat said in all seriousness. 'It will be disappointing. It will be alarming and you will feel enormously let down.'

'Oh.' Hermitage knew what being let down felt like. For some reason, an image of his father came to mind. That hadn't happened for a while.

'You will have a lot of questions,' Wat continued. 'For which I will have answers. Which you will not like.'

Hermitage had forgotten the threat of a letdown and was positively panting to see the tapestry.

'I'll answer your first questions before I let you see this.' He waved the tapestry again.

Hermitage's eyes followed it like a starving man watching a dying cat. Wat touched Hermitage's shoulder with the tapestry and held his eyes with his own.

'Yes, this is the sort of business I am involved in,' he said. 'Yes, these are the sorts of tapestries I make, and the ones I have made all my money from. Finally, yes, they explain the death of Briston.'

With a flourish he closed the wooden box again and threw the tapestry open on top. It covered the surface of the box and trailed over the sides in all directions. The main scene was clear, and Hermitage gobbled it up eagerly. He put his head over to one side and then the other, trying to make sense of the picture in front of him. Wat's head sagged as he saw realisation dawn on the monk.

'Oh my,' Hermitage said, his jaw low and his eyes wide.

'I know,' Wat acknowledged.

'I can see why this sort of thing would be locked up.'

'Of course.'

Hermitage examined the work in some detail, stroking his chin now and nodding.

'So?' Wat asked as the time seemed to be stretching.

'Well,' Hermitage said leaning back, 'as a representation of the destruction of Sodom and Gomorrah, I imagine it is accurate. It appears to be very detailed indeed. All the people are individually picked out at the height of their sin. I can certainly see why Briston needed so much pink thread.'

'It's not a representation of Sodom and Gomorrah,' Wat said.

'Oh?' Hermitage frowned for a moment as he considered his scripture. 'The daughters of Lot, perhaps?'

'No. Not the daughters of Lot. Someone's daughters certainly, but not Lot's.'

'No, I see that now. Too many of them. And the men with them are certainly not angels. Not judging by what they're doing, or what they're doing it with.'

28

Hermitage bent closer still and considered the little pink figures dancing before him. They even appeared to be anatomically correct, which was an awful lot of trouble to go to for a tapestry.

'The wives of Solomon?' he speculated. 'Although I can't see why it would get someone killed.'

'You're on the wrong track altogether.' Wat shook his head at the tenacity of the monk's innocence.

'Really?' Hermitage was fully engaged. What a fascinating puzzle.

'Yes, you're being too, erm, biblical.'

'Too biblical?' Hermitage said. This really did cause him trouble. How could you be too biblical?

'Psalms?' he speculated.

'No, Hermitage.' Wat ran a hand over his face. 'You're being biblical at all is too biblical.'

Hermitage stopped. He really had nowhere else to go.

Wat drew breath and explained, 'It's a Christmas gathering at the hall of the Bishop of Dorchester. The year 1062, if I'm not mistaken, given the number of goats and the jester with that rather unique staff.'

Hermitage looked from tapestry to Wat to get the joke. He saw there was no joke.

'Oh my,' he glanced to the box.

'And the rest of them are the same,' Wat acknowledged. 'Well, different situations and subject matter, but the same quantity of clothing on the subjects.'

'None at all, you mean,' Hermitage said with a touch of irritation.

'Afraid so.'

'Well, I can certainly see what all the trouble is about,' Hermitage was matter of fact. 'Do you make these things too?'

'I do.' Wat hung his head.

Hermitage said nothing.

'Except,' Wat added, 'mine are better.'

'In what way "better"?' Hermitage asked.

'Better quality,' Wat blustered. 'More, erm, realistic.' His voice faded off as he realised this was not a good thing to be talking about with a monk.

'I'd better see another one,' Hermitage said, in that tone parents use when their children have confessed to doing something naughty with their neighbours' chickens when, in fact, they've killed the lot.

Wat's head drooped as he rolled up the Dorchester Christmas, opened the box, and exchanged it for another tapestry. He threw this one open on the top.

'Oh my gracious me, good heavens above, and all the saints.' Hermitage tried to move backwards in his chair.

'Personal, isn't it?' Wat said with a shrug.

'Definitively.' Hermitage tried to make his eyes stop working. This was a much more straightforward image – a simple one of two people. A loving couple, Hermitage sincerely hoped. They had been caught in the middle of their loving, and depicted in the most minute and unnecessary detail.

'And, people pay for these things?' Hermitage asked.

'Very well. Not the sort of thing you can get over the counter in a public place.'

'I should hope not. Who buys them?' Hermitage's voice squeaked with offended disbelief.

'Everyone,' Wat replied.

'Everyone?'

Hermitage could not believe this. He certainly didn't know anyone who'd bought one. He'd never seen anything like it before. Or had he? His mind wandered back to an alarming tapestry he'd seen in his old Abbot's study. That was a depiction of the fate waiting for sinners inside the gates of hell. He'd assumed it was there to focus the Abbot's mind on need to battle evil. Now he thought about it, he recalled that most of the sinners had been women. And none of them had any clothes on. He thought about asking Wat. Perhaps the weaver knew the work.

'That's the joy of it,' Wat was explaining. 'Everyone buys them, but they all think it's only them. It's not the sort of thing they talk about, or show visitors. They certainly don't hang them on the wall.'

Hermitage drew breath at the thought.

'Well,' Wat considered. 'Except in the case of Baron Lasder, of course, but then he is rather unique.'

'I think I may have seen something a bit like this before,' Hermitage admitted.

'Been in a bishop's private chamber after dark then?' Wat asked.

'Dorchester?' This really was too much.

'Most of them actually.'

'Appalling.'

'Anyone who's got any money at all really. From the lowest born to the most high. I did several for King Harold. Very fond of the bathhouse was Harold.'

'But,' Hermitage's thought processes were recovering from the shock, 'if everyone has them, why is Briston dead?'

'Because everyone thinks they are awful and sinful and says so. And of course the guild agrees. In public.'

'So everyone has them, but everyone says they're sinful and no one should have them?' Hermitage's thinking was not built for such naked contradictions.

'That's it.'

'But that's hypocritical.'

'It's what?' It was Wat's turn to be thrown off his stride.

'It means preaching one thing while doing the opposite,' Hermitage explained, 'more or less.'

'Oh right,' Wat nodded. 'Quite common then. Yes, it's hypocritical. Everyone has one in private, but in public they go on about how they should be banned. How the weavers responsible should be punished. How the common man must have nothing to do with this sort of thing.'

'So they can keep it to themselves,' Hermitage concluded.

'Very good, Hermitage. You've grasped a real piece of human nature.'

'I wish I could let it go again.' Hermitage pondered this new found information and concluded it was best left alone. 'But if everyone has them, why have Briston killed? Doesn't that cut off supply?'

'Hermitage, you're thinking like a real merchant.'

'Oh dear.'

'No, it's good. It's the right question. We've been at this business for years. What's happened to bring this about now?'

Hermitage hoped this question was rhetorical. He liked rhetorical questions generally, but he simply didn't want to speculate about the answer in this case. He offered the standard response to a question like this. The words every Saxon used these days when asked "how's things?", or "been up to much lately", or "what's new?"

'The Normans have invaded,' he said.

There was hardly an aspect of life untouched by the new overlords. And their touch tended to be very heavy. He couldn't immediately see why this would have descended on the world of weaving though.

'They have, haven't they,' Wat replied in a speculative tone. 'And we know they don't like this sort of thing.'

'Do we?' Hermitage didn't have any information about Norman taste in tapestry. He and Wat had been together since the invasion and they hadn't discussed Norman decorative arts at all.

'I picked up some useful information when we were at the monastery in De'Ath's Dingle from Brother Amsom after his trip to Lincoln,' Wat explained.

Well, that was a bit much. Hermitage had tried to ask Brother Amsom about his visit to Lincoln, and what the latest developments were in the lexicography of the post-Exodus prophets. The Brother claimed to have bumped his head and lost his memory. Given what he now knew of Wat's trade, it was somewhat vexing that the weaver had been better accepted in the monastery than Hermitage, who was a monk, after all.

'If it's not a representation of a battle, or a horse, or preferably both, they aren't interested. If it's anything remotely intimate, they express the strongest objections. Apparently they found a weaver's apprentice in Lincoln making a copy of an early Briston.'

'Like this?' Hermitage gestured at the work that was still revealing itself to him. He was horrified at the thought of a child being exposed to anything like this.

'Nah,' Wat was dismissive. 'Mild stuff. Could show it to your grandmother. Didn't stop the Normans breaking all the tools of his trade though.'

'His needles and looms?'

'No, his fingers.'

Hermitage shivered. 'So the Normans killed Briston?' He wasn't surprised by the Norman response to things they didn't approve of.

'No, the guild killed Briston.' Wat seemed annoyed that Hermitage had forgotten this. 'Remember? The Tapestry of Death?'

'Ah yes. Maybe the Normans asked them to do it?'

'Or they did it to show the Normans what fine fellows they are. To show how they despise this disgusting stuff and are dedicated to putting a stop to it.'

'Kill one of their own?'

'Better than having the Normans take out their annoyance on the whole guild. They are a bit, what's the word? Unsophisticated?'

'After looking at the works of Briston, I don't think we can criticise the Normans for being unsophisticated,' Hermitage sighed and looked at the field of pink laid out before him. 'Can we put it away now?' He gestured at the tapestry.

'Of course.' Wat rolled up the picture, opened the box, and put it back. He left the lid open and went through each rolled up tapestry, touching them in turn and mumbling under his breath.

'What *are* you doing?' Hermitage asked in some horror.

'Stock check,' Wat replied. 'Making sure they're all here.'

'Are you so familiar with his work?' Hermitage's horror at the subject matter, and his horror at this latest revelation about mankind, was joined by a dawning horror that his friend was up to his knees in this stuff. Even the image of Wat being up to his knees in it was horrible.

'Oh yes,' Wat replied. 'As you've seen, Briston and I were close. We let one another know the sort of thing we were doing so we didn't tread on one another's toes.'

'So your, erm, material is different?'

'Not really. We just made sure we weren't making duplicates. Even though people never talk about their purchases, it would be a bit risky to try and sell the same scene.'

'I can see that,' Hermitage said, 'Oh Wat,' he sighed.

'I know,' Wat shook his head slightly. 'I know it'll be no comfort, but it is just a job. I don't have any of these things myself. In fact, I find it quite hard to understand the sorts of things people want to look at. I can understand their money though. I suppose that's a sin on its own.'

'Yes, it is,' Hermitage was quite clear. 'So why do them?'

Wat left his stock taking, stood, and paced up and down the small space of the tent, pausing each time as he passed by Briston's remains. 'I got dragged into it when I was an apprentice. In fact, I was with Briston. Some freeman came into the shop, asked for something, and the old master kicked him out. Well, you can imagine we were intrigued. We found the fellow and asked him what he'd said to the master. He told us.' Wat shivered slightly at the memory. 'And, when he told us how much he was prepared to pay, we said we'd do it for him.'

'Corruption of the young,' Hermitage commented.

'It certainly was. We didn't have a clue where to begin. We didn't even really understand the full details of what the man actually wanted. Briston asked one of the journeymen and got a clip round the ear. Two young lads being told that something wasn't fit for their ears.'

'You had to find out.' Hermitage shook his head in sorrow.

The tale had a certain familiarity. In his youth, he had been told certain matters weren't for him, ideas and discussions not to be raised or brought into his father's house. Of course, Hermitage's insatiable curiosity could not stand such a challenge. He had gone ahead, deceived his father, and met secretly with people who were prepared to talk on forbidden topics. When he was found out, his father washed his hands of the young man. Why any son of his would want to read, praise God, and do good was beyond him.

'And we did find out,' Wat continued. 'There was an old man in the village called Parbul. He'd sell children mead, buy anything they'd stolen, and show them his...'

'Yes, yes, I can imagine the type.'

Wat stopped pacing and looked into the distance. Which wasn't very far away. 'He told us exactly what the man wanted. In detail. And how much we could really charge for it.'

'And that was it,' Hermitage nodded. 'The downward slope.'

'Helped by the fact Parbul offered to buy three more from us,' Wat grinned. 'Briston and I set to work and delivered them. Word spread and within six months we were as rich as our master.'

'You could have stopped there,' Hermitage suggested.

'We couldn't. For one thing, the temptation of the money was too great. For another, we kept getting more orders. And the people who asked said if we didn't do the work, we'd be reported to the guild. And we all knew what the guild did to people.'

'The Tapestry of Death,' Hermitage concluded.

'Exactly. What could we do? Carry on, take the money, and

stay alive. Or, give up, not have the money, and be dead?'

'A dilemma,' Hermitage nodded.

'Not really.' Wat clearly couldn't see the dilemma. 'We carried on together for a while, but then Briston had a bit of bother. One of his noble clients wanted to make him his personal tapestrier.'

'Isn't that good?' Hermitage asked. 'The security of a great house, a reputation?'

'With no pay, virtual imprisonment, and all the profit from the work going to the noble?'

'Ah, perhaps not.'

'So we split up. He went North, I stayed in the midlands. We created the death notes before we parted and said we'd always leave word of our whereabouts.' Wat gazed at his bundled companion. 'Now I've found you, Briston.' He hung his head.

Hermitage had taken in so much that there wasn't room for any more. He would need some time to think all this through. He also knew he really didn't want to spend time thinking much about any of it. 'How could you make them?' he said, shaking his head at the loss these things had brought to the world. Loss for the spirit of man being led along the road to corruption. Loss for Wat's immortal soul and, of course, the ultimate loss for Briston.

'Well,' he began, 'you start with a preliminary sketch. It has to be pretty accurate so you know exactly what's going where and so the faces are recognizable. It's usually made up to the client's specification but occasionally you do the sketch from life. Can't say I'm fond of that approach.' Wat allowed himself a short shiver. 'Then you transfer the sketch to the cloth with a set of directions for the apprentices. Keep an eye on progress, bit of instruction here, bit of your own work there and…' Wat looked at Hermitage who was gaping at him. 'What?' Wat asked.

Hermitage spoke slowly and quietly, 'I meant how could you make them morally speaking? I don't want specific instructions.'

'Ah,' Wat hung his head again.

'It is a sorry tale,' Hermitage said, glancing towards the recumbent Briston. 'But, you cannot blame yourself for his death.'

'I wasn't going to,' Wat responded with some surprise. 'Like I said, he always was a chancer. Took on more work than he could do, delivered late, poor quality. I told him. I said "quality", Briston, that's the way to profit. Keep the supply short and the quality high and then you get a premium. It's no good turning out acres of the stuff. Just devalues the market.'

'Oh.' Hermitage was a bit disappointed at this.

'I mean,' Wat went on, 'Briston had plans to get the tapestries into the hands of the common man. What good's that going to do, I asked. They haven't got any money.'

'Is that a bit, erm, mercenary?' Hermitage suggested.

Wat paused and his shoulders fell. 'You're right, of course. Briston used his money to buy himself out of his apprenticeship and then bribed the guild for a master's badge. I kept mine. Stashed it away and bought some nice things. What have either of us got to show? I have to keep myself to myself and never trust anyone. And Briston's dead.'

Wat collapsed back in his chair.

'You can trust me,' Hermitage said.

'I know, Hermitage,' Wat replied looking up. Hermitage thought there was a glint of moisture in the weaver's eye. 'I *can* trust you Hermitage, and that's been a great thing for me. I can't remember the last time I was with someone I could trust. Trust not to rob me or worse. I could have gone home several times over the months we've been together. Got back to work and counted the profit, but I stayed.'

'You didn't have much choice most of the time. There's usually someone with a small army and a gallows making the consequences of departure most explicit.'

'I know, but even so. You're an innocent. You're trusting and well meaning and the look on your face when you find out something bad about people? Well, it reminds me of what I've thrown away.'

'Perhaps there is a way back for you,' Hermitage nodded, thinking hard

'Really?'

'Yes, the monastic life offers a wide range of…'

'Oh no. No, no, no. I feel bad about what I've done, who I am, and the people I deal with, but there some things even I won't do.'

Wat opened the box again and returned to checking Briston's stock.

'At least our friendship puts us in the right place to deal with this,' Hermitage said.

Wat looked around the grim scene once more. The inside of the tent was becoming damp with the cold of the January night and the oil was flickering in the lamp casting incoherent yet lively shadows on the tapestries.

'Friendship.' Wat tried the word out. He liked it. 'Yes it does, doesn't it? Having been forced to solve other people's crimes for them, we can now do it for ourselves. Well, for me. Perhaps getting Briston's killer will be some, erm, what's the word when you make up for something bad by doing something good?'

'Penance?' Hermitage offered.

'That's the one.'

Wat's head vanished into the box once more as he rummaged about. There was a sudden stillness to his body then he emerged holding a golden tassel in his hand.

'That's nice,' Hermitage observed. 'I've heard the Bishop of Dorchester has those on his bible.'

'I bet he does,' Wat replied with a bit of a snort.

'Did Briston make it?'

'He did.'

'Why would a weaver make a tassel?'

'All finished tapestries that sell are tied in the golden tassel.'

'How nice.' Hermitage was grateful there was at least one pleasant aspect to this trade.

'The tassel makes customers think the tapestry's worth more than it is.'

'Oh.' Hermitage's gratitude went off to chat with his disappointment.

'It's a bit odd though. You don't bother making the tassel until the tapestry is complete and no customer would leave the tassel behind.'

'Aha,' Hermitage drawled out. 'This could be very significant.'

'Don't see why.' Wat threw the tassel back in the box. 'We still know the guild killed Briston.'

'Well, the missing tapestry could be the chop that choked the dog.' Hermitage nodded as he said this. He nodded knowingly.

'Eh?'

Hermitage stopped nodding, 'Sorry, it's an expression my family used. A rather unfortunate event when one of the hounds got into the meat store. Perhaps the missing tapestry prompted the guild to act?' Hermitage paused, smiling at this neat connection.

Wat looked at him, jaw slack, as if a thought had dropped from his head into his mouth. 'The killer left it behind,' he said, 'but took the tapestry.'

'Erm,' Hermitage didn't see that connection.

'As you said, the customer gets the tassel. If the customer had taken the work, the tassel would be gone. A killer wouldn't be worried about a bit of tassel. All he'd want to do is get the job done and get away.'

Hermitage thought it a bit callous calling the murder of a friend a "job".

'It could be an important image,' Wat speculated.

Hermitage shrugged, 'Just another one of Briston's rather deplorable tapestries, I'd have thought.'

'No it wasn't,' Wat thought out loud. 'If the guild killed Briston to show the Normans how much they disapprove of this sort of thing, why would the killer take just one tapestry away?

The rest of them are much the same.'

'Yes, they are, aren't they?' Hermitage's disappointment gave his head a solemn shake.

'Why leave the rest behind?' Wat's thoughts were not going to be interrupted. 'Perhaps this one was to hand. Perhaps it's just the sort of thing the man went in for.' Wat frowned hard, as he could not bring a suitable reason to mind. 'Who cares?' He concluded quickly. 'The guild committed the murder. It'd be nice to know why, but it won't stop me dealing the man who did it.'

Hermitage was horrified at this. Wat had raised a question and seemed prepared to wander off without answering it. Worse still, the question was why – not knowing why was unthinkable. If something happened, which was not the will of God and so beyond man's reason, you had to know why. Really had to. If you didn't know why, it would rankle and nag at you. Stop you sleeping, upset your stomach, disturb all your thoughts. Until now, he'd been prepared to accept that Briston was killed for the tapestries he created. It was certainly a good enough reason as far as he could see. Now there was the suggestion of some other motive.

'But,' he whimpered, 'we have to know why. It might be the key to everything.'

Wat looked at Hermitage with disappointed eyes and shook his head slowly. He added a sigh to complete the effect.

'I suppose if I find out who and you find out why, we'll have covered everything.' He smiled indulgently as he gave Hermitage this gift.

Hermitage's enthusiasm boiled from him, 'I wonder what it's a picture of?' he bubbled.

'We can ask the murderer when we find him,' Wat replied. 'Remind me not to kill him before we've had a chat.'

Hermitage frowned his best disappointed frown at his companion.

'In the meantime,' Wat rubbed his hands together, 'we need

somewhere to sleep.'

'Perhaps we should keep vigil,' Hermitage suggested, looking round the tent to see how they should organise themselves.

'I'm not staying in here with him.' Wat was horrified. 'He's dead! That peasant who brought us the news can put us up.'

Hermitage was taken aback by this apparent heartlessness, 'I hardly think a poor peasant will be able to provide for two guests, let alone be willing.'

'You'd be surprised what people will do for a browse through the catalogue of Briston the Weaver. We'll take this with us.'

He moved to the box of tapestries and indicated that Hermitage should pick up the other end. Holding the end of the box of sinful tapestries, Hermitage followed Wat, who led the way out of the tent without a backwards glance.

Caput IV

A New Ritual

E HAVE GOT TO FIND THAT TAPESTRY,' the master said to The Hoofhorn.

The cowled figure had stepped down from the chair upon the dais and was pacing between the columns. The Hoofhorn stood in the middle of the room, the ritual middle of the room, and he stood in a very ritual way.

'How did you manage to lose him?' the master demanded.

The Hoofhorn cackled. 'He went beyond the bounds,' it said in wild, yet mysterious tones.

'The bounds?'

'The bounds of the guild.' The Hoofhorn waved his arms wide and twiddled his fingers up and down to indicate the bounds, 'The Hoofhorn may not act beyond the bounds of the guild.' It was a statement of fact.

'Where are these bounds exactly?' The Master asked.

> *The bounds of guild upon the ground*
> *One half league and a sheep's throw from the chair upon*
> *the dais will be found,*

The Hoofhorn recited, hurriedly scanning the last line.

The Master frowned, 'Are you telling me you failed to chase one man with a small dagger while you had a large sword?'

'The Sword of Tup,' The Hoofhorn corrected.

'Of course. You had the Sword of Tup and you chased this man until he got one half league and a sheep's throw away and then you stopped?'

'Of course,' The Hoofhorn answered, as if so much was blindingly obvious, or at least should be to the Master,

> *The powers of The Hoofhorn can only be found*
> *Within the bounds. The bounds. The bounds.*

'You'll have no powers at all in a minute,' the Master snorted.

He stepped up to The Hoofhorn with the clear intention of grabbing the figure by the scruff of the neck. As he got closer, he could see the rags in sobering detail. He gave up on the grabbing.

'So how do you suggest we get the tapestry back?' he demanded.

The Hoofhorn cackled, 'The Hoofhorn cannot do it.'

'What if I grabbed The Hoofhorn by his horny hoof and dragged him over the bounds? Kicking him as I went?' the master suggested.

> *If beyond the bounds The Hoofhorn steps*
> *Into his shoes the Master must, erm, step.*

'Steps and step?' The master snorted at the rhyme.

'The Hoofhorn can never leave,' The Hoofhorn bleated. 'The successor must be here to take on The Hoofhorn's duties before death. Only then can The Hoofhorn depart this place. If The Hoofhorn is forced beyond the bounds, you must take his place.'

'I don't think so.' The Master was pretty clear on this.

'No choice.'

The Master paced up and down the hall. The idea of going after the tapestry himself did not seem to occur to him.

'You must have a ritual,' he mused.

'Ah, many rituals. Many, many.'

'Yes, yes.' The Master tried to shut The Hoofhorn up before he went on an excursion through his rituals. 'You must have a ritual for crossing the bounds. How did you get here in the first place? You must have crossed the bounds on the way in?'

'Only during the trance of transposition can The Hoofhorn move from one guild hall to another. Not much good chasing people when you're in a trance,' The Hoofhorn observed with re-markable sense.

'There's a ritual for everything,' the Master went on. 'Opening the doors, closing them, taking the first step in the morning and the last one at night. That one with the fir branches for the first lamb of the season and the three hundred and twelve rituals for each lamb thereafter.'

The Master ignored the fact The Hoofhorn was glaring at him for apparently making light of the rituals.

'Never mind all that bizarre stuff for polishing the cauldron.' The Master stood with arms folded.

The Hoofhorn continued to glare, but his look slowly light-ened and he turned his head towards the cauldron.

'The cauldron of the boiling fleece,' he intoned.

'I know,' the Master answered.

'There is a ritual,' The Hoofhorn announced with some ex-citement. 'An ancient and mysterious ritual.'

'More ancient and mysterious than all the others?' The Mas-ter sounded incredulous.

'Oh yes,' The Hoofhorn was positively gleeful. 'Much more ancient and wildly more mysterious.' The Hoofhorn skipped off behind the pillars.

The Master had never followed him behind the pillars. He didn't know what The Hoofhorn got up to back there, but it nev-er sounded very wholesome.

The ancient and ragged creature returned with a great book in its arms.

'The book?' The Master was impressed now. 'I thought you knew all the rituals.'

'Not this one. Not been used by a Hoofhorn in a thousand generations.'

'A thousand?' The Master wasn't prepared to accept this ex-aggeration.

'Well, a lot,' The Hoofhorn negotiated.

'Uh huh, and what does this ritual do exactly?'

The Hoofhorn cackled with his book and skipped over to the cauldron.

'It deposits the spirit of The Hoofhorn into the cauldron of the boiling fleece.'

'Does it?'

'Oh yes. It is a measure only to be used in the direst emergency. It frees the Hoofhorn from the bounds to carry out the needs of the guild. The powers are left in the cauldron, but the body that houses The Hoofhorn can venture abroad.'

'Let's get on with it then.' The Master was impatient.

'Oh no. You must convince The Hoofhorn that the emergency is dire. You say you need the tapestry, but The Hoofhorn has been told nothing. There could be an emergency, but is it a dire one? If it is, how dire? Perhaps it isn't dire at all and you only think it is. Do you see dire where The Hoofhorn does not?'

The Master folded his arms, put one hand to his mouth, and considered the shape before him. Finding any trustworthy fellow who could take a secret to the grave was always a challenge. Finding one in this room was impossible. On the other hand, The Hoofhorn was completely mad and the Master really wanted the tapestry.

'Can you keep a secret?' the Master asked.

'Keep a secret? Keep a secret?' the Hoofhorn baa'd like a lamb on a stick. 'I have more secrets than your puny mind could comprehend. I know things of the world even the world doesn't know. And do I tell anyone? Well, I tell the next Hoofhorn, but that's it.' The creature folded its arms.

'Oh well,' the Master shrugged. 'I suppose you'll have to know if you're going to find the thing.'

He stepped up close, well, as close as seemed sanitary, and whispered in the ear of The Hoofhorn.

'Really?' The Hoofhorn responded. 'That doesn't even seem much of an emergency, let alone dire.'

'Well it is to me and I'm the Master,' the Master retorted.

'I s'pose you are.' The Hoofhorn was still not convinced.

The Master whispered again, this time gesturing to the dais and then to the cauldron. The Hoofhorn followed the gestures and frowned.

'Really?' he said, part incredulity, part contempt.

'Oh yes.' The Master was confident. 'Bring down the whole guild and I shouldn't think The Hoofhorn would escape attention either,' he rounded off his mysterious argument.

The Hoofhorn paused.

'Of course, no Hoofhorn has completed this ritual for thousands of generations,' the Master enticed. 'You'd be the first.'

'True.' The Hoofhorn was being won round. 'The Hoofhorn will do it.'

'Excellent.' The Master rubbed his hands together. 'What do we need to do then?'

'You do nothing. You are not The Hoofhorn.' The Hoofhorn glared again.

'Of course, of course.' The Master bowed and gestured that The Hoofhorn should continue.

The ancient shape, somehow standing straighter and taking on even more raggedness, took his book over to the cauldron and laid it on the floor. He read two pages, turning them back and forth to make sure he'd got it, before he began.

'There is something you do,' he croaked,

When The Hoofhorn's dance around the cauldron copper
Is completed and the ritual is to be done proper,

'Done proper? Really?' The Master scoffed at the sacred text.
'Yes,' The Hoofhorn snapped,

When The Hoofhorn's dance around the cauldron copper
Is completed and the ritual is to be done proper,
The Master steps forward from his place on the dais…

46

At this, The Hoofhorn indicated the dais.

The Master indicated that he knew perfectly well where it was.

> *Opens the lid of the cauldron dire*
> *And tips The Hoofhorn in.*

'That's awful,' the Master commented.

'Oh, The Hoofhorn will survive,' The Hoofhorn responded.

'Not you, the verse,' the Master said with a dollop of despair.

'Sometimes I think you don't take the ritual seriously,' The Hoofhorn said in a serious tone.

'Only sometimes?' The Master asked. 'Get on with it then,' he added.

The Hoofhorn read from his book, mumbled to himself, and set off to dance around the cauldron. He gestured that the Master must return to the dais. After a demonstration of dancing that would draw well earned criticism from a three-year-old child with a broken maypole, The Hoofhorn threw off the lid of the cauldron and beckoned the Master to attend. The Master strode from the dais and, following the waving directions of The Hoofhorn, grabbed the rags by the leg and heaved them into the pot. He brushed his hands vigorously on his breeches immediately afterwards.

'Close the lid, close the lid!' the metallic voice of The Hoofhorn commanded.

The Master did so, only now wondering what level of insanity had come over him that he was taking any part in this nonsense.

There was an alarming clanging noise from inside the cauldron, as if The Hoofhorn himself had decided that this was, in fact, a very bad idea. Or, he had discovered that he really didn't like enclosed spaces with dead birds in them. Or both.

The noise stopped. Silence.

The Master was about to step forward and take peek inside

when he actually jumped in surprise. The lid of the cauldron was thrown off and the head of The Hoofhorn emerged. Physically, it was exactly the same. The hair hadn't gone and, as the shoulders emerged, it was clear the rags had not benefited from their time in the cauldron of the boiling fleece. The face had changed though. There was a new shape to the muscles, a new quality of reflected light in the eyes, and a new cut of the mouth that looked almost, well, sane.

'Well,' said The Hoofhorn in a very strange voice as he climbed out of the cauldron.

He picked up the lid and placed it firmly back in place. He then fetched the book and placed it on top of the lid, as if to stop something escaping. The Master appraised him.

'So?' The Hoofhorn asked in his new tones. Normal conversational tones without even the hint of a bleat. Not at all the tones of a mostly mad man who thought he was a sheep. 'This tapestry then? Where do you think they'll have gone? I'd better get after them quickly if they're not to get away completely.' The Hoofhorn, or ex-Hoofhorn, or whatever he was, now became aware of his own appearance. 'Oh dear,' he commented, 'I'd better go and change, hadn't I? What must I look like?'

The Hoofhorn strode off purposefully to the back of the chamber.

The Master watched him go with a slack jaw and a head full of questions. The questions became seriously alarmed when the Master thought he heard the faint, copper-clad cooing of doves coming from the sealed cauldron.

Caput V

The Secret's Out

HE SUN ROSE UPON A DISMAL SCENE, but no more dismal than it saw every other day. The market field of Baernodebi was at least enlivened by the presence of a tent, and two figures that stood stretching themselves outside the hovel of a peasant. The young one was of clear complexion with barely any beard disturbing his clean face. He was bright of eye, in a monk's habit, and was frowning and holding his stomach, as if preventing some awful secret blurting itself all over the bright morning. The slightly older, stubble faced one, very well dressed, ran a hand through a mop of curly black hair and gazed out at the day. He clearly had plans for it.

'Right, back to the tent,' Wat chimed. 'Let's see if there's anything we missed in the dark last night. We'd better take the box with us. That peasant will sell the lot if we don't keep an eye on it.'

They bent back into the hovel and emerged a moment later with the box between them. The peasant, who gave his name as Lolby, followed, still putting the last of the extraordinary works back in place.

'Can't I keep a little one?' he whined.

Wat stopped and looked at the man. 'If you keep your mouth shut and give us any help we need in sorting this business out, I'll see what I can do.'

He winked. Lolby grinned.

'Was that wise?' Hermitage asked as they resumed their walk to the tent.

'He could be useful. He's local. Plus if he knows there's something in it for him he's not likely to talk to anyone who asks. In

49

case the guild come looking, or anything.'

Hermitage nodded then shook his head. 'I was thinking more of his eternal soul and the danger it's in from these things.' He tipped his head towards the box.

'Ah.'

'I really don't want Mister Lolby giving us any more favours from his cook pot.' Hermitage clutched his grumbling stomach.

They arrived at the tent and had to turn sideways to get through the entrance with the box between them. Hermitage went first, threw back the tent flap, took a step forward, and fell flat on his face, the heavy box falling behind him.

'Oww,' a figure on the floor, lying right across the entrance, called out in genuine pain as the weight of Briston's work fell upon it.

'Watch where you're going,' it called angrily as it rolled from under the box and found room to stand.

Hermitage regarded the shape with surprise. The box was still blocking the entrance and there was a muffled cry from outside as Wat's shins found they were a suddenly stopping a box.

'Who are you?' Hermitage asked, the surprise squeaking his voice.

'Who are you?' the shape responded.

The voice was high and unbroken and the figure in front of Hermitage was a good foot shorter than the monk, and slim.

'What are you doing here?' Hermitage asked a second question, not having got an answer to the first.

'I work here. What's your excuse?'

'I am Brother Hermitage,' the monk replied, thinking that one of them had better get this conversation moving.

'Odd name for a monk.'

'It is,' Hermitage acknowledged.

'Well, I'm Briston's apprentice,' the figure announced, 'and I want to know what happened to him.' There was a tremor in the voice at these words.

An apprentice? Hermitage thought this boy could have some very useful information. The child, for child he was, wore breeches, a jerkin, boots, and a hood, but then so did most people. However, most people weren't lying across the entrance of a dead weaver's tent in the middle of Baernodebi market.

The hood was still up, doubtless from keeping the cold of the night at bay. The face in the hood was glum and pale.

'What are *you* doing here?' The young voice was contorted by anger and sadness.

'My child, my child,' Hermitage comforted. He knew apprentices started young. This one must be about ten, by the size of him. And here he was in the tent of a murdered weaver. Awful. A murdered weaver who did awful weaving.

'What's going on?' Wat's face appeared through the tent flaps as he clambered over the fallen box.

'We appear to have found an apprentice,' Hermitage waved a hand of introduction.

'I'm saying nothing,' the young child snarled and spat on the floor.

'Oh really,' Hermitage said in despair.

'What's your name, boy?' Wat asked. He did so in a nice mix of encouragement, friendliness, and threat.

'What's yours?' the impudent boy sneered back. 'What's a monk doing here? Come to bury Briston?'

'I'm Wat. I'm with Brother Hermitage.'

Hermitage gave a short nod to encourage the boy's acceptance of Wat.

'Wat?' the boy asked, his voice rising to a shriek.

'That's right.'

'Wat the Weaver?'

Wat smiled, 'You've heard of me, I expect.'

'You're a bit bloody late!' The boy howled and the tears flowed.

'Eh?' Wat looked from boy to monk.

'Briston sent word. He knew he was in danger. Don't worry, he said, my old mate Wat will sort things out. But when do you turn up? After he's dead.' The boy slumped on to the box and held his face in his hands.

'We only got the note after he was dead,' Wat explained. 'Some peasant brought it over. Found it in the tent.'

This explanation only brought more howls from the young man.

'And you were stealing his work.' His young fist thumped the box ineffectually.

'We were looking after it. Don't want this lot getting into the wrong hands.' Wat smiled the best he could at a crying child.

'So you say.'

'Yes. I do.' Wat's smile was wearing out. 'Briston was my friend. We'd been friends since he and I were your age. If I'd got word earlier, I would have come earlier. Now pull yourself to-gether.'

Hermitage thought this was a bit harsh given the poor child's state. Still, at ten years old, he ought to be a bit more resilient.

The boy sulked and stared some more.

'Anyway,' Wat went on, 'Brother Hermitage and I have some talent in the area of finding killers.'

Oh, Hermitage thought. Yes, we do, don't we.

'If it wasn't you,' Wat probed.

'Me?' the boy almost screamed. 'What would I be doing lying here blubbing my eyes out if I'd killed him?'

'It could be a ploy to cover up the fact you killed your master.'

'Bit of a bloody stupid one.' The boy was contemptuous of such a plan. 'Better ploy would be killing him, taking everything, and running like hell.'

'Hum,' Wat hummed, somewhat appeased, but clearly ir-ritated by the apprentice's attitude. 'I've made a vow to avenge Briston's death and I'm going to find out who did this.' He ges-tured to the bound figure that was just as they had left him.

Hardly surprising really.

'Well, I've been here looking after him all night,' the boy claimed. 'Where were you?'

'In the hideous hovel of a hideous peasant,' Wat responded. 'Working up the strength to give you a clip round the ear for lipping your elders.'

Hermitage looked at the boy, who was genuinely upset at the death of Briston. It must have been a very close relationship. Apprentice to master. Most unusual. Wat had told him of the relationship with his own master, which had been very different. Lots of violence, resentment, spite and hatred. Much more normal.

'I can see Briston was your friend,' Hermitage soothed. 'But if we are going to discover who did this, we need to talk to you and find out as much as we can about his, erm, last hours.'

The howls now filled the tent and even Hermitage was starting to find them annoying. The boy's reaction puzzled him. Yes, it was the death of someone close and yes, you would naturally be upset, but the death was hours ago. He should be over it by now, for goodness' sake.

'When did you last see him, erm, alive?' Hermitage asked as nicely as he could.

The howls became snuffles.

''Bout midday,' the apprentice got out. 'He sent me out to get some fresh water. I ask you, fresh water round here? I couldn't get back before dark because I had to avoid the Normans. I only got back a few hours ago. I think Briston knew what was coming.'

'So, you didn't see who killed him?' Wat asked.

''Course I didn't. If I'd seen who done it, I'd either be lying there with him or still running away.'

'We think it was a guild killing,' Hermitage explained.

'Of course it was,' the boy answered with a sneer at idiocy. 'He was an individual. He didn't go by the rules of others. He followed his own path.'

'We know all the reasons the guild would want him dead,' Wat observed. 'But, we're not asking for the full roster. I don't think we've got the time.'

Wat and Hermitage exchanged knowing glances.

The apprentice observed the exchange and raised his eyebrows in a most suggestive and disgusting manner.

Hermitage was appalled, again.

'Was there anyone peculiar around here over the last few days. Anyone more threatening than normal?' Wat asked.

The apprentice shrugged.

'What's he doing with an apprentice anyway?' Wat remembered who the boy was. 'I never saw Briston as the type to take on an apprentice.'

'He is…was a great master.' The apprentice was defensive.

'Well,' Wat drawled, clearly not prepared to go quite that far. 'I suppose your father paid him a huge sum for the apprenticeship.' Wat nodded to himself, recognising a good scheme when he saw one.

'No he did not. Master Briston took me on for my talent.'

Wat was incredulous. 'So?' He got back on track. 'Did anyone visit yesterday? Anyone odd? Odder than usual, I mean.'

The apprentice frowned, pouted, and sulked all at once.

'Come, my child,' Hermitage encouraged. 'The awful deed is done. The least we can do for Briston is identify the killer and expose them.'

The apprentice still frowned at them both.

'Well? What customers were you expecting?' Wat pressed.

'I'm not telling you that!' The lad was surprised at the question.

'I'm not going to steal them, for goodness' sake,' Wat snapped. 'I want to see if one of them might have killed him. They're not going to be much use to him in this state,' Wat nodded at the bundled body of Briston.

The apprentice just sniffed.

'No one special. Usual mix. The odd Norman, a couple of merchants, a regular. Some new bloke from round here.'

'A Norman?' Wat was interested.

Hermitage's eyebrows rose in accompaniment. If anyone was going to kill anyone these days, chances are it would be a Norman. He did think it less likely they'd know about the Tapestry of Death though. 'What was he like, this Norman?'

'Like I said, odd. Kept mumbling to himself. Took one look at the work on the walls, had a quiet chat with Briston, and left. Walked around the outside of the tent a couple of times and then wandered off round the hovels.'

'Probably measuring the place up for another bloody castle,' Wat grumbled. He thought on. 'The merchants and the regulars wouldn't do for Briston. Where would they get their favourite tapestries?. Tell me about the local. What was he like?'

'Bloody old boy, name of Stott,' was the comprehensive description.

For a moment, Hermitage wondered if Stott had been covered in blood and was therefore a suspect. He realised the child swore and tutted disapprovingly.

'I think we should see him,' Hermitage said.

Wat gave him a look that said the debate about what the missing tapestry looked like was over.

'I must say this weaving of yours is most disappointing.' Hermitage shook his head. 'I was expecting enlightened artisans producing fine works that enhanced the human spirit. Instead I've been shown pictures of things that shouldn't have pictures made of them at all. And the artisans are widely reviled, if not actually hunted down.'

'Oh, and there was Virgil,' the apprentice threw in.

'Virgil?' Wat almost shouted.

'The poet?' Hermitage asked.

'The lunatic, violent giant?' Wat asked.

'No, no, he was a Roman,' Hermitage corrected.

Wat huffed at Hermitage before turning to the apprentice. 'Are you telling me that in all our talk of death and murder and who killed Briston, you didn't think to mention that Virgil had been round?'

'Briston owed him money.'

'Better and better.' Wat threw his hands in the air and walked a small circle round the tent, avoiding the box and the body.

'Who is this Virgil?' Hermitage asked. 'Obviously not the poet. Who's been dead for quite a while, come to think of it.'

'No, not the poet. Not that I knew there was one called Virgil.'

'Oh yes, he wrote the Aeneid.'

'Never mind what he wrote. The Virgil we're talking about is a giant.'

'I got that.'

'A giant, violent lunatic.'

'Yes, you said.'

'A giant, violent lunatic who thinks that our weaving business should be his.'

'Is he a weaver then?'

'Only if you count killing weavers, slicing them into bits, and weaving them together.'

Hermitage considered the proposition for a moment. 'No,' he concluded, 'no, I don't think I would.'

'He knows our market is a profitable one and he wants the weavers to work for him.'

'Why would you do that?'

'Because he's a violent, giant lunatic? Didn't I mention that? When one of them gets hold of you, the inclination is to do as he says.'

'But why's he picked on your trade in particular?' Hermitage was thinking things were getting steadily worse. First there was a killer. A good one. Now a giant that specifically went round damaging weavers and presumably the people who were with them at the time. Being a lunatic.

'Because he knows no one will come to our aid. He can threaten us and steal our work and make our customers go to him because they're too scared of being named.'

'Named and shamed,' Hermitage offered.

'Yes, thank you, Hermitage.' Wat seemed to be getting a little testy about the disparagement of his trade. 'So, when he finds a weaver, he threatens them. Some give in straight away. Others, like Briston and me, avoid him like the plague.'

'Does he have the plague as well?' Hermitage asked, thinking that a giant, violent lunatic with the plague was a bit much.

'No, he doesn't have the plague.' Wat was getting more and more annoyed.

'What the hell possessed Briston to borrow money from Virgil? He knows that's the end. Sorry, knew that was the end.' The question was harsh and was directed at the apprentice.

'I don't know.' The apprentice started howling again. 'Briston didn't tell me anything.'

Wat's irritation was fanned by the crying and he stepped up and cuffed the child round the back of the head. It wasn't hard, more of a push than a slap, but it knocked the hood from the head. The revealed face was grimed with the tracks of ancient tears, but underneath the skin was clear, not yet marked by the passage of time. The child had an elfin chin, a slim nose not yet filled out, and eyes of dark green in a field as white as snow. It gave Hermitage a moment's pause. It was a face of purity. A face of the innocence of youth. As he looked, he realised it was a face of something much, much more significant.

Wat stopped and gawped.

Hermitage, unusually, couldn't think of anything to say.

Some thoughts came to him, eventually.

'Oh,' he said, turning to Wat. 'Apprentices aren't supposed to be girls, are they?'

'No,' Wat said most emphatically, staring hard at the girl, who did not return his look. 'They are not. The guild has very strict rules about passing the secrets of the craft outside the prescribed paths.'

'Do I need to guess,' Hermitage sighed, 'what your book of ritual says the penalty is for having a female apprentice?'

Wat smiled grimly. 'The Tapestry of Death for the master,' he said. 'Just plain death for the apprentice.'

Sullied Stotts

I T'S NO GOOD, PARSIMON. It simply has to go.'
Thelred Stott stood in the main hall of his modest
manor and looked at the tapestry hanging on his wall.
It was on a quiet part of the wall, away from the main thorough-
fares of the room. Certainly not above the fireplace. Even so, the
work did stand out. It was a large piece, much longer than a normal tapestry, but only about two feet tall. It stretched to left and
right. Its purpose was not to stop the draft whistling through
one of the manor's large expanses of stone; it had been ordered
as a decorative piece to be gazed upon, admired, and to bring
happy reminiscence. Now it was just being gazed upon. Admiration and happy reminiscence had been asked to leave.

'It is,' Parsimon, Stott's lifelong servant, just a touch less ancient and decrepit than his master, searched for the right word,
'unique,' he said as he gazed upon the acquisition.

'Unique?' Stott raised an eyebrow in his traditional expression of complete outrage. 'It's disgusting is what it is.'

Parsimon nodded his agreement.

'I mean, for goodness' sake,' Stott grumbled into his grey
beard that seemed to bridle of its own volition at the scene before it. This growth was of such magnificence it could be used
for a tapestry itself and while a field of featureless grey would
make a very boring scene, it would be more acceptable than the
one currently dangling before Stott's eyes.

'All I asked for was a remembrance of my dear wife. I gave
the wretched man a charming description of Lady Lorinda's
manners and pastimes, her appearance, and her favourite dress.

I asked for something of her in a garden, perhaps with a dragon nibbling the roses.'

'Tradition,' Parsimon approved.

'What do I get instead? This monstrosity. I mean, why's it so big for one thing?' He gestured at the picture spread out before them.

Stott had admitted the likeness of his lady was a good one, but that only made it worse. Yes, it was in a garden, yes, there was a dragon, but there was no sign of the dress. Or any dress at all, come to that. There was one other main figure he assumed was meant to be himself, but the likeness was very poor. And he had certainly never done anything like *that*. Neither had Lady Lorinda.

Thelred and Lorinda Stott had been married for thirty years. How this tapestrier could represent bits of his wife he had never seen himself was beyond him.

Next to lady Lorinda, a trail of men stretched off into the distance of the scene, all of them carrying out some act of indecency. It looked like nothing less than a play written from the depths of an imagination upon which its audience floated like scum. The thing had to be large simply to fit all the various activities in.

The figures were all very lifelike and of high quality, but it was pretty obvious they were forming a very sinful queue, waiting to take over once Master Stott had finished whatever it was he was supposed to be doing. The tapestry was vivid and detailed. If it hadn't been hanging on a wall, it could have formed the frontispiece of a physik's directory. The sort of directory physiks kept locked away. The activities of the two figures were complex and intensely personal. Poor Stott had never seen anything like it. He didn't know people could do things like that to one another, let alone that a picture could be made of the frankly revolting result. He'd once seen a contortionist at a fair, but doubted that even a professional could get in the position his dear departed wife appeared to have adopted.

'Lorinda would be appalled,' Stott's beard seemed to mumble to itself.

'Indeed,' Parsimon nodded.

'Why did the man think I wanted something like this? Why would he think anyone would want something like this?' Stott's questions were those of a man who knows only up and down suddenly being asked to move sideways.

'Why would *anyone* want something like this?' His puzzlement was complete.

'I gather there are certain markets.' Parsimon did not complete the thought.

'Really?' Stott was genuinely amazed.

'Yes, sir. A lively trade in images of this nature carries on up and down the country.'

'You don't say?'

'I do, sir.' Parsimon hesitated slightly. 'I also recall mentioning that this Briston character might not be the most suitable artisan.'

'But there are so few who come by these parts. And he did have some charming works on the walls of his tent. Just the sort of thing I wanted.'

'But the bulk of his trade is of a more, erm, personal nature.'

'Who was that other fellow we heard about?'

'Wat the Weaver, sir?' Parsimon enquired.

'That's the one.'

'Oh Lord, no, sir,' Parsimon urged, as if his master was about rest his feet in the fire. 'The work of Briston is, erm, very intimate.'

'I think it goes beyond intimate,' Stott harrumphed.

'Those of Wat the Weaver are of an altogether different order.'

'Worse?' Stott's voice found this incredible.

'Not worse as such, sir, more life-like perhaps. I did see one once and it was if the characters were in the room with you.'

'Without any clothes on?'

'Quite naked.'

'And, erm, doing things?'

'Many things. With many people.'

'Ghastly.' Stott shook his head in disappointment. 'Do people buy these things?'

'Oh they do. In great numbers and at great prices.' Parsimon paused. 'Or so I've heard,' he added quickly.

'They should be ashamed of themselves.'

'I rather think they are, sir.'

'I never thought to see the like in Baernodebi. It's such a charming place. I shall have the fellow banned. I can do that, can't I?' he asked his retainer.

'Oh yes, sir,' Parsimon confirmed. 'The market is yours. The Normans didn't seem interested.'

'Excellent.'

Stott had clearly done with the piece, but could not drag his eyes away from it.

'Take it down, would you, Parsimon?' he eventually managed to mumble.

The servant stepped forward and unhooked the tapestry from the hanger, which had been specially prepared to receive the image of Lady Lorinda.

'Appalling,' Stott mumbled again. 'You don't suppose…'

'Suppose what, sir?' Parsimon asked, as he rolled the offending work up.

'That lady Lorinda? Ever?' He nodded towards where the tapestry had hung, 'you know.'

'Oh no, sir,' Parsimon said with confidence.

Lady Lorinda had come to the Stott house from one of the best families as a young, pure, unadulterated virgin. Parsimon was confident that when she was carried from the place on her last journey, the only change was that she wasn't young any more.

He certainly knew from the maids that the lady allowed them to go only so far when undressing her for the night. After that, it was everyone leave, torches out, door shut. No, the image on tapestry had to be pure speculation, or more likely copied from someone of less modesty. Copied from someone of no modesty at all judging by some of the details.

That the Stotts had no offspring was unsurprising. The master had been brought up in a refined house. His two older brothers had been expected to continue the family line, and had been sent into the world to do so. Stott had remained behind to engage in learning and book work. The Stott house never invited the facts of life to stay overnight. His father was proud of his three strapping sons, but never explained to his youngest where any of them came from. Having survived the birth of three large boys, Stott's mother had retired to her tower and locked the door. When the two older brothers, who were very light on learning, were killed in a hunting accident, having shot one another, the Stott line went with them.

Parsimon suspected that Stott wanted children, but had no idea where they came from or how two adults went about getting one. The old boy probably thought one might still turn up, even though his wife was now dead and buried. Or perhaps because his wife was now dead and buried.

The real world had never impinged on his consciousness. Even this small image of a bit of it, albeit a very uncommon and disreputable bit, had disturbed the old man.

At least he had been too old to go and fight for Harold; he'd never have survived that. All he was good for was pottering around the manor, not doing anything of any value.

'Take it back and have it unpicked,' Stott waved the rolled up tapestry away.

'Yes sir,' Parsimon bowed and left his old master ruminating in the cold hall, alone once more with only the memories of his departed wife. Memories now well and truly sullied.

Parsimon took the tapestry away, but he made no move towards the market at Baernodebi. Instead, he took the roll of material down into the cellar, into his personal area of the cellar, the one behind a locked door to which he had the only key.

At the back of the room there was a stack of shelves, more like open-sided boxes piled one upon the other. Parsimon selected a suitable niche, moved a few objects around, and slid the roll in. He angled it slightly and then moved the objects back so that the tapestry was invisible to any passing eye. The passing eye would have to enter the manor, go down to the cellar, through the locked door, and know which niche to look in, but you could never be too careful. Parsimon was about to leave the room when he stopped. He went back to the niche, moved the objects, and retrieved the tapestry. He unrolled it until the first major scene of the work was revealed. He gazed at the remarkable image of his erstwhile mistress. His prudish, demanding and difficult mistress.

'Oh dear, oh dear,' he grinned. He put the work back in its place and left the room, locking the door behind him.

As he climbed the stairs back to the hall, he continued to comment. The farther he went, the more his words morphed into laughter. 'Dear, oh dear, oh dear,' the tears rolled from his eyes and he was almost in hysterics by the time he got back to his chamber.

Caput VII

The Girl

'S O YOU DID KILL BRISTON,' Wat accused the girl, who had the grace to look down.

'How?' Hermitage asked. 'Could an apprentice do the Tapestry of Death?'

'Didn't have to,' Wat said. 'She did it by being a girl. Why are you a girl?' he demanded of the apprentice, who now sat with head bowed, all resistance gone.

She shrugged.

'She can hardly help her birth,' Hermitage put in. 'The question, my dear, is why you are an apprentice?'

The girl shrugged again.

'Do you have a name?' Hermitage asked.

'Leofcwen,' the child mumbled.

'Well, Leofcwen.'

'Most people call me Cwen.'

'Very well, Cwen it is. So Cwen, how come you are an apprentice?' Hermitage asked, before realising this was the wrong question. 'Are you, in fact, an apprentice?'

'Well,' Cwen began.

'She can't be,' Wat interrupted his pacing. 'She's a girl, apprentices are boys. Therefore, she can't be an apprentice.'

Hermitage raised an appreciative eyebrow, 'While that is a very good argument, it doesn't explain the situation,' he responded. 'What were you doing with Briston? Maybe that's the best place to start.'

'I was his apprentice,' Cwen admitted.

'Ha,' Wat raised his arms.

'I was,' Cwen insisted. 'Briston was teaching me all he knew. I've been with him for two years. He's teaching me the craft.'

'He can't, erm, couldn't…' Wat was exasperated.

'Why not?'

'Because you are a girl,' he reemphasised.

'I don't think that makes sense,' Hermitage reasoned. 'Consider the case. A girl is in the same room as an apprentice, a boy apprentice. The master is talking to the boy, instructing him in some part of the trade. If the girl listens as well, is she not also taught?'

Wat frowned, dropped his head slightly, and looked long and hard at Hermitage. He puzzled the proposal through until he had the answer.

'No,' he said.

'Why not?' Hermitage thought it was perfectly clear.

'Because she is a girl,' Wat repeated slowly, this time for Hermitage's benefit.

'Ah,' Hermitage said with some realisation. 'You mean that if a girl learns something of weaving, she is not being taught.'

'Erm, no.' Wat's frown said he was starting to get lost.

'What is it then?'

'Eh?'

'What is it, if I show a girl how to, I don't know, make thread.' Wat looked puzzled and out of his depth.

'I don't know.' He threw his hands up again. 'Stop trying to confuse me.'

'Let us take it that Briston was, erm, showing Cwen here some elements of weaving.' Hermitage waited for objection but there was none. He went on, 'This explains her presence.'

Wat said nothing but stood, arms folded, glaring at Cwen.

'It also gives us reason to question her about Briston's movements.' Hermitage turned to Cwen. 'You say this Virgil character was here? He surely sounds the most likely killer. He seems to know about weaving. Perhaps he can do the Tapestry of Death.'

'Hardly,' Cwen snorted. 'And he wouldn't kill Briston, would he?'

'Why not?' Hermitage was doubtful. Surely a giant, violent lunatic was just the sort of person they were looking for. Not that he actually wanted to find one.

'Because Virgil wanted his money back. He needed Briston to carry on working so he could pay him back . He's hardly likely to kill someone who pays him, is he?'

'Hum.' Hermitage could see that this was sound. 'What was the conversation with Virgil like? Any promises of death? Or even hints?'

'Oh yes,' Cwen responded with alarming candour. 'It was quite a routine visit, you know, a few threats, shouting, bit of pushing and shoving.'

'Anything about a particular tapestry?' Wat asked, apparently now willing to actually talk to the girl.

She looked at him as if he'd spoken Welsh. 'No.' Her impudence was not diminished and seemed to prefer Wat.

'There's one missing from the box. Where is it?' Wat asked, implying she'd deliberately taken it.

'How should I know?' Cwen replied, implying that she'd like to shut Wat in the box, with a tapestry shoved down his throat.

'Not much of an apprentice if you don't know where the works are.' Wat huffed off on another short walk.

'Briston always dealt with those works himself,' the girl explained.

'I bet he did,' Wat snorted.

'The customers didn't like having anyone else around. It put them off paying.'

'So you know the nature of the works?' Hermitage asked in his reasonable tone, a tone completely out of place in this conversation between the weaving fraternity. Or should that be sisterhood? No. Perhaps association. Back to the point Hermitage, he told his wandering mind.

'Of course I do. Briston wasn't proud of it but it was profitable.' She shrugged a sad and tired shrug.

'There appears to be a work missing, as Mister Wat says,' Hermitage explained.

Even at the mention of the name, the girl snarled slightly.

'Would have been tied up in gold thread?' Hermitage prompted.

'I know,' she reluctantly admitted to Hermitage, making it clear with a glance that she wouldn't have told Wat. 'The Stott work, a reminiscence of Lady Lorinda.'

'You know it?' Hermitage was immediately excited at the prospect of finding out what the thing looked like. He then found himself rather disappointed by the fact this young girl knew of the work, which was bound to be very rude. He now found Wat's trade totally abhorrent. That children should be involved made it worse for some inexplicable reason. Children should be clearing dung, fighting, wholesome pursuits.

'I made most of it,' the girl boasted.

'No,' Wat stated. 'You couldn't have.'

'What was all that poking a needle through the cloth I did then? A needle with thread attached to it? The one I tied off before I did a thousand more? That thing was bloody enormous.'

'It does sound like making a tapestry.' Hermitage thought it pretty closely matched his definition.

'Only masters make tapestry.' Wat's arms must be getting tired of being thrown into the air with every sentence. 'I've got apprentices at my workshop – real boy apprentices. They put needles through cloth, but it's still my tapestry.'

Hermitage was about to bring up Wat's comments of weeks ago when they first met. Wat had never actually been made a master. He'd also said Briston had paid to become one, while he clearly hadn't. By his own argument, he could not make tapestry. He thought his thought and saw that expressing it would not be constructive. It would upset Wat and would probably send the conversation off in a pointless direction. He marvelled at this unusual flourish of perspicacity.

'Whatever you think.' Cwen's face said she no longer cared about any opinion of Wat's.

'The point is,' Hermitage said, trying to get them back to the topic in hand, 'that it is missing. It doesn't matter who did what to it. It's not here.'

'Course it isn't missing,' Cwen explained. 'Stott took it.'

'Why didn't you say so?' Wat seemed unable to classify Cwen. His voice said idiot, fraud and girl, all in disparaging tones.

'He took it?' Hermitage was staggered. This wasn't what he'd expected at all. The killer should have taken the tapestry because its image was the key to the whole affair. It would unravel events, reveal truths. What an awful experience, to be so curious about something that turned out not to matter at all. 'But the golden thread?' he muttered. 'If the customer took it, he would have the golden thread. You know, the erm…'

'Customer fodder?' Cwen offered.

'Yes, quite.' Hermitage acknowledged another disappointment that this girl was being comprehensively corrupted.

'Didn't want it. Funny old boy though. I can't imagine him wanting one of Briston's specials at all.'

'I thought you said you kept out of the way?' Wat asked in some triumph.

'I was looking under the tent. I have to. Briston let me. He said I needed to see how customers were handled.'

'Stott wasn't happy with the work?' Hermitage pressed on, realising that this was a possible motive.

'Nah,' Cwen said. 'He went all shaky and red. Said it was a slight to his precious wife's memory.'

Hermitage nodded in understanding and sympathy. He could imagine. He didn't want to ask the next question at all, let alone of a young girl. He reasoned to himself that this was bizarre, considering the young girl in question had actually made the thing. Still, it didn't feel right.

'I don't need to know *all* the details, my dear,' he began, 'but I imagine the work was of quite a personal nature,' he continued quickly, hoping to put her off giving him an anatomical description, the sort of description he didn't want to hear coming from anyone, let alone the mouth of a child. 'I have seen the other works in the box so I know the general style.'

'Yeah,' Cwen said, undisturbed. 'Usual stuff. It showed the Lady Lorinda in the garden with a great big…'

'I don't…' Hermitage almost yelled. He controlled himself, 'I don't need the full description.'

'I thought it was rather good,' she said, as if describing an apple.

'This Stott fellow clearly did not,' Hermitage commented, with greater sympathy for Stott.

'Nah,' Cwen scoffed. 'Briston still got his money though and he went off.'

'He accepted it?' Hermitage was amazed. 'Why would the man do that?

'Briston told him he had to pay because of all the thread and cloth and work and everything.'

'And how if he didn't pay, Briston would be destitute, the debt collectors would come and beat him half to death, and then his children would starve,' Wat said in a very matter of fact manner.

Hermitage stared at him.

'Standard response,' Wat explained.

Cwen nodded.

'This gets worse and worse.' Hermitage had never expected he could feel such depths of despair at weaving. Hitherto his despair had been applied to much grander concepts, oh like, human nature, sin, corruption, the ultimate fate of the human soul. Not a bit of thread through some cloth.

'So this Stott fellow?' he speculated.

'What about him?' Cwen asked.

'He has a tapestry he doesn't want. More than doesn't want. He probably despises it and himself for ever ordering it.'

'Yeah,' Cwen sniggered. 'I think he expected Briston to be a normal weaver.'

'He's in anguish over the tapestry. He's lost money over it, and it insulted the memory of his wife. Plenty of motive for murder.'

'I doubt it,' Wat dismissed the suggestion. 'He wouldn't know the Tapestry of Death from a cow pat. He sounds like the sort of customer who just blushes and walks away. Never tells a soul what he's ordered. If he didn't throttle Briston there and then, he certainly wouldn't have come back and done it later.'

'He could have got someone else to do it.' Hermitage didn't want to give up on the tapestry being the cause of all this.

'Nope,' Wat knocked this idea as well. 'The people who want other people killed tend not to be the types who go a bit red and then pay up. They tend to be the types who drag you around your tent, having punched you several times in the head to soften you up for the journey.'

Cwen nodded agreement.

'Also, he wouldn't have time,' Wat said. 'He was only here this morning. Finding someone who could do the Tapestry of Death would take ages. Then they'd have to get their killer to Baernodebi and finish Briston off. All by dark the same day.'

'Perhaps he went back to his house and told his guards to go and kill a weaver?' Hermitage offered.

'Like this?' Wat gestured to the neatly bound package that used to be Briston the Weaver.

'One of the guards used to be a weaver? Or Stott is a guild man himself?'

'All a bit unlikely,' Wat said.

'Well,' Hermitage said, whose ideas really were running out of plausibility, 'he may have paid the guild killers directly. Or perhaps he saw something of them. There's only one way to find out.'

'You want to find this Stott character and see what he knows,' Wat summarised. 'While Briston's real killer, the guild man who finished him off for having a female apprentice, gets away.' He glared at them both.

Cwen just shrugged again.

'You were lucky you were looking for water or you'd be dead as well,' Wat said, clearly thinking that's just what should have happened.

'We go to the guild,' Wat said. 'If this Stott's place is *very* nearby, we can go there first. If not, we leave him alone.' He made it sound like he was giving Hermitage a treat, but only if he was very, very good.

'Well, that's excellent,' Hermitage smiled some encouragement. 'We want to get a complete picture. We'll question this Stott fellow and take it from there.'

'We need to go quickly,' Wat added as he stood once more over the body of his friend.

Hermitage looked and nodded in sympathy.

'Briston's starting to smell,' Wat said.

To The Manor Forlorn

I**T TOOK A LITTLE BRIBERY** and corruption to get clear directions to the Stott manor, which was two miles away. Lolby the peasant insisted on being bribed and corrupted before he would say a word. There then followed a lively debate on whether two miles constituted nearby, very close, close, or miles out of their way. Hermitage had a number of sources, most of them biblical, which supported the proposition that a visit to Stott's would actually take no time at all – in a rather obscure and theological sort of timeframe. Wat waved his arms about and tried to indicate two miles by holding his hands apart. Eventually Cwen stepped in and pointed out that they could have got there and back in the time spent arguing the point. They finally set off for Stott's, Hermitage gently satisfied, Wat not at all.

In exchange for the route, Lolby was left once more in charge of Briston's box of bounty. Cwen told him in no uncertain manner that she knew every piece in detail, and that if any of them were missing, damaged, or needed cleaning when they got back, he'd wish his private parts were made of wool.

Hermitage listened to the conversation with his familiar despair. A peasant whose highest ambition was so low. A young woman mired in a trade of such depravity her very thinking and language had become corrupt. And his friend Wat. At least he now knew why Wat never spoke of his work. The great mystery of their relationship had been cleared up. Hermitage rather wished it was still a mystery. He liked a mystery unravelled and revealed, but hadn't thought this one would be quite so revealing.

The members of the little team were in their own worlds and conversation wasn't welcome. Hermitage followed Wat and Cwen as they walked the two miles to the Stott manor. The two weavers, in line astern, were munching on a piece of something Lolby had given them. He had said it was bread, but Hermitage was not convinced. His previous experience had convinced Hermitage that starvation was the safer option. Plus, the 'bread' was a kind of yellow colour and not the healthy kind.

He thought of the two in front of him as weavers, despite Wat's protestations that a woman putting thread in a cloth was not weaving while a man doing the same thing was. Wat had made some truly ludicrous suggestion that perhaps the church should take the lead and say that women could be priests. Hermitage always enjoyed a good debate, but there really was no point if your opponent was going to spout such unintelligible nonsense.

The triumvirate, separate but together, arrived at the Stott manor in the glorious, crackling sunshine of the winter morning. The air was so clear, the cold passed through it unhindered and made straight for the bones. Hermitage shivered in his habit, but then he always did. Wat was covered in thick, well-fitting clothes as normal, but rubbed his hands together to frighten the chill out of them. Cwen had wrapped a cloak around her boyish garb. She pulled it closer as they approached the main entrance.

The manor was modest but solid. A great oaken door studded with black iron work sat in the middle of an expanse of stone that looked like it had been thrown up, readymade, just after God said, "Let there be light". Moss and ivy clad the face, giving it a life of its own. More likely it was the chief means of holding the wall together. Small windows peeped through the ivy, as if ashamed to be spotted, while worn down castellations topped the greenery.

Wat strode forward and hammered on the oak. Hermitage had been about to suggest looking for the tradesman's entrance.

He didn't know about weavers, but monks were never welcome at the front door. After a wait, during which they said nothing but looked around, displaying a hitherto hidden fascination with ivy and moss, steps were heard behind the door. They went on an awfully long time, as if the space inside the manor were far larger than the outside indicated. Eventually the door creaked open and the reason for the steps was displayed.

The ancient Parsimon dragged the door open, taking the slow and tiny steps that were all his legs were capable of.

'Yes?' he asked, frowning at the band behind the door.

'Is your master at home?' Wat enunciated each word loudly.

'I'm not deaf,' Parsimon retorted. 'Everything else, but not deaf.'

'Sorry,' Wat dropped his voice to normal. 'Your master?'

'Who's asking?' Parsimon had not opened the door wide enough for anyone to enter.

'I'm Wat and this is Brother Hermitage,' Wat announced.

'And I'm Cwen, weaver's apprentice,' Cwen added in a loud and clear voice of her own. Mainly for Wat's benefit. Or rather for the benefit of his irritation.

'Ah,' Parsimon hesitated. 'I am confident my master will not want to talk to anyone about weaving. He's had rather a nasty experience lately.' Parsimon's eyes narrowed as he looked from Cwen to Wat. 'You're called Wat, you say? Not Wat the Weaver?'

'I am,' Wat said and bowed a bow of acknowledgement rather than humility.

'He definitely won't want to see *you*,' Parsimon concluded, which rather knocked Wat.

'Does he know me?' Wat wondered.

'By reputation,' Parsimon hissed.

'Oh dear,' Hermitage observed.

'I'm surprised to see a monk in such company.' Parsimon cast a glance at Hermitage.

'We are investigating a death, a murder,' Hermitage answered, hoping to move the conversation away from weaving. Especially Wat's very particular sort of weaving.

'Death, murder, and weaving, eh?' Parsimon raised an interested eyebrow. 'Subjects currently excluded from my master's fireside.'

'We think your master may have some relevant information,' Hermitage put in quickly, as the door began to shut in their faces.

It opened again slowly, 'And who was the victim, exactly?' Parsimon asked with some suspicion.

'Exactly?' Hermitage puzzled, surely the victim was the victim. There was no ambiguity. Who was the victim approximately? Didn't make sense.

'Briston the Weaver,' Wat explained, seeing that Hermitage had been confused to a halt.

'Ah.' Parsimon raised his eyebrows. 'Well, these things happen.' He made no attempt to open the door wider.

'These were very unusual circumstances,' Wat explained.

'I'm sure,' Parsimon's voice shrugged.

'I'm determined to bring the culprit to justice,' the weaver added with some more intensity in his tone.

'Very commendable.'

'So we would like to talk to your master,' Wat growled, trying to make it quite clear that he was going to get what he wanted.

'I'll be sure to let him know you popped by,' Parsimon said, putting his paltry weight behind the door.

'It's alright,' Hermitage whispered to Wat. 'If master Stott doesn't want to talk about it, I quite understand. We still have our killer to go after.' He felt bad about his curiosity now. It was unjust to satisfy it at the expense of an old man.

'I don't like doors being shut in my face,' Wat hissed back. 'The people doing the shutting are usually hiding something.'

'Do you know a chap called Virgil?' Wat asked through the last closing inch. The inch paused.

'No,' Parsimon said, sounding puzzled by such a non sequitur.

'Nasty piece of work,' Wat continued, clearly happy that Virgil wasn't close at hand. 'Big, violent, thoroughly unpleasant.'

'Well, I don't know him,' Parsimon closed the door.

'Not yet, you don't,' Wat spoke in a friendly manner to the sheet of oak that now faced him. 'But he's very interested in Briston and his works. In fact, we hear that Briston owed him money. When this Virgil finds out your master might have information, he'll probably pop by as well. Trouble with Virgil is he can never pop quietly. Always brings a few friends with him and they tend to make an awful mess. Of places, people. No respecter of position is Virgil. Or age, come to think of it.'

'My master has no information for you or for this Virgil character.'

'So he doesn't own a tapestry made by Briston then? A representation of Lady Stott?'

The door opened a touch.

'May I assume that if I let you in, this Virgil character may never hear about my master?'

'Who's Virgil?' Wat played along.

The door was opened very unamicably and Parsimon reluctantly let them in. Wat stood in the doorway as Cwen and Hermitage passed.

'Really, Wat,' Hermitage frowned in renewed disappointment, 'an old man.'

'They're usually the worst,' Wat said as they entered the hall and he closed the door behind them.

Hermitage looked around the place and thought "comfort". They were in the traditional large hall. The door opened directly into this but the chill of the world was left outside. The place was filled with warmth from a massive log fire that looked like it had been burning since September. The fireplace itself was big enough to walk into and a large wooden chair was pulled up close to the flames. The floor was scattered with fresh straw and large tapestries hung from the wall, preventing draughts and presenting a happy scene. Deer leapt, streams tumbled, musicians played, dragons nibbled. Windows with real, unbroken glass let the weak winter sun fall in over their sills. This was reinforced by a huge iron candelabra that hung from the main beam of the ceiling. It was full of candles, even at this hour of the day, and they burned merrily. This Stott fellow clearly had money.

The room was some fifty feet square. The fire was opposite the door and a stone staircase to the right led to upper chambers. In the middle of the room, a large rectangular table held the largest amount of pewter Hermitage had ever seen in one place. There were pots and mugs, cutlery and plates, massive tureens, and serving dishes. There were also things, the purpose of which was beyond Hermitage. Strange shapes that looked like they had started life as something else. Even the something they had started as seemed bizarre. The place was warm and homely. The master who lived in it was gently roasting in the chair by the fire.

'Master,' Parsimon called as he approached the fireplace.

'Ah, um, what?' The master woke into alarmed life. He remained seated but his voice leaped. 'What the devil is it, Parsimon? Dinner?'

'No sir, there are visitors.'

'Visitors?' The master spoke as if a cart load of dung had been poured on his pewter. 'You know my instructions for visitors.'

'Yes sir, but these have a particular reason for coming.'

'Visitors with a reason?' the master ruminated. 'Can't think of one.'

'It's about the weaver,' Parsimon explained.

'Oh, no more, Parsimon! Enough of the wretched fellow.'

'It seems he's dead, sir.'

'Is he, by Jove?' Stott paused for a moment at the news. 'Probably for the best.'

Cwen's grief had been replaced by anger as she prepared to launch herself at the old man by the fire. Hermitage, noticing the movement, grabbed her arms.

'Now then my dear, nothing to be gained from that.'

'Who's that lad?' Stott asked, hauling himself from his seat to see what was going on.

'I'm a woman,' Cwen snapped.

'Oh, I don't think so,' Stott squinted at her. He turned his attention to Wat. 'What is it you want?' He looked the weaver up and down and then noticed Hermitage. 'Good God! There's a monk in here.' He sounded as if he'd just spent weeks exterminating an infestation of monks, only to find they'd been breeding in the wainscoting.

'Brother Hermitage,' Hermitage announced.

'Odd name for a monk,' Stott frowned. 'What are you all doing here anyway? You're in my house,' he announced.

Hermitage was having trouble following this place. The fellow at the door asked odd questions about the victim, now the master didn't seem any better. Of course they were in his house! How else were they going to talk to him?

'We are investigating the death of Briston the Weaver,' Wat explained in loud, clear tones.

'Murder,' Cwen put in.

Stott considered this for a moment. 'Can't say I'm surprised,' he mumbled into his beard.

'Why so?' Hermitage asked, helping himself to a few steps into the room, closer to the fire.

'Did you see the tapestries he made?' Stott's beard was all outrage and offence.

'Yes, we did,' Hermitage sighed.

'Appalling.'

'Quite,' Hermitage glanced at Wat and Cwen with disapproving eyes.

'If I'd been a younger man…' Stott left the thought to the air.

'So he was well when you left him?'

'He had a sore ear from the thick end of my tongue, but I'm old,' Stott sighed deeply in reminiscence of younger years, 'I can't kill people anymore.'

Parsimon coughed loudly.

'If you were offended by his works,' Hermitage asked, 'why did you visit him?'

'Ah, well...' Stott's beard ruffled up and down in a series of incoherent mumbles.

'You had gone to collect a piece from him?' Wat sought confirmation. He had intended to sit down and had pulled a chair out from the table for the purpose, only to find it was covered in bits of pewter.

'All I said,' Stott pronounced clearly, 'was that I wanted a reminiscence of my dear wife, the Lady Lorinda. Garden, dress, that sort of thing.'

'Dragons?' Wat suggested.

'Exactly. So I go to the fellow's tent and what do I see?'

'A rather more explicit reminiscence?' Wat offered.

'Doesn't even begin to approach the scene,' Stott agreed.

'Briston does rather specialise in the reminiscence of the deceased wife,' Wat explained to the room. 'Very popular after a death in childbirth,' he added with an entirely inappropriate grin.

'Obviously, in my younger days, I'd have given the fellow a damn good thrashing and run him out of town.' Parsimon's cough returned. 'But what can an old man do?'

Hermitage had a new thought. He considered that Stott appeared to be a man of some money and therefore influence. He also considered the nature of the offending tapestry. 'Did you by any chance report him to the weavers' guild for the work he'd done?'

Wat looked at his friend with widened eyes. That wasn't a thought that had occurred to him.

'No, I didn't,' Stott was upset again. 'It's bad enough that Parsimon and I know about it. I'm not going to go spreading word of the ghastly thing. At least I know, now the weaver's dead, there's no one else who knows anything of it. No one has any inkling of the foul scene.'

It was Cwen's turn to cough.

'Do you have the tapestry?' Wat asked.

'Certainly not!' Stott was outraged.

'You refused to accept it?' Wat asked.

Hermitage thought this a very clever ruse: see if this Stott fellow was going to lie.

'Ah, well, no, not actually, as such.' Stott returned to his bearded mumble.

'You took it?' Hermitage knew the answer and was grateful to hear the truth.

'Of course, like I said, didn't want anyone else looking at the thing.'

'Can we see it?' Wat enquired.

'Certainly not! I wouldn't besmirch the memory of my dear wife any further. In any case, it's gone.'

'Gone?' Hermitage couldn't imagine the man would have given the thing away to someone else.

'Yes, Parsimon destroyed it, didn't you?'

'Yes sir,' Parsimon confirmed.

'How?' Wat asked, full of suspicion.

'I got him to unpick the thing thread by thread, isn't that right?' Stott and his beard nodded at Parsimon.

'That was my intention, sir, but the thing in question was rather large for such a task. I had to burn it instead.'

'Burn it, you say?' Stott asked.

'Indeed.'

'Good show! Even better.'

'Oh dear,' Hermitage dropped his head in thought.

'Oh dear?' Stott was back in outrage. 'Oh dear, sir monk? You of all people should not be searching after such images as this. Your mind should be on higher things.'

'No, no,' Hermitage protested, 'I don't want to see it. Not really.' He realised that he really did want to see it, but only for entirely selfish reasons. He even realised that if he did get to see it, he'd wish he'd never seen it. 'It's just that it was connected to the murder. It could have been useful to see the original work.'

'Not if you want to go to heaven when you die,' Stott commented. 'Anyway, how could it be a useful?'

'I don't know really.' Hermitage realised he really didn't know. Now he knew Stott didn't report it to the guild and the killer hadn't taken it either, so that was it. No connection. Wat could be right. The guild were just making an example of Briston, or they'd found out about a female apprentice. He really hoped it was the former, for Cwen's sake. 'I just thought there might be something in it,' he tailed off.

'There was far too much in it, young fellow,' Stott bridled. 'And it's best burned to a cinder.'

'You're sure that Briston was alive when you left him?'

'He was counting my money, impudent wretch.'

'Ah,' Hermitage didn't want to press the question about why he paid up for a horrible tapestry he didn't want.

'What time was this?'

'Early morning, soon as the market opened. I was anxious to see the work. Until I saw it, of course. Then I was anxious again but for a different reason.'

'And you haven't seen him since?'

'Never want to see the fellow again. Not that I will now, eh? Came straight back here. Hung it on the wall.'

'You hung it on the wall?' Hermitage couldn't understand why he'd have done this.

Stott's beard flapped about. 'By the time I'd got it home, I'd convinced myself it wasn't as bad as I thought. When I hung it on the wall, I remembered it was worse. Took it down and got rid of it.' Stott was final.

'You didn't go back and visit him again?'

'Certainly not.'

'And you didn't send anyone?'

'Parsimon here?' Stott scoffed. 'He's hardly the stuff murderers are made of.'

'You have no other servants?'

'No he doesn't,' Parsimon said with some feeling. 'There's the old lady's maid, but she really is old.'

Hermitage's mind gaped at anyone this wrinkled ancient would call really old.

'And there's the house maid, but we don't let her go out.'

Hermitage nodded, all well and proper so far.

'Did you see anyone else around Briston's tent?' he asked.

'Absolutely not!' Stott was offended. 'Place was deserted when I arrived and I had to loiter about looking at some pewter before I dared leave. Couldn't let anyone know the sort of thing I'd been given. Heaven forfend I'd meet anyone I know.'

'You didn't see Cwen here?' Hermitage gestured at the girl, who had propped herself on the edge of the pewter-laden table.

'The young man? No.' Stott cast his eyes around the room at the assembly crowding his pewter. His face darkened, under the beard. 'I don't know what's going on here, master monk, but I am not inclined to continue this conversation. In my own home!'

'I am sorry, sir, but if we are to find out who killed Briston, we need to find out as much as we can.'

'Well, you can find things out somewhere else when I have my servant here throw you all out the door,' Stott snapped.

Wat and Cwen eyed Parsimon, who made it quite clear he was going to attempt no such thing.

'You have been most helpful.' Hermitage nodded and smiled in gratitude.

'I hope not,' Stott grumbled as he returned to his seat by the fire. He waved the back of his hand at them, inviting them to leave. Immediately.

Parsimon closed the door dismissively behind them. The three stood in silence for a moment.

'Well,' Hermitage said eventually, 'I think that was very useful. We know that Master Stott left Briston alive in the early morning. Cwen saw him at midday. We found him that night.'

'How's that useful?' Wat asked. 'He died sometime during the day. We knew that already. We knew he was killed by the guild already. I'll admit we now know the tapestry was not reported to the guild, so that can't be the reason for the Tapestry of Death. All we're left with is what we had in the first place. Briston was killed as an example for the Normans, or as an example to anyone thinking of getting a female apprentice.' He glared at Cwen who glared back very effectively.

'Of course, we did get a bit more information,' Cwen said through her gritted teeth; teeth that looked like they wanted to be gritted on some of Wat's more delicate places.

'Which is?' he asked with contempt.

'Parsimon was lying.'

Quarrels

I HAVE GOT TO FIND THAT TAPESTRY,' Eadric mumbled to himself as he stepped as smartly away from the guild as he could without calling it running.

The open road seemed awfully open. All directions held peril – the peril of the guild and The Hoofhorn behind him, and the peril of Baernodebi, and a dead body ahead. The peril of simply running away was equally real. It was clearly the favoured option, but he knew what the guild and The Hoofhorn were capable of. He'd done most of what they were capable of for them. They never gave up. Well, he never gave up, mainly because they kept paying him. He did wonder who they would send. Who they *could* send. Without him doing their dirty work, who would they get? Old Acca, the last guild enforcer, was well past it.

He had seen The Hoofhorn in action. The chase had been very close and if the loony old rag bag hadn't simply stopped for some reason, Eadric's head would be boiling in the cauldron right now. His mind made up, he strode along, anxious to get to Baernodebi and resume his search. The wretched thing must be somewhere.

'Ha, fine fellow!'

A loud voice from behind knocked Eadric from his thoughts with a start. He turned and saw a bright-eyed, smiling figure almost skipping along the road towards him.

'Hi, hi,' the figure called with laughter in his tone.

Eadric watched in some astonishment. He looked warily around the open countryside, but couldn't see anywhere this man could have come from. His eyes twitched back and forth nervously.

'What a relief to find a fellow traveller,' the figure said when it reached him.

'Which noble's table did you fall off?' Eadric asked, eyeing the new arrival.

The clothes were all well fitting and clearly made to measure. Bright breeches and a matching jerkin were cowled in a thick winter coat – the sort of thing that could keep a small family warm. Thick boots at the bottom and a jaunty cap at the top finished the picture. The jaunty cap even had a jaunty feather in it. Slung across the back was a well made and rugged pack. The sort designed for comfort as much as load bearing. The whole ensemble screamed money.

The jaunt of the cap was matched by the figure's stance – right foot back, left slightly forward, as if the fellow was about to start a dance. The left hand was on his hip and the other hung at his side, except it didn't hang naturally – it was posed, palm outwards. The head was held back slightly and the smile on the face was as shallow as a swallow's toilet. The whole ensemble screamed arseling. And a big one at that.

'Firman, at your service,' the new arrival said.

He bent at the waist, leaving his feet where they were, while sweeping the hat from his head with his left hand in a flamboyant bow. Firman's smile spread to a genuine grin of pleasure at meeting Eadric, as if he was an old friend.

Eadric stared in astonishment at everything. The clothes, the stance, the performance, but most of all the face. Firman's face had basically been borrowed from a horse. Very recently. If they'd met in the dark, Eadric would have led the man straight to the stable. His eyes seemed to have wandered to the sides of his head and, in doing so, had pulled the nose up. The complete absence of a chin, and cheek bones that had been lined up with a ruler, meant this man would be very unwise to enter a field of stallions.

'Firman, you say?' Eadric asked.

'Indeed, and grateful I am to find a fellow traveller. We can journey together to avoid the attention of robbers.'

'Robbers?' Eadric said in disbelief, looking around at the open country and the wide road. There wasn't a hiding place for a robber in sight.

'Or Normans,' Firman said.

Eadric did acknowledge this threat with a short nod of his head. 'Where do you travel to?' he asked blankly.

'To Lincoln, but tonight I shall seek an inn or tavern in Baernodebi.'

'An inn or tavern?' Eadric asked in wonder. 'Have you *been* to Baernodebi before?'

'No, but I'm always fascinated to see new places.'

'You'll be warmer sleeping in your coat,' Eadric observed, 'and it's probably more spacious than most buildings in Baernodebi.'

'You're familiar with the place then? Excellent. This is a most fortuitous meeting.'

'Yes, isn't it?' said Eadric without any fortune in his voice.

With a reluctant raise of his eyebrows, he indicated that this Firman character could accompany him. It never did any harm to travel in company and at least Firman didn't present any sort of threat himself. Mind you, he wouldn't be much help if any robbers actually did turn up.

They plodded off along the road to Baernodebi. Eadric said nothing, but his mind cantered around. It was odd enough to meet a stranger on the road, let alone one who wanted to travel with you. His recent experiences had made him nervous and wary. The sight of Firman was enough to put anyone on their guard.

Firman himself kept up a stream of irrelevant and irritating observations about everything. From the spacing of the trees to the surface of the road. From the weather for the time of year to recent developments in timekeeping. The one thing he seemed poorly informed about was silence.

'Why are you travelling alone?' Eadric interrupted a fascinating, one-sided conversation on the best luggage makers north of the Humber.

'Beg pardon?' Firman seemed surprised to be spoken to.

'Why are you travelling alone?' Eadric repeated. 'You are obviously a man of substance,' he gestured at the man's clothes and pack, 'and you are rightly worried about robbers. You seem to be the type who could bring a couple of large fellows with you to keep the robbers away. Not rely on strangers you meet on the road. In fact, I could be a robber.'

'Oh no, no,' Firman laughed. Eadric didn't. 'I could tell straight away you were an upright and decent fellow.'

Both wrong, thought Eadric. 'But you still travel alone?' he pressed.

'To tell the truth,' Firman dropped his voice and stepped close to Eadric, beckoning him to receive a secret, 'I am on a mission,' he hissed.

Eadric's eyes narrowed, 'A mission? What sort of mission?'

'Oh, I couldn't possibly say.' Firman tapped the side of his nose.

'Surely all the more reason to be accompanied?'

'Ah well. Family, you see. Always troublesome, eh?'

'Your family is why you're travelling alone?'

'It's the mission. Can't have them knowing exactly what's going on,' Firman nodded significantly, as if this explained everything.

'A secret family mission in Lincoln makes you travel the road alone, dressed in your finest? The mission is so secret no one can come with you, yet you tell a total stranger?' Eadric had stopped walking and had folded his arms.

'Who safer?' Firman was amiable. 'I don't know you, you don't know me. Worst case would have been meeting someone I knew. They'd have put two and two together.'

Eadric stood frowning.

'Shall we?' Firman gestured to the open road and stepped off along it.

'I don't believe a word of it,' Eadric muttered.

✦   ✦   ✦

'So,' Hermitage tried to sound bright, but didn't feel it, 'what do we do now?'

His urge to interrogate Cwen about Parsimon's lying was like an unreachable itch. It burned his tongue, which almost writhed in his mouth, wanting to throw the necessary question into the cold air. He did feel rather ashamed at having dragged them all this way for nothing. Anyway, Cwen and Wat had returned to their hostile, staring silence. Hermitage thought if he asked Cwen a question, Wat would only dismiss it as nonsense.

'Back to Baernodebi for the box and then the guild,' Wat said.

As they walked, Hermitage did try to prompt some lively conversation about the information they had got from Stott and Parsimon. Despite his making it entirely relevant to the matter in hand, he couldn't get Cwen and Wat to engage. Basically, he couldn't get them to speak to one another at all. At one point, Cwen had a bit of a coughing fit and Wat scoffed as if she was doing it just to get attention. They would both speak to him, but only separately. And when they did, they were full of sympathy that poor Hermitage had to speak to the other one. After a spell of flitting to and fro, which achieved nothing, Hermitage walked ahead a few steps and stopped in the middle of the road. The others had no choice but to stop too.

'You two are a disgrace,' he lectured.

They looked at him in surprise and actually stole a glance at one another.

'Wat, are you dead?' Hermitage asked.

'No, of course not,' Wat replied, not understanding.

'Cwen? Have you been bound in tapestry and left in a tent?'

'No,' Cwen replied, anger conquering grief.

89

'Are we together in this place to resolve the apprenticeship issues of the weavers' guild?' Hermitage carried on before there could be an answer, 'Or are we here, perhaps, to determine the relative merits of the acquaintances of Briston? No. We are here to find his killer. I admit we got little from Stott, but we are on the trail again, so you two need to cooperate.'

'If he'd turned up earlier, Briston wouldn't be dead at all,' Cwen accused Wat with a dismissive gesture of her thumb.

'And if she wasn't a girl, the guild wouldn't have had a perfectly good cause to kill Briston in the first place,' Wat spat back.

Hermitage folded his arms and glared. He'd never done real glaring before. He knew what the physical process was – he'd been glared at enough in his time, and had even tried to copy the effect when alone in his cell. Now he felt there was something authentic in his look. The slight narrowing of his eyes, the hardening of his mouth, and the stiffness in his neck came from somewhere inside. It wasn't a physical imitation of someone who was good at glaring; it was a sincere, heartfelt, pointed glare.

Wat and Cwen swayed backwards slightly and looked at the road.

It had worked. Hermitage could now glare. He would have to remember the moment.

'So?' he asked.

Wat and Cwen mumbled through their dropped heads.

This was most gratifying. He would have to try it out on some of his more troublesome Brothers if he ever met them again.

'If we could leave behind our personal animosity and concentrate on the journey at hand, we might make some progress.'

'Yes, Hermitage,' Wat said.

Cwen nodded.

'Good.' Hermitage lightened and his glare lifted.

He turned his back on them and walked on along the road,

'Cwen,' he prompted, 'you were suggesting that Parsimon might be lying?'

'Oh, erm, yes. He did seem a bit fidgety, not quite looking at anyone, stepping from one foot to the other. Like some of the customers.'

'The ones who don't want anyone else to know they *are* customers?' Wat added.

'That's them,' Cwen confirmed. '"Oh it's not for me, I'm just getting one for a friend", or "it's a joke for my cousin's wedding". I've heard them all and seen them all. Fidgety, never look you in the eye, can't wait to get away.'

'I can imagine,' Hermitage said, thinking such behaviour would be perfectly reasonable if you were buying one of those awful tapestries.

'I mean, if Stott found the tapestry so shameful…' Cwen went on.

'Which we know it was,' Hermitage put in.

'Yes. He could really have ordered it to be destroyed. But it was one of our best and most expensive works, even for someone with Stott's money. Big step for a chap in Parsimon's position to burn something that was worth a month's food. Or maybe Stott's lying?' Cwen's eyes widened as her own thought processes raced along. 'Maybe he really did want it. Paid for it, kept it, and all the rest is show. Complaining to Briston, making a fuss about how disgusting it is. Then he's gloating over it by the fire?'

'He did seem genuine in his disgust,' Hermitage observed. 'In which case, he's probably telling the truth. He ordered it destroyed and wouldn't dream of telling anyone about it.'

'I'd say it's very likely,' Wat nodded.

'Cwen?' Hermitage sought the girl's attention even though Wat was largely ignoring her.

'S'pose so,' she grunted. 'Stott does come across as a mush head.'

'I concur,' Hermitage put his hands behind his back as he

strolled along. 'I did not detect anything in Master Stott's nature to indicate scheming or dishonesty. He was slightly put out at our appearing in his home and interrogating him, but apart from that, nothing.' He furrowed his brow and thought as he walked.

'Let us assume then,' he carried on, 'that, as far as Stott is concerned, the tapestry is destroyed. Stott himself is shamed by the whole event and simply wants to be left alone. If Parsimon is lying and has kept the piece for himself, he's hardly likely to report it to anyone, let alone the guild. And I don't think Master Stott is the type to go and directly hire a killer.'

The others nodded their agreement.

'Mind you,' Cwen added a thought, 'if Parsimon did want to steal valuable tapestries, the old man had a very good collection on his walls.'

'I noticed that,' Wat nodded agreement. 'Some very good examples and a very old work by the fire. I'd say he knows his tapestry.'

'Enough to arrange for the murder of a weaver?' Hermitage couldn't make the connection from tapestry lover to weaver murderer. 'Offended that the whole of tapestry was besmirched?'

'Well,' Wat thought and clearly couldn't make the connection either, 'no.'

'Marvellous,' Hermitage said in a very heavy tone. 'We are no further forward. Briston was alive when Cwen left him and dead by evening when Lolby found him.'

'And the guild killer did it.' Wat was insistent and final.

They took a few steps in silence.

'I think,' Hermitage said, but knew that his thought was not going to be welcome. 'I think it's time to talk to the other person we know was there, this Virgil character.'

'Oh, Hermitage, give it a rest.' Wat did sound annoyed now. 'We know the guild did it. We've looked at your Stott and that's taken us nowhere. We go to the guild, we find the killer, and that's that. I know you'd like it to be more complicated, more motives, more suspects, more interesting facts to hammer to death, but really, this one is very straightforward. Find guild killer. Kill guild killer. Go home.'

Hermitage studied the ground.

'If Virgil is as you say, he might know who the killer actually is,' he offered quietly. '*We've* got to go to the guild to find out. Perhaps we could find out straight away if we ask Virgil?'

'I wouldn't advise it,' Wat replied, putting his irritation behind him in the face of Hermitage's persistence. The persistence of a puppy trying to climb on its mother's back.

Cwen coughed sarcastically.

'Well, you go and ask him if he knows who killed Briston then,' Wat snapped at the girl. 'When he says he does, and asks what you're going to do about it, you'll have your answer.'

'It's you who's supposed to be avenging your friend,' Cwen snapped back. 'If you think Virgil knows, we should ask him.'

'Right!' Wat threw his arms up in loud surrender. 'Let's go after Virgil then. The biggest, maddest killer in the kingdom. We'll ask him if he knows Briston's killer and then see if he'd like to kill us as well.'

'Stop,' Hermitage said.

He didn't say it loudly; he wasn't even aiming it at the squabbling weavers. They had arrived at Baernodebi and the sight before his eyes put fear where his stomach used to be. He knew they'd been seen. The loud argument had drawn attention their way. There was no chance of walking quietly from this ghastly situation.

Wat and Cwen removed their attention from one another and gazed across the market field.

'Oh, bloody hell,' Wat gasped as he saw what had filled the space.

Coming up the road from the other side of the market field, Eadric and Firman had stopped as well. Looks flew between the two small parties. Looks of sympathy and resignation. The sort of looks people probably exchanged when they entered opposite ends of a bottomless bog and knew there was nothing for it but to drown together, yards apart.

'What do we do now?' Cwen asked.

'Pray?' Hermitage suggested.

Caput X

Castigatori

OU!' A LARGE FINGER on the end of a large arm pointed straight at Hermitage. 'Come here,' the voice was large as well.

Hermitage's old feelings of insignificance swamped him. His knees trembled, his stomach grumbled and he felt as if he was back in the monastery of De'Ath's Dingle, about to be damaged in some way. He looked briefly to Wat and Cwen. Not in hopes that salvation would come, or that they would step forward in his place, more as a sort of resigned goodbye.

Wat looked at him with sympathetic eyes. Hopeless and resigned, but still sympathetic.

Cwen was looking backwards and forwards from Hermitage to the gaggle of figures gathered around what was now the wreckage of Briston's tent.

'Coming, Father,' Hermitage called as he left the comfort of his friends and strode as obediently as he could towards the large priest – owner of the finger, the arm, and the voice.

The large priest was accompanied by three figures all dressed in ecclesiastical garb. The garb had to be large, simply to accommodate the men inside. Hermitage recognised the habits. The cuts of the cloth and the quality of the weave said they were Castigatori. The girdle that closed their waists confirmed the fact: it was blood red. These select few spent their time visiting brothers around the country, castigating them. Obviously this was a good thing as even devout monks need to be reminded of their path now and again.

The problem was the Castigatori only carried out castiga-

95

tion. Occasionally, an exemplary religious house was found, where everything was correct and proper, where the leaders of the community and the brothers themselves spent their lives in true devotion and dedication. The Castigatori would naturally find little to criticise in these institutions, but that didn't stop them castigating. It was reported such places inspired them to exceptional vigour, as if they'd been irritated by finding good work. It didn't do to irritate the Castigatori.

If appearance was anything to go by, the tent of Briston the Weaver had irritated them to the end of their wits – which they kept close by. The Lord, while blessing their physicality with a surfeit of treasures, had been positively parsimonious when it came to the power of thought. It was said their leaders simply pointed them in the required direction and let go. Stopping was not part of their training.

As Hermitage drew up to the priest, the motto of Castigatori came to mind: "If it moves, castigate it." He also recalled the motto of those about to receive a visit: "If they can string two words together, they aren't the Castigatori'."

'Father.' Hermitage kept a safe distance from the priest and bowed his head. All around him was the ruin of the tent. To his right the fabric, the tent poles, and the camp chairs were piled up, just waiting for a torch to set the lot on fire. Neatly stacked to his left were the tapestries that had hung on the walls. The Castigatori were gathered around these, turning them over one by one. Each image was examined as if they were unable to understand how pictures worked. Most incongruously of all, the bound body of Briston still rested where it was, the world around it having been well and truly dismantled.

'What do you know about this, Brother?' the priest asked, spreading his arm to take in the devastation.

Hermitage looked up from his bow and appraised the fellow. At close range, the voice was a lot smaller and it was educated. Granted, the frame was huge, probably six feet tall at least, but the face was not that of the Castigatori. This face displayed the spark of intelligent awareness. Hermitage couldn't help but think the man was too good for this place. There was no smile or welcome in the features. Hermitage detected a sort of disappointed resignation at the events of the day. Probably of the world in general. It was the look his father usually carried whenever Hermitage tried to talk to him. Unlike his father, this priest's eyes were focussed on Hermitage and were waiting for a reply. This was most unusual as none of the priests Hermitage ever met listened to anyone.

The man was quite young, perhaps only a year or two older than Hermitage. Young to be a priest and have charge of a band such as the Castigatori. He was clean shaven and his cowl was thrown back across his shoulders. Most alarmingly of all, he was completely bald. No monk's tonsure, of course, but Hermitage could see traces of stubble on the man's head where he had clearly shaved. Remarkable. It certainly made him look intimidating. Well, more intimidating. That was probably the idea.

'I don't know, Father,' Hermitage followed the beckoning arm. 'The place was certainly intact when we left it.'

'It was intact when we arrived,' the priest explained with some impatience and a troubled glance towards the Castigatori.

'Ah,' Hermitage said, remembering what the Castigatori were best at.

'What's your name?' the priest demanded.

'Brother Hermitage, Father.'

'Odd name for a monk,' the priest frowned.

'Indeed.'

'What are you doing here, Brother Hermitage? And what were you doing here when the place was intact?' He said these last four words loudly and directed them at the Castigatori. Hermitage detected criticism, but the Castigatori took no notice.

Without Wat at his side, Hermitage had only one course of action in a situation like this. Tell the truth. The skills of deceit and misdirection he had gained in Wat's company washed away in the face of religious authority. Any authority would do, but religious was best.

'I was summoned here by a villager,' he said. 'I was at Castle Grosmal when word of the death of Briston the Weaver was brought.'

'And why would this villager immediately run for a monk, rather than, say, a shovel?'

'Briston told him to.' Even to Hermitage's ears this exposition was not going well.

The face on the front of the bald head frowned. 'A dead man sent a villager to fetch a monk?'

'Well, not exactly, I suppose.'

'Well, what exactly then?'

'Yes.'

'Pardon?' It seemed the priest was losing both patience and interest at the same time.

'It was Mister Wat. Briston left a note to be read upon his death. The note said to fetch his old friend Wat. And I was with Wat.'

The priest frowned, 'Shouldn't you be in a monastery?'

'Oh, I was but, erm…' Hermitage didn't like to mention the king and investigating. His natural modesty meant he would not bring the topic up voluntarily. He also knew some people reacted badly if they thought someone was trying to threaten them with authority. This priest looked like he could react badly to the very widest range of circumstances, and that surely would not go well for anyone around him.

'Are they with you?' The priest pointed over to Wat and Cwen, clearly thinking that Hermitage was some sort of idiot. That suited Hermitage down to the ground.

'Oh yes,' he said, 'that's the Wat I was telling you about.'

The priest beckoned them to come over. His beckon was instruction rather than invitation. Hermitage watched as Wat looked behind him, trying to see who the priest was beckoning to.

The priest rested his hands on his hips to give his impatience expression. 'I can ask my Brothers to come and get you,' he offered across the market place.

Wat's face lit up in recognition of the request and he strode happily across the space.

'Sorry,' he said as he and Cwen arrived. 'Thought you wanted another monk.'

'This one's quite enough.' The priest tipped his head towards Hermitage, who tried to look helpful.

'And who are they?' The priest pointed to the space where Eadric and Firman were wandering slowly away, looking with interest at the ground and the trees, apparently in deep conversation.

'No idea,' Wat said. 'Definitely not with us.'

The departing pair had their backs to the tent so the priest could not beckon them over. He drew breath to call out and thought again. He looked to his Castigatori, who were now starting to push and shove one another around. He sighed deeply and closed his eyes for a moment.

'Brother,' he said very reluctantly towards the band of jostling monks.

One of their number threw his head up and looked expectantly at the priest, rather like a dog who's just heard the word "ball".

A nod towards the two figures sent the castigator scurrying across the field to invite the two men to join his leader. He rubbed his hands in some pleasure at the prospect.

The priest sighed again. Hermitage interpreted it as the sigh of someone who thought all this was beneath them. He'd come across that quite a lot as well.

Wat was about to speak when the priest held up his hand for silence. 'We'll wait for this pair,' he said. 'Don't want to go through this more than once.'

Hermitage got a sinking feeling about what "going through this" might mean.

The new arrivals were herded like sheep by a dog, if the dog had hands and continually cuffed the sheep around the ears to make them move faster.

One of the men kept up a fairly constant stream of complaint about this treatment. The other just rubbed his ear each time it was struck.

'Right,' said the priest when they were all gathered, 'I am father Dextus.'

'Dextus?' Hermitage interrupted, unable to contain himself. 'How fascinating. A Roman name, if I'm not mistaken.'

Father Dextus stopped and looked at Hermitage, his weariness with the world falling upon the young monk like a pillow smothering a kitten.

'It is, and if you interrupt me again, I'll get one of my Brothers to do to you what the Roman at the foot of the cross did to our Lord.'

Hermitage gaped. Violence and blasphemy. From a priest. The violence obviously, but the blasphemy was shocking. He kept quiet.

'Good,' Dextus went on. 'I am here on church business and you are going to help me.'

Faces fell at the thought of helping the church with anything. People who went to help the church with its business tended not to be seen again.

'Oh, anything at all,' Wat offered.

Dextus frowned at him. 'Why are you here?' He directed the question at Wat.

Wat gave Hermitage the briefest of glances during which the monk gave his shrug of the shoulders and innocent face look. The one that said "whatever it was you would rather I hadn't said, I have probably just said".

Wat returned to Dextus. 'I was called here by Briston the Weaver. He and I had an arrangement if harm should fall.'

Dextus's eyes narrowed. 'Wat? The monk said you were called Wat.'

'Did he?' Wat said while casting a sharp look in Hermitage's direction.

'Wat the Weaver?' Dextus enquired.

Eadric's face showed surprise. Even Firman seemed impressed.

'Yes,' Wat replied with confidence. The sort of confidence that said he knew people, people more important than some priest with a funny name.

'That's handy,' Dextus responded. 'I've got a bishop who'd like to know where you are.'

'Many of them do,' Wat said. 'He probably wants to pay me.'

'No,' Dextus said quite explicitly, 'it definitely wasn't that.'

'And you?' Dextus turned to Cwen.

'Leofcwen, weaver's apprentice,' Cwen held her ground and her head high.

'I hardly think so,' Dextus guffawed slightly.

'Now, you two who aren't with this lot,' Dextus addressed Eadric and Firman. 'Although it's a bit of a coincidence this many people arriving in Baernodebi at the same time. Bit odd this many even being here at all.'

'I'm Eadric and I'm just passing through. Mister Firman here just joined me on the road for safety.' Eadric shrugged.

'That didn't turn out well, did it?' Dextus arched an eyebrow towards the castigator who still stood at their shoulder.

Eadric grinned weakly while Firman's attention flew all over the place, taking in the tent, the tapestries, all the people.

'Back to business then. What are you doing here?' The question returned to Wat.

'Like I said, Briston and I had an arrangement. Word was sent and I came. Too late, it seems. What brings a major expedition such as yours here?'

Dextus looked at Wat. Just looked. There was no way on earth he was going to answer any questions.

'I imagine you know the works of Briston well, being in the same line of business. He said the word "line" as if it was the border between Sodom and Gomorrah.

'I'll be sure to pass your observations to the bishop,' Wat quipped. 'He's such a devotee of my line of business that he funds a lot of it. When he pays.'

It was clear from his face that Dextus was tempted to release the Castigatori and let them do their favourite thing – to Wat. He controlled himself with some effort.

'The works of Briston we have found here are all pretty harmless. Not very good, but harmless. Where are the rest of them?'

'The rest?' Wat sounded as if butterflies could nest in his soft and innocent words.

'Yes, the rest.' Dextus pulled the wings off the butterflies before eating them, 'You know exactly what I mean. The personal works. The sort of thing *you* do.'

'Ah, commissions,' Wat said with realisation. 'I'm sure I don't know. Perhaps he didn't have any on at the moment. We don't make these things up you know,' Wat explained and excused himself. 'People ask us for them. Nobles, bishops, priests even. Ordinary men. They tell us what they want.'

'And you do it,' Dextus said, as if this were sufficient accusation. 'And I don't think the ordinary man can afford your prices.'

There was no reply Wat could give so he just smiled a bit.

Dextus sighed his sigh again. He beckoned the loitering castigator with one finger and the man stepped smartly to his master. The master whispered in an ear and the man obeyed. Ignoring Wat and Hermitage, this monster monk grabbed Cwen by the throat and lifted her from the ground with one arm. She tried to cry out but her voice wouldn't work.

'Stop,' Wat called as he stepped forward, only to bump into

another huge castigator who stepped in his way.

'What are you doing?' Hermitage called in outrage.

Eadric and Firman stepped back.

'This one says she's a weaver's apprentice,' Dextus observed, as if he was chatting round the camp fire instead of a dangling girl. 'Nonsense, of course, but she probably knows where the other works are. I'm sure my Brother here will wring the details out if he squeezes hard enough.'

'They're in the hovel,' Wat blurted, looking with alarm at Cwen's reddening face.

Dextus shook his head and nodded to the wreckage of Briston's tent. 'We looked.'

'Not that. The hovel, over there.' Wat pointed anxiously to Lolby's hovel.

Dextus nodded and Cwen was dropped. Wat immediately ran over to her and put a comforting arm across her shoulder while she coughed and choked the air back into her meagre frame.

'Your actions are intolerable,' Hermitage bridled. If he'd been twice his own size, he would have castigated Dextus there and then.

Dextus ignored him and indicated that the Castigatori could investigate the hovel.

Lolby, who had been loitering outside his dwelling watching the goings on with some enjoyment saw large monks coming his way. He left home and hearth at a fast run. The Castigatori turned questioning heads to Dextus who indicated they did not need to follow.

Two of the largest monks Hermitage had ever seen entered the hovel. Two of the largest people he'd ever seen at all, really.

The hovel of Lolby was not built to contain such bulk, and as the figures inside moved around searching, the walls of the place bulged and stretched. Chunks of mud fell from the sides and the goat-skin door fell off.

'Ah!' An exclamation of discovery burst from the inside of the hovel as the head of a castigator popped up through the roof.

The man tried to move forward, seemingly ignorant of the fact that he was now wearing a hovel. The building did actually move a couple of feet before the man's ponderous mind realised that ducking down would be more effective. He did so, and there was a groan from inside as he had clearly ducked on to his fellow Brother. There was more struggling as two large monks tried to exit a small hovel at the same time. The small hovel wasn't up to this and simply collapsed back to the pile of mud and twigs of its natural state. Lolby's rude cot and pot were all that remained standing of a once disgusting home.

The monks returned across the field, one of them carrying the box of Briston on his shoulder.

'Happy?' Wat asked from where he was still tending a recovering Cwen.

'Not usually,' Dextus replied.

'Well, perhaps you'll be on your way now you've got what you want,' the weaver invited.

'I don't know that I have got what I want yet,' Dextus replied. 'I need to examine the box. And, as I say, my bishop would like a word with you. When I do go on my way, you'll be on it as well.'

'Wat is with me,' Hermitage piped up. He was nervous and apprehensive. This was not something he had done before so he had no idea how it was going to turn out.

Dextus appraised him with a look of unworried surprise. 'You can come if you like,' he said, 'not that I'd advise it.'

'I mean,' Hermitage stumbled slightly over his words and drew breath, 'Wat is with me, on my official business.' He still couldn't bring himself to utter the words, even though he knew they were essential.

'Official business?' Dextus was disbelieving. 'You should be in your monastery, little monk. What official business are *you* on?'

Hermitage tried to draw his shoulders back and look commanding; he suspected he just looked odd.

'I am the King's Investigator,' he announced.

Dextus just kept looking.

'The King's Investigator,' Hermitage repeated.

'I heard,' Dextus said. There was a bit more steel in his voice now.

'So,' Hermitage hadn't thought beyond this, he imagined that would be enough. 'I am on the king's business and Mister Wat is on that business with me.'

'Which king?' Dextus asked, narrowing his eyes.

'Both of them,' Hermitage answered immediately, warming to his task. 'King Harold appointed me some months ago and King William repeated the honour. Yesterday,' he felt this added weight to his position, 'at Castle Grosmal, in fact.' Hermitage's first experience of pulling rank was proving exhilarating. 'It's just round the corner. He might still be there. Perhaps you'd like to come and check? Lord Grosmal was there, William's personal guard, everyone.'

There was a snort from Wat as Dextus stared hard at Hermitage. The priest seemed very unsure.

'You don't strike me as the type who could make something like that up.'

'Thank you,' Hermitage said with gratitude.

Wat snorted again.

'So what's the King's Investigator doing here?'

At least the fellow seemed to know what an investigator was.

'We're looking into the death of Briston.' Hermitage felt very bad saying this. Of course, it wasn't strictly true that Hermitage was looking into the death of Briston as King's Investigator. He was doing so as Wat's friend. He just happened to be King's Investigator while he was doing it. He didn't feel that this was outright lying, but it wasn't outright truth either.

'Are you?' Dextus asked with a curious tone.

He walked over to the still bound corpse, which now rested in the open air. He squatted at its side and looked it up and down. He then stood and looked at the wreckage of the tent. His brow furrowed and he looked back at Briston. He then stepped back and appraised the corpse from a distance. He tipped his head over to one side slightly. Then he approached again and paced out the length of the body. He put his hands on his hips and looked at Wat. 'This thing?' he asked and gave the dear departed a hearty kick.

'Oy,' Wat called out.

Cwen had recovered enough of her strength to jump from the floor and glare at the priest with clenched fists.

'A little respect please,' Wat insisted. 'That's the body of my friend.' He sounded genuinely upset.

'No it isn't,' Dextus said.

'Yes it is.' Wat clearly couldn't understand why he was being contradicted.

'No it isn't.'

Wat shook his head rapidly, 'Why are you saying it isn't?'

'Why are you saying it is?'

'Because it is.' Wat reacted as if he'd just been told the grass was made from slices of sky painted green by pixies. He was clearly dealing with the priestly equivalent of the village idiot. 'He's tied up in the Tapestry of Death, his hair is sticking out the top, and his feet are sticking out the bottom.'

'No they aren't,' Dextus said.

Wat had rapidly reached the end of his tether. He stamped his feet on the spot in frustration and pointed at the end of the bundle. 'Look,' he shouted, as if getting louder would make the presence of the clearly visible sticking-out feet more obvious.

'Ah,' Hermitage said in some recognition.

'What?' Wat shouted, 'Ah, what what?'

'Go on, King's Investigator,' Dextus challenged.

'Briston's boots are sticking out the bottom of the binding, not his feet.'

'Exactly,' Dextus said, impressed.

'Arrgh,' Wat screamed and tore at some of his hair. 'What difference does that make?'

'How do we know his feet are in them?' Hermitage asked in his intelligent way.

Wat was dumbstruck for a moment. 'Where else would he keep them?' he cried in exasperation.

'Well, on the end of his legs obviously,' Hermitage answered, rather puzzled himself now.

'You're all mad,' Wat concluded, getting a little calmer.

'If his feet aren't in his boots, but his legs are still joined on…' Hermitage left the question for Wat.

'Eh?' Wat was having a lot of trouble with this.

'Exactly,' Dextus commented.

Wat's head transported his eyes back and forth between these two idiots.

'It's the sort of question we had in the investigations of Brother Ambrosius and Henri de Turold, you know? The what if?'

'What if what?'

Hermitage caught Wat's wandering glance and held it. 'Wat.'

'Yes?'

'What if Briston's feet are not in his boots but are still attached to him?'

'Erm.'

'Think about it.'

Wat thought. He looked over the bound body once more and reached his conclusion. 'The bastards have cut off his legs!' he wailed

'No, no, no. I realise the man is your friend but think hard.'

Cwen had come up to Wat's side and was peering around him at the bundle of tapestry on the floor.

'If his feet aren't in there,' she speculated.

Hermitage nodded encouragement.

'And his legs aren't there either, perhaps the rest of him isn't there as well. Erm, either. Neither.'

'Precisely.'

'The bastard,' Cwen hissed.

'But the hair?' Wat clung on to his version of events.

'Easy enough to cut off some of your hair and stick it in the tapestry,' Hermitage explained. He was glad his friend seemed to be getting this now.

'Are you saying this is not Briston's body?'

'Well done,' Dextus said in a very patronising tone. He applauded slowly. Even his hands were patronising.

'But...' Wat's face still contorted with the ideas being bandied about.

'How tall was Briston?' Dextus asked him plainly.

'Oh,' Wat said, thrown rather by the question. 'Erm, about five three, I suppose. Quite tall.'

'So why is his corpse four foot two at best? Did he shrink when they tied him up?' Dextus now added sarcasm.

Wat simply stared at the Tapestry of Death, which he now seemed to accept did not contain the body of his friend. He had the fact, but he didn't have the understanding. 'But...' he whimpered slightly. His "but" wandered off on the breeze.

'You bastard!' Cwen's voice was in full flow, as were her feet as she stepped forward and gave the erstwhile corpse a solid kick. 'Ow, bloody hell,' she cried as she grasped her toe.

'You didn't know about this then?' Hermitage asked her.

'No of course not,' she snapped back. 'He was always going on about the Tapestry of Death, what it was, what it looked like, and how one day he'd be caught by the guild and they'd do it to him.'

'Ah.'

'Yes, bloody ah. He was obviously using me for just this moment. If he isn't actually dead, I'll kill him myself.'

'As you please, young lady,' Dextus offered. 'The Castigatori would like a few words with him first though.'

'As *you* please,' Cwen said with a horrid gleam in her eye.

'Well,' Wat recovered his composure very quickly, 'I can see that Briston may not be dead after all so there's really nothing to investigate. I imagine you've probably got a lot on. Hermitage and I can pop off back to King William and erm, await his bidding.'

He rubbed his hands and made to move off.

Eadric and Firman had been watching all this with ever widening eyes and retreating steps; they made to leave as well.

'Oh no,' Dextus said, and his Castigatori turned their heads like a flight of buzzards spotting rabbits. Baby rabbits. Baby rabbits with bad legs. Baby rabbits with bad legs and poor memories who couldn't remember the way back to the burrow.

'My business here is not finished. In fact, it's only just started. You're not going anywhere.'

There was movement on the outskirts of the field as more people arrived.

'Oh, what now?' Dextus said in exasperation. 'Does the whole country want to come and join in?'

'Have you got Briston?' a voice boomed across the space, a voice full of intent. A deep voice that must have originated from something very large.

'Great. Just what we need,' Dextus said. His day was clearly getting worse and worse. 'Virgil.'

The Giant

HERE IS HE?' the mammoth figure of Virgil demanded, each syllable clear and weighty.

'That's what we'd like to know,' Dextus answered in
some irritation.

'We wouldn't,' Eadric put in, trying to look disinterested and
disconnected from events.

'Never even heard of him.' Firman nodded agreement.

Hermitage was feeling positively tiny. He wasn't small himself, about average height. He could hold his own against most
other monks. Well, in a tallest monk competition, at least. Yet,
he had been dwarfed by Dextus and his Castigatori and now
they in turn were dwarfed by Virgil. It wasn't just that the man
was tall, he was too tall. His legs were too long, his arms and
hands were too big, and his head was simply monstrous. It was
only the fact a voice came out of his mouth that made Hermitage believe the shape before him was human at all. He was more
like something out of the Old Testament. He probably did a lot
of smiting. He knew human measurements typically didn't go
this far, but he thought Virgil must be seven feet tall. Wat was
right, the man was a giant. He just hoped his companion wasn't
quite so accurate about the violent and lunatic bits.

Virgil had a contingent with him, much as Dextus had his
Castigatori. At least Virgil's band weren't a patch on their master; the three men who accompanied him looked clean, intelligent, and normal size. They were looking carefully at everyone in
the field as if taking notes. Occasionally they huddled together
and whispered. One of them approached Virgil and tugged at

his sleeve. The giant bent a giant ear down the level of the normal man. The normal man whispered in the giant ear. The giant head turned towards Wat.

'Well, if it isn't little Wat,' Virgil boomed with pleasure.

Hermitage was rather taken aback to hear this Virgil character talk in a well rounded and clear voice. It spoke of learning and even erudition. He really should not judge a book by its cover, even if the cover was absolutely massive.

'Virgil,' Wat called with apparent glee. 'How are you?'

'Oh, the usual,' Virgil replied, rather resigned to his lot. 'Angry, disappointed, you know.'

'Oh dear.'

'Quite. Still, I have you now. That'll cheer me up.' Virgil beamed and reached out to slap Wat heartily on the back. Wat ducked as if he'd practised.

'Ha ha,' the weaver laughed lightly but with little pleasure as Virgil's attention moved on to the crowd.

Wat sidled over to Hermitage. 'Don't tell him we're on king's business whatever you do,' he whispered.

'Really?'

'Yes. He hates kings. They make him very cross.'

'Not good, I imagine,' Hermitage speculated, looking at the giant figure.

'Not good at all,' Wat said with real sincerity. 'If he'd joined Harold at Hastings as he was asked, we probably wouldn't have a King William now,' Wat shrugged.

'And Dextus,' Virgil went on, holding his arms wide as if waiting to embrace the priest. Or crush him. 'You and your band of nasty habits. Still doing the Lord's work without being asked?'

The Castigatori looked as one at Virgil. Their physical presence wasn't a patch on his, but their absence of intelligent thought probably meant they would dive in anyway.

Hermitage noticed Dextus shake his head very slightly and the Castigatori relaxed.

'I hope you're not going to disturb church business, Virgil,' Dextus said quite seriously. He seemed completely unbowed by the size of Virgil.

'I can't imagine the church wanting anything to do with the likes of Briston,' Virgil replied, in apparent surprise. 'Surely men of piety wouldn't dabble in his awful trade. It's bad enough that the rest of us have to engage in it, but then we're really only performing a public service.'

'Our business with Briston is ours. Once we've concluded that, you can do what you like with him.'

'So that's not him then?' Virgil nodded towards the bound shape on the floor.

'We thought it was,' Wat grinned. 'We wondered whether you'd done it to him.'

'The Tapestry of Death? Oh, good Lord no,' Virgil was contemptuous. 'Complete waste of good thread. Plus, killing a man tends to make him less profitable.'

'I suppose so,' Wat said in some quiet and apparently unpleasant reminiscence.

Virgil nodded his great head to one of his men, who advanced towards the tapestry bundle with a knife. This man, who seemed to sneak across the ground, even though there was no need for sneaking, stopped at the bundle and appraised it. He looked to the boots and moved to that end. He bent and grasped the sole of the left foot and heaved. The top of the boot was caught up in the tight binding of the Tapestry of Death and did not want to move. Instead, the whole body shifted towards him.

Hermitage, Wat, and Cwen grimaced slightly, still thinking that this was the body of Briston, even though the evidence was now against it.

Virgil's man straightened, planted his own left foot against the right foot of the corpse and heaved again on the left. This time it shifted and the man staggered back, holding an empty left boot in his hand.

'Ah,' Wat said in acceptance of the fact that when he had known Briston, his fellow weaver's left leg did not end in a pig's trotter. Or at least as far as he could be sure, never having closely examined his friend's feet.

The man now moved to the head with his knife and dug it in, slicing the top knot open and allowing the rest of the thread to fall away. He even started rolling it up to save it.

Despite the pig's foot at one end of the body, Wat and Cwen still drew breath as the knife went in. Hermitage wasn't sure whether this was because they were worried the man might be stabbing Briston's head, or damaging hours of a weaver's pains-taking work.

Even Eadric and Firman winced as the weapon was plunged.

'Pig,' said the man as the body was revealed. 'All the way up.' He wiped his knife on the grass and put it away.

'Nearly Briston then,' Virgil commented with a hearty laugh. His men joined in, but no one else.

The giant cast his large eyes around the field. 'Seems to be a great deal of interest in the whereabouts of the missing weaver. Everyone wants to know where he is.'

'We don't,' Eadric put in.

'Yes, and who are you?' Virgil asked, clearly wondering what strangers were doing here at all.

'No one, no one at all. And neither is Mister Firman. He's absolutely no one either.'

'What are you doing here then?'

'Pure coincidence. Just travelling and happened upon the place.'

'Happened upon Baernodebi?' Virgil looked to his audience for agreement that this was a ridiculous suggestion. 'You're after Briston.'

'No, no, I assure you.'

'I'm sure you do, but I simply don't believe you. Of course, I could hit you until you tell or get one of my men to stick things in you, but it doesn't matter really. Briston isn't here. As long as I get to him first I'll be happy. I won't be happy if anyone else gets to him. All sorts of horrible things happen when I'm not happy, don't they, Wat?'

Wat nodded.

'Might as well be on your way then,' Dextus suggested as if it was already decided. 'Start looking.'

'Oh, I think I need to keep an eye on you. Don't want you finding him on your own. I know of the amount of damage your stupid monks can do once they get hold of someone. I want Briston in one piece, all his fingers working, that sort of thing.'

Dextus tutted as if this was outrageous nit-picking. 'And if you find him, I can imagine he'll be working away for the rest of his life. Never seeing anyone again, probably not even daylight. The bishop *will* have his conversation.'

'Which will be so one-sided it'll render Briston speechless. And probably lifeless.'

There was much glaring in the silence. Virgil turned his attention to the others.

'Who's the rather dim-looking monk?' he asked, his eyes having found Hermitage.

Hermitage could take many insults. In fact, he *had* taken most of them at one time or another. He'd got used to them all and they flowed like water from a water vole's willy. He always bridled at being called dim though. Or stupid, or thick, or an idiot, or ignorant. He knew pride was a sin, but still liked to consider his own intelligence from an objective standpoint. Standing next to anyone he had ever met, his was bigger.

It wasn't his fault; it was like saying his hair was more black. When someone accused him of being stupid, they were being stupid. True, he didn't know things that Wat knew, but then most of the things Wat seemed to know were bad things. He had a lot of knowledge of more serious facts. Biblical most of them, but still serious. And he could piece information together. He could see the holes in arguments. He could pierce to the heart of ill-formed judgement and point out the weaknesses – which usually led to more insults. Thus he took offence at Virgil's assessment of him as dim. He looked at the mountain of man and decided not to debate the issue just now.

'The King's Investigator,' Dextus replied with mock awe.

Wat winced at the word "king" being spoken out loud in front of Virgil.

'Brother Hermitage?' Virgil asked with happy recognition.

'Erm, yes,' Hermitage replied, quite sure that being known by Virgil was not a good thing.

'De'Ath's Dingle,' Virgil said, as if the name of Hermitage's most recent monastery was impressive in its own right.

'Erm, yes?' Hermitage repeated, rather worried where this conversation was going.

'I had some business lined up there. For the refurbishment, you know. I heard all about it. The old dead monk, the abbot, the king.' Virgil sounded as if he was about to re-tell some myth, 'Absolutely fascinating and all solved by Brother Hermitage, the King's Investigator.' Virgil smiled at Hermitage. Actually smiled. Right at him. It was rather disturbing.

'Aha!' Hermitage smiled back very thinly. He couldn't tell if Virgil's was genuine enthusiasm or if he was about to be picked up and snapped in half.

'There's no one needs investigating like a king,' Virgil added with feeling.

'Oh.' Hermitage saw the misunderstanding and wondered about correcting it. He quickly reached the conclusion all by himself that this would be an incredibly stupid thing to do.

Dextus was looking backwards and forwards. He was clearly surprised at Virgil's confirmation of the monk's title.

'But that was Harold?' Virgil questioned Hermitage's appointment.

'Erm, ah yes, it was,' Hermitage stumbled, wondering how he

was going to be able to explain this without it coming out that he was on the king's side. 'But then I had some business at Castle Grosmal,'

'Robert Grosmal?' Virgil asked.

'That's right.'

Virgil, the giant of a man who could surely squash most other people under his feet without noticing, shivered at the name, 'Ghastly man,' he concluded.

'And, erm, King William was there,' Hermitage shied away slightly as he said the words. 'So I was investigator again, only with the new king.' He felt this was as close to the truth as it was sensible to get. He was the investigator with a new king. Saying he was the investigator *for* the new king might make things difficult.

Wat nodded encouragingly at his efforts.

'You idiot,' Dextus put in. 'It doesn't mean he investigates kings. It means he does their investigating for them.'

Virgil looked backwards and forwards between monk and priest.

'Does he?' Virgil asked with a worrying grumble in his voice. 'And what's the king's interest in Briston?' he asked with menace in his voice.

His body was clearly large enough to hold an awful lot of menace, but this little hint was quite sufficient for Hermitage. Oh dear. He felt the world fall away from him. He had sinned and the devil was about to hurl his punishment from the depths of his dark kingdom. And it was all he deserved. He had told a fib, he had broken sacred vows, and departed from his own best judgment. Retribution was at hand. A very large hand.

He had only paddled in the murky shallows of dishonesty, yet here he was up to his neck. To Dextus he had implied that he was on the king's business. Now that falsehood was going to bring a very big and heavy man down on his head. He cursed himself. He knew he was doing wrong at the time, he knew he was being led astray by Wat's worldly ways. He should have stuck to his principles. The truth in all things and always the truth.

He felt true regret for the first time in his life. Perhaps that only came when you knew you had done a wrong, and then got the opportunity to watch while it came back and bit you. All the other times things had come back to bite him, he knew he had been true and honest and open. The bruises were still the same, but at least he didn't feel so bad about them. He wouldn't be caught out again. Of course, there was a good chance he wouldn't live long enough to have the opportunity for any more falsehood anyway. If Virgil bit him, he'd probably take his head clean off.

'Quite straightforward,' Wat spoke up, taking Virgil's attention. 'Poor Hermitage here was *made* King's Investigator. The first time as well as the second. You know what kings are like.'

Well that was true really, Hermitage thought, grateful that a more experienced dissembler was taking over. He immediately felt the regret for this gratitude sharpening its teeth for some future occasion.

'He didn't want the job at all,' Wat explained. 'Then, when we'd finished at Grosmal's place, word about Briston came, so as King's Investigator, Hermitage had to look into it. And it was a favour to me.'

'Eh?' Virgil was looking puzzled at this explanation.

As was Hermitage.

'Both kings forced Hermitage to become investigator. You know what happens when you try to say "no thank you" to a king.'

Virgil grumbled. There was clearly some recognition of the situation. Albeit reluctant.

'I say!' Virgil's face lit up. 'I've had an idea,' he announced, rather surprised at himself.

'Oh?' Wat said. 'Good.'

Dextus folded his arms and gave Virgil a look that said his

expectations were very low.

'We want Briston, this priest and I, right?'

'Yes,' Hermitage said with caution. He was very worried about where this might be leading.

'And these two dung sorters want him as well.'

'No, no I assure you,' Eadric pleaded. 'Just passing through, and we can carry on passing immediately.'

'Do shut up.'

'Right.' Eadric shut up.

'Now, both Dextus and I want Briston alive and functioning. I'll keep him that way because I have great plans for the young man.' The words were those of a benefactor expressing nothing but the best of intentions for his protégé. The tone said that sticking your naked bottom in a viper's nest was preferable to being Virgil's protégé. 'On the other hand, Dextus will wheel him off to the bishop, like the lackey he is, and then Briston's works will grace the world no more.'

Hermitage thought this was probably a good thing. Keeping Briston alive was obviously important, but if the man could be persuaded to stop producing his horrible tapestries, the world would be a better place. Killing him to achieve this did seem a bit extreme.

'So?' Wat prompted.

'Well, we've got an investigator, haven't we?'

Hermitage now saw where this was going and didn't like the view at all.

'If I go off to look for Briston, I might find him. Problem is, Dextus might find him first. Sort of even chance. If we all stay here, where we can keep an eye on one another, Brother Hermitage can go and find him.'

'If he's still alive,' Hermitage put in, hoping this might put Virgil off his plan.

'He'd better be,' Virgil explained, already holding Hermitage personally responsible for Briston's health.

'A fascinating proposal,' Dextus reasoned. 'Which I have absolutely no intention of taking part in. If you want to stay here while the monk goes looking, good luck. We'll follow our own plan.'

'Well, that's not very friendly,' said Virgil.

Wat took two steps back and pulled Hermitage with him.

Dextus now nodded to his Castigatori, who leaped towards Virgil as one.

His own party gave their leader some space as Virgil faced the oncoming monks. Three of them. All large. All experienced in the ways of violence. And all of them asleep on the floor in the twinkling of a tree-sized fist.

Hermitage found it hard to recall exactly what had happened. He thought Virgil had grabbed the first two by the scruffs of their habits and banged their heads together. They certainly dropped to the ground as one. The third man had launched a vicious attack on Virgil and landed two good blows with his clenched fists, one to the midriff and one to the table-like chin. Each had the same effect: they got Virgil really annoyed. The giant looked down as if he had dropped crumbs on his front. He raised his fist to drop it on the man's head, then took a glance at Dextus but thought better of it. Instead he swung his massive right hand on the end of his massive right arm back behind him. The fist came forward and hit the monk. The monk flew. For a big monk, he flew very gracefully. It was clear that unconsciousness had arrived with first contact. The monk flew backwards in an arc that deposited him at Dextus's feet.

Dextus coughed. 'Well, if you're going to be like that,' he nodded as he surveyed his damaged Castigatori.

'Excellent,' Virgil nodded back and didn't even bother to rub his hand.

'What if I can't find him?' Hermitage asked before Wat could stop him.

'Oh, I wouldn't do that if I were you,' Virgil replied, nodding at the very large sleeping monks.

Hermitage was resigned. He'd only done murders up to now. The body didn't tend to move in those cases. This time, there wasn't a body at all. What was he going to do? He didn't even know where to start. Yes he did. 'I'll need Wat,' he said.

'Why?' Virgil's cow-sized eyes squinted in suspicion.

'He helps me. When I'm investigating,' Hermitage explained.

'What's to stop you just running away?' Virgil asked.

Hermitage was shocked. 'I wouldn't!' he said.

'He wouldn't,' Wat added in a rather resigned tone.

Virgil frowned. He summoned his little men to his side and they engaged in whispered conversation.

'Alright,' Virgil accepted, 'but we'll keep your little friend with us.'

Wat and Hermitage turned and saw that one of Virgil's men had slipped away from the discussion and was now standing behind Cwen. With a knife pointing at her side.

'There's no need for that,' Wat barked.

'Of course not,' Virgil agreed, as if his threatening Cwen was really nothing to do with him. 'You come back with Briston and all will be well. Don't come back with Briston and all won't be well.' He left the thought with a shrug.

'In fact,' Virgil added thoughtfully, 'let's add a little urgency. It's what, about three-o-clock now?' He glanced at the sky, and then at one of his men. The man made a gesture.

'Two o'clock,' Virgil corrected himself. 'If you're not back by dusk tomorrow, we'll, erm, what shall we do? Oh yes. Kill the girl. Then the next morning we'll kill one of them.'

'I say,' Eadric protested as he was pointed out.

'And then we'll do the rest until they're all dead. If you're still not back, we'll come for you and kill you as well.' Virgil seemed very satisfied with this comprehensive proposal.

Hermitage simply looked on in horror. Virgil had said all of this as if he was inviting them to a party. They were right about the violent lunatic stuff.

'But…' he began but didn't know where to end.

'But how soon should you start?' Virgil prompted. 'I'd suggest about now,' he growled. Which he did very well.

'You're not going to wait exactly here?' Wat waved his arms around to cover the market place.

'Course not,' Virgil said. 'We'll go and find the local manor. Invite ourselves to stay the night. Come and find us there. Whose is it, by the way?'

'Chap called Stott,' Wat said reluctantly, imagining how old Stott and Parsimon were going to cope with this lot. Not at all, probably.

'Excellent,' Virgil said. 'This is much better than traipsing about the countryside myself. Well, go on then.'

Hermitage looked at him.

'Investigate!' he instructed.

✦　　✦　　✦

As Hermitage and Wat plodded away from the sorry scene, not really sure which direction they were going or why, Lolby emerged from some trees to survey the wreckage of his home. He picked his way through the tumbled mass of mud and not many sticks, eventually locating his rude cot and pot. The cot was so rude it now resembled the fallen bits of tree it had once been. The pot was intact so he pulled it from the pile, tipping mud and twigs from its inside. He looked with as much contempt as he dared towards the monstrous figures that had done this to his home. Monstrous figures, some of whom were wearing church garb, so needed to be given a very wide berth. Even if they were lying down.

He noticed the revealed body of what had been Briston. He dared a few steps to get a closer look. No one seemed bothered about him and so he peered over the reclining Castigatori and examined the contents of the Tapestry of Death.

'Oh,' he said, in surprised observation.

Virgil and Dextus forgot their mutual glaring for a moment and looked at Lolby. Their looks were of complete indifference.

Lolby looked to Dextus and then to Virgil.

'This looks bad,' he said with all the nonchalance of a fellow in the tavern hearing about the woes of his enemies. 'Real mess.' Now he tutted and drew his breath like a wheelwright looking at a perfectly good wheel that doesn't need any work at all. 'I could, erm…' The peasant hesitated and adopted his own pose of indifference as if he was thinking whether he could be bothered to help out. 'I could take the pig, if you like?'

Caput XII

Peasants, the Lot

HAT ON EARTH DO WE DO?' Hermitage surveyed the now empty site of Baernodebi market. Empty apart from Lolby, happily stripping bits of high quality pink fluff from a pig carcass.

He and Wat had circumnavigated the market while Virgil, Dextus, and the others gathered for their journey to Stott's. The Castigatori had been woken, Eadric and Firman had tried to continue their passing through, to which Virgil had put a very rapid and rude halt. Eventually the band set off to disturb, if not actually destroy, the life of a harmless old Saxon and his ancient servant.

'De'Ath's Dingle and Castle Grosmal were easy.' Hermitage went on, 'There was a body. A dead one. We could look at it, what had been done to it, and figure out what had happened. Who had been there, who wanted the dead, well, dead. What do you do about a missing person? He could be anywhere. And he's probably gone of his own volition.'

'No doubt about it,' Wat added with a scowl.

The wreckage of Briston's tent was heaped like a lazy monument. Virgil had taken the box of special tapestries and Dextus had been allowed to keep the harmless ones. One of Virgil's men had carefully gathered the pink Tapestry of Death and stored it away.

'Nothing to go on at all,' Hermitage wailed, holding his arms out to encompass the scene.

'At least we can be fairly sure of what actually happened,' Wat said. Hermitage looked at him.

'Briston had everyone after him,' the weaver explained. 'Virgil, the church, the customers, everyone. Some wanted him dead, others wanted a refund. Knowing Briston, I'm not sure which'd worry him most. What to do? Disappear. Get a pig, tie him up in the Tapestry of Death, send me the note, and problem solved. Quicker than an arrow in the eyeball.'

'Wat!' Hermitage reproved his friend. 'Surely he'd be discovered when the tapestry was opened?'

'Ah, but it shouldn't be. That's the point of the Tapestry of Death. Once bound up, the victim is dead and buried. The ritual doesn't allow the tapestry to be opened again.

> *If opened be*
> *The tapestry*
> *Of death once it is woven*
> *Great evil will*
> *The world up fill*
> *Unless it is recoven.'*

'Recoven?' Hermitage was aghast at this nonsense, and the appalling use of the language.

'Don't know,' Wat shrugged, 'I think it's a sort of mix of recovered and re-woven. Most of the guild ritual is in awful rhyme.'

'So, he'd have got away?'

'Yep. We'd all have gathered round the graveside. The church would have lost their man, Virgil would have lost his income, and the guild would bury a pig. I'm sure there's something in the ritual about that being a bad thing,' Wat mused. 'Meanwhile, Briston's away and clear.'

'He left everything.' Hermitage wondered if the man would do that. 'His normal tapestries, the other ones, a whole box full. They must have been worth a lot. His tent, chairs, everything.'

'Small price to pay for all your enemies forgetting about you.'

'And Cwen!' Hermitage thought this was the worst of all.

'Yes,' Wat looked at the ground. 'She wasn't happy, was she? Clearly had no idea. Briston used her to make it all more realistic. What better than to have someone genuinely weeping at your departure?'

'Heartless,' Hermitage concluded.

'And he sent me the death note. We'd agreed that should only be used for the real thing.'

Wat was clearly angry at this. Hermitage imagined the poor fellow must be in turmoil. To find your friend dead is awful. To find he's not dead must be good. To find he's tricked you into thinking he's dead, when actually he's alive and has used the trick to let everyone else think he's dead, well? Hermitage had completely lost track of his own thought.

Wat must be confused. Or annoyed. Or something. Hermitage had never been very good with emotions. His own were bad enough but other people's were a closed book with big locks on.

'He's deceived us all,' was all he managed to come up with.

The two men stood in disheartened silence.

'It's not enough.' Wat had come to some conclusion.

'Not enough?'

'The church, Virgil, a dodgy customer or two? Should be normal business to Briston. I said he's a chancer, so he spends his days avoiding people like that without any trouble. What's changed? Why would he suddenly go to extremes?' Wat took to pacing up and down by the pile of discarded tent. 'The Tapestry of Death is bloody expensive,' he mused. 'I really can't see Briston making that sort of investment over a bit of customer trouble.'

'We still have nothing to go on,' Hermitage complained. 'It's all very well knowing why he did what he did, but the fact is he's gone. If we don't find him and take him to Virgil, Cwen is in trouble.'

'I know,' Wat grumbled back. 'What would he have done?'

'Who? Virgil?'

'No, not Virgil,' Wat was impatient, 'Briston. What would Briston have done?'

'How do I know?'

'We have to put ourselves in his shoes,' Wat thought out loud.

'Are they still by the tent?' Hermitage looked over to the pile.

Wat sighed and closed his eyes for a moment. 'We have to imagine that we are Briston. Perhaps if we do that, we'll have an idea what he did.'

'Ah.' Hermitage saw that the idea was a good one, but imagination was another problem area for him.

As a child, he'd been expected to pretend he was in a castle or somewhere. He then got in trouble for walking through the imaginary walls or off the top of the imaginary battlements. He couldn't fight imaginary dragons if he didn't know how big they were, and he certainly couldn't rescue the maiden. He hadn't been given her name, any indication of her life history, or a credible explanation for her incarceration. He stopped being invited to play.

'So,' Wat said, 'here I am in the middle of the tent.' He stood in the place the tent used to be. Hermitage was impressed.

'Stott's got his tapestry, Cwen's gone for the water, I'm on my own with a good stretch of time before anyone comes back. Which way do I go?'

Hermitage looked around. All directions seemed the same.

'Not north,' Wat concluded.

'Why not north?'

'He's well known in the north. That's his territory. He wouldn't go north if he wanted to get away from everyone.'

Hermitage nodded. Using someone else's imagination was much easier than using your own. He followed this thought and came to a wider conclusion. If you could use another's imagination, their inmost thoughts, you could use their outer bits as well. Like eyes.

'South then,' Hermitage concluded, ready to set off.

'Or East or West?' Wat proposed. 'Maybe across to Wales or a ship from the coast?

'Ah,' Hermitage paused, he hadn't considered Briston would

go to such extremes. To take your life in your hands by travelling such distances, to be threatened by the monsters everyone knew lurked in those parts, to risk being eaten by giants or incarcerated by witches? And if he didn't go to Wales, the boat trip would be even worse. Hermitage hated the sea. It was so messy, moving about all the time, coming and going. No order at all. His thoughts meandered on.

'What time is it?' he asked.

'What?' Wat was thrown off his imaginary stride.

'What time is it? In the tent. When you're getting ready to leave, as Briston?'

'Oh, erm. Don't know. Does it matter?'

'I think so,' Hermitage pondered. 'We know Cwen left at midday and Lolby found what we now know to be a pig in the evening.'

'Yes.'

'So what was going on here in between? The evening arrives early at this time of year. I know it's not a busy place, but there must have been other market stalls. Perhaps someone actually saw him leave?'

'He could have wandered off at any time. Could have gone into the woods to relieve himself. Gone backwards and forwards several times.'

'Even so, it might help?'

Wat glanced at Lolby. He wandered over nonchalantly and squatted at the peasant's side. Hermitage joined him and stood looking down.

Lolby had removed all the thread and was stroking the pig, using his own imagination to predict the taste by the look of it.

'When did you last see Briston alive?' Wat asked.

'Eh?' Lolby jumped, all his attention being focussed on his future dinner.

'You found this thing in the evening, with the note stuck in the thread?'

'The note was on the ground, not in the thread,' Lolby corrected.

'It would have to be,' Hermitage said. 'How could Briston have stuck the note in his own Tapestry of Death?'

'Alright, you found the note on the ground,' Wat sighed at apparent pedantry.

'Yeah?' Lolby was suspicious, mostly of someone stealing his pig, judging from the way he wrapped protective arms around it.

'When did you see him before that?'

'I didn't have anything to do with him.' Lolby was full of pride, expressing standards far higher than those who visited a weaver such as Briston. Not too proud to hug a dead pig in a field of mud though.

'You noticed Stott coming and going. You noticed the apprentice,' Hermitage observed. 'You're clearly a very observant fellow, keeping an eye on the market like that.'

Wat raised eyebrows at this tactic of flattery.

'Well,' Lolby softened. 'You never know when there might be a profitable errand to run.'

Hermitage picked up this thread, 'So who else was at the market? Who might have errands for you?'

Lolby looked at them through screwed-up eyes. He clearly thought these questions were suspicious and dangerous, but couldn't quite figure out why. 'There was the pewter stall, of course,' he said. 'Clopper. Regular he is. Usually does some business. Tries to bring something unusual for Stott if he can.'

'And others?'

'There's Master Baker.'

'What does he do?'

Lolby surveyed the idiot monk. 'He's the baker.'

'Ah, oh. I see.' Hermitage blushed.

'And Briston?' Wat prompted.

'He came and went. Arrived before dawn like normal. The apprentice set up the tent and Stott turned up first light.'

'And when did Stott leave?' Hermitage asked.

'Don't know exactly. He was picking over Clopper's stall for a bit before he went off.'

'Did he find it?' Hermitage asked.

'What?'

'The bit he was looking for on Clopper's stall?'

'Eh?'

'For goodness' sake, Hermitage,' Wat half growled, half sighed.

Hermitage looked to his friend for an explanation. There was none so he just shrugged. He'd ask later.

'So Stott goes off home, then what?' Wat pressed Lolby.

'Dunno. Coming and going. The apprentice goes off about midday, I suppose.'

'To get some fresh water, we know,' Wat said.

'Round here?' Lolby was incredulous. 'Oh, the big fellow came after Stott had gone.'

'Which big fellow?' Hermitage asked.

'The one who was here, throwing the monks about.'

'Virgil,' Wat explained. 'Yes, we know about him as well.'

'Big, isn't he?' Lolby was impressed.

'Very,' Wat agreed. 'And he wants to find Briston. And he's told us to do it.'

'Well, good luck,' Lolby said quite genuinely.

'If we don't manage to do it, big Virgil is going to start killing people.' Wat stood up to give his words added emphasis.

'Ah.'

'And once he gets started, he tends not to stop until there's no one left to kill.'

'I can imagine.' Lolby still didn't get it.

'And he'll kill you as well.'

'Me?' Lolby's voice rose to a shriek. 'Why would he kill me?'

'You can ask him just before he does. So? What else happened at the market? Who else was there?' Wat spoke slowly and deliberately, making it clear that the answers were as much in Lolby's interest as theirs.

At least the man had developed a sense of engagement now.

'I suppose there was the usual crowd of locals. People getting bread and stuff. The ones who could afford it. No strangers.'

'How many?' Hermitage asked. 'How many locals were there?'

'Over the course of the day? 'Bout twenty, I suppose. They come in from all around for the market.'

'Oh, Wat, this is hopeless,' Hermitage wailed. 'Twenty people? That's a whole throng. And they came from all over the place. We don't have the time to go and find them all and ask them if they saw Briston.' He looked around the space, almost hopeful that Briston was going to pop up from behind some bush now that everyone had left.

Wat too looked rather despairing.

'What about other stalls?' he asked Lolby.

'Like I say, just the usual.'

'Yes,' Wat ground out through his teeth, 'but we don't know what the usual is, do we? We're not from round here, thank God! So you have to tell us.'

'Oh right,' Lolby nodded with understanding. Wat buried his face in his hands and Hermitage sighed and looked to the sky.

'You only had to ask,' the peasant grumbled. 'So, who we got so far?' Lolby counted the stalls off on his fingers, 'Clopper, Baker, your Briston.'

'Yes,' Wat and Hermitage encouraged together.

'Then there'd be Tailor, Wheelwright, and Grocer,' Lolby finished.

'And what are their names?' Hermitage asked.

Lolby just looked at him.

'Ah, of course, Tailor, Wheelwright, and Grocer.' The monk nodded. This information about the workings of the modern market was fascinating. Perhaps he should have called himself

Brother Monk all those years ago instead of Hermitage.

'Where do they live?' asked Wat

'All over, really.'

'Did any of them see Briston?'

'How the hell should I know?' Lolby was defiant.

'You didn't see them talking? Sharing information? Chatting like market folk do?'

'People tended not to share or chat with Briston.'

Wat walked round in a small circle. Hermitage followed him with his eyes.

'What are we going to do?' Hermitage was lost and in despair. He always found his way there eventually.

'Why don't you talk to Mister Butcher? Lolby suggested.

'The butcher?' Hermitage checked.

'Of course.'

'Why the butcher?' Wat asked with the suspicion Lolby knew something he wasn't telling.

'He's local, lives in the next valley. You'd get to him quick.'

'But we'd have wasted our time if he has nothing to tell us,' Wat hissed.

'It wouldn't be a waste of time though, would it?' Lolby said as if they were being stupid.

'Why not exactly?' Wat demanded.

'Because he must have spoken to Briston.' Lolby seemed confused that they weren't following him.

'If he spoke to Briston why didn't you tell us?' Wat shouted in frustration.

'I don't know that he did,' Lolby shouted back.

Wat's frustration rendered him speechless. Hermitage drew up to Lolby. 'What makes you think that speaking to the butcher will help?' he asked in reasonable tones. 'What makes you think Briston and the butcher spoke?'

Lolby pointedly stroked his treasure and shrugged. 'Where else is a weaver going to get a pig?'

Caput XIII

Loins

'WHY DIDN'T I THINK OF THAT?' Hermitage was crying out and beating his sides with his fists as he and Wat left Lolby behind and strode as fast as they could into the next valley. 'The man had a pig. A large dead pig. Where else was it likely to come from? Was it just walking by when Briston persuaded it to help him with a devious plan? Perhaps the pig tied itself up and Briston had nothing to do with it.'

'Hermitage, you're getting hysterical,' Wat chided.

'I'm entitled,' Hermitage responded. 'I'm supposed to be the King's Investigator. What sort of investigator doesn't wonder where a fully grown pig has come from? In a weaver's tent?'

'Good heavens,' Wat said. 'I've never seen you so excited. It's only a pig.'

Hermitage paused for a moment. It was true, he had never been so excited. Why was that? 'It was a pig, Wat,' he moaned. 'That was it. It was the pig.'

His new career as an investigator appealed to him in many ways. Dealing with dead people, kings, and killers didn't appeal at all, but the intellectual exercise was stimulating. Just as he hated misreading a piece of scripture or overlooking a poorly structured argument, so he found irritation when facts he should have seen emerged.

'A butcher's tent, fine. If Briston had been the butcher, his whole tent would have been hanging with pigs and we'd have wondered where the tapestry came from. Why did I not ask the immediate question. Immediately?'

'It's not the sort of thing you expect to see. A pig tied up in a

tent? I've got a collection of the very strangest people in the kingdom for my clients and none of them ever asked for anything
like that.'

'Really, Wat,' Hermitage frowned his distaste at the weaver.
'The point is it was out of the ordinary.'

'I'll say.'

'So, I should have spotted it and then asked why it was there,
where it came from, who brought it.'

'Well, you found out.'

'Only after Lolby told us. I shall have to pay more attention
to the details in future.'

'*More* attention?' Wat gave a little sigh, as if having Hermitage pay more attention to details was going to be a bit of a trial.

Their journey had taken them south from Baernodebi into
woods, but the trail was strong. Following Lolby's directions,
they turned off the main track and headed up a short rise on a
well-beaten path. The path lifted itself over a hillock of sorts after only a few hundred feet and the next valley was revealed. The
trees were thin and scattered and the view opened before them.

'Ah,' Wat said.

'Oh,' Hermitage said.

The valley was not much of a valley really. The land herea-
bouts was only undulating at best, so there was no expectation
that valleys would be great gouges cut from the sides of monstrous mountains. This place was more a dent, and a small one
at that. The two companions could see why the butcher lived in
the next valley. On his own. The best description that came into
Hermitage's head was that this was the site of a battle. Probably
an Old Testament battle. Great forces had been unleashed and
thine enemies had been well and truly scattered. The butcher's
enemies were scattered everywhere.

Hermitage wondered for a moment why this man had become a butcher as it looked look like he wasn't very good at it.
On the other hand, it may have been his only choice.

Perhaps he had been sitting in his house one day when a limitless army of animals appeared through the trees. House was a very generous description of the assembly of rubbish piled slightly higher than the surrounding ruin. The man had leapt to the attack, slaughtering everything mercilessly. Then he simply left the dead where they lay and went back indoors.

The man probably emerged every now and then to drag some remains away and do whatever it was he did to them before he took them to market. Hermitage was no victualler but he was certain nothing here would be bought by anyone with the smallest iota of discernment. He wondered how Briston had got such a neat and new looking pig. The things that lay on the valley floor bearing the strongest resemblance to pigs were hard to discern from the things which bore resemblances to sheep or cows. Or cats? A creep ran down Hermitage's back and he looked away.

'Blind me,' Wat said, as he wrinkled his nose and gazed about. 'This man is a butcher?'

'Plainly.' Hermitage's eyes were still wide from the first revelation.

'I mean butcher in the sense of someone who prepares meat for consumption, not someone who just kills things.'

'Perhaps he started with the latter and moved into the former.'

'Sell meat as a way to support his little...' Wat searched the valley for the right word, 'hobby?' he suggested. 'Who'd buy any of this stuff?'

They exchanged looks, realising there was nothing to do but walk through the scene of animal destruction. If this man had anything to tell them about Briston, Hermitage was determined it would be done quickly.

As they passed the outer reaches of the deceased, swarms of insects rose around them.

'Flies,' Hermitage observed. 'In January,' he shivered again.

'Hi,' Wat called loudly, with a slight tremor in his voice. He was clearly hoping the owner of this appalling scene would come to them, so they wouldn't have go any deeper into his diseased realm.

A man emerged from the shapeless shape in the middle of the destruction. He had a knife in his hands.

'Good morning,' he called in a round and well-filled voice. He waved his knife in what appeared to be a friendly greeting. Bits of stuff flew off the blade, anxious to join the larger heaps scattered on the floor. Unfortunately, the man made no attempt to come to them so they picked their way through the fleshy obstacles.

'Are you the butcher?' Hermitage asked rather pointlessly when they reached the knife wielder.

'I've got a lot of explaining to do if I'm not.' The butcher grinned and held out his arms to encompass his demesne.

Wat looked at the man as one can only look at a man who appears to be mad while holding a large knife covered in blood.

'We, erm, just wanted to ask about the pig,' Wat said. 'Erm, Briston. Briston, the pig, erm, his pig. Briston's pig. The pig Briston the Weaver got from you. May have got from you. Possibly.'

Hermitage looked at Wat with some anxiety. The weaver was always so controlled and calm, but he seemed positively jumpy.

'Did you supply a weaver at Baernodebi market with a pig?' Hermitage asked more reasonably.

Wat was staring around as if the bits on the floor were about to leap up.

'Oh yes,' the butcher replied. 'Fine specimen. One of my best.'

'Your best?' Wat's voice broke into two squeaks.

'Absolutely,' the butcher nodded as if this would be clear to anyone. 'Come see.' He beckoned them to join him inside his dwelling, or slaughterhouse, or whatever it was.

'I'm not going in there,' Wat mumbled so only Hermitage could hear him.

Hermitage tutted and followed the butcher to the interior of what could only be described as a shack.

The inside was remarkable. Not for the fact that it was basically a continuation of the outside with a roof on, but because in one corner was an immaculate scribe's lectern, complete with parchment, inks, and quills. Hermitage was so taken aback by the unexpected piece of furniture that he didn't immediately notice the rest of the place.

As his eyes got used to the gloom, he saw that the lectern had a half-completed drawing on it. He drew close and found it was an anatomical diagram – one of remarkable accuracy and detail. He then noticed that the thing of which it was a remarkably accurate and detailed drawing was lying on a table to the side, gently leaking on to the floor.

'My gracious me!' Hermitage found it hard to reconcile the scene of destruction and death with the fine work. 'Are you a butcher or a scholar, sir?'

'Ah well,' the fellow replied in his educated voice. 'That's an interesting tale.'

Hermitage found himself weighing the man up now. He acknowledged that when he had thought the fellow a simple butcher, perhaps a careless and slovenly one but nonetheless a tradesman, he had given him little heed. Now it was clear there was more to him, Hermitage paid attention.

The man was dressed in a butcher's apron, but his feet were shod in solid black shoes that rose to his ankles and then turned over in the fashionable manner. An expensive use of material. The head was a mop of straight, dark hair, tied in a tail behind him. Presumably to stop it dipping into the gore. His face was clear and seemed untroubled by the wreckage around him. The skin was wrinkled with age rather than worry. He must have been at least forty, but still looked to be in good health. The eyes though were much younger; they bubbled with enthusiasm and commitment. Hermitage recognised something of himself in them.

136

'I have always had an interest in the workings of the body,' the butcher-academic explained. 'My first choice was to become a physik, which I did. Briefly.' The words tailed off.

'Why briefly?'

'There were, erm, unfortunate incidents with some of my patients.'

'Ah.'

'Yes. One or two of my treatments proved to be, what can we say? Harmful.'

'Oh dear.'

'Well, quite a lot of them did, really. Word got around. Outrageous exaggerations, of course, but you know what the common folk are like. Don't go there, you'll get poisoned. Never ask him to fix your foot, he'll chop your leg off.'

'I say!' Hermitage expressed sympathy at the outrageous impact of gossip.

'I know!' The butcher was defensive. 'And that only happened the once. Or twice,' he added. 'Some of them even objected to me making a record of their parts with my drawings, can you believe?'

Hermitage was not surprised. The common folk were always suspicious of developments in thinking.

'How are we ever going to advance the practice of medicine if we don't have details of the injuries people suffer and the route to their cures?' he said. 'I can see it would be essential to have comprehensive notes and diagrams of the affected parts.'

'Oh, I do all the parts,' the butcher smiled his enthusiasm. 'Affected or not. I wanted the whole picture.'

'Oh.' Hermitage could see that this might cause some offence.

'It was the husbands who caused most of the trouble.'

Hermitage's mind hopped back to some of the tapestries he had seen. Perhaps this fellow and Wat ought to get together. On the other hand, no, they most certainly should not.

'So, driven from my study of the human body, I turned to

animals. No one makes a fuss about them. I got hold of some for my research and then folk started asking if they could have the leftovers.'

'For food,' Hermitage understood.

'Oh!' The man seemed surprised. 'Yes, I suppose that must be it.'

'So, you sell the parts to fund your study.' Hermitage saw this as a most constructive arrangement.

'No,' the butcher replied. 'Money's not really a problem, the family support me. I rather suspect they pay me to stay away. I am quite grateful when the locals come to take some bits. It is getting a bit messy out there. Problem is they've even stopped doing that since this Norman business.'

'The invasion?'

'Yes, that's it. Some Normans did turn up, but they didn't stay long.' The man shrugged.

'In my experience, they have no great interest in learning,' Hermitage shrugged himself.

'I'm happy enough here so I shall just carry on.'

'What about your family, though? Will they be safe?' Hermitage knew the whole country was in turmoil. There was no guarantee this man's money supply would be safe in a Norman country.

'Ah, I hadn't thought of that.'

This man reminded Hermitage of himself in so many ways. The enthusiasm for his subject, the single-minded devotion, the complete absence of common sense. He realised how much he had changed since meeting Wat. Looking at this man, he saw that most of it was actually for the better. Besides the topics of Wat's tapestries.

'What *is* your name?' Hermitage asked the blunt question.

'Hamard,' the butcher replied. 'Hamard Godwin.'

'Oh,' Hermitage managed to say while his mind was screaming, "Great God Almighty and Lord preserve us." The old King's family. If the Normans had known who this man was, they'd have left him in the same state as his meat.

'So, your erm...' Hermitage didn't know how to frame the question.

'Uncle,' Hamard answered.'Harold, yes.'

'You heard that he, erm...'

'Yes. Hastings, I gather. I've never really been one for all that family business.'

'Might I suggest you take that a stage further? Change your name. Never tell anyone you are called Godwin. Certainly never mention it to a Norman.'

'Do you think so?'

'Most assuredly.'

Hamard looked at Hermitage, clearly grateful for the advice, but not absolutely clear why it was needed.

Hermitage recalled the reason why they had come here and combined it with a new-found need to leave quite quickly. He didn't want to be within a mile of this place when any Normans came back.'So this pig?' he asked.

'Which one?' Hamard looked around clearly trying to recall which bits had been pig.

'The one for Briston?'

'Ah yes, the weaver. Charming fellow, I must say.'

'You gave him a pig?'

'Yes, a whole one. It was slightly disappointing as I was planning to get a fine representation of the fiery humours of the loins.'

'Loins?'

'Yes, it's a favourite topic of mine. First male, then female, make a detailed comparison and determine where exactly the procreative fundaments are located.'

Hermitage felt his eyebrows raise of their own accord. 'And this was your topic with your human patients as well, was it?'

'Oh yes,' Hamard answered, 'but it caused no end of trouble.

People are awfully sensitive, don't you think?'

Hermitage easily cast his mind to when his own simple enquiries into the scriptural justification for an individual's action had led to a punch on the nose. He could only imagine the consequences of enquiring about the fire of someone's loins. Let alone ask to draw a picture.

'Did Briston say what he wanted with the pig?'

Hamard shrugged and looked away to his drawings. 'Only that it was vital to his plan.'

'Really?' Hermitage was encouraged. Hamard could be a source of useful information.

'I say,' Hamard said with excitement. 'You're not Wat the Weaver, are you?' He looked at Hermitage's habit. 'Ah, no. Of course not.'

'No *I'm* not,' Hermitage said with equal enthusiasm, 'but the fellow outside is.'

Hamard's eyes lit up. 'How marvellous. I've got a message for him.'

Hermitage quickly ducked out of the hovel-heap.

'Wat,' he called and beckoned over the distance the weaver had put between himself and the dwelling of Hamard.

Wat looked very unhappy at being called back.

'Hermitage,' he called and beckoned in the opposite direction.

'There is information,' Hermitage shouted.

'Good,' Wat called back. 'It'll sound much better over here.'

Hermitage put his head back in the building, 'I'm sorry Mister, erm, Hamard. Would you be able to join Wat outside?'

'Of course, of course,' Hamard wiped his hands on his apron, which did little for his hands, but added ruin to the apron.

Picking their way through the wreckage of research, Hamard and Hermitage joined Wat on top of the rise out of the valley.

'Oh dear,' Hamard said looking back. 'It is a mess, isn't it?'

'You wanted Wat? This is he,' Hermitage introduced the two.

Hamard held his poorly cleaned hand out. Wat bowed his head.

'You had a message?' Hermitage prompted.

'Ah yes,' Hamard brought his attention back to the situation. 'Master Briston told me you might have some fine sketches of loins.'

No words came out of Wat. He looked from butcher to monk and back.

'It's Hamard's special area of research,' Hermitage explained. 'Purely academic interest.'

'That's what a lot of 'em say,' Wat sneered.

'Was that the message?' Hermitage was disappointed.

'Um, eh?' Hamard stumbled through reality. 'Oh no. Just a personal question. Master Briston explained his work and we had a fine discussion on detailed points of anatomy.'

'I bet you did,' Wat leered now as well.

'The message?' Hermitage prompted.

'Ah yes. Master Briston said you might find me.'

'Did he?' Wat was sceptical.

'Absolutely. He said Mister Wat was working with the King's Investigator and would trace his steps in no time at all.'

Hermitage and Wat just exchanged glances.

'Good job you didn't bring this king's fellow with you. Might have been awkward. Anyway, Briston said that he had to leave.'

'Because people were after him?' Hermitage prompted.

'No, apparently that was quite normal. He said to look out for a churchman called Dextus and for Virgil. I assumed the poor fellow thought the poet was still alive, but it seemed not.'

'Most assuredly not,' Hermitage confirmed.

'Briston said not to worry about them. He asked if you could look out for someone named Cwen,' Hamard went on.

Wat cast his eyes down at this request.

'He apologised for using the death note, whatever that means.'

'I understand it,' Wat said.

'Good. He then said not to look for him. You would understand if I said that he had made the Tapestry of Death.'

'We know,' Hermitage put in. 'It's a special weaver's binding for the dead. Covers the body completely. That's what Briston put on the pig to make everyone think it was him.'

'How clever,' Hamard appreciated.

'That's not it,' Wat said.

'Not what?' Hermitage was confused.

Wat breathed deeply and had a significant frown on his face. 'The Tapestry of Death that wrapped the pig is woven, never made.'

'I don't understand.'

'There are really two Tapestries of Death,' Wat explained. 'It's all in the ritual. The first is the one we saw, the second is a joke.'

'A joke?'

'Or is it a myth? Whatever. It's suggested that a tapestry can be made that brings death to its creator. It is an image of the truth of the world.'

It was all Hermitage could do to gape rather openly. This wasn't making any sense at all.

'A weaver could make the Tapestry of Death either by chance or deliberate act. The image in the second reveals everything. The truth. The ultimate scene. God, if you like.'

'How could a weaver make an image of God?' Hermitage was disbelieving. 'No one knows what God looks like.'

'And no one knows what the tapestry would look like. That's why it's a myth. We use it to frighten apprentices. Weave what you're told or you might create the Tapestry of Death by mistake and you'll instantly burst into flames.'

'Nonsense.'

'Of course it's nonsense. A fairy tale and clearly not true. This is what he told you to say?' Wat asked Hamard, apparently convinced the butcher had got this completely wrong.

'Exactly his words. Tell Mister Wat that I have made the Tapestry of Death. He was quite explicit that I got it right.'

Hermitage rubbed his hand across his tonsure absentmindedly, wondering if this would help his thoughts move about.

'When did all this happen?' he asked.

'Yesterday,' Hamard replied, confident in his memory.

'Yes, but when yesterday, what time?' Hermitage pressed.

'Oh,' Hamard replied, finding this question a bit trickier. 'Let me see. He glanced at the sky. 'I think he came to collect the pig about midday, or soon after.'

'After Cwen had left for water,' Hermitage exclaimed.

'I'm sure I wouldn't know,' Hamard replied in some confusion.

'Did you see him again?'

'Oh yes, he came through on his way. That's when he left the message.'

'When would that have been?'

'You worry about the time too much,' Hamard noted.

'It is important. Please think,' Hermitage encouraged the rather vague butcher.

Hamard looked to the sun again, 'About this time, I suppose.'

Wat thought quietly for a moment but nothing seemed to come to him. 'Which way did he go?'

'He said not to tell.'

'I expect he did. Unfortunately, the Cwen he asked us to look out for is currently in the hands of a deranged killer.'

'Oh my! There are so many about these days.'

Wat asked again, 'If I assumed it was south, would I be right?'

'Obviously I can't say you're right, that would be breaking my word.

'You could tell us we're not wrong,' Hermitage suggested, 'that wouldn't be telling us which way he went, which would be breaking your word, but would, in effect, be *not* telling us in which direction he *didn't* go!' Hermitage smiled.

143

Hamard smiled as well. 'How erudite,' he said.

'What?' Wat said gaping at the pair.

'It's quite straightforward,' Hermitage started off. 'You see, if we aren't told in which direction…'

'Shut up,' Wat interrupted. 'We're going south. Quickly. We have to find him and bring him back before tomorrow evening.'

Wat made to leave, while Hermitage paused to check with Hamard.

'Would you be in a position to not tell us where he wasn't going? Exactly.'

'If such a question were posed,' Hamard responded, 'I would only be able to not tell you that he wasn't going to Bigby. It's the next village down the road and has a renowned inn. Many travellers make for it.'

'Thank you.' Hermitage nodded his head.

'You two deserve one another,' Wat snorted.

'Oh, before you go?' Hamard asked.

'Yes?' Wat snapped as he was clearly anxious to get away.

'You look like a fit young man. I don't suppose I could do a drawing of your loins?'

Caput XIV

Cellars

ＴＨＥＬＲＥＤ Ｓｔｏｔｔ's ｖｉｅｗｓ on visitors are already well known. The very low level of Parsimon's desire to meet Virgil has been indicated. Both old men suffered disappointment through a single knock on the door. Only one knock was required to get the old retainer running. It was of such violence that some of the pewter fell off the table.

'Normans?' Stott cried out as he leapt from his chair by the fire. Well, lifted himself as quickly from his chair as his aching bones allowed.

Parsimon shrugged a shrug of worry. He opened the door his usual half an inch only to find the thing nearly thrown from its hinges. In place of the door was another door. This door was just as big and strong, but it was man shaped. Apart from the fact men didn't come in shapes this big.

'Yes?' Parsimon asked with remarkable poise for a gnat about to be blown away by a gale.

'Correct answer,' the giant replied. 'I'm Virgil and these are variously my friends, enemies, and complete strangers. We've come to stay.'

'How lovely,' Parsimon replied. 'Unfortunately, it's not con-venient. My master is unwell and the house is small.'

'Most kind,' Virgil said as he strode past Parsimon into the body of the hall with his little band in tow.

Dextus at least nodded an apology to Parsimon as he entered accompanied by the Castigatori, who were still rubbing various damaged parts. Two of Virgil's men sidled past the door as if they were hoping the room wouldn't spot them. They meandered off left and right, examining everything and peering eve-rywhere. The last of their number brought up the rear, his knife still out and still pointed at Cwen, whose continuous sulking grumbles had prompted a couple of sharp jabs with the weapon. They were all followed by Firman and Eadric, who looked like they were about to walk away rather than enter. A glance back from Virgil changed their minds.

'Who the devil are these people?' Stott demanded as he stood, master of his hall. For now.

'The devil?' Virgil asked amicably. 'Yes, not far off, as it hap-pens. We've come in out of the cold to wait for a delivery.'

'This is my home,' Stott wailed.

'Hold on to that thought,' Virgil responded with mild nu-ances of menace.

'Well, what are you having delivered?' Stott asked. 'I'm sure I can send it on somewhere. Anyway, what are you doing having things delivered to my house?'

'My my, you are a curious old fellow.'

Virgil approached Stott. He held out his hand to shake, which Stott refused. Disappointed, Virgil grasped the Stott beard firmly in his right hand. He lifted the ancient Saxon from the floor and ignored the ancient Saxon squeaks that came from the mouth. Holding Stott face to face, the old man's feet a good two feet off the floor, Virgil explained.

'Shut up,' he said. 'With any luck, we'll be gone by tomorrow evening.'

Stott spluttered and threw both hands to his agonised face, as Virgil lowered him to the ground.

'Without any luck, we'll take a shine to the place and keep it.'

'Are you Normans?'

'Good God, no,' Virgil spat on the floor.

'I say,' Parsimon piped up looking at the mess the massive mouth had deposited on his flagstones.

'Well, what are you doing threatening good Saxon folk?'

Stott demanded.

'I'm just generally threatening,' Virgil replied, stating a fact. 'It's what I do. Being my size, I find it comes easy.'

Stott just stood and blustered through his beard. It was obvious neither he nor Parsimon had the power to make this man do anything other than exactly what he wanted.

'Well then, who are all these other people?' Stott seemed to need an outlet for complaint.

'Oh, the usual bunch. A priest, some violent monks, my associates, a couple of strangers from the road who are up to no good, and a hostage.'

'A hostage?' Stott was shocked. 'What sort of man are you?'

'Oh, nasty.' Virgil nodded at this happy description.

Stott scanned the assembly. Most of them had slumped to the floor and were resting against the walls. Particularly the Castigatori, who needed to rest their bodies somewhere. Dextus stood in silence by the door, arms folded, while Eadric and Firman had approached the table and found all the seats full of pewter. Cwen was seated on the floor, but curled up with her arms across her knees and her face buried. Her guard stood over her. Stott frowned at the shape with some glimpse of recognition. He was about to say something when one of Virgil's men approached his master.

The great head sank in the room and words were whispered.

'Fine collection of tapestry you have,' Virgil observed.

Stott said nothing.

'I have an interest in tapestry myself.'

'Really?' Stott pondered, in the disbelieving tone that comes out when your garderobe cleaner tells you he could value your jewellery for you.

'Oh yes,' Virgil now looked around the hall, where the words of his man had directed him. 'I see you have an early Mundham.' Virgil gestured at one of the largest works on the wall.

This was at least ten feet square and insulated the outside

wall of the hall. It had maidens and roses and dragons galore.

'Erm, yes,' Stott said, taken aback somewhat that this monster actually knew what he was talking about.

'I met him once, you know. Mundham.'

'Really?'

'Yes. Just before he died, as it happens,' Virgil nodded sagely to himself. 'Great work though. Had a very fine green, did Mundham.'

'He was known for it,' Stott commented, glancing at the vivid greens that danced from the foliage of the tapestry.

'Yes.' Virgil was reminiscing about something. 'Wouldn't share it with anyone.'

'Ah.'

'More than his life was worth, he said.'

'Did he?'

'He was right.'

'Ah, and is that a Blazon?' Virgil gestured to an old and ragged hanging, which clung to the wall to the right of the fireplace. This was much smaller and was so faded it was hard to see what the image was.

'It is.' Stott was cautious. 'It was handed down from my great grandfather. Made in the time of Alfred, they say.'

'You should hang on to that.'

'I will,' Stott said in some defiance.

'My delivery's to do with tapestry.'

'I still don't see what it has to do with me or my house,' Stott grumbled quietly, finding being lifted by the beard an uncomfortable experience.

'You're just in the wrong place at the wrong time.' Virgil smiled. 'Bad luck.'

'What do you propose to do? Just loll about here and get in my way?'

'Oh, not at all.' Virgil was accommodating. 'We'll have a nice meal, fine conversation, get warm by the fire, and lots of drink.

You do have lots of drink, I take it?'

'I...' Stott began.

'Excellent. My men have gone to explore your cellars. I'm sure they'll come up with something suitable.'

'Parsimon,' Stott called, but Parsimon had already set off after the men exploring the cellars.

He found them tapping barrels, lifting sacks, and opening crates.

'Be careful,' he called.

The men looked at him but made no visible attempt to increase their care.

'What's round here?' one of the men asked in tones so nasal Parsimon assumed he was doing a funny voice. Hardly the time for humour.

'Nothing,' Parsimon answered as calmly as he could. "Round here" was his locked corner with its shelves of treasures. He imagined these men liked treasures. Especially other people's. 'Just some new wine, not ready yet. The good stuff is this way.'

He beckoned to the other end of the vaulted cellar and was gratified to get the appropriate reaction to the expression "good stuff". He did indeed lead them to the good stuff, reluctantly. Stott's personal collection of beers and wines. The man may hate the Normans, but he didn't mind drinking their wine. Parsimon leaned against a wall with folded arms while the men went from barrel to barrel, tapping each in turn with leathern mugs until they found one to meet their approval.

'We'll take this one,' the second man whispered. Where his companion's voice seemed to be generated, rounded and delivered entirely by his nose, this fellow spoke as if he only had so much voice for one lifetime and was saving it for something important.

'Beg pardon?' Parsimon asked, partly because he couldn't make out the quiet voice and partly because he wasn't sure what he was being asked.

'We'll take this one,' the quiet one repeated.

'All of it?' Parsimon couldn't believe the request now he had heard it.

'You have seen the size of Virgil?' the nasal one asked.

'How am I supposed to get the barrel upstairs?' Parsimon asked.

'Don't mind,' the whisperer answered, as if it was some sort of quiz.

'I'll fetch Virgil.' The one with the talking nose scurried back up to the main hall.

Some moments and several loud thumps, crashes, and significant bits of damage to the fixtures and fittings of the Stott Manor later, the barrel of wine sat on the main table in the hall. Virgil had simply lifted it from its resting place and carried it upstairs. He had also drunk about a quarter of it already. Much of Stott's pewter collection lay on the floor and Virgil had ruthlessly scooped the stuff from the chairs to join it.

'What do you want all this stuff for anyway?' he had asked Stott.

The old man had tried to answer, but it was clear Virgil wasn't really interested.

After he had quenched his thirst on Stott's finest French vintage, he invited the others to take their fill. Even Dextus and the Castigatori were instructed to drink.

'Come, girl,' Virgil called to Cwen who was still hunched double. 'No good sulking yourself to death. Your friends think you're still alive so will be carrying out my little errand. Personally, I don't care if you live or die.'

Cwen's eyes peered out over her arms. She looked at the barrel with obvious thirst and reluctantly unwound herself. Her body tried to make it clear that she wasn't doing this because Virgil said so, but because she wanted to.

'It's that boy again,' Stott called. 'I thought I recognised him.'

'Ah,' said Virgil, massive eyebrows raised in massive interest.

'You've seen this slip of a thing before then? It is a girl, by the way.'

'No it isn't,' Stott simply explaining the fact.

'Boy or girl, where have you seen her before?' Virgil asked.

'Here of course. She was with that nosy man and his monk.'

'A monk?' Virgil was very interested, 'Brother Hermitage, the King's Investigator.'

'No, there was only one of him. Most impertinent pair.'

'What brought them here?'

Stott paused for a moment. The wobble of his beard said that he rather wished he hadn't said anything.

'Come now, Master Stott, I want to know.' Virgil's voice said that he always got what he wanted.

Stott tried to sound dismissive, 'They were asking about some weaver or other. I forget his name.'

'Briston,' Virgil prompted.

'That's the fellow.'

'Why did they come here to ask you about Briston?'

'That's what I said. Most impertinent,' Stott huffed.

'We assume it was simply because we are the local manor and Master Stott owns the market,' Parsimon spoke up for his master. 'Apparently this Briston was murdered at the market.'

Virgil glanced to Parsimon with suspicion. 'When I want you to speak, I will make it quite clear,' the giant said. 'When I don't want you to speak, I will pull your tongue out.' He finished the threat with a quality glare.

'Only trying to help,' Parsimon muttered under his breath.

'Well, don't.' Virgil turned his full attention to Parsimon. 'Killing old people should be less of a crime, you know,' he proposed.

'Really?' Parsimon asked, a slight choke in his voice.

'Yes, you've not got many years to go anyway. If I kill you, I'm only robbing you of what? Three or four years at most. If I kill a baby, I'm taking away forty, maybe even fifty years. If it's a high born baby.'

Parsimon seemed quite content that Virgil could kill old people and babies, and anyone in between if he put his mind to it. He closed his lips tight, giving every impression that he was never going to let another word pass through them.

'Good.' Virgil turned back to Stott. 'You were saying, Briston the Weaver and this girl?'

'Boy,' Stott corrected.

'Boy then.' Virgil raised his eyes to the ceiling in exasperation at the old man's idiocy. 'This boy. Why were they here?'

'Well,' Stott said. Parsimon held his breath. 'It's as my man says. I own the market and where else would you go to report a death?'

Parsimon breathed again.

'The monk is the King's Investigator. Why would he report to anyone? People should report to him. And you said they were impertinent. They weren't reporting a death. You can't report impertinently.'

'I just didn't like them,' Stott shrugged as if Virgil would understand this.

'So who is the girl, boy?' Virgil asked the direct question.

'How should I know?' Stott replied.

'He came with the impertinent monk and you seemed quite surprised to see her. Him.' Virgil seemed to be getting quite frustrated at having to deal with Stott's wandering mind.

'Well, I am. I sent them away. I don't expect people I send away to come back.'

Virgil threw his large arms in the air and paced backwards and forwards. 'I'm worried that if I hit you to tell me the truth, you'll drop dead. Perhaps if I hit your man and he drops dead, you'll tell me the truth.'

'Now you're being impertinent,' Stott grumbled.

Virgil stepped forward and took hold of the Stott beard once more. He didn't lift this time but his face was threat enough. 'Why were they here?' he spelled out.

'I told you,' Stott retorted, attempting to brush Virgil's fist out of his beard. 'They came to report the death and wanted me to do something about it.'

'What?'

'Tell them who was at the market, where people lived. They wanted to investigate. Apparently the other fellow was Wat the Weaver and he was a friend of this Briston, the dead one. Quite frankly, they're both disgusting and if I'd known, I wouldn't have let any of them into my market.'

Virgil released the beard, turned around, and grabbed Cwen, who had been standing with her back to the room, helping herself to the wine. She squeaked as she was lifted from the floor by her tunic.

'So girl boy,' Virgil snarled, 'who are you?'

Cwen looked at the man in defiance, even though her feet were a good distance from the ground.

'I am Briston's apprentice.' She held her head as high as possible.

'No you're not,' Virgil replied.

'Because I'm a woman?' Cwen asked sarcastically.

'Yes, of course,' Virgil answered, lowering her again.

She straightened her tunic and stared challengingly at him.

'Whoever you are, you know where he's gone,' Virgil replied.

'I don't,' Cwen snapped back. 'He tricked me as much as anyone. I thought he was in the Tapestry of Death.'

'Or it was all an act. You're here to make sure we accept he's dead and then you run off to join him. His little woman.'

'I am not his little woman,' Cwen flared. 'I am his apprentice.'

'He is married, you know,' Virgil stated for the record.

'I don't care if he's The Queen of Sheba's pussycat,' Cwen shot back. 'I am his apprentice, learning the trade. If you can't cope with that, it's your problem. I do not know where he is. If I did, I would be with him. If I found out where he was, after he had run off, I would still be with him, kicking him hard in the soft bits.'

'Oh, there is more going on here than meets my eye,' Virgil said slowly, glaring at everyone in turn. 'And my eye is very large indeed. My arrival here seems to be at a moment of good fortune. These old men are hiding something and I don't believe the girl is telling me a word of the truth.'

The giant's tone was serious and even his acolytes seemed tense, wondering what was going to happen next.

'Bring the girl to the cellar,' he commanded.

'Why the cellar?' Parsimon asked, forgetting his promised silence.

Virgil gave him a horrifyingly frank stare. 'Because I always do my best torture in a cellar.'

Caput XV

The Other Village

HE SUN WAS RETREATING towards the safety of the horizon as Hermitage and Wat left the site of Hamard's charnel enquiries. Their pace was quick, Wat having argued they would be able to catch up with Briston if they moved fast. More importantly, he indicated the likely outcome of being found by Normans while travelling at night. Hermitage hurried.

'He's had hours of advantage,' Hermitage panted as they stepped briskly. 'We know he left here this time yesterday. He could be, erm…' Hermitage paused and did the necessary calculations. 'Fifteen miles away by now. An impossible distance.'

'There is one fact about Briston you aren't aware of yet,' Wat said as he negotiated a pile of horse dung in the middle of the path. 'Bloody Normans,' he swore at the obstruction.

'What's that?' Hermitage asked.

'He is enormously lazy. Monumentally, fundamentally idle. If he can find a reason not to do a job, he will. Even better, he'll find a reason for someone else to do it for him.'

This puzzled Hermitage. It didn't seem to fit the image he'd built up. 'But all the tapestries, the business, the tent, the apprentice and all the people after him. He seems to have been quite busy.'

'Like I said, a chancer. Gets other people to do most of the work, and if people are after him, it's probably because he hasn't delivered. I can see why he'd be terrified of getting in with Virgil. The giant man would make him do a day's work for once in his life. Followed by another one and another one. Poor Briston.'

Wat smirked. 'If he put as much effort into doing his work as he does into avoiding it, he'd be rich and safe.'

'Oh.' Hermitage tried to reconcile this with all the other information he had. 'Perhaps that explains Cwen? Get someone else to do the work for him.'

'And a, erm...' Wat couldn't bring himself to say it.

'Woman?' Hermitage offered.

'Quite. Someone who couldn't go complaining to the guild, fraternise with other apprentices, or be likely to inflict the Apprentice Complaint on someone twice her size.'

'Apprentice Complaint?' Hermitage asked, wondering why the phrase was being given such prominence.

'Just a means of complaint that apprentices can use in extreme situations. When their master is really getting out of hand. It is very rare though.'

'How does it work?'

'Oh, well, the apprentice just kills the master,' Wat said.

'What?' Hermitage was horrified. 'An apprentice kills their master?' He could only imagine that this was over and above the simple sin of murder. Any guild worth its name would certainly want to take action to stop that sort of thing. It was like a novice killing an abbot. Mind you, there had been a few occasions... Hermitage put that thought out of his head immediately.

'Not usually one apprentice on their own, of course,' Wat explained. 'They'd have to get together to take out a master. Particularly in this case, what with Cwen being so small and Briston being quite a big chap.'

It was all Hermitage could do to gape at this information. He would have to examine it in detail when he got his mind in order. There were more pressing matters to consider. Though what could be more pressing than apprentices killing their masters, he couldn't immediately bring to mind. The problem of Briston was here and now. At least that was something to be dealt with immediately.

'So you think Briston may not have gone far?' he asked.

'That's why we'll catch him. He wouldn't *run* anywhere. Out of sight out of mind isn't an expression to Briston. It's a way of life. As soon as he can't see the people chasing him anymore, he stops and puts his feet up. Then he seems surprised when they appear again.'

'I imagine he will think people are still after him though.' Hermitage thought Wat's description was of a very foolish sort of fellow.

'Not with his pig trick. He'll think that's put them off the scent and he's set us after him and knows we won't do him any harm.'

'This Tapestry of Death that he claims to have made seems to be at the heart of it, at least according to Hamard.'

'It's a fairy story. It certainly isn't the reason behind all this.'

'Then what is?' Hermitage was anxious to know. Just like a child pretending to rescue the maiden, or defend the castle, he had to know *why*. Chasing errant weavers across the country was fine, as long as you knew why.

'Who cares?' Wat replied, which was not the answer Hermitage needed. 'We're just worried about finding him and bringing him back. If we don't, Cwen gets the Virgil treatment.'

'If Briston is as lazy as you say, we may find him well within the allotted time.' Hermitage nodded some comfort.

'If Virgil hasn't finished her off already, along with the rest of them.'

Hermitage was appalled. 'I'm appalled,' he said. 'The man told us to find Briston or Cwen would suffer, not find Briston *and* Cwen will suffer.'

'He is a violent, giant lunatic,' Wat explained.

'He wouldn't,' Hermitage said.

'Why not? Save all the trouble of looking after her until we get back. We do his searching for him, find Briston, deliver him, and Cwen turns out to be dead. What's he lost?'

'His eternal soul.' Hermitage felt rather sick.

'That's long gone,' Wat said, and strode on.

'So why?' Hermitage couldn't bring himself to ask why they were bothering.

'Because he might not have done anything. It's the chance we have to take and the one Virgil knows we have to take.'

'The others will protect her.' Hermitage spoke solely to give himself some assurance.

'Stott and Parsimon?' Wat laughed, 'I don't think they'll be protecting much. You saw what he did to three Castigatori. Dextus and those two strangers will be no contest.'

'Yes, who do you think they were?' Hermitage's bottomless well of curiosity bubbled once more.

'Probably customers after Briston as well.'

'So Virgil was right on that account.'

'Once again,' Wat said with some finality, 'who cares?'

'So we just need to save Cwen.' Hermitage nodded to himself.

'That's it.'

'Rescue the maiden,' Hermitage mused.

'Hardly that,' Wat protested. 'Just, erm, avoid an innocent party coming to a nasty end.'

'Yes,' Hermitage said, smiling out of Wat's view.

Night was falling now, the sun having abandoned its daily doomed attempt to shed light on the world. Darkness swam across the land, hiding those things from sight that were best hidden. Creatures that used the night to cover their activities scurried from their holes and homes. The creatures that liked to jump out on things that used the night did likewise. Tiny mice scurried through the undergrowth, seeking insects to grasp in their tiny paws before nibbling them with sharp but tiny teeth. Massive owls sat in trees, waiting to descend in deadly in silence on tiny mice, like God throwing houses at people. Houses with razor sharp feet, ready to snatch a mouse before swallowing the beast whole. The digestive system would do the rest. Inequity was everywhere.

Fortunately, a large moon provided some pallid light to the scene, only hiding every now and then behind convenient clouds.

'I say we press on,' Wat said. 'No way will Briston walk anywhere at night.'

'What about the Normans?' Hermitage asked, looking round as if the conquerors came out of holes in the ground at night.

'Bigby's not far. We'll definitely make it,' Wat said. His legs did not share his confidence and he broke into a slow trot down the road. Hermitage followed suit.

'I don't know if I can keep this up,' Hermitage panted after a few minutes. 'I declined any of the foods the peasant Lolby offered. I know he ate them, but he was probably used to them.'

'We'll keep on to the inn at Bigby. I'll bet you his pig that Briston's there.'

They hurried on through the encroaching night in silence. The path was clear and the moon made their going easy. Scrub and trees crowded the way but didn't overgrow the road. In places, bits of stone emerged from the ground and some places were almost paved. Another Roman highway fallen into complete disrepair.

At least this gave Hermitage's mind something to ponder as they made their way. He needed something to ponder, silence not being his natural state. He wondered about the men who had made this road. Of course they'd probably been slaves, local people forced into labour, but time had taken the edge off such inhumanity and given it a warm historical glow. Common thought was that these historical figures had all been brilliant minds and outstanding engineers. Every Roman who ever trod the shores of Albion was raised to the status of genius/saint. Hermitage was sure that couldn't be the case. Some of them must have been normal people like him. Well, like Wat, perhaps.

No, not Wat. Maybe like, erm… He thought for a moment trying to recall if he actually knew anyone normal.

Maybe, in years to come, history would look back on this time with similar eyes. People of some hugely distant future, say the year 1250, would think of Hermitage's folk as mythical creatures, possessing great knowledge, wisdom and insight. He thought he better write something down to make sure they got the true picture. It would be a great disappointment of course but the truth had to be known. Or at least it did to Hermitage. No one else seemed that bothered. This prompted a new thought. Maybe it was him who wasn't normal? Maybe all the wrong people were normal? It was a ghastly thought.

His musings had achieved very little but had passed sufficient time for them to arrive at the gates of Bigby.

These gates were high, and black in the night, and shut.

'Hi,' Wat called over the ten foot high barrier that barred their way.

The village must be very proud of its protective shield. There weren't many these days that retained their defensive capability. The Normans took a dim view of such things and brightened their outlook by tearing them down and setting light to them.

'Ho,' Wat called. 'Anyone there?'

'They may not admit visitors after dark,' Hermitage proposed.

Wat was not interested in this idea and hammered on the door with his fist and kicked it with his right foot. There was no response and he stepped back to look left and right.

The gateway was fitted tightly between two buildings. Large planks of ancient wood were firmly fixed to the buildings and looked like they had been so for some time. In the middle of their expanse, which must have been nearly twenty feet across, the outlines of the two main gates could be seen. These, once open, would be large enough to admit a whole cart. As long as it took the gap slowly and carefully.

Set into one of the gates was a smaller version of the same thing. This was plainly for people only, and could doubtless be opened separately. As if completing the set, an even smaller door sat high in the woodwork, probably the peep hole from which the village guard would be able to judge visitors. Wat thumped them all to the same effect.

'This is ridiculous,' he complained. 'Where is everyone?'

Hermitage could only shrug. Of course he had no idea. How could he have? He didn't live here. He realised this was one of those moments not to take things so literally. He nodded sagely to himself.

Wat strode off first left and then right to see if there was a way round the gate. The buildings were solid.

'Come on,' he said to Hermitage. 'Let's go round the walls and see if there's another gate.

Choosing the direction to his right for no particular reason, Wat led away from the gate. They left the path and walked across some rough ground. Hermitage trod in something soft and remembered what villages tended to use the rough ground outside their walls for. He would wash his feet when they got inside. If they got inside.

The moon lit their way past the first building, after which Hermitage expected to see the next one closely butted up.

In fact, there was a gap. More than a gap: it was the end of a street. The street led out of the village on to a track that snaked off into the darkness. Its other end opened on to the main road they had been on, where torches hung from a few buildings, lighting the way for strangers.

'What?' Wat cried in frustration. 'What was the point of the bloody gate if the next street round is wide open?'

'Perhaps it's a relic,' Hermitage suggested. 'It could be that, in historical times, the whole village was surrounded but the rest of the walls have fallen? Or the Normans took them down?'

'Then why close the bloody gate and make us walk round?'

Wat was clearly very unhappy with this arrangement. Perhaps he'd trodden in something as well.

They trudged up the street to the main road and looked left and right. To the left, the place was deserted. The inside of the gate they'd been hammering on could be seen only a few yards away. It too was deserted and so Wat's calls and knocks had been for nothing.

The weaver, with an angry look on his face, strode off down the road. He grasped the wooden bar that held the gates closed, lifted it from its iron cradle, and threw it into the road. He then dragged the gates open and strode back to Hermitage.

'Stupid bloody people,' he muttered as he headed off in the other direction.

Hermitage scurried after. He was desperate to ask if Wat was allowed to open the gates, but had a pretty clear idea of what the answer would be.

The village was made of so few buildings, all of them poor, that Hermitage wondered what the gate was for anyway. The two either side of the gate looked like homes of the very poor. Probably quite a lot of them. The next two, one of them next to the street they'd come up, at least had torches and looked lived in. Lived in by people of little pride and with no time for maintenance, but nonetheless, they were signs of reasonable habitation. Only two more structures sat in the road before another gate could be seen, straddling the highway. This one was wide open.

'For goodness' sake,' Wat exclaimed at this frustrating sight.

The house to their left was ablaze with light. Torches hung on the outside and more light staggered into the night from an open shutter. A sign above the door declared this to be The Green Man, and although wood smoke poured from a chimney and a steam of heat rose through the window, the place was remarkably quiet.

The smell of a large cook pot introduced itself to Hermitage and his stomach groaned. Without word, he and Wat made for the door. They pushed it open and were greeted by the traditional silence reserved for strangers in small villages.

They'd expected no less, but they noticed that no one even bothered to look at them. No heads turned at the unexpected opening of the door. No glares from locals were thrown at the newcomers. Even the landlord, whose job it was to check arrivals, making sure they weren't going to rob the customers or wreck the place, paid them no heed. This was bizarre.

Hermitage had not entered many inns in his life at all. This number was in single figures since putting on the monk's habit. Every occasion had been the same though. He'd been invited to leave. Immediately. Monks always put a curse on an inn. They either lectured the locals or drank the place dry without paying. His exits had mostly been rapid and many had been violent.

He exchanged a puzzled look with Wat and they surveyed the crowd.

It was a crowd. Everyone from the village and probably the farms nearby must have been here. Every seat was taken and people were standing around the edges of the room.

This was not a large place, perhaps twenty feet across at best. Off to the left was the landlord's window, the small opening through which the man could serve his customers. Small enough to stop the customers getting through and helping themselves. The window was currently full of the landlord. A red faced, whiskered fellow whose head and shoulders were so tightly framed it looked as if the window would go with him when he moved. Across one corner of the room was a large rounded bench with a high back, doubtless the usual resting place for the regulars. It was big enough for three but five were squeezed in now.

In front of this, a table had created a seat for three more. The floor was covered with cross-legged men and Hermitage noticed that those gathered round the edge of the room were women. It was not unusual for women to visit the inn; their toil was hard and the reward of the inn was shared across the population. Tonight it looked like the whole population was being rewarded.

There must be thirty people in the place. Remarkable. All of them were facing the large fire that blazed in the wall opposite the landlord. Seated in a most comfortable padded chair, drawn up close to the fire, with the best mug of the best ale in his hand, a figure sat. The figure was talking quietly and the audience was rapt. The chair was angled to the door so Hermitage could not see who sat there. He and Wat sidled into the room to get a better view.

This was doubtless some travelling storyteller. A wandering character that would appear in villages such as this perhaps only once a year. He would tell tales of the world, bring news of great moments from distant parts, or even just some gossip from the nearest town, which many of the poor local folk would likely never have seen.

He would, of course, tell the traditional stories, the ones demanded by every audience. King Arthur and his knights, lost Roman legions, saints, and dragons. Each individual would have his own theme though. One might be renowned for bizarre encounters with mysterious creatures from the magical realms of Africa and Scotland. Another might have adventures from the east with awful revelations of heathens and how they could fly and eat rocks.

This would explain why the whole populace had turned out. Hermitage would be most interested to hear what this fellow had to tell. Previous experience had showed that many of these men were, at best, ill-informed or, at worst, downright liars.

Hermitage had himself exposed a so-called story man in his local village. It transpired this fellow only ever moved between the same four villages. This didn't stop him reporting on the most outrageous events from wildly far away with apparent authority. His fabrication even led to a small war between two towns. Hermitage still felt the injustice that it was he who was run from town, not the storyteller.

The audience gasped as he and Wat got within sight of the figure in the chair. The quietly speaking figure had clearly reached the denouement of his narrative and expertly led his listeners to the peak. It must have been a tremendous tale, judging from the silence that reigned. Only one member of the audience, a young man of some twenty summers, spoke out.

'Phwooar,' he said, in a crude and lascivious manner. 'With both of them? At once?'

Hermitage was taken aback somewhat and looked to Wat.

The weaver was standing with hands on hips. He gazed across the seated throng straight at the storyteller.

'Hello Briston,' he said in a loud, clear voice. 'I heard you were dead.'

Briston the Weaver grinned at the words.

Wat was not grinning at all. 'In fact, it was you who told me.'

Caput XVI

Back to the Cellar

HE STOTT MANOR WAS IN UPROAR. Well, it was bubbling along just below uproar. The massive figure of Virgil had made it clear he was not going to accept any uproar. There were protests at least. Stott's beard grumbled and mumbled and intimated that torturing young women was not a decent sort of thing to do. At least he now seemed to accept that Cwen was a girl. It wasn't clear if he thought torturing boys was any better.

Dextus had stepped forward from his standing place by the door and the Castigatori had gone to his side. Eadric and Firman had muttered some words of disapproval. They indicated that if they had been in a position to do anything about this, they would do something about it. What a pity it was that they weren't, so they couldn't.

Parsimon was giving Virgil a very hard stare.

Cwen was pale and shaking.

'What is it exactly you hope to achieve?' Dextus demanded.

'Pass the time?' Virgil suggested.

Dextus glared.

'I will find out where Briston has gone and what he's up to,' Virgil glared back, more fiercely and from much higher up.

'You've already sent the monk and Wat to find him. What's the point?'

'Oh, come on,' Virgil responded. 'You know how this works, Dextus. You've been in the church long enough. How do I know those two are going to come back at all? It turns out this girl is closely connected to Briston. She'll tell me things if I cause her some pain. They always do.'

'I don't know anything.' Cwen's voice was half terror, half anger.

'They all say that,' Virgil admitted. 'Then they find that they do know something after all. Bring her!' He gestured to his men who stepped from the shadows to grab Cwen by the arms and lead her after Virgil towards the cellar steps.

The Castigatori stepped forward to block their way.

Virgil turned and looked to Dextus. 'I'll kill them this time,' he said in all seriousness.

Dextus looked and reluctantly nodded his men back to his side. He whispered fiercely as they joined him.

Virgil took two heavy and flaming torches from high on the wall and led the way, his men dragging Cwen between them. Dextus and the Castigatori followed with Parsimon in tow.

'Where do you think you're going?' Virgil asked.

'We're going to stop you,' Dextus said, as if it was decided.

Virgil laughed and carried on down the cellar steps.

Dextus turned and glared his glare at the others in the room. Stott, Parsimon, Eadric, and Firman looked guilty and reluctantly followed.

The cellar itself was large enough for a decent torture chamber, but was very poorly equipped. Music, tapestry, riding, and the collection of pewter had been the main activities of the Stott manor. None of which required much in the way of torture. Stott had once described Parsimon's lute playing as torture, but that was as close as it got.

The space was lined with barrels of wine and beer and, of course, Parsimon's secret corner was in the corner. Secretly.

There was a table in the middle of the space, which was itself dominated by arches of stonework leaping from the floor and running across the ceiling before diving into the ground again. The table was mainly for putting the jugs on before and after they were filled with wine or beer. In fact, that was all it was for.

Virgil cast about the place with his eyes, searching for something.

'Where are your irons?' he demanded.

'Irons?' Stott asked as he joined the group gathered around the table.

'Irons, man. Your instruments?'

'I've got a lute upstairs,' Stott replied, hopelessly out of his depth.

'What do you use for punishing your staff?' Virgil was insistent.

'My wife tended to deal with that side of things,' Stott sniffed in reminiscence.

'Well, what did she use?' Virgil pressed.

Stott thought for a moment. 'Sarcasm, mainly,' he shrugged.

'Oh, this is hopeless. Bring the girl over here and I'll just hit her a bit.'

'If you tell me what it is you want to know, I'll tell you, if I know.' Cwen stifled her fear. 'I've got no loyalty to Briston. He ran off and left me here. If it was him on the table, I'd fetch the irons myself.'

Virgil looked at her. There was something in the shape of him that said he wanted to hit something. And soon.

'Where is he?' he asked instead.

'That I do not know,' she said as honestly as she could.

'Ah, what a shame, because that's what I want to know.' Virgil reached out a great arm, grabbed Cwen by the scruff of her neck, and sat her on the table.

'I know all about his tapestries,' Cwen said, clearly hoping this would stop whatever it was that was about to happen.

'So do I. In fact, I've got them now.' Virgil was weighing up Cwen's figure as a stonemason weighs up a wall, working out just how hard to hit it.

'In fact, I made most of them,' Cwen blurted out.

Virgil had been reaching out to take Cwen's arm, presumably

to break some bits of it. He paused.

'You?' He was both mocking and disbelieving.

'Yes.' Cwen's old defiance surfaced. 'I don't know why everyone finds it hard to believe I could make a tapestry. My hands are smaller than Briston's, my eyesight's better, I've got a better eye for colour, and I'm a damn sight less lazy.'

Virgil nodded slightly at this last point.

'So, if you damage me, you'll be damaging the one who creates the Briston tapestries,' Cwen went on. 'It's no good getting hold of him. I can't remember the last time he put thread to needle.'

Virgil was thinking. At least he wasn't hitting at the same time.

'Even if I assume that what you say is true, I still need Briston.'

'Why?'

'Because no one is going to buy a tapestry made by a girl, are they?' Virgil stated a plain fact of life. 'They want to know they came from the workshop of Briston.'

'They buy tapestries made by a girl now,' Cwen retorted. 'They just think they're made by Briston.'

Virgil looked around the cellar. Dextus and the Castigatori were close, presumably waiting to pounce the moment he made his move. The rest of them were either looking at Virgil or gazing around the place, looking everywhere, but at Virgil.

'No, no, no!' Virgil seemed to shake his thoughts away. 'This is ridiculous. I don't know who the hell you are. You're telling me you make tapestries just to stop me breaking your fingers. It seems you know Briston and that's enough for me.'

He reached out again for Cwen's arm.

His own arm was pushed aside as Dextus came in from behind. Virgil was forced to turn slightly, exposing the ribs under his right arm. Dextus drove a devastating blow into this sensitive area and was gratified to hear a grunt from the giant. Virgil turned full circle and surveyed the room. Dextus nodded and indicated the bottom of a pillar where Virgil's men lay. They had clearly been dealt with quite effectively by the Castigatori. Cwen scurried from the table, which Virgil knocked aside.

'I say,' Stott complained, seeing his furniture maltreated.

'About time we sorted this, Dextus,' Virgil snarled as he turned and stepped forward, arms outstretched to grasp the priest.

He was surprised as Dextus actually stepped towards him and ducked instead of running away. The great arms closed on nothing, but Dextus's sprang up and head-butted Virgil cleanly on the chin. The massive head went back and a Castigatori leapt on it from behind. While he pulled, his colleagues attacked the legs. They struck hard behind his knees and Virgil could do nothing but buckle. With a Castigatori pulling his head, two pushing his legs, and Dextus adding to the lever, he went down.

He only went to his knees though, which still left him as tall as most in the room. His arms were free and he used one to grab the Castigatori still clamped to his head. He pulled this man over his shoulder and threw him into the opposite wall. Dextus and the remaining Castigatori threw their weight against Virgil, trying to get him on to his back. Presumably so they could kick him to death.

'Could do with some help here,' Dextus grunted to Eadric and Firman.

The two men checked with one another and acknowledged that they really had no choice. They added their weight to the pile and Virgil roared his resistance.

Stalemate.

That was good. It was clear Virgil was applying all of his massive strength to the task of getting a load of people off his chest. He was achieving nothing. Neither was Dextus. The whole press of priest, the two conscious Castigatori, Eadric, and Firman were a perfect balance for the giant's strength.

Stott and Parsimon stood by, knowing that hopping from one foot to another was not really helping much. They also knew that stepping into this fray would be the end of them.

The struggle was going nowhere, but was doing so very noisily. Both sides grunted and strained as they tried to achieve superiority. Out of sight to their side, Cwen had found a bucket. It was wooden and it was heavy, but she swung it easily. Approaching the struggling mass of men, she took a careful aim and swung her weapon, ready to bring it over on to Virgil's head. She chose her moment, let the bucket fly up and over her head, and brought it down.

Virgil caught sight of it from the corner of his eye and relaxed. The force of Dextus's party pressed forwards as the resistance faltered.

The grin of triumph on Dextus's face was fixed, so fixed that it didn't even fade when he was hit on the head by a bucket and collapsed to the floor.

'Oh!' Cwen called out, as her rescuer rolled onto his back.

Virgil threw the remaining restraints off, stood and neatly despatched the Castigatori with hearty blows to the heads. Eadric and Firman retreated quickly and joined Stott and Parsimon, trying to look as if they'd never been involved in the first place.

'Now then,' Virgil said as he stood once more, his head brushing the cellar roof. 'Where were we?'

He grabbed Cwen with one arm and lifted her from the ground. With the other, he put the table back on its legs and sat her on it once more.

'I can prove it,' Cwen gurgled as the neck of her jerkin started to throttle her.

'Prove what?' Virgil asked, his voice full of impatience and the desire to get on with things.

'That I did the tapestry,' Cwen tried nodding but Virgil's great hand was in the way.

'I'm starting not to care anymore,' Virgil growled. 'I'm being mucked about and I don't like it. If I break your arms, I can always find another weaver. Briston may be laziest in the kingdom but I'm sure I can persuade him to greater efforts.'

'But if I can make tapestries as well, that would be even more profit,' Cwen offered.

Virgil paused slightly at this. 'Suppose I could always break your legs. Don't need them for weaving.'

'Unless I need to do treadle work?'

Virgil said nothing, but his brows drew together as if in secret conference.

'You make Briston's tapestries?' Virgil was at least trying the concept out.

'I do.'

'The real ones, not the roses and dragons?'

'The real ones.'

'Right!' Virgil was scoffing now.

'Yes, right. I'm not as young as I look. I can pass for a ten-year-old boy, but I'm seventeen. I've been around a bit, seen things, been told about others. Takes a lot to shock me. And I have one major advantage over most of the men I've ever met: I actually know what a naked woman looks like.'

'The Garden of the Seven Eunuchs?' Virgil threw in.

'Oh,' Cwen blushed. 'Yes, that one was a bit of a surprise.'

'I'll bet it was.'

'But I did the leather work and some of the equipment.'

'You said you had proof.' Virgil was at least pursuing this idea.

'I do. There's a tapestry missing from the box.'

'I saw the golden tassel,' Virgil sneered.

'It's an important work. The most important I ever did. Briston did give me clear direction for this one. He didn't just say he wanted this many of those, and that many of these, and those should be doing that to these.'

'Very clever, I'm sure. And this proves you made it, does it?'

'It's got my mark on it.'

Virgil released his grasp and looked at Cwen through hooded eyes. 'You have a mark? A weaver's mark?'

'I do.' Cwen held her head high.

'How?' Virgil was still having trouble.

'Briston taught me about them, how a weaver always puts one in every tapestry. Mark of the maker.'

'And what's yours?' Virgil asked. 'And what's Briston's?' He tested Cwen's knowledge.

'Briston's is an antler. Mine's a holly leaf.'

Virgil just looked now. 'Show me,' he instructed.

Cwen turned to survey the room. One of Virgil's men was just coming round, but the Castigatori slept. Dextus was still on his back, but stirred and groaned as encroaching consciousness sent advanced word of the pain he was about to be in. Stott, Parsimon, Eadric and Firman occupied the far wall, trying to vanish between the barrels.

'Mr Parsimon,' Cwen called. 'Would you fetch the tapestry?'

Parsimon looked genuinely nonplussed. He scanned the room, but could see no tapestry.

'You'll have to go and fetch it,' Cwen pressed.

'Fetch what tapestry, young lady? From where?'

'The reminiscence of Lady Lorinda. And fetch it from where ever you've got it.'

Stott now looked startled and worried. 'My dear young man,' he said, confusion returning, 'I don't know what you had to do with that ghastly work, or even how you know of it at all, but it is gone. Destroyed.'

'I know of it because I made it,' Cwen said.

'What?' Stott's horror took over his face and beard. Both writhed in agony. 'You made such images of my own dear wife? Such intimacies.'

'I am a woman myself, you know,' Cwen explained.

Stott could only make noises.

173

'And it's not destroyed. Mister Parsimon has it.'

'I can assure you…' Parsimon began.

'And so can I,' Cwen interrupted. 'I've been around this trade long enough to know the customers. They're all deeply ashamed, deceitful liars. I can spot them a mile off. When we were here with you before, you were lying. Shifting about on your feet, looking out of the window, or up at the ceiling. It got really bad when you told your master you'd burned the tapestry, which means you hadn't. You've still got it.'

'Parsimon! Is this true?' Stott asked his servant with disappointment.

Parsimon was clearly not a very good liar, and went completely to pieces when challenged by his master.

'Well, erm, you see. The point is. I…'

'Parsimon,' Stott said. 'How could you?'

The servant hung his head in shame.

'Well, go and get it then,' Virgil demanded.

Parsimon sidled off to his secret corner.

Dextus had recovered enough of his senses to sit up. And enough of them to know he shouldn't try to do any more. Eadric and Firman approached the table now. Threats of revenge on Virgil's behalf had not materialised and the appearance of the tapestry seemed to motivate them to action.

Parsimon reappeared with the rolled up work.

'Parsimon, really!' Stott's head shook and Parsimon's sank further. 'What were you thinking?'

'That it was a Briston, an original,' Parsimon mumbled. 'They're worth quite a lot, you know.'

'Money,' Stott spat contemptuously.

'It's different when you haven't got any,' Parsimon mumbled under his breath.

He laid the roll on the table and Virgil threw it open. He seemed surprised when it spilled over the side of the table and on to the floor. He immediately moved the thing around to look in the lower left corner. Cwen's slim fingers pointed out the antler of Briston and her own holly leaf.

'Hum,' Virgil thought and looked at Cwen with more interest.

He returned his attention to the work and took in the whole scene.

'Oh, I say!' His eyes widened and his mouth followed them into a grin.

Cwen frowned this time. Surely Virgil had seen far worse than this.

'Put it away, for God's sake,' Stott pleaded, averting his eyes.

Eadric and Firman were all attention and poured over the picture.

'Oh Dextus,' Virgil had a laugh in his voice. 'You've got to come and look at this. No wonder the church want to get hold of it. I can see why Briston's run away now. This is incredible.'

Tapestries in Tapestries

RISTON WOULD NOT TALK TO HERMITAGE or Wat until he'd collected all the donations from his audience. For this purpose, he had a young woman with him, who shuffled amongst the crowd, making sure she got them before they had a chance to leave. Hermitage assumed she was the landlord's daughter or maid. Each person in the room gave very little but it soon added up. Even with the tales told and the money gathered in, he made them wait until he had secured the room for the night, which seemed to be part of the package.

With all of this sorted, he still gestured them to silence until they had followed him to his chamber, he had closed and bolted the door, and shuttered the windows.

A pair of candles sitting on a crude chest behind the door lit the reunion scene. There was straw on a cot in one corner and on the floor and it looked relatively fresh. The room was barely big enough for the three of them, but at least Hermitage could say this place was better than Lolby's hovel. Before it fell down.

He stood back and observed as the two weavers, friends from boyhood, made their greetings. Briston was not at all as Hermitage had imagined. His mind's eye had the man a slight and twitchy fellow. Briston should be nervous and watchful, bowed down by his worries and his conflicts. His cheeks would be sunken and his eyes darting and hooded. The weaver's frame should be almost wasted by the need to be constantly on the move, and by the trade he followed. Hearty meals should not be enjoyed by any who profited from sin.

In fact, Briston looked more like a jolly friar. The sort who ate too much and drank fully from the cup and from life. The eyes were merry, the cheeks red, and a laugh hid behind the tongue, ready to emerge at any moment. The head was partly bald, but wisps of hair seemed to dance, leaping from the scalp in spikes of amusement. Hermitage could not reconcile the man before him with anything he had heard.

Wat stood with arms folded. 'You bastard,' he said.

'Now, now, Watty,' Briston lowered his plump frame on to the cot. 'Is that any way to greet your old mate?'

'It is when the old mate has sent me a death note and dragged me across the country into the hands of people I really don't want to meet only to find he's faked it all.'

'Would you rather I were trussed up in the tapestry then?'

'I might do it myself if there isn't a damn good explanation.' Wat took half a step back and lowered himself on to the chest. He shuffled over to make room for Hermitage.

'Where would you like me to start?' Briston asked as he pulled his boots off and put his feet up.

There was a knock on the door before Wat could answer.

Briston jumped up, drew back the bolt, and opened up to find the landlord's girl bearing a tray. There was a large pot of something that smelt to Hermitage very much like food. Edible food. A jug, a stack of plates with a loaf on top, spoons, and cups completed the set.

'Stick it on the chest,' Briston bubbled with good cheer.

The girl smiled winningly and put the tray down as Hermitage and Wat made room. The woman looked at the monk with a frown.

She returned to the door and closed it. From the inside. She grinned at Briston and sat next to him on the cot.

'Eat and drink,' Briston commanded. 'Conversation always goes best with victuals.'

Wat gaped at the girl. 'Who the hell is this?'

'Perhaps she's my new apprentice,' Briston roared with laughter and patted the girl on the knee.

Hermitage took the time to examine the girl now that she seemed connected to Briston. Connected in a rather intimate manner, judging from where Briston was now resting his hand.

She was young, probably about Cwen's age or a bit more, but there was no doubting she was a girl. No one was going to mistake her for a male weaver's apprentice. She was garbed in fine clothes and shoes. A long, heavy winter dress hung to the floor, with embroidery tumbling from shoulder to hem. It must keep her legs and body very warm. She was obviously less concerned about the temperature of her chest. Her neckline was bare and plunged like a waterfall – a waterfall that disappeared between two round ponds that seemed anxious to break their banks.

Hermitage thought perhaps part of her dress was missing. Above a long neck, a clear, intelligent face sat beneath very well-tended dark hair. This had clearly been professionally arranged, although that was some time ago. Strands were making a break for freedom and might be thought of as unkempt on the whole.

Hermitage looked back to the face and concluded that such comments would not be welcome. The intelligence flitting between brown eyes and smiling lips was clear. It was also clear that the intelligence knew best. Probably about everything. It had that distant, slightly contemptuous cast to it. The one that said, "I shall smile and laugh but if you stop me getting what I want, I will do something quite awful. And unexpected."

Hermitage swallowed. He swallowed again when he considered the nose. It was the only feature to spoil this vision of domineering beauty. As the intelligence flitted from eyes to mouth, it had to take a not insignificant detour round the nose. And once it reached the mouth, it probably thought night had fallen, such was the shadow. Hermitage thought he recognised the shape but couldn't recall who had a similar appendage. Apart from a sundial, perhaps.

It was clear that Wat could not think of anything to say as he appraised the girl. His mouth moved about, but the right words wouldn't come out. Eventually he just shook his head in despair and reached for a plate. Hermitage followed the lead and they piled up a passable looking stew. Real vegetables and a piece of meat for each of them. Genuine meat, recognisable as an animal, and one which hadn't passed away under suspicious circumstances. Hermitage wasn't sure whether it was mutton or beef, but to have that choice was a huge improvement.

The jug contained wine. It was a similar colour to that provided by Lolby, but this stuff was just more wholesome somehow. It had a tang of fruit to it rather than the cloy of the mould that remained after the fruit was long gone.

Hermitage and Wat sat down on the floor, filling the available space, but finding it was the only way they could accommodate the feast. Briston and the girl shared a plate on the bed, offering one another titbits of food in a most revolting manner.

Hermitage thought about asking several interesting questions, but his stomach rejoiced at the experience of eating and he wondered how long it was since he had a decent meal. Well, half decent. Days, he was sure.

The two men focussed on the task at hand, happy to make interrogation wait upon their stomachs' convenience. As they mopped the last gravy with the final crumbs of bread, belches of comfort invited explanations to enter the room.

'You were about to explain yourself?' Wat prompted as they rested after the meal – Briston on the cot with the girl at his side, Wat with his back to the chest, and Hermitage resting against the wall by the single window.

'Ah yes!' Briston's voice was full and round as if it came from the depths of his stomach. Which was itself full and round. 'I have made the Tapestry of Death. I suppose that's where it all starts.'

179

'Rubbish,' Wat replied with a snort of derision – a snort which also contained a goodly spread of undigested crumbs. 'For one thing, the Tapestry of Death is a fairy tale to frighten apprentices, and for another, if you had made it, you'd be dead. Hence the name: Tapestry of Death.'

'Well, obviously I haven't made *that* Tapestry of Death!'

'Obviously.'

'But I've made *a* Tapestry of Death.'

'Also rubbish.'

'It's a marvellous idea,' Briston went on, ignoring Wat's disbelief. 'I've made a tapestry that will bring death to my enemies. One which gives me the chance to vanish and start again.'

'Sounds like a very interesting tapestry,' Wat said, clearly still not believing such a thing existed.

'It is.'

'And the pig in the tapestry?' Wat asked.

'Gave me time to get away. I was hoping I wouldn't be discovered at all. You know, buried with all due ritual and, low and behold, Briston the Weaver is no more. Might even get The Hoofhorn to officiate at the ceremony, death of a master weaver and all that. Few months later, I pop up down south somewhere. New name, new life. And if anyone from the old world pops up to bother me, I slap them with the Tapestry of Death and they leave me alone.'

'So why send me the death note? Why not just vanish with your pig and leave me out of it?'

'What's the first thing Virgil would do if he got word and found me wrapped up in the tent?'

'He'd unwrap you.'

'Exactly, but with you there, death note in hand to testify, he might not bother.'

'He did bother,' Wat said.

'Oh bugger,' Briston said, but he still seemed unreasonably cheerful about the whole business. 'Bit quicker than I thought.'

'And what about Cwen?' Hermitage put in. 'Was it necessary to trick her into believing your death as well?'

'She's a bright kid, that one. She'll go far. Wasn't much more I could teach her.' Briston continued to smile.

'A female apprentice!' Wat shook his head in despair. 'And one who cared for you. Deeply upset at your death. And all to allow you to have what you want.'

Briston simply shrugged and belched again.

'Briston all over!' Wat was contemptuous. 'And you've got another woman within a day. I don't know what it is they see in you, really I don't.'

'Good times Watty. Sophistication, the pleasures of the day. You were always too restrained, understated, quiet, unassuming,' Briston paused for another word, 'dull,' he paused again, 'dull, dull, dull.'

'I imagine she's modelling for new works?'

Hermitage was horrified at this disgusting suggestion, but Briston didn't deny it. The girl giggled.

'Why try to escape now? You've been in worse scrapes than Virgil and Dextus looking for you.' Wat's face showed his puzzlement.

Briston looked at the floor. 'I've been planning it for a while. Virgil was getting closer and closer. I knew I wouldn't be able to avoid him much longer. Dextus's interest was new and you know what the church is like when they take a shine to you. I'm getting tired, Wat. I'm heading for thirty. How much longer can I go on before someone finds me in an alley one morning? Then I thought of my Tapestry of Death and knew it would work.'

'Yes.' Wat was still full of contempt. 'This Tapestry of Death. What sort of tapestry is going to stop Virgil and the like from hunting you down, or even better, bring about their own death?'

'Oh, you ought to see it, Watty. A stroke of genius, if I say so myself. To be honest, I'm not sure I could have done it without Cwen. It's almost as good as some of your stuff. You know that one with the fifteen novices and the sheriff?' Briston was reminiscing happily.

'What do you mean, without Cwen?' Wat demanded.

'Well, she made it, didn't she?' Briston explained. 'She's really very good indeed.'

'But,' Wat clearly objected, 'she's a girl,' was all he could say.

'And a very good weaver. Tiny little hands, good eye for thread. I just gave her the sketches and she did the rest.'

'The guild will have your guts,' Wat muttered.

'They probably think they've already got them, but I've got a Tapestry of Death, haven't I?'

'It works against the guild?' Wat was very surprised.

'Oh yes, very well indeed.'

'You still haven't said what this tapestry is or how it could possibly work,' Hermitage asked as Wat seemed once more dumbfounded by the concept of a female weaver.

'No I haven't,' Briston replied. 'And, of course, I won't.'

'Oh.' Hermitage was rather disappointed. It all sounded terribly exciting and new. He liked to hear about new things.

'That's part of its magic. You don't get to see it. You just have to hear about it.'

'We haven't even heard anything about it.'

'Even better. Lots of mystery. Build up the legend. All I can say, and I can say it because I want you to repeat it, is that it works. The Briston Tapestry of Death will bring death to my enemies. You aren't my enemies and so I can't tell you about it. No, I mean I won't tell you about it. That's right.' Briston nodded to himself as if checking he'd got his own plan right.

'I have to say,' Hermitage had to say, 'it does seem rather unbelievable.'

'Because it is,' Wat interrupted. 'The whole thing is just a trick. Typical of Briston. Like the time he told the moot court in Hull he'd done intimate tapestries of the blacksmith's wife when she was young. And how if they didn't let him leave town, instead of hanging him as they planned, he'd pin it up on the church door.'

'That's awful!' Hermitage breathed in sharply at the thought of anyone even thinking such an appalling thing.

'Particularly as it wasn't true.'

'He hadn't made the tapestry?'

'Blacksmith's wife had been dead for years,' Wat said.

'But then?' Hermitage thought this most odd.

'Blacksmith wasn't part of the moot court and everyone was too embarrassed to ask him. Typical Briston. Chancer.'

'This one is different,' Briston argued. 'The tapestry is real and it does what I say.'

'Where is it then? This magical tapestry.'

'Safe,' was all Briston said.

'I hope it's not in your box.' Wat looked at Briston seriously.

'Nah,' Briston smirked. 'I've put it somewhere no one would ever think of.'

'Hermitage will,' Wat said.

Oh, that would be good, Hermitage thought before he remembered that meant him.

'I will?' he asked in surprise.

'Of course. This is the King's Investigator,' Wat boasted. 'He solves puzzles like this all the time.'

'He can have a go if he likes,' Briston smiled his constant smile. 'He'll never get it.'

Hermitage looked to the weavers in the small room and felt the familiar weight of expectation. He never carried this weight particularly well. He looked at Wat with hopeless eyes.

'It could be anywhere,' he said, his eyes having leant their hopelessness to his voice.

'Exactly,' Briston smirked.

Even the girl poured her scornful look on the monk.

'No, it couldn't be anywhere.' Wat was confident. 'It can only be in the place it's in.'

'That's not much help,' Hermitage moaned.

'Think of it as one of your puzzles, an argument to be dismantled. Where is the last place anyone would look for a tapestry?'

Hermitage looked blank and his mind followed suit. He had no ideas. Not even one. He even lost the idea of having an idea. This was followed by the disappearance of any awareness of where he was and who was with him. His mind often went like this when he was considering some particularly ticklish issue. The spelling of Nebuchadnezzar, for example.

He found his thoughts in this empty space once more. All the pieces of the question before him were out of sight – there was only a big blank. Into this space, an ancient and never-before-recalled memory popped up. It leapt around in the vacancy of his thoughts, waving at him. An old riddle, told by the ancient priest who had been his guide and mentor and, yes, his friend. In fact, the only friend prior to Wat. The riddle had been about the books of the bible being in the book that was the bible. It wasn't a very good riddle.

'In a book,' he said, as much surprised by the words coming out of his mouth as the others in the room.

'Beg pardon?' Wat said, not getting it at all.

Briston guffawed loudly.

'Sorry, I mean the books of the Bible are hidden in a book, which is the Bible. You see?'

Wat was shaking his head in disbelief. 'You are supposed to be thinking about the tapestry, not the Bible.'

'Oh yes,' Hermitage shrugged. He really didn't have any more to offer.

'What made you *say* that?' Wat really was quite cross.

'I don't know really. It's an old riddle. Where do you keep the books of the Bible? In a book. The Bible. Don't know why I thought of that really.'

'The books are in a book?' Wat's face was stiff and unfriendly.

Hermitage shrugged hopelessly.

The face of the weaver softened. 'The books are in a book,' he repeated, this time with some enthusiasm.

Hermitage nodded without any idea where this was going.

'So where is the tapestry?' Wat asked. 'In a tapestry.'

He turned to look at Briston, who had gone very pale all of a sudden.

'Aha!' Wat said in long drawn-out triumph.

Hermitage smiled broadly. 'Beg pardon?' he asked, when he realised his happiness had overtaken his understanding.

'Within the picture of one tapestry lies another tapestry.'

'Oh,' Hermitage said, getting it now. 'Like a tapestry of a castle wall that has a tapestry hanging on it.'

'Exactly.'

'Clever.'

'Yes,' Wat said. 'I might use that myself.'

'But, which tapestry?' Hermitage wailed. 'Mr Briston must have done hundreds.'

Wat's thoughts ran ahead. 'Except, of course, he didn't make this one. He said that Cwen did it. So it must have been recent.'

'I knew we'd get there,' Wat sneered at Briston.

Hermitage nodded, still smiling, but still not quite sure why.

'The one that went to Master Stott,' Wat concluded with a flourish.

'Oh bloody hell,' Briston wailed now.

Wat went on, 'When you think about it, it's a bit of a coincidence, Briston being in Baernodebi when all this happens. It's not the sort of place a lot of his customers would live. So, if he decided to escape his life at this moment, the tapestry in question must be very recent indeed. Not only did Briston hide this Tapestry of Death within the tapestry of Master Stott, he then sold it to Stott. What better place to hide it? In the manor of an old widower who probably has very few visitors.'

An idea struck Hermitage. 'And you said pieces like this

weren't shown in public, so no one would see it. Master Stott was rather ashamed of the piece anyway.'

Wat nodded now. 'I reckon Briston knew that. It was exactly as Stott said, he only asked for a pleasant reminiscence of his wife and that was what Briston promised. When he delivered the work, Stott would have been appalled, but it was exactly what Briston meant to create all along.'

'Alright, don't go on,' Briston sulked, all good cheer firmly put in its place.

Wat folded his arms and stared. 'That didn't take long, did it?

Briston quickly recovered his composure. 'Doesn't matter,' he said. 'So you two figured it out. No one else knows and I'm sure my old friend Wat and a devout monk wouldn't breathe a word.'

'Don't have to,' Wat replied. 'There's a whole host of trouble you don't even know about.'

'Such as?' Briston was contemptuous, clearly thinking Wat was making this up.

'Oh, the fact that Virgil has just gone to Stott's manor along with Dextus.'

'What?' The colour left Briston's face once more, probably looking for somewhere a bit less changeable.

'Except, of course, that doesn't matter so much because Stott's burned the tapestry.'

'He what?' The pale Briston had started to shake slightly and his full and wholesome voice sounded like the death rattle of an emaciated wren.

'Oh, it gets worse.' Wat seemed to be taking some pleasure in this. 'Virgil sent us to find you, and if we don't take you back, he'll kill Cwen.'

Briston had no words left. No sounds at all judging by the state of him. He even seemed to have lost weight.

'Good plan though,' Wat nodded. 'Looks like the Tapestry of Death might work yet. On you.'

Caput XVIII

That Cellar Again

EXTUS WOUND HIMSELF TO HIS FEET and woozily wandered to the table. He rested his hands on the edge to stop himself falling down again. He blinked several times and gently shook his head to make his eyes work. They eventually focussed on the tapestry.

'Ah,' he said, clearly recognising something he didn't really want to see.

'Does your mission make sense now?' Virgil asked.

'Yes,' Dextus admitted. 'I rather think it does.'

'A quite remarkable piece, wouldn't you say?' Virgil asked.

Dextus simply grunted.

'No wonder the church wants to get hold of it. At all costs, I would think.'

Eadric and Firman were at the table, but the tapestry was up-side down in front of them. They twisted their heads to take in what was presented.

'Oh my,' Firman's educated tones were surprised. 'Is that…?'

'Yes it is,' Eadric broke in. 'And there's another one.'

'Well, I never.'

'No,' said Eadric. 'I don't think many people have.'

Firman continued to turn his head this way and that, trying to accommodate all of the details. The Castigatori and Virgil's men were coming to their senses now and they made it to their feet one by one. They wandered over to see what the fuss was about, brushing Eadric and Firman aside. There was much muttering and pointing and some elbows dug playfully into sides. Virgil took one end of the tapestry and held it up to the light of the torches. The colours in the piece leapt to dancing life. Flesh pink mainly, but a splash of dark hair here and there. Mostly there. The crowded cellar gathered round like peasant villagers in front of a mummers' play: eyes slack and jaws wide.

'This is appalling!'

Stott burst forward and brushed people aside with remarkable strength. He snatched the tapestry from Virgil's hand and started to roll it up again. It took quite some time and the rest of the audience watched as the very widest variety of scenes disappeared into the rolling cloth like boats passing the bend in a river. Boats full of very rude people in full display. 'I will not have the likes of you gazing upon the likes of the parts of my wife.'

'Your wife is the least of it!' Virgil laughed.

Stott glared and used the finally rolled up tapestry, which weighed quite a bit, to smack Parsimon firmly on the head.

'It's not really her,' Cwen tried to sooth the old man. 'I used your description for her face, but it isn't her body, erm, parts, erm, person.'

'Hardly the point, young lady. How would you like it if I put your head on something like this?'

Cwen shrugged as if it had already happened.

'Ha ha!' Virgil rubbed his humungous hands in glee. 'Oh, this is too marvellous. Everyone upstairs again. Torture's off! There's so much to be achieved with this one work. I take it all back, Briston isn't a lazy, good for nothing pimple on the face of weaving. He's a genius.'

'I made it,' Cwen put in.

'But he thought of it,' Virgil laughed.

He ushered everyone back towards the stairs. Parsimon went first, his head still hung low, but not so low that Stott couldn't smack it firmly with his hand as he followed his servant. As the master of the manor passed Virgil, the tapestry was snatched from his hands. Stott gave Virgil a hard stare, but the stony face made it clear the work was Virgil's property now. The Castigatori and Virgil's men departed, exchanging unhealthy looks and threatening gestures. Eadric followed with a look of deep thought on his face. He stole glances towards the tapestry in Virgil's hand and flexed his fingers, as if half thinking of snatching the thing and running. Virgil gestured Cwen and Dextus to go up the stairs ahead of him. Cwen did so but Dextus loitered.

'It's no good loitering,' Virgil told him. 'There's no way you're getting your hands on this.' He waved the tapestry tauntingly.

'We'll see,' Dextus mumbled as he took to the cellar steps.

The giant looked back round the space as Dextus disappeared. 'Come on you,' he called to Firman. 'Now I've seen this thing,' he waved the tapestry, 'I'm very much inclined to find out exactly who you are. Perhaps we'll have some torture after all.'

Firman smiled at Virgil. 'I wonder if I might have a word, Mister Virgil,' he said in a conspiratorial manner, looking round the cellar himself to make sure everyone had gone.

Virgil half closed one eye, looking at Firman as you would at a cat that's just barked. He turned from the steps and approached the table.

✦　　✦　　✦

Stott was berating Parsimon up in the main hall. The slap on the head had just been the start. There were fierce whispers, smacks on the shoulder, arms thrown in frustration, and small circles walked in. Lectures were started on a variety of subjects – lectures that would clearly be repeated many times over the days to come.

Parsimon stood taking it all, gazing at the flagstones. When Stott started an exposition of Lady Lorinda's wonderful qualities, the servant did raise his eyes to the ceiling but it went unnoticed by his master. Dextus and the Castigatori were huddled by the fire, the fighting force recovering its senses. The men stretched and flexed their arms and legs, silently preparing for the next round. Virgil's men sat at the table among the disordered pewter. They were similarly rubbing injured limbs but were whispering fiercely. Every now and then one of them would look over to the Castigatori, as if taking note of a face. Eadric stood alone, deep in thought. Cwen joined him, having looked around the room and weighed up the alternatives.

'What *is* your interest in all this?' she asked.

'Me?' Eadric expressed surprise. 'Exactly as I said. I was travelling the road and got caught up in this ghastly business. Now I've seen that tapestry, I can see how ghastly it really is.'

Cwen frowned at him, 'And Firman?'

'Not a clue. Seems to be a bit of an idiot. Wandering about the highway dressed like that. On his own.'

'It's a bit suspicious, isn't it?' Cwen asked.

'You know, I think it is.'

'I mean, both of you. Like I said downstairs, this trade has made me a pretty good judge of character. Firman is odd but so are you. You don't look like a humble traveller going from here to there. I hate to agree with Virgil, but I think you're looking for Briston.'

'I can honestly tell you that I am not, but it doesn't matter really, does it?'

'Why?'

'Because the only thing that does matter is whatever our friend Virgil believes. If he thinks I'm the pope, we can have mass.'

'Where is Firman anyway?' Cwen asked, 'and Virgil? What are they up to?'

'Search me,' said Eadric, glancing round the room to confirm the two were missing. Firman could be missed in a room full of people, but Virgil couldn't be missed in a room full of anything else at all.

The two frowned at one another, but then their eyes widened and the frowns transformed to looks of horrified surprise. A sound inveigled its way into the space of the main hall. It was an unexpected sound and it made the entire company stop what they were doing. It was a sound that brought the Castigatori to tensed readiness. It made Virgil's men stand and form a defensive triumvirate. It was a sound of pain.

That it appeared without warning, without anyone in the room actually being in pain, caused the surprise. No one had fallen or got in some new fight. That it was authentic and heartfelt caused the horror. It began as a low moan, the moan of realisation that comes in the moments after you've turned your ankle and look down to see your foot dangling from the end of your leg.

Then it grew. It grew into the scream of someone having the offending foot ripped off by an enormous strength. The volume increased so rapidly that no one in the room could do anything but listen. The sound seemed to have no particular source. It raced and bounded round the room like a wounded animal trying to shake a bear trap from its limb. This was no animal though: it was human. Only a creature with an immortal soul could wrench such agony from its lungs and force it upon the ears of others.

This was worse than Virgil's threat of torture. The imaginations of everyone in the room drew their own picture of what had made this demented noise. None of the pictures were at all healthy. Childhood nightmares, remembrances from the heat of battle, the anticipated beating from deranged parent, all fed the images that spun in their heads as the sound filled the room.

Dextus was the first to move, but all he did was turn to try and locate the source of this torment. It faded as he did so. Not instantly. It rose to a shriek of simple disbelief at whatever was happening to this ravaged soul then it descended to a strangulated, gasping choke before there was silence. Even the silence held threat. Whatever had happened was horrible and could be looking for somewhere to happen again.

'Firman,' Cwen called when she at last drew breath.

'He's with Virgil,' Eadric said with urgency.

'Not anymore,' one of Virgil's men said with a slight snigger of nervous relief.

Eleven heads turned to the cellar entrance as one. Everyone in the room simultaneously wanted to know, and not know, what it was Virgil had done to Firman. Eadric and Cwen looked to one another, their question was why? What on earth could the harmless clothes-horse Firman have done to prompt such awful violence.

There was no movement from the cellar door.

Eight of the heads turned to Virgil's men. They all tried to look in other directions.

'Go on then,' Dextus commanded, with a nod of the head towards the cellar.

The Castigatori growled. Two of Virgil's attendants gave the third and smallest a strong shove towards the cellar. He looked back in anger at his fellows, mouthing deprecations. They waved him away and he trod cautiously toward the door. The man peered into the depths from which the lights of the torches flickered, as if held in the cellar against their will.

'Master?' the man called in a soft and friendly tone, raising the expectation that his next sentence would be "would you like any help with the dismembering?"

There was no reply and so he took the first step, calling hopefully and forlornly at each stair as he descended.

Once out of sight, the group in the main room breathed more normally. No one moved to offer the man any support, either moral or physical, least of all his companions.

After a moment, there was a new sound. This too was one of pain, but heavily tainted with anguish. Looks were exchanged across the room and as one, the group moved towards the stairs. They were bowled backwards by Virgil's man coming back out of the cellar at speed. The look on his face was one they would all remember for years to come. The man glanced nowhere, he stopped for no one. He went straight to the door of the manor, threw it open and ran, howling, into the night. The remaining men of Virgil's band gave snorts of contempt. They were not confident snorts though, and they did not offer to go next into the cellar.

Dextus gathered the Castigatori and they slowly descended the cellar steps. The rest of the company formed a line behind them, safely in the shadow of large monks.

'It could be a wolf,' Stott helpfully observed.

'A wolf?' Dextus stopped going down the cellar steps and looked at the master of the house in complete surprise.

Stott was unmoved. 'Yes. One got in the cellar once. In the worst of winter. Devil's own job to get the thing out again. Had to kill it.'

'A wolf?' Dextus was now disbelieving. 'In Lincolnshire? When was this?'

'Oh, not long back. Fifty, sixty years? My grandfather told the tale every Christmas.'

'You idiot,' Dextus muttered. 'I think a wolf would make more wolf-like noises. What we heard was a man. Or rather used to be a man. What the hell is Virgil doing down here?' he asked, as he resumed the descent. 'Eating the remains?'

There wasn't room for them all to get down the steps at once so they formed a line behind Dextus. The line bumped to a halt as the priest had clearly stopped at the foot of the stairs.

'*Deus salvabit nos,*' the priest's voice passed along the line like a grieving relative.

Everyone pressed forward to see what had been found. Some of them didn't really want to see what had been found. A verbal report would have been quite sufficient.

As they dislodged Dextus from the bottom step, the group crowded into the space and gawped at the sight that greeted them. Despite herself, Cwen clapped an appalled hand to her mouth and swung her eyes quickly away. So did Stott and Parsimon, the latter letting out a small squeak of disgust.

'Good God,' Eadric said as he looked at the body on the table.

He pushed passed Dextus and stood by the corpse he had been speaking to moments before. It was clearly a corpse even though there was no break in the skin, no sign of obvious attack. Certainly no wolf bites. Rather, it looked as if the skin had been put over the wrong body. The bits inside no longer fitted properly, and jutted and prodded out in various places. It was only moments after death and so the bruising would probably come out very soon. From the state of the body, it was reasonable to assume the bruises would be forming a very long queue and would be coming out for hours.

They had all seen the results of a beating. It was quite a common sight since the Normans arrived. The swollen lips, deformed cheeks, and half-closed eyes distorted a face until it could be unrecognisable. That had happened to the whole body in this case. From head to little toe, there didn't seem to be a single part left untouched. And that touch had been one of incredible strength. The victim had clearly stood no chance and had probably not even been able to put up much of a fight. At least in this case, despite the damage, the victim was recognisable.

'How could anyone do this?' Cwen demanded, part in horror at the damage inflicted on a human being, and part at the strength and determination required for this particular damage.

'I think we better go back upstairs.' Dextus was clearly scared. He glanced around the cellar space and could not see anyone else. Perhaps after a monstrous frenzy such as this, the killer had retreated behind one of the barrels, or into one of the darker corners of the cellar, to recover from the insane rage that had clearly possessed him.

Dextus ushered them towards the stairs once more.

'But,' Cwen interrupted, 'what about Firman?' She looked back at the table.

'Believe me,' Dextus said, laying a comforting hand on her

shoulder. 'Whatever man or creature did this to Virgil, he's probably done the same to Firman. Wherever he is.'

Cwen gave a last shivering look at the giant's body and scanned the room. 'Whatever did it took the tapestry,' she observed.

Plans Afoot

HAT DO YOU MEAN, YOU WON'T GO? You will go!' Wat was more than insistent. He was instructional, demanding, and threatening all at once

He and Hermitage were standing over Briston, appalled at the man's blank response and that he was staying exactly where he was.

'If I go, Dextus will kill me,' Briston reasoned. He hadn't got up from the cot and was still cuddling the girl, making it clear he had no intention of going anywhere.

'And if you don't go, I'll kill you.'

'Ah, but you won't. Not really. You'll be very cross and shout a lot, but you wouldn't actually kill me. Not to death. Dextus would do the death bit. Not personally, of course. He'd take me to some church institution and do it there. And you know how they take their time over killing people.'

Wat looked to Hermitage for some answer. The monk had none and just looked blank. People not doing as they were asked was quite a common experience for him and he'd never figured out what to do about it.

'Virgil will kill Cwen,' was all he could say.

'Yes,' Briston did at least have the grace to cast his eyes at the floor at this, 'that's probably true.'

'And you're going to let him!' Wat snarled the accusation.

Briston held his arms out to indicate helplessness. 'What difference would it make if I was there? Virgil's a big chap. He can kill who he likes.'

'I hope you're listening,' Wat said to the girl. 'Cwen first and it'll be you next.'

The girl simply looked as if all this was terribly exciting and said nothing.

Hermitage continued to plead, 'Virgil is holding Cwen against your return. We take you back and he lets Cwen go. We don't take you back and he kills her.'

'Oh come on!' Briston was contemptuous of such naivety. He turned to Wat, 'You know perfectly well he's probably killed her already. And if I do turn up, he'll kill her anyway. He's like that.'

'He might not.' Wat seemed to admit the strength of Briston's argument.

'So, on the basis of "might not", I'm to throw myself on Dextus's sword? Or knife? Or whatever it is the church uses to help people leave the world these days?'

'Dextus wouldn't kill you. Not personally. And Virgil wants you alive.'

'I think I'd rather Dextus killed me.' Briston leaned back on the bed and gazed at the ceiling as if the matter was decided.

Wat looked again at Hermitage. Who again was no help. He looked at Briston. He looked at the ceiling. And then at the floor.

'There must be a way. There's always a way,' he said mostly to himself.

'We'll figure it out while we travel,' he said after a moment's thought. 'We take you back. Get Cwen released if she's alive and then get you out of it.'

'How?'

'Erm, a trick.'

'What trick?'

'A good one.'

'Obviously. And what is this trick? The disappearing weaver?'

'Well, I don't know. I haven't thought of it yet,' Wat snapped his frustration. 'We'll think of something though.'

'I'm not comforted.' Briston folded his arms.

'We let Virgil take you and then kidnap you back.'

'Got a record of taking things from Virgil, have you? Things that he wants to keep?'

'I cannot believe you are going to leave Cwen to die!' Wat's anger was real.

'Ahh,' Briston said in that manner people use when trying to imply that the weaver they are talking to has a soft spot for an illegal female apprentice.

'What does that mean?'

'You've gone soft on Cwen,' Briston accused with a laugh in his voice.

'I have not,' Wat bit back. 'I'm just appalled at yet another example of you not thinking things through. Of you taking what you want because it's in front of your eyes, while you leave everyone else to clear up your mess. Except, in this case, she won't be able to clear up your mess because she'll be dead.'

'You're still going on about Leamington!' Briston's voice was high and accusatory.

Hermitage was intrigued. Leamington? What had happened in Leamington, he wondered. He once knew a novice from Leamington. Perhaps it was to do with him? He glanced at the arguing weavers and recalled their trade. No, definitely not. The novice had been a rather obsessive character, Hermitage recalled, kept going on about the size of Noah's ark and how all the animals wouldn't fit.

Wat's voice had risen to a crescendo, 'It is not about Leamington. I told you, I've forgotten about Leamington. I don't care about Leamington any more. It's just the perfect example. I was lucky to escape Leamington with my life, while you…'

'While I left with the profits in my hand and a trail of destruction behind me,' Briston mocked.

'Well you did. Have you been back to Leamington?'

Briston looked horrified, 'No! Of course not. Are you mad?'

'There you are then. A whole town you can't visit any more.

CAPUT XIX

This time, if you want to visit Cwen, you'll have to look for her grave.'

Wat breathed deeply and recovered himself. A bit. 'Briston, whatever this plan is of yours, whatever this Tapestry of Death thing is, it'll end the same. In another six months, you'll be running away again. From a different set of problems, I grant you, but they'll be just as deadly. It'll be just as important and there'll be just as much wreckage behind you. And this girl will probably be in the middle of it.' He gestured to the still smiling girl.

'So, let me get this straight,' Briston reasoned. 'You're suggesting that I should face up to Virgil and Dextus. Take my chances because I have to get it over with some time. That if I carry on, there'll be another Virgil and another Dextus down the road. That if I deal with them now, I really will be able to change my life forever.'

Hermitage thought this was a very mature and sensible approach.

'Absolutely,' Wat confirmed.

'Ha,' Briston burst out. 'You may be mad but I'm not. Remember that stupid phrase you were always quoting?'

'Which one?'

'Never put off 'til tomorrow what you can do today?'

'Yes?'

'I've finished it off.'

'Go on then,' Wat said.

'Never put off 'til tomorrow what you can do today. Avoid it altogether and it might go away!' Briston chuckled at his own cleverness.

'You talk to him, Hermitage,' Wat said in resignation.

'Me?' Hermitage was not at all prepared to be drawn into this.

'Yes. Tell him about his eternal soul and damnation and all that stuff.'

Hermitage thought for a moment. He weighed up Briston's

responses thus far and drew his own conclusions about the man's priorities. 'I rather think damnation at the end of his life is less troublesome than Dextus's ministrations in the next day or so.'

'Spot on, monk.' Briston congratulated Hermitage with a wink.

'So that's it then, is it?' Wat looked down at Briston sitting on the cot.

'I think we've covered everything,' Briston nodded.

'I'd better go back and tell Virgil you aren't coming. Perhaps I can intervene.'

'I wouldn't if I were you. You know what Virgil's like once he gets going. He'll more than likely kill you as well. In fact, he's bound to. It's his standard response to bad news.'

'Come on, Hermitage,' Wat said.

Hermitage stood ready to leave. He looked out the window at the dark. He glanced at Wat, hoping to bring his attention to the dark as well.

'One last swig of wine and we'll risk the darkness and the Normans to go back into danger.' Wat gestured at the jug which sat empty on the chest. 'In fact, I don't even care about the Normans,' he added with remarkable recklessness.

Hermitage's curiosity about all of this trumped the prospect of tramping in darkness in which danger lurked. He took the jug and handed it to Wat.

'Good luck,' Briston said with a guffaw at the pomposity.

'We'll need it,' Wat said as he brought the jug crashing down on Briston's head.

The weaver slumped over.

The girl screamed and leaped up.

'Wat!' Hermitage exclaimed.

Wat shrugged. 'Not the first time I've had to do that,' he said. 'Let's get him tied up and head back. You've seen what trouble he is when he's awake.'

'You can't do this,' the girl hissed an objection, pushing Briston's shoulder to see if he would wake.

'Just have,' Wat shrugged again.

Hermitage looked at the recumbent weaver and weighed him up. 'We'll never carry him all the way back to Stott's,' he argued. 'Not at all, never mind in the dark. He's a big chap.'

'What about me?' The girl's voice remained a hissing rasp of hatred. Hermitage thought this was more in anger at the inconvenience caused to her, rather than the damage caused to Briston's head.

'Count yourself lucky.' Wat gave her a sideways glance. 'His last girl lived about two years. With him out of the way, your life expectancy's gone way up. I should just go home if I were you.'

'Right!' The girl scoffed at the idea.

Wat frowned at Briston but did seem to realise the problem. 'We'll get a trolley.'

'A trolley? We're going to wheel an unconscious weaver down the road in the middle of the night? That'll take some explaining to the Norman patrols.'

'What do you suggest?' Wat put his hands on his hips and glared at Hermitage.

Hermitage thought. This wasn't the sort of thing his mind was used to. Getting unconscious people from one place to another was a very practical problem. He didn't do practical.

'Erm, wait till morning, get a bier, and tell the Normans he's a leper we're taking on pilgrimage?' he offered with a flash of very practical inspiration.

Wat's eyebrows rose. 'Very good,' he said.

Hermitage grinned.

'Where do you take lepers on pilgrimages round here?' Wat asked.

'Well, I suppose the closest religious institution is the monastery at De'Ath's Dingle.'

They looked at one another in silence at the mention of that place.

'No,' they said together.

'I suppose the sea is always good for healing,' Hermitage admitted. 'But then I don't think the Normans will know any better.'

'Good point. We'd better tie him up though. First thing he's going to do when he wakes is try and get away.'

'Right,' Hermitage said, oozing positivity.

'Right,' Wat said with enthusiasm.

They looked around and at one another. And then at the girl.

'I think you'd better go,' Wat told her. 'We're dealing with some very bad people. If they get a sight of you, they'll do some of their very best bad things.'

'Where am I supposed to go?'

'Anywhere that isn't here, really. Go and help the landlord.'

'He's disgusting.'

'And Briston isn't?'

She didn't move.

'Tell you what,' Wat proposed, 'you stay here with Briston, we'll knock you out as well and take you to the mad Virgil and the dangerous priest. Assuming we don't get killed by the Normans on the way.' He smiled broadly and reached for the pot that had contained the stew.

The girl glared at them both, looked at the recumbent Briston, and stamped her foot. She seemed most angry with Briston for letting her down like this. She strode from the room with a snarl and slammed the door behind her.

'Young people these days,' Hermitage tutted as if he knew a lot of them. Or any of them. 'So,' he turned to Briston. 'What, erm...' he hesitated to ask, 'what do we, erm, tie him up with? I mean, what do you generally tie people up with?' He assumed Wat was familiar with this sort of thing.

Wat scanned the room, 'Your belt?' he asked, pointing at the thin piece of rope that bound Hermitage's habit to his waist.

'I don't think so,' Hermitage reasoned. 'It's not very strong at all. And if I take it off, my habit blows about all over the place. What about your belt?' Hermitage pointed out the fine piece of leather embroidered with delicate weaving that circled the weaver's breeches.

'Oh no,' Wat said. 'This is a precious piece. Can't have it damaged. Is there any other rope?'

Hermitage looked around the room now. 'No,' he concluded, not really expecting to find a handy coil of rope nearby. 'Perhaps we could ask for some.'

'There must be some somewhere,' Wat said as if rope was always close to hand.

'I wouldn't know,' Hermitage replied. 'It's never really played a significant part in monastic life. It's the sort of thing Brother Ambrosius might know about.'

'Really?'

'Yes, you know, the monk who died in the debate about sandals? He tended to focus on domestic supplies. Only in the context of their biblical significance, of course.'

'You don't think his being dead is going to put a dampener on his helpfulness?'

It was Brother Ambrosius's death that first brought Hermitage and Wat together. Wat had been contemptuous of the deceased brother's interests then. Perhaps he wasn't feeling so clever now.

'Well, what do you normally do in these situations?' Hermitage asked.

'It's not a normal sort of situation,' Wat shot back. 'I don't regularly need to tie people up.'

'I have seen those tapestries, you know.' Hermitage brought one of Briston's works to mind. That had involved quite a lot of tying up. He tried to persuade it to leave his mind again.

'What about some thread?' Hermitage suggested. 'Have you got any of that we could tie him up with?'

'Tend not to carry large quantities around with me.' Wat

seemed to be getting frustrated at Hermitage's lack of cooperation.

'People are always getting tied up in tales. You know, the thieves tie up the lord of the manor before taking his treasure. The evil knight ties the maiden to the tree. The sheriff's men tie up the outlaws. How do they do it?'

'I rather think they go prepared. Take the rope with them. After all, if you're a thief, an evil knight, or a sheriff, tying up is likely to be a routine requirement.' Wat was getting positively snappy.

'I'm only asking,' Hermitage responded with his own brand of impatience. This went unrecognised.

'Go outside and look around. See if you can find some,' Wat ordered.

'Why don't you go outside?' Hermitage asked.

'Because one of us has to look for rope while the other stays here and hits Briston on the head again if he starts to wake. Which do you think you'd be best at?'

Hermitage looked at the sleeping weaver. 'I'll look for rope,' he said as he headed for the door.

Hermitage stepped out into the darkened landing and let his eyes adjust. The weak red glow from the fire below illuminated the scene very slightly. Everyone had left the inn for the night and the place was deserted. At least no one was going to challenge him. He crept along a very short passage to the top of the stairs that led down to the main hall. Stairs was a bit of a generous description for the rickety ladder propped up against the eaves of the roof into which Briston's chamber had been squeezed.

Putting his hand out to steady his descent, Hermitage grabbed hold of the simple banister that hung at his side. The simple banister made of rope. He got to the bottom of the steps before he realised the thing he had been clinging on to for dear life was made of the stuff he was looking for. He unhooked the bottom of the rope from the ladder and used it to haul himself up, releasing it from the top as well. He entered the room rather triumphantly with his rope in hand, just as Wat hit Briston again.

'Was he waking already?' Hermitage asked.

'Nope,' Wat said without the slightest hint of guilt. 'Ah, excellent,' he smiled at the rope.

Taking it from Hermitage, he quickly and expertly bound Briston's legs and arms with the single long length.

'You *have* done this before,' Hermitage accused.

Wat said nothing.

'How are we actually going to get him out?' Hermitage recalled his experience on the ladder. 'He won't want to go and he's going to be difficult to manoeuvre. The landlord might have a cart we can rent, but he's not likely to look the other way as we carry his tied up guest out of the place.'

'You'd be surprised what landlords turn blind eyes to,' Wat said, patting the small but heavy purse tied to his belt. 'As for getting him out of here…' Wat walked around the small room. He opened the door and looked out before closing it again with a frown. He looked Briston's recumbent form up and down. He then went over to the shutter and opened it, stretching his head out to look below.

'If he cooperates, we'll take him down at first light.'

'I don't think he'll cooperate,' Hermitage said.

'In which case, at first light you go and get a cart and bring it round to the side of the building.'

'What are you going to do with Briston?'

'Throw him out the window.'

Hermitage was shocked, but thought it through. The building was not large. Their window was probably only some seven feet from the ground. 'I could load the cart with a bed of straw,' he suggested.

'Nah,' Wat said, accidentally kicking the unconscious Briston as he climbed over him to get to the cot. At least Hermitage assumed it was an accident.

'He'll bounce.'

Caput XX

Knock Knock

HIS TIME, THE STOTT MANOR really was in uproar. Full blown, out of control, hide-the-children uproar.

Virgil's men had gone. As soon as they came up the cellar steps from the body of their master, they headed straight for the door. It was dark and dangerous outside at this time of night. Clearly they thought it not as dangerous as being inside a house containing something capable of killing Virgil. The remainder of the company gathered by the fire.

'Well, really,' Stott mumbled, offended that someone had the temerity to commit murder in his own cellar. Without asking.

'What do we do?' Parsimon's voice squeaked and shivered despite the warmth of the fire.

'Don't move until daylight,' Cwen said. 'Hermitage and Wat will be back by evening. Then we can all go our own way and forget about Virgil. Good riddance,' she added as an afterthought.

Dextus was pacing up and down in front of the fire, which now blazed with the fresh logs Parsimon had piled on. The Castigatori formed a protective ring, their faces turned to the body of the hall, their bodies ready.

Eadric sat on the hearth stone, his legs stretched out in front of him.

'There is one problem,' Dextus said. 'Whatever it was killed Virgil took the tapestry.'

'Good luck to them, erm, it,' Cwen snorted.

'The tapestry I must have,' Dextus finished off.

'Well, good luck to you as well,' Cwen answered.

'My tapestry,' Stott put in, 'which I shall thank you for its return.'

Dextus ignored him. 'We must find whatever it was that killed Virgil and took Firman.'

'We?' Cwen questioned. 'I don't want to find it at all, thank you very much.'

'What could do such a thing?' Parsimon whimpered. 'Virgil was a giant. A massive, strong giant. Mister Wat said he was a violent lunatic and I concur. What on earth is there in the world capable of doing that to him?' He pointed a shaking finger to the cellar door. 'It looked like he'd been battered to death.'

'Yes, it did, didn't it?' Eadric spoke.

'Whatever it was, it has taken the tapestry.' Dextus was a man with a mission. So far, he was the only one. 'Perhaps it was taken by design, perhaps by accident.'

'Accident,' Cwen said, 'definitely accident. Mister Parsimon's right. Virgil must have been killed by a what not a who. An animal. No human could have done that. But, animals don't steal tapestries,' she followed her trail of thought. 'An animal might eat a tapestry . Perhaps it was a goat?'

'A goat?' Stott was contemptuous. 'I don't keep goats in my house, young lady.'

'And it would have to be a very large goat to finish off something the size of Virgil,' Eadric observed. 'And a very clever one to lay him out on the table afterwards, stop for a nibble of tapestry, and then make off with Firman.'

'I don't hear anyone else coming up with ideas,' Cwen retorted.

'Perhaps it was Firman?' Parsimon put in.

'Don't be ridiculous,' Cwen replied. 'That's even more stupid than the goat. Mister Firman couldn't have knocked Virgil's foot off a stool, let alone break all his bones in one go.'

'Maybe he just fell?' Stott proposed.

'He'd have to fall several times from a very great height for that amount of damage. Bit tricky in a cellar. And he landed on the table every time?' Eadric dismissed that idea.

'Could it be an ague?' Parsimon piped up. 'I heard of this old man in the woods who caught an ague from Oak bark beer. Came out in boils all over.'

'Virgil didn't have any boils,' Cwen observed.

'I'm not saying it was the same ague. Obviously it wasn't the same ague. I'm just saying that they're funny things, agues. You never know what you're going to get.'

'I once had an aunt who got an ague of the leg,' Stott began.

'It was not an ague.' Dextus was firm, trying to get the subject back to his mission.

'Medical man as well now?' Stott mumbled.

'No, just brimming with common sense. There is no ague in the world that breaks a man's bones.'

'Maybe the ague made him thrash about until he broke them himself,' Stott persisted.

'Then where is Firman and what happened to the tapestry? Or is this an ague that makes giants thrash about until they break their bones but makes other men disappear and devours clothwork?'

Stott returned to mumbling.

'Are you saying it was a man?' Cwen asked Dextus.

'Who or what it was does not matter. What matters is the tapestry. We must search for that.'

'There you go with that "we" again,' Cwen said.

Dextus turned to Stott, the old man having returned to his seat by the fire. 'Is there another way out of the cellar?'

'Oh, several.' Stott sounded as if he was going to set off on another tale of olden times. 'There's the hole in the wall for the water. The well's just outside and there's a very sophisticated piece of machinery that actually brings water directly into the house without anyone having to go outside.'

'A bucket and a channel?' Dextus suggested.

'How did you know?'

'Everywhere has them.'

Stott seemed disappointed at this. 'Then there's the old chimney. Not used anymore, but it runs the full height of the house.'

'Why would you have a fire in the cellar?'

'Great grandfather had it put in. He, erm, tended to live in the cellar, mostly.'

'Any more?' Dextus's tone said he hadn't expected a comprehensive directory of all the exits from a simple cellar.

'Just the steps and the hole in the wall.'

'A hole in the wall. Not very secure?'

'It's been there years. Just never got round to mending it.' Stott turned to gaze into the fire.

'So whatever did that to Virgil could be anywhere. It's probably not in the cellar as we didn't see or hear anything. If it could kill Virgil, it wouldn't hesitate with the rest of us.'

'Charming thought,' Eadric said.

'Or, it could have simply left and be miles away by now.' Dextus expressed his frustration by pacing up and down with more conviction.

He beckoned the Castigatori to him and they gathered in a huddle. After some whispered instructions, they split up. One man returned to the cellar, one headed for the main door, and one for the upstairs chambers.

'I say,' Stott started to rise from his chair.

'Do you?' Dextus asked with an insistent stare.

Stott did some more mumbling and sat down again.

Within moments, the castigator from the cellar returned shrugging his shoulders and shaking his head. Seconds later, the one from upstairs did likewise. Dextus gestured they should join their fellow outside.

'What are they going to do if they find it?' Eadric asked. 'Run?'

'Report back and then we can all tackle it. Recover the tapestry.'

Eadric looked about the small gathering, 'I think you're on your own there, friend.'

'Absolutely,' Cwen seconded the motion. 'If the thing wants tapestry, give it tapestry. It can have these as well.' She gestured to the hangings on the wall and to the box on the floor that contained Briston's works.

'Now then, young man,' Stott mumbled. 'Can't be giving away me tapestry.'

'Perhaps we could lure it into a trap,' Parsimon suggested. 'Lay out a trail of tapestry. When it follows the trail, we drop a box on it or something.'

Cwen snorted, 'Or perhaps we just give it all the tapestry it wants in one go and then run away?'

'And I rather think a box or something isn't going to hold it,' Eadric added.

'Silence,' Dextus called and held his hand up.

They listened. All of them seemed expectant that the quiet was going to be torn by the screams of another Virgil.

Ears were cocked, heads tipped over as if to help any sound drop into ears.

There was a very faint rustling sound, like leaves circling in a wind dance, or running away from something horrible. Three loud thumps on the main door made them all jump. They'd been listening so intently for any sound that they'd stopped expecting one. Everyone looked to Dextus. He didn't hesitate and strode across the room to fling the door open.

Someone had used the Castigatori as door knockers. The men lay in a heap on the floor as if each one had been simply cast aside once his head had been smashed into the door. Other than the crumpled pile of habits, there was nothing to be seen.

'Are they?' Cwen asked as she peered around Eadric, the rest of the band having gathered to see what was going on.

Dextus knelt at his pile of men and rolled them over until he could get at each one. He examined heads and lifted eyelids. He laid his hand on chests and lifted arms to let them drop again.

'No,' he said, 'just badly damaged. Let's get them in.'

'They must be getting used to it by now.' Eadric arched an eyebrow.

He and Dextus made rapid trips from door to fire, depositing two of the Castigatori in front of the blaze. Cwen and Parsimon struggled with the last one, half dragging him across the floor and doing more damage as they bumped the body into most of the furniture on the way. Cwen said sorry every time this happened, but the castigator didn't seem to mind.

Back at the door, Dextus looked out but could see nothing. He stood at the entrance, challenging whatever it was to try the same thing on him. After a few moments of nothing, he swung the door closed and turned back to the room.

'What was that?' Cwen cried out.

'What?' Dextus was alert.

'That noise.'

'What noise?' Eadric asked, 'I didn't hear anything.'

'Just as Dextus closed the door,' Cwen insisted. 'It sounded like a sort of bleat.'

'A bleat?' Parsimon was scornful. 'Young lady, you have goats on the mind.'

'Probably just the hinges of the door,' Dextus said, although he didn't go back to open it again to prove the point.

'We're doomed,' Cwen tried to intone, but her voice was too high and anxious to bring it off.

'Doomed?' Eadric asked, clearly thinking the word ridiculous.

'Of course. There were thirteen of us to begin with and one of them was a giant. All awake and fully functional. Now there are five. All in the space of half a candle. Who's next?' She looked around the room nervously. 'Probably the old men.'

'Now look here!' Parsimon and Stott objected together.

'Or maybe not.' Cwen's nervous look twitched about the room. 'It started with Virgil, then his men and then Dextus's. It'll probably have Eadric or Dextus next. You know, leave the weak behind, easy pickings.' She drew closer to the fire.

'It's nothing of the sort.' Dextus sounded calm and confident. 'Yes, something killed Virgil. These things happen.'

'Not to giants who love nothing better than hitting things and killing people. And then your men get it. They're supposed to be strong and powerful, I suppose.'

'Of course.'

'They don't look it,' Cwen gestured to the sleeping forms on the floor.

Dextus shrugged. 'The point is, whatever killed Virgil escaped the cellar and went outside. My men found it and it took them by surprise.'

'Surprise?' Cwen squeaked again. 'It used them to knock on the door, one at a time, and then piled them up for collection.'

'They probably disturbed it.'

'It disturbs me.'

'I assure you there is nothing to fear.' Dextus reinforced his statement by holding his hands out, palms down.

'Excuse me, yes there is.' Cwen was not placated. 'I've been in many situations when there was something to fear, and believe me, this is another one.'

She was even more disturbed when Dextus headed back to the door.

'Where are you going?'

'I'm going to find the tapestry. It's probably outside somewhere.'

'How are you going to find it in the dark? When your head's been caved in by the, the...' she searched for the best word, 'the giant battering goat monster,' she blurted out.

Everyone raised their eyebrows at this.

'I shall be prepared,' Dextus said. 'I will not be surprised like the Castigatori.'

'You don't know they were surprised,' Cwen persisted. 'Perhaps they were introduced to whatever it was bashed their heads in. Maybe they had a nice chat before the head bashing started. Maybe this thing is stronger than all of us.'

'I'm gratified by your concern,' Dextus bowed slightly.

'I'm not worried about you. The question is, who's going to protect me if you're dead? Eadric will be next and that's that.'

'Well then, what do you suggest, young lady?' Stott was impatient, but was at least getting the gender right.

'Bar the doors, shutter the windows and wait 'til daylight. Hermitage and Wat will be back before dark and we'll at least be able to see what we're dealing with. Or run away, obviously.'

Dextus just shook his head. He stopped shaking it when there was massive blow on the main door. One that shook the hinges and knocked a chunk of plaster from the wall.

'There's no one left out there to use as a knocker,' Cwen observed. 'This must be the real thing.'

The door shook again.

Dextus glanced to the cellar door and back to the main entrance.

'Bar the doors and shutter the windows,' he said, as if it was his idea. 'We'll wait 'til daylight.'

Caput XXI

Weavers

HE NEW DAY MADE CAUTIOUS advances into Briston's chamber, as if concerned it might get hit on the head and tied up. It gently illuminated a scene that might have come from a tapestry in Briston's box. One weaver lay on the cot, another was tied up and unconscious on the floor, while a monk snored in a corner. Whatever had gone on the night before must have been pretty riotous.

Hermitage was first to stir as the light bothered his brow. He didn't know where he was for a moment. Was this his chamber at the monastery in De'Ath's Dingle? No, far too warm and comfortable. His first thought on waking was not that he was on the verge of starvation. Could it be some dark corner of the castle of Robert Grosmal? No, his waking mind seemed to recall leaving that place. He had to back track the events of the day. Was he in the hovel of Lolby the peasant?

Ah, now it flooded back, and he wished the tide would go out again. His task on this morning was to take a bound and reluctant weaver and deliver him to the hands of a deranged killer.

He knew his life at De'Ath's Dingle had been harsh and horrible and he had often longed for any change. Yes, he had now escaped the place and had even eaten and slept comfortably, but was he putting his soul in peril? The chain of events that led to this sorry morning was simply incredible. His monastic life had at least been one of order and obedience. Cruel order and frequently pointless obedience, but even so. He sighed before moving and looking over at Briston.

At least he was taking a thoroughly disreputable weaver, who made the most disgraceful images, into the hands of the killer to save a young woman's life. That was alright then. Actually, he was rather sure that it wasn't alright at all, but didn't have the capacity to analyse the theological issues at this hour of the day.

He couldn't tell whether Briston was still unconscious or just asleep. Wat clutched the jug in his arms as he snored on the cot. He looked rather guilty, like a cat sleeping amongst the bones of a fish intended for the family dinner.

'Wat,' he hissed.

There was no response so he dragged himself to his feet and tip-toed over to give the weaver a nudge.

At first contact, Wat flapped into life as if the fish had been resurrected. 'What, what?' he cried out, brandishing the jug.

'It's morning.' Hermitage gestured to the rising sun to prove his point.

'Oh, erm, right.' Wat shook sleep from his head and tried to make wakefulness take its place. The bleary eyes said it was a struggle.

'Shall I go and get the cart?' Hermitage offered.

Wat looked at him as if he'd just been asked if he'd like a cart for breakfast.

'To put Briston in?' Hermitage explained.

'Ah, yes,' Wat said, sense forcing its way past his numbed senses. 'Here, take this.'

Wat thrashed around on the cot for a few moments as he recovered a purse from his belt. He emptied the contents into his hand and Hermitage gaped at the bright and shiny things nestled there. As a monk, he had made a vow of poverty – it had never taken much effort to stick to this, as no one ever gave him any money. He had seen coins of course, even used them in his younger days. They had always been battered and damaged things. Usually long overdue their return to the king's mint for re-issue.

As an intelligent and intellectual person, he understood the uses of gold and silver. He knew their role in the economy of nations; he even understood something of the methods of production. He'd heard of the gold mines in Wales and the silver in the far south. He had never realised that he would drool when he actually saw some. No words came out of his mouth as Wat popped most of the haul into another purse. He handed the one now containing two silver coins to Hermitage.

'Give this to the landlord. It should ease our passage.'

'Ah,' Hermitage said. It wasn't an "ah" of understanding, it was an "ah" of oh-my-goodness-I've-got-some-real-live-silver-in-my-hands.

'Well, go on then.' Wat waved the monk away as he looked at the still recumbent form of Briston, and hefted his jug once more.

'Go on then,' Hermitage repeated rather mindlessly as he stepped from the room, carrying the silver as if it would break.

Down the rickety stairs he went, nearly breaking his leg because some fool had taken away the banister. In the main room, he came face to face with the landlord who had risen to start the fruitless task of trying to clean the place before the dirt of another day moved in.

'Oh, yes, good morning, landlord.'

The landlord frowned at the monk.

'How many people been sleeping in my room?' the man rumbled.

'Oh, erm, we're just on our way.' Hermitage scrabbled for the purse, which he thought would ease his passage. 'I was just wondering to myself,' he paused and waited for the reply, "what were you wondering."

He got a slightly revised version of the frown. Revised downwards.

'I don't like monks in my inn. It's a reputable house.' The landlord was rumbling and frowning at the same time now.

'Aha, yes indeed,' Hermitage nodded agreement. 'I was wondering whether there might perhaps be something, anything really, in the form of a, erm, sort of cart available?' He tried grinning.

'A cart?' The frown of the landlord deepened into a scowl of suspicion.

'For rent, of course,' Hermitage added, holding out the purse.

A scowling face extended a suspicious arm and took the purse. It tipped the contents into an open hand and promptly transformed into gap-toothed grin.

'Cart, sir? Of course,' the man said, with what Hermitage supposed passed for a smile in these parts. It was still rather alarming. 'How big?'

Hermitage was about to reply that one big enough for a large sleeping weaver would do the trick, but caught himself just in time. 'Oh, I don't know. What have you got?'

The landlord led him from the inn to the stable next door. This wasn't really a stable any more as the Normans had taken all the horses. It still had a flat-bedded cart in it though, and Hermitage saw it would do the job.

'You'll have to pull it yourself,' said the landlord in a rather odd tone.

Hermitage interpreted this as an indication that if enough silver were available, the man would strap himself into the harness and drag the cart up a mountain or two.

'Yes, that's fine,' Hermitage said, noting the disappointment. He was just starting to think of an excuse for the cart, a rather complex web of half truth that would satisfy the man's curiosity and avoid too much interest in their nefarious plan.

'Please yourself,' the landlord said as he wandered off counting his silver. He only needed to get to two so it was a pretty straightforward task. This didn't stop him repeating it over and over again.

Hermitage shrugged his shrug of bewilderment at the behaviour of people and pulled at the cart. It wasn't actually a bad piece of machinery. Hermitage's normal dealings with people ended with him being supplied with all sorts of rubbish. If he got fish for the monastery, it would be rotten. If he was sent by the victualler to get game from the butcher, it would be hung the requisite time. Then some more time. Then it would be taken down because no one wanted it. Then it would be hung up again and finally it would be sold to Hermitage.

He fully expected all the wheels of the cart to fall off the moment he tried to move the thing, but it stayed intact.

He loaded it with a gathering of straw left over from the horses and dragged it round to the window of Briston's chamber.

'Wat,' he hissed.

'Wat,' he hissed again, as he climbed on to the cart, his head just a couple of feet below the window.

'Wat,' he said normally and with some impatience.

Wat's head appeared at the window and he looked down at cart and monk.

'Well done.'

He sounded surprised that Hermitage had actually achieved this simple task. He raised a hand, and ducked back into the room. The next thing to appear, after a few moments and some rather odd noises, was the still sleeping head of Briston. Hermitage suspected that the fellow might have been on the receiving end of the jug again.

'Hadn't you better lower him feet first?' Hermitage reverted to hissing.

'He's heavy enough as it is, never mind getting his feet out of the window.'

Wat was struggling with the bulk of the weaver, but managed to push and pull until the man was balanced on the window ledge. The large stomach took the weight – head dangling out of the window and feet presumably dangling inside. Hermitage stood on the cart ready to lower the figure into place on the straw. Wat simply tipped the legs up, and down came the weaver.

Hermitage realised two things as he looked up at the descending mass. One, his outstretched arms and slender frame were not sufficient to the task of stopping the body of a large weaver as it fell from an upper storey window. Two, it was too late to get out of the way.

He closed his eyes, at the same time wondering, from an intellectual standpoint, what effect closing the eyes could have when someone was about to land on you.

The unstoppable weaver hit the immovable monk.

'Well caught, Hermitage,' Wat said from his window, as he watched a Benedictine habit disappear under the significant bulk of Briston. He vanished from the window as the fallen weaver started to make stirring noises. Wat headed for the cart and fell down the stairs. He grumbled and moaned his way to the cart where Briston was now awake. He was not happy.

Hermitage wasn't very happy either. The two men had spent some uncomfortable moments extricating themselves from their jumble. This was not a straightforward task when the larger of the two was tied up.

'Wat, you untie me,' Briston demanded as his fellow weaver arrived.

'Erm,' Wat thought about it for a moment. 'No,' he thought some more. 'I could knock you out again if you like?' he offered, holding up the jug he had brought with him. Hermitage wondered how many more times this jug could be used for the purpose. It must be of remarkably robust construction.

'What the devil are you playing at?' Briston strained against the rope that was not going to give way.

Hermitage wormed his way off the cart and stood next to Wat.

'You have got to go and see Virgil,' Wat explained in clear and serious tones. 'You wouldn't do it of your own volition, so you're going to do it of my volition. You can either sit on the cart and enjoy the journey or I can keep hitting you on the head until we get there.'

Briston glared.

'Personally, I'd prefer to keep hitting you.'

'What's happened to you, Wat? This monk has been a bad influence, I can tell.'

Hermitage looked surprised, he was sure this had nothing to do with him.

'You're the influence, Briston.' Wat was suddenly fierce. 'You always have been. You got us into this.'

'Me?' Briston would have held his hands out in innocent supplication, if they hadn't been tied behind his back. 'I was minding my own business and *you* came after *me*.'

'Not just this,' Wat snapped, 'everything. Virgil, the tapestries, everything. It's all your fault. You were the one who had to find out what that man wanted.'

'What man? I think you've lost your wits.'

'It's not all I've lost. If it hadn't been for you, I wouldn't be in this wretched trade. I wouldn't even know Virgil and Cwen wouldn't be at risk of death.'

'And you wouldn't be wearing all those fine clothes, have a large house in Derby, and a purse full of gold,'

'There's more to life than that,' Wat said with some feeling.

'No there isn't,' Briston replied, clearly not understanding the concept.

'There we are then,' Wat concluded. 'You stay tied up, I take you to Virgil, and we see what happens next.'

They glared at one another.

Wat broke the silence, 'I think I'd like to hit you again now.'

Hermitage took his arm and gave a slight shake of the head.

Wat considered for a while and eventually put the jug down on the back of the cart.

They rearranged Briston and used some of the rope around his wrists to secure him to the vehicle.

'Virgil will only kill you both as well. And he's probably already done Cwen in,' Briston argued.

'Maybe not,' Wat replied. 'Maybe we'll all stay alive and you'll end up in one of Virgil's smaller dungeons. Such a happy outcome has got to be worth a try.'

'Let's assume you're right. Everything goes according to your plan. You'll end up with Virgil at the very least. I hope his little dungeon's big enough for two. In fact, he'd probably rather have you than me. More profit in a scene of Wat's than one of Briston's.'

'It's a risk we'll have to take. I'm sure I'll think of something. Perhaps we could just call from a distance, get Cwen, and then send you and your cart rolling down the hill into Virgil's arms.'

Briston looked at Wat with his best loathing face, which was very loathsome. He drew breath to continue the argument.

'Help,' he yelled. 'Help, help! I'm being captured.'

Hermitage jumped in alarm and stepped towards the cart with arms outstretched, waving about in those gestures that say "be quiet". He didn't really know why Briston would respond in any way other than get louder, but it seemed the right thing to do.

Wat wasn't concerned at all.

Hermitage got in a positive panic when the landlord appeared around the corner.

'Mornin',' the landlord said as brightly as a shiny piece of silver. The man appraised the situation before him. He looked at Wat who was simply standing at the end of the cart. He looked at the monk, who seemed to be dancing from side to side, trying to obscure the contents of the cart with his habit. He leaned around the monk and observed his erstwhile guest now tied up in the cart.

'You off then?' he asked.

'Oh yes,' Wat replied. 'Our friend's got an appointment at Stott Manor.'

'Ah,' the landlord nodded. 'Fine old gent, Mister Stott.'

Briston gaped at the conversation. 'Get me out of here,' he demanded.

The landlord looked to Wat who flipped another coin into the air.

The landlord's hand moved and the silver vanished in mid air. One moment it was glinting in the early sun, the next it was gone, the glint having transferred to the landlord's face.

'You have a safe journey then,' he nodded and turned whistling back to his cleaning.

'Come back here, you rogue,' Briston called.

Wat lifted the jug again and Briston fell to silence.

Hermitage joined Wat at the front of the cart and they stood where the horses ought to be. They got the vehicle moving with a hearty tug and rolled it round into the main street. They turned right in the direction of Baernodebi and heaved away.

'Good gracious,' Hermitage said as they came upon the wreckage of two houses at the end of the road. The buildings on either side had collapsed into the roadway and were being examined and kicked over by a gaggle of locals.

'Perhaps there was an earthquake?' Wat suggested as they drew close. There was room between the bits of wreckage to negotiate the cart and the locals were far too engrossed in their fallen buildings to take any notice of the shouting weaver who claimed he was being kidnapped.

'Never mind you,' one old man snapped at Briston. 'Look what's happened to my house. Some bloody idiot opened the gates last night. They were the only thing holding my home up.'

Hermitage was about to open his mouth when he found it clamped by Wat's hand. 'Walk on,' the weaver instructed very clearly, 'just walk on.'

What Animal?

HE SAME MORNING SUN gently tested the walls of Stott manor. There had been sleep, but Stott and Parsimon had done all of it. They had snored like pigs with terminal congestive disorders, one in his chair and the other curled in front of the fire. The sleep had been fitful though. And so it should be.

The barring of doors and shuttering of windows had been carried out in double quick time and though this secured the room, it didn't stop the hammering from outside.

Dextus, Eadric, and Cwen sat, paced, stood, and then did it again. In the black heart of the night, the noises had stopped. Whatever it was realised it was not going to get past the barriers. Unless it had found another way in, of course.

Caution rose with the silence. Knowing where the thing was when it was hammering to get in was more comforting than thinking it might be silently behind you.

The first rays of light lifted loads from backs and raised furrows from brows. Cwen, Dextus and Eadric exchanged looks of careful relief. As the light bled into the room, Dextus approached the door. Even for a large, strong and threatening priest he was tentative, as if expecting the thing to fly off its hinges at any moment. Cwen and Eadric gave him strong support. They stood where they were and silently urged him on.

He reached out and lifted one end of the substantial oak beams that had been laid across the door, slotted in metal brackets built into the wall for just this purpose. He rested one end on the floor and turned to the other. This too was removed without incident. Eadric gently kicked Parsimon into wakefulness and they waited to see what would happen next.

Dextus leaned forward and lifted the latch of the main door then pulled gently. Nothing moved so he pulled harder. He frowned at the door and pulled hard again. He then stepped back, appraised the door, and kicked it hard.

'Damn thing's stuck,' he called. 'All that thumping to get in must have wedged it. Give me a hand.'

Dextus looked at Eadric, who looked at Cwen, who looked at Parsimon. They all looked at Stott, who slept on. With a resigned and unenthusiastic shrug, Eadric went to the door.

Together the two men pushed, pulled, kicked, prised, and persuaded the door to creak open a crack for the daylight and then get hands around it and heave. To great splintering noises, the thing eventually opened enough to let one man pass through.

The noise had woken Stott.

'What are you doing to my door?' he demanded, instantly awake.

'Opening it,' Dextus replied.

'Well, it certainly doesn't sound like it. Parsimon, go and open the door properly.' He waved an instructional hand at his servant.

'I'm not going anywhere near it,' Parsimon replied as if the request was outrageous. 'Not with that thing out there.'

'Good God, man. This is all your fault,' Stott explained and continued the previous night's berating just where he had left off.

Dextus looked at the old men with contempt and squeezed himself out through the door.

'Ow,' came from outside, and it was not Dextus's voice.

The others made for the door and peered out as best they could.

'Firman?' Cwen asked as she saw a figure on the floor just moving after Dextus had tripped over him.

'I believe so, my dear,' Firman replied as he got to his feet. 'To be honest, I'm not entirely sure any more. Not after the night I've had.'

Dextus now put his back to the door and heaved it from the outside. It opened some more, reluctantly.

Firman stretched and tested his limbs and muscles and then limped his way back into the hall.

'What happened?' Cwen asked, when the man had deposited himself on a chair.

Dextus, having surveyed the outside and found nothing, joined them.

'I simply do not know,' Firman replied looking at them in turn. He noticed the pile of Castigatori. 'Where are the others? Mister Virgil and his little men?'

'They ran off,' Dextus answered before anyone could get a word in, 'Virgil's still here.' His look said there should be silence about Virgil's fate.

'You were with him, Mister Firman, in the cellar. Do you remember?' Cwen asked.

Firman looked to the flagstones as if they held the answer.

'I don't,' he said. 'I remember seeing that awful tapestry of Mistress Stott. I'm ashamed to say I was going to tell Virgil this was really nothing to do with me. I thought perhaps he would let me go now he had his tapestry. I do know the Bishop of Dorchester, you know,' he nodded around the assembly, none of whom were remotely interested in which bishops he knew.

'And then?' Dextus demanded.

Firman's face said he was thinking hard. His frown said nothing came to him. 'It's all a blank.' He sounded puzzled. 'I remember waking up outside and it was dark. There was lots of noise and I hid a bit, to be honest.'

'Hid? From what?'

'I don't know. There was just lots of thrashing about going on, like an animal in a bush or something.'

'An animal in a bush?' Dextus was not impressed. 'Big animal? Big bush?'

'Well obviously, or I wouldn't have hidden. After a while, there was some running about and some banging.'

'Probably your men's heads on the door,' Cwen told Dextus.

'Really?' Firman was interested.

'And then?'

'Then it all went quiet and the sky was just starting to brighten so I headed for the door. It was stuck but I could see the lights inside. I just lay down for a moment and must have dropped off.'

'Dropped off? In the night? With animals in bushes and banging going on? Not having a clue what had happened to you, you fell asleep?'

'I was tired,' Firman defended his actions.

'I don't believe it,' Dextus summarised. 'Come and see Virgil,' he instructed, taking Firman by the arm.

'Must I?'

'You must.'

Dextus led the man across the room. Eadric and Cwen followed. Stott and Parsimon stayed by the fire. Down in the cellar, Dextus spread his arm to introduce the new Virgil.

Firman looked and then looked back to Dextus. 'What?' he whispered, trying not to wake the giant.

'Look more closely,' Dextus spoke. 'Give him a poke if you like.'

Firman looked very puzzled but approached the body.

The bruising really had come out now. It had come out and was parading up and down the main street of Virgil's body. It was livid bruising and was shouting angrily at anyone who looked in its direction.

'Oh my goodness,' Firman's voice was a shocked whisper when he took in all the details. 'Who could have done all this?' He held his hands out to encompass the "all" that had been done to Virgil.

'That's what we'd like to know,' Dextus asked. 'You were the one with him before this happened. Then you vanished. You say you're outside all night, outside with all the noises we heard. My men go out and are piled up by the door. When we eventually get it open what do we find? You. Asleep.'

'My dear fellow,' Firman protested, 'I don't know what you think I'm capable of but it certainly isn't any of this. I mean, look at me.' He held his arms out to offer himself for inspection.

The others looked and shoulders sagged as they all accepted there was no way this character was capable of killing Virgil and despatching three Castigatori. His clothes weren't even out of place.

'Perhaps you're possessed at night,' Dextus proposed.

The others looked at him. He was serious.

'Are you serious?' Cwen almost snorted. 'Possessed?'

'It's perfectly reasonable,' Dextus explained in a weary tone that he obviously used when he was speaking to the uneducated. 'Possession is a fact,' he said, 'Mark, Book Five, Chapters one to twenty.'

His audience looked blank

'The region of the Gadarenes?' Dextus clearly could not believe the ignorance around him.

'For goodness' sake, the man from the tombs who was possessed and could not be bound? Do none of you listen to your priests when they warn you of the dangers of the devil?'

There was a sort of mumbling assent. The sort people use when they want to give the impression that they understand when actually they don't have a clue.

'In fact,' Dextus was following his own trail, 'the Lord cast the devils into the bodies of pigs. That's suspicious.'

'Yes,' Eadric said, taking half a step away from the priest who seemed to be getting quite excited.

'And Briston used a pig. It all fits.'

'Does it?' Cwen asked in the sympathetic voice saved for the dying.

'I'm not mad, you idiots,' Dextus proclaimed.

The others did not look convinced.

Dextus counted on the fingers of his left hand, 'One, Briston the Weaver, who we know does works of sin, if not actual evil, uses a pig to attempt his escape from justice. Two, pigs were the animals our Lord chose to host the devils named Legion before they drowned.'

'Drowned?' Cwen was getting lost.

'Of course. They all threw themselves in the sea and drowned.'

'All? How many were there?'

'Two thousand of course.'

'Two thousand! Two thousand pigs?'

'Naturally.'

'That's a lot of pigs.'

'It was a lot of demons.'

'Did no one object?'

'What?' Dextus was an intelligent man losing control of his own conversation.

'I mean, drowning two thousand pigs?' Cwen asked as if it had happened yesterday. 'That must have been most of the pigs for miles around. Wasn't there a fight or something? I heard of a preacher over Grimsby way who tried to baptise a lamb in the sea and drowned that. The shepherds nearly murdered him.'

'We are talking about our Lord, you foolish girl. The populace rejoiced because he had rid them of a legion of demons. A legion! Not one or two causing a bit of trouble here and there but a whole legion. A couple of thousand pigs was a small price to pay.'

Cwen shrugged, still not happy. 'If you say so.'

'Yes I do.' Dextus glared his priestly glare, which was very good. Cwen averted her eyes.

'Now,' the priest tried to recover his composure, 'where was I? Ah yes. Briston uses a pig. Then Virgil, an out and out sinner if ever I met one, gets done to death in mysterious circumstances. By some creature of immense strength, you see?'

The audience didn't see.

'One who could not be bound even with chains?'

'You've lost me.' Cwen was shaking her head.

Dextus sighed and explained, as if to children, 'In the Book of Mark, there is a man who lives in a tomb, who is possessed and cannot be restrained even by chains. Our Lord meets him, casts the demons out of him and into pigs that then drown themselves. Clear?'

Eadric and Cwen nodded, trying to look agreeable.

'So the connections here are obvious. Firman could be the one possessed who cannot be restrained. Someone like that could easily have killed Virgil and knocked out my Castigatori.'

'But,' Eadric was thinking, 'he's only possessed at night?'

'Yes.'

'And he doesn't damage his clothes while he's running around killing giants and knocking Castigatori about?' He gestured at Firman who displayed himself to show that all of his fine attire was undamaged from this supposed night of mayhem.

'Not if he has the strength of Legion, no.' Dextus was clear.

'Well,' Firman said in the silence no one was able to fill. 'If it was me, I'm terribly sorry.'

'You don't seriously believe this?' Cwen asked.

'Who's to say? I certainly don't remember what happened last night. And Dextus is a priest, an educated man. If he says that's what happened, who are we to argue?'

'Look at Virgil,' Cwen pleaded. 'I mean look at him. Unless your fists are going to grow when you're possessed, how could you do this to him? The man was a monster. But, I can't believe that demons, even legions of them, pop in for a bit of possession during the night but then clear off when the sun comes up.'

229

'Well, that's perfectly reasonable.' Dextus scoffed at her ignorance.

Cwen went on, 'I know everyone laughed, but I said it had to be an animal. Something like a goat with great big horns.' She demonstrated what great big horns would look like.

'A goat,' Dextus snorted. 'It was a devil.'

'Perhaps I simply don't know my own strength?' Firman suggested.

Eadric was silent. He was looking at each of them in turn. 'Something like a goat,' he mumbled, 'big horns, hooves.'

They looked at him and he focussed his gaze on Firman, 'Or like a sheep,' he said.

They all laughed at this.

'Now you're being ridiculous,' Cwen spluttered.

Normans

ORTUNATELY FOR HERMITAGE AND WAT, the road was clear and the cart was good. Briston kept up a stream of moaning wails as they headed back for Baernodebi. He had begun the journey with a series of very reasonable arguments for his release. These had subtly transformed into mild threats after only a few paces. Then they became very explicit threats. The threats were followed by offers of bribes for his freedom, which became progressively more extravagant, and eventually he resorted to plain begging. When this failed, he simply wailed like a child who didn't want to go and see his toothless and stinking old grandmother.

'Has he always been like this?' Hermitage enquired as if they were talking about a horse with a mangy coat.

'Oh yes,' Wat nodded. 'Always wants what's best for Briston and will lie, cheat, and cajole until he gets it. Never cares a hoot about what damage he causes and never takes responsibility.'

'But he's your friend?' Hermitage couldn't quite follow this.

His history was full of people with the most appalling personal qualities and he wouldn't count any of them amongst his friends. Actually, he couldn't claim anyone at all amongst his friends until he met Wat. Of course, there had been boyhood fellows with whom he ran the woods and fields of home, but usually he went home and read a book by the fire after. There was only the one book in the house but he read it many times.

The fellows went home and practised fighting, or breaking things, or tormenting sisters. They wouldn't have dreamt of going home and reading a book. Obviously they couldn't because Hermitage had the book.

'Well…' Wat was giving careful thought to his answer. 'We go back a long way. We're both weavers. We shared the same master.'

'Who died just before we left,' Briston called from the back of the cart with a great weight of suggestion in his voice.

'These things happen,' Wat replied without apparent interest.

Hermitage felt a connection traipse across the back of his head but Wat was still talking.

'I suppose we were sort of thrown together. I don't know if we'd have struck up a friendship if that hadn't been the case. In fact, we spent most of our time arguing and fighting. It was alright when the money was coming in, but we split up as soon as trouble came along. Briston had his own ideas about how to live his life and I had mine.' Wat lapsed into quiet thought for a moment. 'No actually, I don't think we are friends.'

'Thank you very much,' Briston called from the back of the cart. 'So the death notes mean nothing.'

'You know I don't think they do.' Wat was quite equitable in his reasoning, as if the conclusion that he didn't really like Briston had cleared his head. As the cart approached a bend in the road, he craned his neck round to address the bound weaver. 'I came for you when I got the note but I'm pretty damn sure you'd have been off in the opposite direction before you could say "watch out for that Norman" if I had sent mine to you.'

'Watch out for that Norman,' Hermitage repeated.

'Yeah,' Wat sniggered.

'No,' Hermitage said. 'Watch out for that Norman.'

Wat turned to face forward and saw the Norman.

It was a big Norman. It was on a big horse and it had some other Normans standing at its side. It was in the middle of the road and it was looking at them with interest.

As Hermitage considered man and horse, he could see why Harold lost the battle at Hastings. As the Briston-pig had been bound in soft pink tapestry thread, this fellow was bound in shining metal and he could have looked down on Virgil from the height his saddle and hit him with one of the many bits of metal that hung at his side.

The head was gloved by a sparkling Norman helmet that protected ears, neck, and most of the skull. The front was open to reveal a face that said all it needed to. It was a mature and ragged face that looked like it had seen far too much to worry about anything. Light chain mail ran down the right arm and loitered on the handle of a sword in its scabbard at the side of the horse. This weapon did its best to reach the ground. One glance told Hermitage he was perfectly happy if the thing stayed exactly where it was.

The Norman's chest was emblazoned with a fine coat of arms. This looked like nothing more than a Norman sinister rampant trampling a field of Saxons dormant.

The legs were clad in metal work and hung around the sides of the horse as if ready to crush the beast to death at any moment. Four men were standing by the horse and they all had weapons of their own. They wore the same blazon and looked just as relaxed about this encounter.

Briston was silent. Hermitage was silent. Wat opened his mouth to speak.

'A strange group of travellers?' the Norman asked, although it seemed he was asking his men rather than the travellers themselves.

All Hermitage could think of to do was smile. So he did.

'A grinning monk, a well-dressed man, and a fat fellow tied to a cart. I imagine the explanation for this would be fascinating.'

'Well, sir,' Hermitage began.

'I said *would* be fascinating,' the Norman interrupted, 'if I wanted one.'

'Ah,' Hermitage tried smiling again, even though it hadn't helped the last time.

'You are travelling from Bigby to Baernodebi.' This was a statement.

'Yes, sir,' Hermitage confirmed.

'Having just travelled from Baernodebi to Bigby.'

'Oh,' Hermitage wondered how the man knew that. 'Yes, we did.'

'To fetch the fellow tied to the cart.'

'Erm, yes, I suppose so,' Hermitage shrugged.

'You suppose so? You have a fat man tied to a cart you are pulling along the road and you *suppose* so?'

'Well, he didn't want to come,' was all Hermitage could think of.

'Is there some trouble, sir?' Wat asked, as if pulling carts with fat men tied to them was perfectly normal.

'Not yet.' He waved Wat to silence, his eyes boring holes in Hermitage. 'I assume that you are the investigator.'

Hermitage was surprised. First Virgil now a Norman on a horse. He had a reputation and it seemed to be spreading. Perhaps the king had put out an edict announcing that Hermitage was his investigator. He could be known the length and breadth of the land as the King's Investigator. As he considered this more, and took into account the current popularity of the king, he thought this might be a bad thing. A very bad thing. There were those in the land who resisted the Normans still. They attempted to wreak great damage on the property and symbols of the new king. Hermitage did want any damage wreaked on him.

'I, erm…' He supposed that a Norman wasn't likely to wreak damage. 'Yes, that's right, but how did you…?'

'Come with me,' the Norman on the horse instructed.

'Actually, we've got to get back to Baernodebi,' Hermitage answered. 'You see, we're dealing with something at the moment.'

'Really,' the Norman said, with little interest.

'Yes, and a young lady's life is in danger. We have to get back with the fellow on the cart to make sure that a great wrong is avoided.'

'Very commendable,' the Norman commented. 'Problem is, if you don't come with me, I'll do a great wrong as well, probably use my sword. Then my fellows here will make sure you come with me anyway.'

This was a very reasonable Norman, Hermitage thought, in the sense that he reasoned well, not that he was being reasonable.

'Lead on, sir,' Wat gestured.

The Norman swung his animal around and the four men turned and followed. None of them even cast a glance back at the cart so sure were they that they were doing exactly as they were told.

'Wat,' Briston hissed.

Wat turned his head.

'Let me go,' Briston whined. 'I don't think they want me.'

'Oh, yes we do,' the Norman on the horse said without a head turning or step faltering.

'Bugger,' Briston hissed again.

♦   ♦   ♦

They didn't go far down the main road from Bigby to Baernodebi before they turned off on to a track that ran into the woods. They tramped on for a couple of hundred yards or so, no one saying anything, until they emerged into a clearing. Or rather what had once been a clearing. A stockade now dominated the area. High wooden walls went off to left and right, circling round to enclose a space at least a hundred yards across. The wall was about seven feet high, just tall enough to make someone pause before trying to scale it, followed by death, most likely.

The traditional Norman construction could be seen in the middle of the space. Hermitage thought it interesting that the Normans had established tradition in so short a time. That's what came of making sure all the people of alternative traditions were dead, he supposed. As soon as the Normans arrived, the locals would have been forced to build this massive heap. It was at least thirty feet tall, and about a hundred across the bottom. On top of the pile there was another palisade of fencing with a reasonably substantial wooden keep inside it.

They passed through a gateway in the outer wall and the Norman got off his large horse and handed it to another soldier who led it away. Without issuing any further instructions, the Norman made for steps cut into the side of the mound and headed for the top of the hill. One of the attending men cut Briston free and indicated that they should follow by jabbing them with his pike. They followed.

It was a steep climb. The mound was high and the steps were few. Both Hermitage and Briston were panting when they got to the top. The Norman led the way through the upper palisade gate, across only four or five paces of open ground and into the keep.

This was a simple building – the building of a soldier at camp – more substantial than a tent obviously, but with little more comfort. A fire blazed in the place, but unlike Stott's manor, this one did so in the middle of the floor and most of its smoke hung around in the room, as if waiting for something exciting to happen. They all coughed and spluttered through the fog that headed straight for the open air as soon as the door was opened.

'My Lord,' the Norman from the big horse gave a short bow, turned and left.

Hermitage peered through the murk. The keep was basically a wooden box. It was about thirty feet square and fifteen or so tall. It was built for defence and so only had slim arrow slits as windows. The smoke from the fire was queuing up at these for a way out. A couple of torches hung on the walls, but all they did was light up the smoke.

This really was a soldier's camp, meant for hardened men who were defending a lawless country. It could defend from attack and be a source of offence when the conditions were right. The Normans had thrown them up all over the place and they were usually filled with very hardened men indeed.

Hermitage almost jumped out of his skin when a definitively hardened man appeared out of the gloom and reared towards them. If war could be said to toughen men, this one looked like he'd been dunked in a blacksmith's quenching tank and then had all remaining softness beaten out of him on an anvil. His face was rough and weather beaten, probably from being outside for days – while he killed people. His war clothes hung on him like a second skin, and he looked like he took them off as often as his skin.

'I am Gilbert,' the man announced.

Hermitage wasn't sure if this was a first name or a surname; the Normans were odd about this sort of thing. Gilbert looked at them all long and hard.

'Brother Hermitage,' Hermitage put in. He thought about holding out his hand, but feared Gilbert might take that as a threatening gesture.

'Odd name for a monk,' Gilbert observed. His glare moved on.

'Wat,' Wat said when the glare came his way.

'Briston,' Briston said.

'Are you all together?'

Hermitage wondered at this. Well, of course they were. They'd been dragged here together, why wouldn't they be?

'Oh yes,' Briston said. 'All together.'

Gilbert frowned while Hermitage and Wat did their own glaring at Briston. He smiled happily back.

'Right. I've got a job for you.'

Hermitage gulped. He'd heard what it meant when a Norman said they'd got a job for you. This man probably wanted some more mud piled on top of his hill. The old joke "what did your last slave die of" was seldom used these days. It had stopped being funny.

'Well actually, we're on our way to Baernodebi,' Hermitage started to explain. 'Got rather an important matter to attend to. Someone's life at stake, you know? We really ought to be getting back.'

'Oh, I know all about people's lives being at stake,' Gilbert nodded agreeably. 'In fact, I've got one of the stakes at the bottom of my hill.'

'Always glad to help,' Wat tried to sound positive.

'Excellent,' Gilbert scowled. He stepped across the fire and came straight up to Hermitage. 'Where's my daughter?' he demanded.

Caput XXIV

At Home with the Normans

OUR DAUGHTER?' Hermitage looked around the smoke shrouded room as if he'd been asked to play spot-the-daughter. 'Erm,' was all he could come up with.

'Come on,' the hardened Norman demanded as if Hermitage was deliberately holding back.

Hermitage was completely lost. He looked to Wat and Briston for help. The fat weaver was scanning the room, presumably for a way out. Wat was looking as non-plussed and confused as Hermitage felt.

'I'm, erm, not sure that I know her,' Hermitage offered as a sort of humble question/excuse.

'Well, of course you don't,' Gilbert snapped back. 'You better bloody well not.'

'But then?' Hermitage was so far out of his depth he started to get panicky. It was bad enough when people confused him, let alone when they were big Normans in dark and smoky keeps.

'Why erm…' Wat spoke up as respectfully as he could. 'Why would Brother Hermitage here know where your daughter is? Sir. My Lord.'

Gilbert glared at Wat with the sort of look that could knock sparrows out of trees. 'He's the investigator, isn't he?' he said.

'Oh, erm, yes. I suppose he is.'

The lord took a deep breath and explained reluctantly, 'My man's been looking for her. He went to the wretched market in Baernodebi, checked the place over, nothing. Well, apart from some disgusting Saxon selling the most revolting tapestries.'

'Really?' Wat enquired with interest, trying not to look at

Briston. Hermitage managed to keep his mouth shut, although his eyes were wide open.

'You're all sick in the mind.' Lord Gilbert took in the whole Saxon race. 'Having stuff like that passing about.'

'You're absolutely right,' Wat agreed.

'At least that's one weaver we won't be seeing around here anymore.'

'Glad to hear it.' Wat did now look at Briston with a now-I-know-what-you're-up-to look.

'Anyway, my man passed through again on his way back and the place seems to have been wrecked. Apparently some peasant with a pig said the King's Investigator-monk was around and had gone off looking for someone. He got directed to some loon in a field who plays with meat and *he* told my man you'd gone to Bigby to bring back some fat man.'

'Did he?' Wat asked, clearly suspicious as Hamard hadn't even wanted to tell Hermitage where Briston had gone.

'Well, he told my man eventually,' Gilbert acknowledged.

'Ah.' Hermitage felt relief as a palpable warmth spreading through him – relief that his discovery as the investigator was simply a chain of events. His relief cooled rather as he wondered what had persuaded Hamard to tell. 'Yes, Briston the, erm, fat man,' he just stopped himself saying "weaver". We found him,' he gestured to Briston who had sidled towards the door.

'There you are then!' The Norman was pleased. 'You found him! Now you can tell me where my daughter is.'

'I'm afraid I don't know,' Hermitage held out his arms, as if showing that he wasn't hiding the Norman's daughter in his habit.

'Well, work it out then.'

'Work it out?'

'Yes!' Gilbert was losing patience. Hermitage felt a large Norman soldier with no patience inside his own keep was probably quite dangerous.

'You're the investigator. You find people. Find my daughter.'

Hermitage felt rather despondent. The first death, of Brother Ambrosius, he had investigated because he was there. Right there. At the time. The exact time.

The second, Henri de Turold, he had solved because he was made to. The supposed death of Briston was his own investigation, which was rather satisfying. Since then, Virgil had forced him to look for Briston and now this Norman was demanding he find a missing daughter.

He didn't think much of being King's Investigator if everyone with a problem could just demand he sort it out for them. How could he manage if he was in the middle of one job when someone demanded he do another one, and demanded that the old one still be done as well, without giving him any more time to do either of them?

Bit like being back in the monastery actually.

Still, he reminded himself, this was a large Norman soldier in his own keep. Surrounded by his own men. And very willing to do horrible things to people. He probably took priority over the mad, giant lunatic who was miles away. Another piece of thinking he would have to file away. He had a feeling it might come in handy.

'If you gave me some details, I could keep my eye out for her as we go on our way. Perhaps consider the facts and see what might have happened. Get back to you in a day or so?'

Gilbert lowered his head slightly and looked at Hermitage through his eyebrows. Which were copious. 'Now,' he said.

Hermitage noted that he'd never seen angry eyebrows before. He looked once more around the smoke-filled room. This simply wasn't possible. How could he find someone who wasn't here and about whom he knew nothing? At least with Briston he had Wat to ask. And Hamard. Who would he ask here? The Norman?

Yes, of course he'd ask the Norman.

'Where did you see her last?' he asked, not immediately able to come up with anything better.

'What?' Gilbert roared, as if he'd been accused of misplacing his daughter.

Hermitage answered quickly, hoping to divert any physical manifestation of Norman rage. 'It's a standard question,' he gabbled. 'I need to know where she was last so we can work out where she is now.'

'It is the sort of question Hermitage uses,' Wat explained, 'even when he's working for King William.' Wat nodded encouragingly.

That seemed to placate Gilbert somewhat. He calmed down to a simple rumbling discontent with menaces.

'Over there,' he said, gesturing to a corner of the room.

Hermitage looked to the corner and thought it quite possible the girl was still there. It was just that no one could see her.

'May I?' Hermitage nodded towards the corner.

Gilbert grunted, which Hermitage took as consent, and he stepped cautiously over to the corner. Wat followed, all the time smiling and making conciliatory gestures towards the smoky Norman in his smoky room.

'How old is she?' Hermitage asked as he walked across the room.

'Sixteen,' the old war horse replied. 'Just turned.'

Wat raised his eyebrows and rolled his eyes at Hermitage. The monk wondered if the smoke was getting in them.

Once in the corner of the keep, the two men looked in some surprise at what they saw. This corner was an oasis of order and civilisation in a room of ruin and squalor. A cot hugged the wall, covered in a fine embroidered blanket. This was neatly laid and tucked into the corners of a feather mattress. The cover had a single charming scene of a princess in a tower looking down at a field of unicorns, each one ridden by a handsome knight in shining armour.

By the side of the bed, laid out in a neat row, were three pairs of shoes. Next to these were several bottles of perfumes or unctures of some sort. The bottles were lined in ascending order of height. The whole presented a scene in stark contrast to its surroundings. It didn't help that all of the objects in this charming corner were covered with a fine layer of soot.

Wat looked from the bed to the room in which it sat and whispered in Hermitage's ear. 'I'm not surprised she's gone.'

'She, erm, normally lives with you then?' Wat asked as if this was perfectly routine and quite proper.

'Of course,' the Norman replied in the same tone. 'Her mother passed on years ago and she's been with me ever since.'

'On campaign.'

'Always on campaign,' the Norman said as if this was right and proper too.

'Looks like she's quite the lady,' Wat commented.

'Ah yes,' the Norman spoke with pride. 'Always well turned out, neat and, erm, that.' It was clear that Gilbert didn't have any other words for neat. One was probably all he ever needed, not being involved in situations where it was applicable.

'And when was it you saw her last?' Hermitage asked.

The Norman paused in thought. 'Would have been last gutting day,' he said.

'Gutting day?' Wat tried not to snort.

'Yes, my little Aveline insisted we do the gutting on just one day instead of every day. It was day before yesterday.'

'How charming.'

'Did she have any friends?' Hermitage asked.

'Certainly not!' The protective father was outraged.

'None of the other girls?' he asked.

The Norman frowned deeply. 'What other girls?' he asked, rather confused.

Hermitage hesitated to ask the next question. Not for long though as he needed to know. 'Did she ever express any wish to, erm, leave?' He tried to sound as humble as he could.

243

'Leave?' Gilbert had some trouble with the concept. 'Leave her father?' He gestured to take in his magnificent surroundings.

'Hard to imagine, I know,' Hermitage said, imagining it very easily. 'Children, eh?' he said, as if he had dozens of them.

'She left her shoes behind?' Hermitage observed.

'Only the spares,' Gilbert explained. 'Never knew why she needed more than one pair anyway, but everywhere we went, another pair of shoes.'

'Really?'

'Even after battles, I had to bring her back a pair of shoes.'

'Ah.'

'None of them any good in the mud either.'

'Perhaps she's only stepped out and will be back soon?' Hermitage offered.

Even his naive and innocent eyes could see what had happened here. Wat's frank and suggestive glances helped, but he would have got there on his own. This poor Gilbert's daughter had run off from an unbearable life. A life lived in unbearable circumstances. She had shoes, nice embroidery, liked the finer, ladylike things in the world and was forced to live in a smoke-filled box with a soldier. Probably several soldiers, one of whom was her father. The question was how to get this message over to the soldier. The large soldier who was right in Hermitage's face. And Hermitage was in his line of fire. Best not to tell him at all, probably.

'Did she ever comment on her life?' Hermitage tried instead of a direct approach.

'What sort of question is that?' The soldier clearly found this concept beyond him.

'Well, what child doesn't?' Hermitage encouraged. 'You know, did she want to go out? Did she want to stay in? Did she want things? Other than shoes?' He cast his mind back to his own childhood when all his requests for a second book were dismissed out of hand by a father who noted that a book wouldn't chop down trees for you.

Gilbert's eyes narrowed aggressively but they were narrowing from recognition. 'I mean, obviously she's not a soldier.' The man seemed to consider this a full and frank explanation.

'Obviously,' Hermitage encouraged.

'She'd have her little moans about the keep, and the men.'

Hermitage nodded his encouragement now.

'And the food, and the travelling. And the smoke, and how she never met anyone.' The man was on a roll now. On a roll down a large and long hill. 'And how she never got to do what she wanted, or have the things she needed.' The Norman paced away from Hermitage and then strode back, arms waving. 'And how I never let her go anywhere. And when I asked where she wanted to go she said anywhere. So I said, tell me somewhere and she said I was ruining her life and didn't understand.'

Hermitage tried to do sympathy now.

Gilbert was glaring, but it wasn't at Hermitage. It was a distant yet introspective glare. The glare of a soldier with nothing to hit.

He took a breath. 'You can see,' he gestured over to the cot, 'she liked nice things.'

Hermitage nodded sympathetically.

'But we'd have lots of nice things after another five years of campaigning or so.'

Hermitage nodded some more. It seemed to help.

'But she said she'd be dead by then. Who'd want her when she was twenty? She'd be an old crone.'

'So she wanted a life other than this one,' Hermitage prompted.

Gilbert's shoulders sagged as if he'd been broken somehow.

'Dull?'

'Dull?' Hermitage hadn't followed.

'I ask you. How can this life be dull? But she'd just sit there on the cot, night after night. Dull, dull, dull, she'd mumble.'

Hermitage felt his head light up. He tried to stop the light pouring from his eyes so he frowned them closed. He looked to Gilbert's rugged Norman face and more recognition flowed through his brain. He turned quickly to catch Wat's eyes. The weaver's visage looked as if all the muscles had been so surprised they had forgotten they were supposed to hold his face up. He gawped at Hermitage and then turned and gawped at Briston, who was now right by the door. Persuading his face to at least close his mouth, he sidled away from Hermitage and Gilbert and made for Briston.

Hermitage muttered sympathies and walked about a bit, examining things in what he hoped was an investigatory manner. He asked Gilbert to show him the shoes and the bottles and considered them closely, keeping the Norman's attention on him.

Over by the door, Wat, now back in control of his facial expressions, spoke quietly to Briston. He spoke reasonably, calmly and gently. But he spoke with fierce determination.

'Briston, my old friend.'

Briston looked at Wat with worry. It was clear from the tone of voice that the man had a new-found power. Briston didn't encourage any further conversation.

'Briston, Briston, Briston,' Wat patted Briston on the shoulder and used a voice that put Briston firmly in his place. That place was under Wat's foot.

'If I tell gorgeous Gilbert here,' he gestured towards the large Norman soldier, 'that his lovely daughter ran off with the very weaver who did the disgusting tapestries of Baernodebi, and that this weaver has seen more of his daughter than is right, proper, or even legal,' Wat let the thought ferment, 'and that said weaver is likely to distribute tapestries that will let the rest of the world see as much of his lovely daughter as well, he *will* kill you. He'll have killed lots of people he doesn't even know. The only motivation he needs is that they're on the battlefield. Or that they're on the wrong side. Or perhaps just that they're in the way. Imagine how inspired he'll be by you.'

'I don't know what you're talking about,' Briston tried.

'Oh, come on,' Wat scoffed. 'You can do better than that. A lovely young girl turns up in Bigby. Well dressed, looking for a life less dull? When just such a girl has recently gone missing from the home of the nearest professional Norman killer? I don't think this part of the country is swimming with them. Who is she then? The Queen of the May?'

'Could be anyone,' Briston shrugged.

'With that nose?' Wat gestured to Gilbert and used his hands to mime the presence of a large Norman nose, the sort which sat happily on Gilbert's face – not so happily on the face of the girl in Briston's chamber.

'So?' Briston avoided Wat's eyes.

'So off we go to Baernodebi.' Wat rubbed his hands as if they were having a trip to the seaside. 'You cause no trouble. You come nice and quiet and take what's coming to you. We get Cwen back and everyone lives happily ever after,' Wat paused for thought, 'except you obviously.'

'And Gilbert?' Briston nodded towards the Norman.

'Hermitage will work out where his daughter is and he'll be very happy. Of course, if anything goes wrong, young Hermitage will suddenly recall that he actually saw the charming Aveline. Where was it? Oh yes, with that fat man, Briston. Of course, he's the one who makes the filthy tapestries. Oh, and he's the one sitting by the door of your fortress.'

'You do the same work.'

'Not of the daughters of Normans, I don't. It's because I'm not, what's the expression? Oh yes, bloody stupid.'

'I haven't made any tapestries of her,' Briston growled, but had clearly given up the game. 'Only just met her.'

'I bet you've made a few preliminary sketches though,' Wat nodded.

Briston's scowl said that was exactly what he had done.

Wat returned to where Hermitage was examining Aveline's

shoes, while regaling Gilbert with the detailed theological arguments surrounding our Lord's footwear during the forty days and forty nights in the wilderness. He hadn't even got as far as the opening references when Gilbert already looked like he would collapse on his daughter's cot muttering dull, dull, dull.

Wat caught Hermitage's eye and nodded. Hermitage inclined his head in return.

'And so,' Hermitage said, in a complete non sequitur to what he had been saying, 'we can thus estimate the location of your daughter.'

Gilbert woke up. His eyes widened, 'What?' he asked, clearly not having been listening to a word.

'Oh yes,' Hermitage smiled as if it had all been perfectly clear. 'Bigby. At the inn.'

'How, did you?' Gilbert started but then stopped.

Wat could see that the man had listened to enough of Hermitage to know that he didn't want to get the full explanation.

Gilbert turned and strode quickly from the room.

There was some yelling of instructions outside, followed by the noise of horses being quickly mounted and ridden away.

Hermitage and Wat exchanged looks of quiet satisfaction. They looked to Briston, who didn't exchange anything.

'If this is true, sir monk, you are a great man,' Gilbert beamed.

'Of course, I've no guarantee, but if my reasoning is sound, your men will find her there.'

'And if they do, I shall owe you a great favour. If there's anything I can do for you, you will only have to say the word.'

There was lots of mutual smiling and grinning at the prospect of the return of the daughter of Gilbert. The daughter of Gilbert probably wouldn't be smiling quite so much, but then she wasn't there.

'Actually,' Wat said raising a finger, 'there might be something you can help us with.'

Caput XXV

How to Disguise a Hoofhorn

YOU'RE HIM, AREN'T YOU?' Eadric demanded fiercely.

He had taken Firman to one side as soon as the laughter, which flowed like a stream about Virgil being killed by a sheep, had died down. Now it was just like a bucket emptied of water – occasionally, another drip would fall out.

The company sat in silence, grinning at one another until some other hilarious pun or ribald comment occurred to one of them.

'Perhaps he was fleeced,' Cwen suggested to wide chortling.

Even Dextus found it hard to resist. 'He may have recognised his killer and said, "Oh, it's ewe", you know, like the sheep spelling.'

Stott still seemed offended they were suggesting his house was the regular haunt of livestock. Parsimon just gave Eadric the sympathetic look reserved for all idiots. Eadric had taken it all in, ignoring them in the way people do when they know they'll be proved right. Eventually. He had suggested they leave the place as whatever Virgil's killer was could come back.

The Castigatori were still out cold. Whatever had done in their heads had done them in pretty thoroughly and Dextus refused to move without them. Stott and Parsimon weren't going anywhere and Cwen refused to walk in the woods with a man who was worried the sheep might attack. Firman said nothing, he just smiled at the comments, like a parent laughing at a three-year-old's joke. Eadric had taken his elbow and walked him away from the flock.

'Admit it, you're him. I mean, you're it!' Eadric stared hard at Firman, who looked back with as much vacancy in his face as the empty bucket.

'I'm who, what?' Firman looked around as if the room would offer some explanation.

Eadric leaned in and whispered hard, 'The Hoofhorn.'

'Beg pardon?' Firman showed no sign of recognition.

'Very clever. You can't fool me.' Eadric too looked around the room, worried that someone might hear him. 'I know.'

Firman leaned in and whispered as well, 'What's a Hoofhorn?'

'It's no good playing the innocent with me. I was in the guildhall after all. I've seen the cauldron.'

Firman's eyes flickered over to Cwen and Dextus.

'Cauldron,' Firman said in the encouraging voice applied to religious enthusiasts who approach you with a knife, offering to send you to heaven one bit at a time.

'Absolutely. I didn't believe it at first, but that stuff with the sword was quite impressive. Why did you stop following me?'

'My dear fellow, I really think you've mixed me up with someone else.'

'Oh no. It all fits.' Eadric paced up and down two or three paces and wrung his hands. 'Soon as I get away from the hall, you turn up. Apparently just off on some secret mission.'

'I am.'

'Yes, to get the tapestry. And me. It was a good idea. You probably knew I didn't have the thing myself but thought I would lead you to it. Pretend to be a harmless traveller and you might get your hands on it.'

'Master Eadric,' Firman tried to interrupt.

'Don't interrupt,' Eadric snapped, a rather wild gleam in his eye. 'For some reason, you couldn't come after me as the Hoofhorn, so you went back to the guild and came in disguise.'

'Disguise?'

'Or maybe this is you and The Hoofhorn is the disguise.' Eadric was now casting his eyes around the room as if more Hoofhorns were going to appear.

'Eadric,' Firman said in all seriousness. He caught Eadric's eyes and held them. 'I do not know what you are talking about. What guild, what Hoofhorn? What *is* a Hoofhorn? I really do not know what you are talking about.'

'That's exactly what you would say,' Eadric shot back. 'You got instructed by the master of the guild to recover the tapestry. It is rather unique, but I don't exactly know what's so important about it.'

Firman opened his mouth to speak.

'It'll come to me,' Eadric spoke mostly to himself. 'Of course you have to keep yourself secret. Can't let the guild ritual get out.'

'What guild?' Firman pleaded.

'The weavers' of course. Don't play the innocent with me.'

'The weavers' guild?'

'Who else?' Eadric spread his arms wide as if so much was blindingly obvious.

'You think you're being followed by the weavers' guild?'

'I know it!' Eadric was intense. Intense and slightly twitchy now.

'And that the guild sent a sheep to kill Virgil?' Firman kept a straight face.

Eadric's face dropped. 'Don't be stupid.' He looked at Firman as if the man was mad. 'That's ridiculous. How could the guild send a sheep to do anything? Do you know how stupid they are?'

'The guild?'

'No, the sheep. They need a dog just to make them go in the same direction. God above, Firman, are you some sort of loon?'

'Me?'

'Did you really think I'd fall for this idiot dressed in his finest who just happens to be walking the same road as me?' Eadric took a step back and appraised the man.

'I told you, I am on a mission for my family.' Firman sounded sincere.

'Oh, give it up,' Eadric scoffed. 'Travelling alone? Out here? Going to Baernodebi of all places? Just when I happen to have escaped the Hoofhorn?'

'Yes, this Hoofhorn, tell me about him, erm, it.' Firman smiled encouragement.

'You tell me,' Eadric hissed. 'Virgil gets battered to death. You're nowhere to be seen. A heap of sleeping Castigatori turn up and then you. It must be part of the ritual.' Eadric was thinking hard. 'What did you do to yourself?' He reached forwards and pinched Firman's arm.

'Ow, do you mind?' Firman brushed his sleeve where Eadric had creased it.

'Where's the beard?' Eadric peered closely at Firman's face. 'Did you shave it off or does it grow back in?'

'Father Dextus?' Firman murmured.

'It's no good calling him. I know all about you. Why don't you tell me? It's only us. You can tell me, you know. I know you're the Hoofhorn and you know you're the Hoofhorn. The others don't need to find out.'

Firman tried a loud cough.

'Of course, you don't need me anymore.' Eadric smiled broadly. 'You've got the tapestry. You took it from Virgil when you killed him. Take it. I don't want the thing anymore.' Eadric was rubbing his hands as if washing something unpleasant from them. 'Take it and go back to your master. You don't need to kill any more of us.'

Firman smiled and nodded. 'Father Dextus,' he called louder through clenched teeth.

'Oh my God, that's it!' Eadric had reached some revelation. 'You're going to cover the tracks. Make sure that no one can talk about the tapestry. You're going to kill us all. Dextus, Dextus,' Eadric shouted as he skipped back across the room to the safety of the fire.

'What?' Dextus asked without looking up.

He then looked up, saw Eadric and jumped to his feet.

'Good Lord, what is it man?' the priest cried out when he saw the look on Eadric's face.

Cwen rose as well, while Stott and Parsimon looked on from the fire.

'It's him, it's him,' Eadric yelled and pointed at Firman who simply shrugged a sympathetic shrug.

Eadric ran back to the fireside and hid behind Dextus.

'What's him?' Dextus looked from the cowering man behind him to the useless looking Firman.

'I can't say,' Eadric whined, 'he'll kill me. He's going to kill us all. Like he killed Virgil.'

'Firman?' Cwen asked, indicating that Eadric should examine the man.

'I can't say, I can't say,' Eadric howled and buried his face in his hands.

Firman stepped forward and spoke in soft and sympathetic tones. 'Poor fellow seems to think I'm some sort of creature from the weavers' guild. A Hoofhorn, whatever one of those is.'

'You know, you know,' Eadric whimpered.

'The weavers' guild?' Dextus was puzzled.

'So it seems,' Firman explained. 'Apparently they sent a sheep to kill Virgil.'

'Not a sheep,' Eadric snapped. 'I told you not a sheep. A sheep couldn't do it,' Eadric paused for a moment, 'unless it had the sword?' he speculated. 'No Eadric, you idiot. How could a sheep hold a sword? It was the Hoofhorn.'

'What is a Hoofhorn?' Cwen asked.

Eadric looked to Firman to answer.

Firman didn't answer.

'Keeper of the ritual,' Eadric almost yelled. 'There. I've said it. Ha ha. Do what you want, Hoofhorn.' He did a little dance around Dextus.

'Master Eadric, are you alright?' Cwen asked.

'Oh yes, fine now. Now it's all clear.' Eadric's voice seemed to have stuck in a higher register. 'The world must know. There's no hope for me, but you can save yourselves. The Hoofhorn is the keeper of the ritual of the weavers' guild. He has powers. Strange and mysterious powers. And he's got a sword. Bloody big sword. First you think he's a harmless old man and then he comes after you with the sword.'

'Does he?' Dextus asked quietly of the man who seemed to claim the sheep were following him, or something. Armed sheep apparently.

'And don't forget the pigeons.'

'We won't forget the pigeons,' Dextus promised, edging closer.

'They were dead!' Eadric cried in anguish. And wrung his hands, which were now well and truly wrung.

Dextus smiled. 'We can bury them,' he offered.

'Bury them?' Eadric demanded. 'Bury pigeons? You're as mad as he is.' He pointed at Firman.

'He's got the tapestry though.' Eadric nodded knowingly at them all. 'He could leave us alone and be gone. Return to his master. But he won't.'

'Won't he?' Dextus was very close now.

'Of course not. He's got to kill us all. So we never talk. Like the pigeons.'

'The pigeons could talk?' Dextus asked as calmly as he could.

Eadric stood up straight. 'What is the matter with you?' he asked the priest. 'First you want to bury the pigeons now you want to talk to them? What is it with you and pigeons?'

'What is it with you and sheep?' Dextus responded. 'Start at the beginning.'

Eadric scanned the room as if he was a lamb at a wolf reunion.

'I had to get the tapestry,' he eventually mumbled, averting his eyes.

'*You* did?' Dextus asked.

'Yes.' Eadric continued to twitch. 'The master of the guild made me do it. Only when I got to Baernodebi, Briston was already tied up. The Master hadn't given me details of the tapestry, just that Briston would know which one it was.'

'So Virgil was right, you were after Briston,' Cwen accused.

'Not now, not now,' Eadric responded looking at the tapestries on the wall as if they were ganging up on him as well.

'So I went back to the guild and the Master set the Hoofhorn on me.'

'The one with the sword?' Dextus checked.

'And the powers, don't forget the powers.' Eadric pointed a shaking finger at Firman.

'And what did this Hoofhorn do, exactly?' Dextus was contemptuous of the whole story.

'He came at me with the sword,' Eadric nodded violently.

'The Sword of Tup,' Stott spoke quietly from his fireside retreat.

They all turned to face him.

'Yes, yes,' Eadric blurted. 'The Sword of Tup. He knows, he knows.' He pointed his accusatory finger at Stott now. 'Oh my God, maybe he's one of them.' He hid behind Dextus.

'The sword is true,' the old man nodded slowly as he appraised them all. 'The Stott family has always been connected to tapestry. We've commissioned some of the finest works in the land. Naturally that gives you good access to the guild. The keeper of the guild's ritual is called The Hoofhorn and he carries the Sword of Tup. Usually for ceremonial use, but I don't suppose the sword minds one way or the other.'

'Are you saying that our rambling friend Eadric here really

is being chased by this Hoofhorn?' Dextus still didn't believe it.

'That I cannot say.' Stott was sombre. 'All I can say is that there is a Hoofhorn, or rather was.'

'Did you ever see him?' Cwen asked in some awe.

'Oh yes. The Stotts were allowed to attend some of the rituals. Only the minor stuff of course, but I saw the Hoofhorn in, oh, when was the last time? Sixty Two?'

'So it would have been the same Hoofhorn,' Cwen concluded, apparently content that there was such a being.

'Could be,' Stott acknowledged. 'It was a job for life.'

'And is Firman the Hoofhorn?'

'Good Lord, no,' Stott responded without looking. 'The Hoofhorn was an ancient old boy, beard to the floor, all rags.'

'He's shaved,' Eadric protested, 'and he's in disguise.'

No one said anything. No one seemed to have anything to say. Looks of befuddlement and sympathy crossed from face to face. Eadric wasn't going to come out from behind Dextus until Firman was dealt with.

Firman's face was the picture of befuddlement and sympathy.

Stott had relaxed back to his fire that Parsimon was tending. Dextus for once looked like he was completely out of his depth. Only Cwen was thinking about it.

'Think about it,' she prompted the company to do the same. 'Eadric was at the weavers' guild and was instructed to get the tapestry from Briston. Briston was tied up so Eadric couldn't complete the task. He goes back to the guild and the Master isn't happy. We know there is a Hoofhorn now, so the Master sets him on Eadric.'

'An old boy with a beard and all in rags?' Dextus said. 'Shouldn't be much of a problem for Eadric.'

'But he has special powers,' Cwen said in a voice labouring with intensity.

'Special powers?' Dextus almost laughed. 'What? The Hoofhorn, the pixies, and the Green Man?'

'He might have,' Cwen protested.

'No. He might not,' Dextus contradicted. 'Ghouls, ghosts and weavers' ritual keepers, none of them have special powers. There's no such thing as special powers. Believe me.'

'Mister know it all, eh?'

'No, mister done it all. The Castigatori and I have dealt with things that would scare the trousers off a four-legged man. And in none of them did we find "special powers". Came across lots of people who claimed to have special powers, of course. Lots of them. Trouble was their powers weren't special enough to stop them being castigated. One could talk to dogs, one was the son of the mountains of Wales, one was even King Arthur. None of them had enough special power to stand up to a slap around the face. Loons, all of them. If there is a Hoofhorn, and I'll take Stott's word for it that there is, he is a man. A normal man, prone to the vagaries of a normal life. Broken fingers, bleeding noses, normal.'

'But he could be after Eadric,' Cwen persisted.

'He could. And if he turns up, we can give him a bloody nose and send him on his way. He's not going to have the power to smash Virgil to a pulp. Not unless he's nine feet tall. Is he nine feet tall?' he asked Eadric.

'No,' Eadric had to admit.

'There you are then. Mister Firman is not nine feet tall either. He'd have to be *really* good at disguise.'

'But if Firman isn't the Hoofhorn, the real one could be out there. Perhaps he did in your Castigatori,' Cwen proposed.

'Ridiculous!' Dextus dismissed the suggestion.

'What was it then? What was it beat a giant to death and knocked your men into next week?' Cwen asked. 'Eh? What was it?' she asked some more.

'Not an old man in rags with a beard to the floor,' Dextus insisted.

Firman took a step towards the fire.

'I really don't know where this is getting us,' he said. 'Whatever the truth or otherwise of Mister Eadric's tale, we don't have a killer for Virgil.'

Eadric, seeing Firman approach, skipped away towards the still half-open door.

'Why were you on the road then?' he demanded in a voice with the barest hint of sanity. 'Now I've said that I was after Briston, what's your tale?'

'I've already told you,' Firman sighed.

He folded his arms as he saw that Eadric was not paying attention any more but was looking out the door.

Eadric turned to face the group. The madness had returned to his face.

'What is it?' Dextus snorted. 'The Hoofhorn?'

Eadric shook his head in despair, 'Worse,' he croaked. 'Normans.'

Caput XXVI

Once a Norman, Twice a Norman

HILE THE OCCUPANTS OF STOTT MANOR were worrying about who or what killed Virgil, not far away, Hermitage and Wat were squatting by the fire in Gilbert's keep considering a much more physical problem.

'You know,' Hermitage whispered, 'I'm not sure we should be here for the triumphant return of little Aveline.'

'Why not?' Wat whispered back. 'Take all the credit for your thinking. Besides, we need the little favour.'

'But,' Hermitage responded, holding up the fingers of his left hand to count points of interest, 'one, her father is going to ask her where she's been. And she'll say at the Bigby inn. Two, he'll ask her who she was with. She could say she was with the fat weaver who's currently sitting by the door. Three, he'll ask what she was doing. It's possible she'll say she was letting the fat weaver make rude tapestries of her. Four,...'

'He'll ask if anyone else was there,' Wat took up the count, 'and she'll say yes. The monk and that other man were there as well.'

They looked at one another.

'Five,' Wat concluded, 'he'll kill us all.'

'She might not say anything,' Hermitage offered. 'She'd be too embarrassed. Hardly the sort of thing you tell your father.'

'Oh yes? How many sixteen year olds do you know wouldn't try to blame someone else if they were in trouble? And who wouldn't say something shocking to their parent just to annoy them.'

'I don't know any sixteen year olds,' Hermitage replied,

'Well, think of yourself when you were sixteen and got into trouble.'

'Trouble?'

Wat appraised Hermitage, 'Forget it.' He gave up on the concept of Hermitage doing wrong, unless it was an accident.

'I don't think Gilbert will be keen on us leaving until his daughter is safely returned,' Hermitage suggested.

'You don't say.' Wat's scorn warmed itself by the fire.

'I do.' Hermitage was sincere. 'What are we going to do?' he squeaked. 'If we hadn't found his daughter, he'd probably have killed us just for being Saxon and not finding his daughter. Now we have found his daughter, he's going to kill us anyway.'

Wat was decisive. 'We've got to get to the daughter before he does.'

'What good will that do?'

'If we get her story straight, we can all walk away.'

'What?' Hermitage screwed his face up. 'Get her to lie?'

'Erm,' Wat paused, knowing what offence this would cause his companion. 'Yes.'

'Oh, Wat.'

'Look,' Wat explained, 'if she tells him all we've just assumed, he'll kill us, right?'

'Right,' Hermitage said, as if this was actually the correct thing to do.

'But what do you think he'll do to her afterwards? A hefty punishment, I should think. One she'd be best to avoid.'

'More likely give her a new pair of shoes to cheer her after such an awful experience?'

'Oh,' Wat said. 'Yes, could be. Not much incentive to keep quiet then. Bugger.' He lapsed into thought again.

They peered at the fire, hoping it might inspire them. Or perhaps leap out and burn Gilbert to death.

'I've had an idea,' Wat said in some shock.

'Go on.'

'It's awful.'

'I rather thought it might be.'

'No, I mean really awful. It's sinful and just horrible.'

'I don't suppose there's any chance of you keeping it to yourself?' Hermitage asked.

'I don't think I can. You'll need to know so you can play your part, and then you can pray for the forgiveness we'll need.'

'Wat,' Hermitage said. 'I have seen the sort of tapestries you do. You make them and I've looked at them. I'm already praying for our forgiveness.'

'Ah,' Wat smiled. 'That's good then, I suppose.'

'Just tell me what it is, for goodness' sake,' Hermitage was resigned to hearing it. 'If it stops us getting killed, I suppose it might have its merits.'

Wat told him.

'Wat, that's awful!' Hermitage breathed in some awe that a human mind could come up with such things.

After a few hurried and shameful whispers, Wat stood.

'Excuse me, my Lord.'

'What is it?' Gilbert called from the corner where he was sharpening his sword.

'Where's the privy?' Wat asked.

'Over there,' Gilbert gestured to the corner of the keep opposite Aveline's cot.

'No, I, erm, mean the, erm, garderobe.' Wat sounded embarrassed.

Gilbert snorted, probably at such soft civility. 'Bottom of the mound,' he said, 'Aveline made us move it outside.'

'Thanks, back in a bit.' Wat scurried from the room, bypassing Briston but giving him a warning stare as he went.

✦　　✦　　✦

The return of the lady Aveline was an event of considerable moment. The horseman despatched for the task had clearly set about it with a will. He was returning through the stockade gate just as Wat got to the bottom of the hill.

The Lady Aveline was not happy.

Everyone knew that the Lady Aveline was not happy.

Even the horse that brought her home knew she was not happy.

The Norman on the horse had taken some pleasure in throwing Aveline over its neck and holding her there with a mailed glove. The grin on the man's face said that this was the sort of opportunity he'd been praying for. The horse's flanks told it not to go near the small human in the frock ever again. The long dress made it look as if Aveline had no feet at all. The horse knew different.

'Come on then, my lady,' the Norman horseman called as he brought his reluctant beast to a halt. He swung himself from the saddle and dragged the lady down. As he did so, he accidentally cuffed her round the head with his mailed glove.

'Oh, pardon me,' he said, clearly not asking to be pardoned at all.

The Lady Aveline stamped and fumed like the horse. Wat almost expected to see steam rising from her head. He really didn't want to talk to her at all, but his life was on the line.

'You,' the Lady Aveline spat as she saw Wat approach.

'Lady Aveline, as I now know. I need a word with you before you see your father.'

'My father cuts people's heads off, you know,' Aveline said, looking at Wat's head and assessing the level of force required to remove it. She also gave encompassing glances to the Norman and the horse.

'I'm sure he does, and that's what I need to talk about.'

Wat got as near to Lady Aveline as he dared and whispered urgently.

In the face of Wat's whispered onslaught, the lady's face remained as stern as the back of a boat. The hissing words were accompanied by a variety of gestures and indications. At one point, Wat stepped back slightly and used his hands to indicate the entirety of the lady's person. He then pointedly looked around the stockade and noted several of the Norman soldiers milling around. Finally he looked to the keep and shrugged a shrug of helplessness.

During the tirade, if tirades can be delivered in low voices, Aveline's face transformed. From affronted innocent about to do harm, or rather instruct someone else to do it, she went as pale as a bucket and her mouth fell open. She too looked at the soldiers milling about and then at the keep.

'You wouldn't,' she said without really closing her mouth properly.

Wat simply shrugged and nodded. Whatever it was she thought he wouldn't do, he was reluctantly confirming that actually, yes, he would.

A calculation seemed to pass across her face, but it was a short journey. The lady stiffened and her mouth now clamped shut, forming a very straight line. She gave Wat a look she had clearly inherited from her father, picked up her skirts, and made for the keep.

Wat followed close at heel, anxiously appraising Aveline's face and posture to see if he could read her intentions. They weren't friendly but then that seemed normal.

At the top of the mound, she threw the doors of the keep open, nearly taking Briston completely out of the picture.

'Aveline,' Gilbert cried out and strode through the smoky murk to embrace his daughter.

The daughter stood and took the embrace, much like a stinking dog takes a bath. She allowed a kiss on each cheek and then stood as stiff as a day-old corpse and folded her arms.

'I haven't decided if I'm staying yet,' she said.

'Where have you been?' Gilbert asked. It wasn't clear whether he was ignoring his daughter or was simply too pleased to see her.

Wat held his breath. Hermitage looked at Wat holding his breath and held his breath. Briston rubbed his head and looked in alarm at the woman who'd come closest to removing his need for it. He gaped at Wat in genuine alarm. Wat gestured him to silence.

'I've been to the town,' Aveline grumbled.

'Why? What's the town got that we haven't?' Gilbert held his arms wide to indicate the magnificence of his surroundings.

'Other people. People who aren't all soldiers. People who don't spend their days in conversation with their horses. People who laugh and talk about clothes and things. People who go to the tavern and hear stories. Travelling merchants with wild and exciting adventures.'

If Wat and Hermitage could have done, they would have held some more of their breath.

'I know what happens to girls who mix with merchants. They come to a sorry end. And if my girl mixes with a merchant, the merchant will come to a sorry end as well.'

'Oh, don't worry about me,' Aveline whined.

Wat and Hermitage breathed again.

'I'm back again, aren't I? Back in this hole on a hill, just one of the many I've been dragged around. Back to lead a dull and pointless life with a bunch of dull and pointless soldiers, who wouldn't know how to treat a lady if they found one lying in a ditch. Mind you,' she said and strode off towards her cot, 'women lying in ditches are probably all they do know. I'm a lady now and I'm not going to stand for it. What on earth do we have to have a fire in the middle of the room for when we've got no chimney? Have you seen the state of my clothes? And we're not having the privy in here anymore. You can get a pot like town folk do, and clear it out every morning. And another thing…'

The voice of the lady droned on, expressing its deep and heartfelt dissatisfaction with everything and everyone about her.

The look on Gilbert's face, which had been one of joy at the recovery of his daughter, was now one of recollection of what it had actually been like when his daughter was here. He sighed and followed, mumbling the odd "yes and "no" as required.

He glanced up at Wat and Hermitage, who detected a faint ghost of regret on his face. A look that said the man would rather be facing a host of Saxon rebels than a single dissatisfied daughter.

Wat raised his eyebrows and nodded, trying to indicate that everything was well, now that the place was back to normal. He tipped his head towards the door, like grandparents leaving the house just as the baby has started to cry. Gilbert gave them a shrug that said that he'd really rather be going with them, but he nodded them a goodbye with his thanks. These particular thanks were rather less ebullient than they had been when the prospect of his daughter's return was just a prospect.

Wat made a collection of gestures to confirm that the favour was still on. Gilbert nodded once more and went over, as requested, to examine the appalling state of Aveline's shoes, which, for goodness' sake, had only been there two days and now look at them.

Closing the great doors behind them, Briston still rubbing his head, the complaints of the lady rose to such a pitch that they brushed the woodwork aside and went straight for the irritation centre of the male brain. Even Hermitage shuddered.

Down at the bottom of the mound, amongst the soldiers and their horses, Wat looked for what he'd been promised.

'Ricard?' he asked of the first man he saw.

This man gestured him towards the makeshift stables, which were actually better constructed and more comfortable than the keep.

Hermitage looked at them and wondered if Aveline didn't have a point.

A large Norman was tending a large horse inside the generous space.

'Ricard?' Wat repeated.

'What?' The large man turned to face them.

They all paused for a moment, Gilbert had kept his promise: this man was the biggest, scariest looking Norman any of them had ever seen.

Even his horse looked ready for a fight.

Caput XXVII

To the Manor Shorn

HE OCCUPANTS OF STOTT MANOR gathered around its rather tattered doors and looked out. Actually, they peeped and peered out, subconsciously hoping that if their heads couldn't be seen, they wouldn't get cut off. If the Normans were coming.

'Where's the rest of them?' Dextus asked as he surveyed the approaching figure.

'Don't tell me you can't see him?' Eadric sounded worried. 'Maybe I really am going mad.' He rubbed his eyes.

'Yes, I can see *him*,' Dextus was rather dismissive. 'What I can't see is any others. I can see a Norman, not Normans. I see one Norman on a horse, riding rather slowly and looking rather bored.'

'But still,' Eadric encouraged alarm, 'a Norman!'

'I think we can deal with one Norman on a horse.' Dextus dismissed the alarm and turned back into the room.

The others followed in both relief that this wasn't a horde of Normans, and disappointment that Eadric had raised the alarm unnecessarily.

'He's a pretty massive and scary looking Norman,' Eadric commentated from the door as the Norman got closer. There was no response. 'And his horse looks really cross.'

'We'll give it some hay,' Dextus suggested. 'That'll cheer it up. And if we throw you to the Norman, perhaps that'll cheer him up.'

'A horse!' Cwen called out.

'Yes, know it?' Dextus replied. 'Large animal, used for transport?'

267

'Really? I never knew that,' Cwen's sarcasm rolled back. 'I mean, a horse could have done Virgil in, not a sheep.'

'Ah yes?' Dextus did not sound convinced.

'Of course. Hard hooves, kick a man like Virgil to death in no time.'

'Quite big, this horse then?' Dextus enquired.

'Oh yes,' Cwen was enthusiastic. 'Just like the one the Norman's on. And we all know that if there's a dead Saxon, there's going to be a live Norman not far away.'

Dextus looked at her with the thoughts making visible tracks across his face. He turned to the door to consider the Norman and horse now approaching. Eventually he reached a conclusion. 'We may have our killer then,' he said, in a rather odd tone.

Cwen beamed and searched the room for approbation.

'Yes,' Dextus went on, 'the large horse that climbed down the chimney into the cellar kicked Virgil to death, laid the body out, stole the tapestry, and then made off with Firman. All without so much as a whinny.'

'Perhaps Firman climbed on.' Cwen defended her assumption.

'Firman?' Dextus enquired. 'Did you climb on a large horse in the cellar after it kicked Virgil to death?'

'No,' Firman said without having to think about it much.

'The horse that then climbed back up the chimney with you on its back?'

'Definitely not.'

'Oh dear,' Dextus said in mock disappointment.

'It could have gone out through the hole in the wall,' Cwen insisted. 'I know horses can't climb chimneys, I'm not stupid.'

'Maybe it ate the tapestry thinking it was forage?'

'Could be,' Cwen nodded.

'Interesting,' Dextus rubbed his chin in thought. 'However, I think I would have to disagree with you on one key point,' he reasoned.

'Which is?'

'You *are* stupid. A horse did not lay Virgil out on the table. We heard no horses. They go clip clop when they move about. We heard no goats and no sheep. We haven't tried a pig yet. They seem quite popular in this business. And I'm told they're quite intelligent. Not quite made it into the tapestry business yet though.'

'Alright,' Cwen grumbled.

'I mean pigs can be pretty vindictive beasts.'

'Yes, yes.' Cwen had given up.

'Perhaps we could find reference in the Bible to them being great despisers of tapestry, sent forth by the Lord to wreak havoc on weavers of evil.'

'There's no need to go on.'

'After our Lord forced the demon named Legion into the pigs and they drowned, they came back to life as a massive scourge of tapestry.'

Dextus folded his arms.

'There are no animals in my cellar,' Stott insistently mumbled. 'No sheep, horses, pigs, cattle, nothing. This is a manor house, not a farm.'

The debate on the homicidal proclivities of the farmyard had taken their minds off the approaching Norman, and so there was general surprise when a heavy, pounding knock shook the door. This was not the sort of knock that enquired if entry was possible. This was the knock of someone who wanted the door taken out of their way. Someone who expected the door to be taken out of their way. Quickly.

The company exchanged glances before Dextus acknowledged that he was the one who was going to get the door.

'Hello,' a friendly cheerful voice called as a figure squeezed through the door.

'Wat!' Cwen called and ran over to the weaver. They embraced and Wat lifted the girl from the ground, swinging her round in joy at seeing her still alive.

'Told you,' Briston snorted, as he forced his bulk through the doorway.

Wat put Cwen down and the two of them looked away from one another as if any expression of mutual interest was entirely coincidental.

'I'm erm, glad to see that you're still alive,' Wat said.

'Thank you. I'm pleased that your journey was completed satisfactorily.'

'Thank you.'

'Don't mention it.'

Hermitage now entered the room, his slim frame having no trouble at all with the hanging door. He took in the assembly.

Stott and Parsimon still by the fire as if nothing had changed.

Eadric on his own in a corner of the room, which seemed a bit odd.

Firman was with Dextus and the Castigatori were piled up on the floor as if nothing had changed for them either.

He scanned the room and frowned. As he opened his mouth to speak, the door moved. It moved completely off its hinges and came to rest on a pile of peculiar pewter.

'I say,' Stott said.

The figure of Ricard strode into the room and he looked around as he pulled his massive mailed gloves off.

Hermitage looked through the entrance to see where his horse had gone after it had kicked the door down. The horse was grazing some way off. He looked at Ricard's metal boot and the metal boot-shaped indentation in the door.

'This is Ricard,' Wat said, introducing the huge Norman to the rest of the room. The rest of the room nodded politely at the huge Norman, his gloves, his sword, his dagger, and his armour plating. 'I borrowed him.'

'Borrowed him?' Dextus clearly found this concept too much. 'You borrowed a Norman?'

The Norman growled. Dextus tried smiling, but it didn't come out right.

'Yes, we were able to do a favour for a local Norman, Lord Gilbert? Do you know him? Nice chap. Lovely daughter.' Wat laid his good relations with the Normans on very thick indeed. Entirely for Dextus's benefit.

'Why did you borrow a Norman?' Cwen asked, also having trouble with the idea.

'To deal with Virgil,' Wat grinned. 'I mean, who better? I've bought Briston as well but we'd already found him. I was worried what Virgil's going to do when we hand him over so I borrowed Ricard. I'm sure he'd stick his sword in Virgil if we asked nicely.' He caught Cwen's eyes and held them, his voice dropping into serious huskiness. 'And I half suspected he would have already killed you. So I brought Ricard along to finish him off.'

Cwen's eyes held Wat's close and the world fell into silence.

Ricard coughed as he rested his hand on his sword and looked at the company as if he was ready to stick the thing in any of them. Or all of them.

'Where is Virgil?' Wat asked as he dragged his attention away from Cwen. His frown said he couldn't understand why the cause of all their trouble would be missing.

Hermitage looked around the room. The cause had gone and the cause's three men had gone with him. The unconscious Castigatori were one thing, but if Virgil had gone out for something, visit the privy perhaps, why weren't his men guarding Cwen? And if Virgil and his men had gone, why hadn't everyone just run away?

Had some other business come up that required Virgil's presence? It seemed unlikely. From the little Hermitage had seen of the man, he was very committed. And what were all these bars and shutters doing on windows and doors.

'He's dead,' Hermitage announced. 'Isn't he?'

'How?' Cwen's surprise stopped her finishing the sentence.

'He's not here. His men aren't here. We've only really been gone one night and he'd hardly be likely to go off and do something else when he was supposed to be holding you. You've barricaded the windows and doors, which could have been for Virgil to keep you all in, but the door was open. You locked yourselves up all night to keep something out.' he paused for a concluding thought. 'Virgil isn't here. He would hardly leave so you could lock him out. Therefore the something you locked out killed Virgil.'

'Very good!' Dextus was genuinely impressed.

'Or perhaps he's incapacitated?' Hermitage added.

'Where is he?' Wat looked around the room as if the giant lunatic was hiding and the whole thing was some bizarre parlour game.

'He is dead,' Cwen confirmed.

Wat looked at her. 'No, come on, where is he?'

'Dead,' Dextus nodded.

'Dead?' Wat was still disbelieving.

'I think that's what three separate people have told you so far,' Dextus calculated.

Wat looked to Stott, Parsimon, Eadric, and Firman. They all gave him nods of confirmation.

'Dead,' Wat said, still in disbelief, but it was now accepting disbelief. 'He can't be.' The words were those of someone who's just been told their favourite dog is dead when he was only chasing sticks half an hour ago.

'Why's that then?' Dextus asked.

'I don't know,' Wat came to his senses rather. 'He was just too, well, big.'

'And big people don't die?'

'Not easily.'

'Oh, he didn't die easily, believe me.'

'Did you do it?'

'Me?' Dextus was flattered. 'My Castigatori and I couldn't

knock a hole in his hat, let alone do him to death. You can see the body if you like, smashed to pieces from the inside out by the look of him. Your Brother Hermitage is right. Whatever did it was outside and we barricaded ourselves in.'

'To avoid it?' Wat was disparaging.

'Wouldn't you? A thing that could beat Virgil to death?'

Wat thought again, 'Good point.'

'You know what this means,' he added as an afterthought. 'I borrowed a Norman for nothing.'

'Oh, I don't know,' Briston piped up. 'He could still come in handy.' He nodded his head to indicate Dextus.

Everyone looked at him.

Stott rose and spoke, having just focussed on the man who was now in his hall, 'You sir, are the cause of all this trouble.'

'Well, I don't know about that,' Briston answered, rather proud of himself.

'I do. You are the wretch who did that appalling tapestry of my dear Lorinda. Who brought monks and the like into my home. Who made that ghastly giant man come here to cause wrack and ruin, to drink my wine and get himself killed in my cellar. To get my door knocked off and my pewter bent.'

Briston shrugged.

'If I've been paying attention, I gather Father Dextus here wants a word with you. Well I say let him carry on and please God it's the last one you ever hear.'

'Now then, now then,' Briston said, trying to calm the conversation. 'Let's not get carried away.'

'Yes, let's,' Dextus said. 'I'll wake the Castigatori and they can carry you away. And Wat,' he added with a pointed stare.

Wat and Cwen were still examining the backs of one another's eyeballs, but the weaver came round when he heard his name.

'We'd better have a look at Virgil,' he said.

'Why?' Dextus asked.

273

'Curiosity?'

Dextus frowned as if calculating what it was Wat was up to. 'Hmmm, alright,' he said.

He gave his Castigatori gentle kicks, as if they shouldn't lay there unconscious all day. He beckoned towards the cellar door. Stott and Parsimon indicated they'd had enough of looking at dead Virgil. Ricard stood like a statue, seemingly unaware and uninterested in what was going on around him. He eventually noticed the fire and moved to stand near that. He unsheathed his sword, dug its point in the floor, and rested his hands on the top, like some knight, carved into the lid of his own tomb.

The others looked at him in some puzzlement about why he would want to just stand there like that. Even Hermitage realised that a huge Norman with a sword could do pretty much anything he liked.

Though Cwen, Eadric, and Firman had already seen the body, they joined the viewing as Dextus led the way past the table that had been upended as a barrier across the door. Once down the steps again, Dextus held his arm out to show dead Virgil on his slab.

'Well, I never,' Wat breathed, now accepting that the man really was dead. 'What a mess.'

Virgil *was* a mess now. All the damage done to his body had come out to show the world. The giant's blood had clearly stopped pumping and so the bruises were starting to fade. This still left them very widespread and visible.

Swellings, which in life would have been debilitating in themselves, were now simple lumps and bumps. The problem was Virgil had a very big body and every single bit of it appeared to have a lump or a bump. Sometimes both.

'Who could have done this?' Wat breathed, clearly impressed.

'That's what we wondered,' Dextus replied. 'We've been through most of the animal kingdom without an answer.' He raised his eyebrows at Cwen.

'Still,' Wat said, who was smiling thoughtfully.

'Still what?' Dextus asked after there was no further word from Wat.

The weaver looked up from his thought and shrugged, 'Who or what killed Virgil, eh?'

'Yes?'

'Who cares? The man's dead. Nobody liked him. Good riddance.'

'Wat!' Hermitage reprimanded his friend. 'The man still had an eternal soul and he has been murdered.'

'He certainly has. Not sure about his eternal soul though.'

'We must not speak ill of the dead.'

'Why not? We all spoke ill of him when he was alive. I should think it bothers him a lot less now.'

'That's not the point. We will all go where he has gone. What do we want people to say about us?'

'Doesn't really matter.'

'It certainly does. If people are thinking ill of you after your death, your soul will suffer. Earnest prayer will see you enter paradise. You really don't want to consider the alternative.'

'As far as Virgil's concerned, the alternative is all he deserves.'

'Hear, hear,' Briston chimed in.

'Forgiveness,' Hermitage suggested and instructed at the same time.

Wat simply rolled his eyes at such an apparently stupid idea.

'Come on then,' Dextus interrupted. 'You've seen he's dead. Time to go.'

'Was Virgil found like this?' Hermitage asked.

'We're hardly likely to try and move him,' Dextus replied.

'Then we have a mystery,' Hermitage concluded. 'A murder by person or persons unknown. We should investigate.' Hermitage was sure about this. Having dealt with murders, deaths, and dead bodies – which turned out to be pigs – he knew this sort of thing needed resolution. More than that, he knew that he needed to resolve it. He could not leave things unanswered. It would be like leaving a parable uninterpreted. Unbearable. It would rankle and wrinkle inside him. He had to know.

'It's as the weaver says,' Dextus stepped into Hermitage's reverie. 'Who cares?'

'Who cares?' Hermitage was horrified at such things coming from the mouth of a priest. In his short acquaintance with Dextus, he was beginning to wonder if the man really was a priest.

'Could have been one of Virgil's many enemies coming to finish him off. If the bad men kill other bad men, we can but rejoice.'

Hermitage gaped. This was appalling.

'Come on,' Dextus pressed. 'Wat and Briston here have appointments.'

'Ah,' Wat said. 'About that. I'm so sorry but I don't think we're going to be able to make it,' he said as if he was reluctantly declining an invitation to dine.

'Very funny,' Dextus was all seriousness now.

'No really. You see, this great big Norman, you know, the one upstairs with the great big sword? He sort of looks after us now. Lord Gilbert, I did mention him, didn't I? Well, Lord Gilbert sent young Ricard with us to make sure no harm befell us. After we'd done our little favour for him.' Wat shrugged, 'What can I say?'

Dextus was dismissive. 'I think my bishop takes your knight,' he said simply. 'After all, he's a Norman bishop now. Probably sends knights to hell every day of the week.'

Wat was still polite and explanatory. 'Yet, your bishop is so far away and our knight is right upstairs. With his sword. I did cover the sword, didn't I?'

'Oh, I'm sure the Castigatori can discuss the matter with your knight. He may be big but he's still not a patch on Virgil, is he?'

Hermitage was looking backwards and forwards, unable to comprehend how these people had their priorities so wrong.

'There has been a murder,' he spoke up, unnecessarily pointing out Virgil's dead body. 'Murder! Someone has been killed. Done to death!'

All these horrible phrases seemed to have no impact on his audience. They were all quite pleased the murder had been committed. Awful. He considered his duty, physical and spiritual. He thought about what was expected of him, as a devout monk and as... ah, yes, he remembered what he was.

'I am the King's Investigator,' he announced, 'and I think that beats a bishop and a knight. This act of evil must be resolved.'

The group in the cellar looked at him as if humouring a rambling loon.

'No, really,' Hermitage tried to sound serious. 'Whatever did this might still be out there, ready to do it again.' No reaction. 'To one of you?' This did provoke a bit of a reaction, but still not much.

'I insist we remain here to determine who the killer was and bring them to justice.' He did the most serious, insistent voice he could.

No one took any notice.

'It's all right, sir monk,' a new voice boomed from the hole in the wall at the back of the cellar. 'I did it.'

Caput XXVIII

Aha!

 SAY!' FIRMAN WAS THE FIRST TO SPEAK as the new arrival strode into the cellar. 'Who are you? Clear off. This is a private murder.'

Firman strode towards the man, trying to shoo him out of the hole in the wall he'd come through.

'It's alright,' the man held up placatory hands. 'It needs to be made clear.'

He came close to Firman and clapped him on both shoulders.

'I,' Hermitage started. 'What?' he continued after a pause for thought. He looked back to the cellar steps and to the man. This did not fit his expectations and he was unable to function while he waited for his mind to catch up with reality. It was a familiar feeling.

'It's alright, Brother,' the man nodded. 'I saw you and friend Wat arrive with Briston. When I overheard Father Dextus's plans, I thought it only reasonable to make myself known.' He nodded a greeting to the others in the room, most of whom looked from him to Hermitage for some sort of explanation.

'I appreciate your concern for the unbearable Virgil here and you are right. The mystery of his murder must be resolved.'

Hermitage was grateful for this support.

'But your colleagues are right as well. He was an evil man who would have come to his end by foul means at some time or other.'

'But why?' Hermitage asked, now that he could speak again.

'Would you mind telling me just who the hell this is?' Dextus demanded of Hermitage in a most unpriestly way.

Hermitage looked to the man, who nodded assent.

He then looked all around the room to check no one could overhear. Apart from the six people with him. He gathered them into a huddle.

'This,' he announced, 'is Hamard.'

The huddle broke up.

'Who?' Dextus was unimpressed.

'Hamard Godwin,' Hermitage concluded.

Everyone in the room gasped and took a step back, except Firman who was still standing with Hamard.

'It's alright,' Hamard held out calming hands. 'I know the family has a bit of a reputation. Harold's fault really, but we're not all like that.'

'The Godwins,' Dextus confirmed. 'And the Godwinsons!' His face was rather pale. 'Not the same Godwins who put King Edward on the throne and Harold there after him? The Harold who fought off the Danes? Not all completely ruthless killers then,' he swallowed his words quickly and clamped a hand over his mouth to stop any more coming out.

'Really,' Hamard was calm and polite. 'I assure you there's no need to worry about me. Is there, Firman?'

'Absolutely not,' Firman confirmed.

'Firman?' Eadric enquired, hesitating and nervous, 'Firman Godwin?'

'Godwinson actually. Cousin on my mother's side.'

'God preserve us.' Eadric crossed himself vigorously. 'So you weren't just travelling to Lincoln?'

'Oh, I was, that's all true. Family business, exactly as I said. The business being to try and keep the remaining members of the family alive. And I have to travel alone as people don't want to be seen with Godwinsons these days.'

'And you can take care of yourself anyway.'

'There is that,' Firman acknowledged.

'But Mister Hamard is a scholar,' Hermitage argued. 'He's not a Godwin like the others. He studies the workings of the body.'

'And probably how to break them,' Dextus added.

'Firman and I have gone our own way. Why do you think we're not lying on Hastings field at the moment? Or rather six feet underneath it? The main family wouldn't have anything to do with us anymore. Gone soft, they said.' Hamard and Firman exchanged smiles.

'But...' Hermitage started. This time his thoughts had run so far ahead of his mouth that the words weren't in the right order to make sense. Also a common experience.

'Why did I kill Virgil?'

'Erm, yes.' Hermitage was grateful.

'I would have to say that I didn't do it all by myself.'

'Firman,' said Eadric.

Firman acknowledged his role with a gentlemanly bow.

'Even though the Godwins are brought up for this sort of thing, Virgil was a big fellow. One of us would have done the job eventually but two was quicker. The Godwins always work well as a team.'

'Not ruthless killers at all then,' Dextus mumbled.

'But he was enormous,' Cwen breathed. 'And you're not exactly, erm, you know.'

'Not built like Ricard the Norman upstairs?' Hamard gave Cwen a friendly smile.

'Well, yes.'

'But we are Godwins.' Hamard exchanged a knowing look with his cousin, knowing and poignantly reluctant. 'It's the sort of thing we were brought up with. The family trade, if you will. Strike first, strike fast, and strike until they stop moving. As my old mother used to say, "A man will more readily give you what you want if he's unconscious." I would have to say Virgil did take quite a lot of our attention. Most impressive. But he succumbed in the end. They all do.'

'So you came in through the hole in the wall, attacked and killed Virgil and then left again to run around all night banging on the walls, scaring the life out of us?' asked Cwen.

'We had to stop those monk fellows as well,' Hamard observed as if the Castigatori were a spot of light weeding.

'You would have killed us all,' Cwen shrieked slightly at the realisation. 'Cover your tracks and get away clear.'

'Only out of necessity, I assure you,' Hamard excused himself. 'It was nothing personal.'

'That makes me feel a lot better.'

'But then I saw Briston and Mister Wat come back with our friend Brother Hermitage.'

'You're welcome,' Hermitage said, although he didn't know why, as it made no sense.

'The young monk is an erudite fellow and a like mind. I couldn't possibly kill any friends of his.'

'Very kind, I'm sure,' Wat spoke up.

'Why would you want to kill anyone?' Hermitage asked, thoroughly unable to make sense of any of this. His reasoning was flapping around like a fresh trout in a frying pan. He had lots of facts but couldn't get them into any recognisable shape.

'I won't take all the credit. Mister Briston gave me the idea.'

'Me?' Briston stopped his sneaky sidle towards the staircase. 'Nothing to do with me, I assure you. I didn't even know he was a Godwin. I only left a message with him, for goodness' sake.'

'Ah, but it was a very interesting message. About your Tapestry of Death.'

'Ha! Trust Briston to blab his mouth off.'

'I didn't say anything,' Briston pleaded.

'Just enough, I'm afraid. The idea that you had made a tapestry that could scare off your enemies was fascinating.'

'It's rubbish,' Wat explained. 'There's no such thing as the Tapestry of Death.'

'Briston believed there was and so I had to look. As you can imagine, we have a lot of enemies in the country at the moment. Brother Hermitage was kind enough to suggest I keep my surname to myself to avoid the attention of the Normans. It was a charming thing to say.'

'How lovely,' Dextus sneered.

'It saved your life, priest,' Hamard said. His tone of voice, his manner, everything about him changed in those five short words: from harmless to a Godwin of the blood. Hamard took a short breath, tamed the animal and smiled. 'When I had the tapestry itself, I saw how it worked.'

They breathed again as the friendly Hamard was back.

'See,' Briston gloated. 'It does work.'

'Right.' Wat did not see.

'Let me show you,' Hamard said, pulling the thing from a pack across his back.

They stepped back as the familiar sight of Lady Stott spread across the table.

'Oh, my goodness me,' Hermitage stepped back and averted his eyes. 'Is that really necessary? I mean, is any of it really necessary? At all? I mean,' he sneaked a look back, 'I can see why poor Master Stott was so upset. That is the most appalling thing. I've seen some of Briston's other work, but this really is the most revolting object. Demeaning, insulting and just plain foul. How could you?' He turned his gaze to Briston. He felt the power of his glare return.

'She made it!' Briston pointed defensively at Cwen.

'Cwen?' Hermitage was shocked, horrified, and appalled all at once.

'He made me,' Cwen muttered, pointing back at Briston.

'I don't really care who did what. The whole thing is just, well, it's... Words fail me.'

'It's brilliant,' Wat breathed.

Hermitage looked in even more appalled shock to see his friend examining the piece closely.

'Told you,' Briston gloated again.

'Oh, Briston,' Wat was all admiration. 'I see what you've done here. It's marvellous.'

'It is, isn't it? I got the idea from old Screpton down Grantham way.'

'The one who liked the nuns and the antlers?'

'That's him, wanted me to keep everything quiet.'

'They usually do. Ah,' recognition came to Wat, 'I see.'

'Of course,' Briston nodded. He and Wat clearly understood one another. Everyone else in the room looked around, hoping they weren't the only one who wanted to ask what the hell was going on.

Briston held his arm out to encompass his mighty work. 'You see this fellow at the front?' he asked, as if he was conducting a guided tour of the Roman ruins in Lincoln.

The group leaned forward and examined the man who was next in line to engage with lady Stott. Very closely engaged with her by the manner in which he was preparing himself. Even Hermitage stole a glance. He had to admit the character was most lifelike – if he ignored the bits of life no one should talk about really, let alone see.

The man was large, he was facing the viewer, and every line and mark on his face was clear. He was old, about fifty probably, far too old to be getting up to anything like that. His head was bald save for wisps of grey hair. A close trimmed grey beard adorned his chin.

Briston explained. 'The Bishop of Dorchester,' he said.

Hermitage looked around to see if the bishop had entered the room.

'No, Hermitage,' Wat pointed at the tapestry. 'That's the Bishop of Dorchester. Even anatomically correct, if what I hear is true.'

'Spot on,' Briston confirmed.

Hermitage had never met the Bishop of Dorchester and so wouldn't recognise him anyway. He was positive he wouldn't recognise him naked and doing what he appeared to be doing.

'Look,' Wat enthused, 'he's even got a little bishop's mitre in his hand.'

'Just to make sure people get the message,' Briston commented.

'But,' Hermitage said. It was the only word he could get out at that moment. He had lots of words for questions constantly running round his head, ready for action at any moment. The problem was none of them had been trained to ask about naked bishops in tapestries.

'Why is the Bishop of Dorchester in the tapestry?' he eventually got out.

'Very good customer, the bishop,' Wat explained. 'Very particular interests. Peculiar as well.' he frowned as some thoughts about the bishop forced their way into his head. 'But discreet, of course, can't let the common folk know the sorts of things the bishop likes. They might drag him from his pulpit and hang him.'

Hermitage looked at the tapestry and wondered if that might not actually be for the best. He chided himself for thinking ill of anyone, let alone a bishop.

'And don't forget the Normans,' Wat prompted.

'What about them?' Hermitage asked, looking round again to see if any Normans had come along.

'We know their views on this sort of thing,' Wat explained. 'Gilbert had Briston run out of town. At least we now know why he chose this moment to vanish. Very funny bunch the Normans, not like the Godwins before them.' He nodded to Firman and Hamard, who acknowledged with a smile. And not a guilty smile, either. 'Very broad minded, the Godwins,' Wat said with a rather lewd tone to his voice. 'Not so broad minded, the Normans. If they found out their bishop was a customer for this sort of thing, well, they'd probably... what do you think they'd do, Dextus?' Wat directed the question at the priest. Dextus glared back and refused to answer.

'That's right,' Wat said. 'They'd kill him. Horribly and slowly. And then they'd have a jolly good purge of the church. They like a purge, the Normans. No wonder Dextus and his Castigatori got sent to find the tapestry. Briston blabbing again. Didn't think the very subjects of your work would have a go at removing it from the world, along with its maker?'

Briston shrugged, 'Calculated risk.'

'So,' Hermitage paused for a spot of reasoning. 'Whoever had the tapestry could hold the bishop to ransom. Hamard will be able to say "Leave me alone or I'll show my tapestry to the Normans".'

'Who will kill you,' Briston concluded. 'See, Tapestry of Death. Ta da!'

Hermitage wasn't satisfied this was enough, 'But that's only the Bishop of Dorchester. I'm not sure why Hamard would be worried about him anyway.'

'Always good to have friends in high places,' Hamard noted. 'Even better if you hold their life in your hands. They're so much more cooperative.'

'Look at the rest of the tapestry, Hermitage,' Wat encouraged.

'I'd rather not. I thought the thing was revolting in the first place. Now I see it has a whole new layer of sin beneath its surface.'

Wat ignored him. 'You see the men queuing up for the lady?'

'I can hardly ignore a long line of naked men.'

'And neither would anyone else.' Wat bent to examine the scene. He picked out individual figures. 'That's the Earl of Leicester, here's Robert de Beaumont. My goodness, is that Le Pedvin, William's man?'

'Yup!' Briston was smug. 'Only been in the country a few months and already falling into bad habits.'

'Good God. Imagine if the King found out.'

'I have,' Briston grinned.

Wat peered very closely and stuck a finger on one small naked man towards the back of the queue. 'That's not?' he said.

'It is,' Briston grinned. 'I told you. Would you believe me? Oh no. Stupid Briston. Tapestry of Death? What nonsense. Now who's laughing?'

Wat shook his head in admiration.

'Who is it?' Hermitage peered in.

'Master of the weavers' guild,' Wat snorted. 'I never knew he was that way inclined.'

'One of the country's leading authorities, apparently,' Briston commented.

Those in the know looked at Eadric, who had the decency to examine the floor quite closely.

'I think the Normans would be particularly keen to get hold of him after seeing this,' Wat said as he examined the picture. 'I mean, they're very fond of horses, but not in that way.'

The analysis of the tapestry died down to a few mumbles and close examination.

'Well,' Hamard said. 'I'm glad this has been so very educational. You can see now why the tapestry is so valuable and why I have to take it away.'

Dextus took half a step forward.

'I wouldn't,' Hamard said, laughing slightly at the priest's intentions. 'Really, I wouldn't.'

Dextus looked at Firman and Hamard and thought better of it.

'Well, it's been lovely,' Hamard said, as he rolled up the tapestry and made for the hole in the wall with Firman behind him. 'Don't hesitate to drop by if you're passing. And do mention the tapestry to your friends. The more who know about it the better.'

With that, they were gone.

'Well,' Hermitage said, as if the whole experience had been very exciting.

'Well, well, well,' Wat said, marvelling at the revelations that had come thick and fast.

'Well?' Cwen asked, wanting to know what they did next.

There was a clatter at the top of the stairs and three bleary eyed Castigatori stumbled into the cellar.

'You're a bit late,' Dextus chastised.

Wat and Briston sniggered.

Dextus turned his eye on them. 'Take these two to the bishop,' he instructed.

No Cunning, No Plan

ERMITAGE WAS LOST FOR WORDS as the Castigatori scuttled into the room and took Briston and Wat by the arms. Words never stayed away from Hermitage for long.

'What are you doing?' he demanded.

Cwen tried pushing the nearest castigator away, but all she succeeded in doing was bouncing off the man.

Eadric stood off to one side, fascinated by some of the barrels Stott had, and by the stone work of the cellar walls, and the beams of the ceiling.

Dextus looked very puzzled. 'I'm taking them to the bishop, of course,' he said, clearly wondering why Hermitage couldn't grasp this simple fact.

'You can't,' Hermitage insisted.

Dextus looked around the room, 'Erm, Yes. I can.' He gestured his men to the steps.

'Ha ha,' Hermitage announced as he skipped around in front of them to stop their passage.

'Ha ha, what?' Dextus sighed.

'What about the tapestry?' Hermitage folded his arms in some small triumph, 'Briston made the Tapestry of Death.'

'What tapestry's that then?' Dextus asked.

'*The* tapestry. The Tapestry of Death. The Tapestry of Death Hamard took.' Hermitage couldn't follow Dextus.

The priest looked to the ceiling, apparently deep in thought, 'No,' he said eventually. 'Doesn't mean anything to me.'

'You were just here,' Hermitage squeaked. It really was infuriating when people behaved like this.

'We don't have the tapestry, Hermitage,' Wat said gently.

'But it exists.'

'Who knows? If we say don't take us to the bishop or we'll tell everyone about the Tapestry of Death, who'd believe us? We can't produce it. We vanish into the bishop's cellar and no one's any the wiser.'

'That's dishonest.'

'Surprised?' Wat asked.

'No,' Hermitage's shoulders fell, 'probably not. Not after what I've seen and heard already.' he turned his attention to Dextus. 'And you a priest,' he scolded.

'I know. Awful, isn't it? Not for long though.' Dextus rubbed his hands as he scoured about the room. Eventually he found some old rope under a barrel of beer. He extracted it and gave it to the Castigatori to tie up Wat and Briston.

'What do you mean, not for long?' Hermitage had always had his suspicions about this man. Now it turned out he was only a temporary priest. 'You're either a priest or you're not. You can't change your mind.'

'I mean, I shall be a bishop soon,' Dextus replied.

Hermitage was mightily offended. 'I hardly think so with conduct like this.'

'You think I should conduct myself more like the Bishop of Dorchester?'

'Yes. I mean, no,' Hermitage corrected himself, having the seen the tapestry of how the Bishop of Dorchester conducted himself. 'What I mean is, it's hardly up to you to decide whether you're going to be a bishop or not.' Hermitage folded his arms.

'I always thought he was too good for the Castigatori,' Wat observed as his arms were pulled behind his back and his wrists were bound together. 'Just serving time, eh, Dextus? Got to be a priest for a few weeks before they give you the bishop's mitre you've paid for.'

Hermitage was lost again. 'You don't pay for bishop's mitres,' he corrected Wat. 'Well, I mean obviously you do because you have to buy them. What I mean is, you don't pay to be a bishop.'

'Poor Hermitage,' Wat sighed. 'The world just keeps letting you down, doesn't it?'

Hermitage looked from Wat to Dextus and back again several times. They both shrugged amicably.

'Oh, this is disgraceful.' Poor Hermitage really did feel poor at the moment, and let down. And now Wat was going to be taken away. Well, he wouldn't stand for it. Thoughts about what he could actually do about this were not exactly tumbling through his head to get to the front though.

If he were a bigger fellow and there weren't three Castigatori, he might try something physical. No, he thought. He wasn't the physical type.

What if he and Cwen ganged up? He looked at Cwen who was smaller and lighter than he was. No, that wouldn't work either.

Eadric was a good fighter, but he seemed to be wandering off towards the hole in the wall, nodding with interest at old bits of wood.

Stott and Parsimon? Hardly.

Once Dextus got up to the main hall, there'd be no stopping the abduction. Apart from Ricard, of course. Who was probably still there, standing like a tombstone with his massive sword.

'Right,' Hermitage said in a huff. 'Have it your own way. It's your eternal soul.'

'I think he's probably sold that already,' Wat observed.

'Well, I'm not going to any bishops,' Briston spoke up. 'They give me the runs.'

'That's alright,' Dextus said. 'The bishop'll probably take your trousers off before he gets started.'

The Castigatori emitted their low grunting laughs.

'Look Dextus,' Briston wheedled, 'Father Dextus. No, Bishop Dextus, of course. You see the thing is, I can put my hands on a rather substantial amount of gold. You know, squirreled away for a rainy day? Well, as far as I'm concerned, it is now pouring down. I'd be willing to share this with you in a proportion of say.' Briston appraised Dextus whose face was a picture.

Hermitage saw a picture of something dark, miserable, and unwholesome.

Briston was attempting to negotiate with the picture. 'A proportion of, what shall we say? All of it for you? How does that sound?'

'I suspect,' Dextus said, apparently mulling the offer over, 'that long before the bishop's finished with you, you'll be telling us where the gold is anyway.' He smiled and beckoned that the Castigatori should take them up the stairs.

Hermitage skipped on ahead as the two men were dragged and pulled up the cellar steps. As suspected, Ricard was standing exactly as he'd been left. Parsimon and Stott were now dozing by the fire. Hermitage beckoned fiercely to Ricard before the others could get to the hall.

'Ricard,' he hissed. 'Come here. Quickly!'

The big Norman looked over at Hermitage and frowned. He seemed to recognise the monk and strode across the room in two languorous steps. His sword was in his hand being a lot less languorous.

'We need to rescue Wat and Briston,' Hermitage whispered, as the noise from the cellar grew. 'The two men who were with Lord Gilbert?' He confirmed this with a nod as the expression on Ricard's face changed not one jot. 'Good.' Hermitage said. He hoped it was good. Ricard didn't seem terribly engaged somehow.

Dextus and the Castigatori emerged from the cellar with Wat and Briston between them. Cwen bought up the rear, pounding pointlessly on the priest's posterior.

'Stop that,' Dextus snapped and cuffed her round the ear.

Eadric was nowhere to be seen.

'Not so fast,' Hermitage said with confidence as he stood by the huge shape of Ricard.

'Oh, what now?' Dextus was clearly impatient to be off.

'Ricard here is going to stop you.'

Dextus did at least pause to look at Ricard who stood still, sword resting on the ground again.

'Is he?' the priest asked. He didn't seem to believe it.

'Where big man?' Ricard asked in a very heavy Norman accent.

'Pardon?' Hermitage asked, disappointed that Ricard had not immediately leapt into battle, or something.

'Where big man?' Ricard repeated.

'Ah,' Hermitage nodded. 'The big man is gone.' His words were clear and slightly louder than normal so that Ricard would understand them. 'The big man we talked about was dead when we got here. We don't need you to put your sword in him now.'

Ricard coughed once, sheathed his sword and turned to go.

'Where are you going?' Hermitage asked in a panic.

'No big man, no sword? Ricard go.'

'No, no, don't go. You can stick your sword in one of these men,' Hermitage offered the Castigatori and Dextus, although he did feel bad about doing so.

'Priest? Monk?' Ricard seemed horrified.

'Well, erm, sort of,' Hermitage had to admit.

'No,' Ricard said in finality and took his massive body and massive sword out through the gap previously filled by the door.

'Bad luck,' Dextus commiserated when the Norman had gone. 'Good idea though.'

That was it then. There wasn't anything else Hermitage could do. Obviously he would accompany Wat on his journey. He would plead with the bishop. Try to use his position as King's Investigator again. Other than that he was out of ideas.

Of course, there was one other possibility, but he couldn't

possibly use that. Could he? It had worked on the Lady Aveline but Hermitage had been appalled at the idea when Wat mentioned it. But then Hermitage seemed to have spent most of the last few days being appalled in one way or another.

Wouldn't it be lowering himself to the standards of those around him? All of which were extremely low. Wouldn't it be a sin? Well, of course it would, but what had Dextus said himself? We should rejoice when the bad start killing one another? Something like that. Surely that could apply in this situation. Do bad unto the bad. As ye sow, so shall ye reap. Hermitage thought of as many justifications for his plan of action as he could. They were all rather weak and he knew he would suffer later. Still, nothing ventured, nothing gained. This really was new territory for Hermitage.

'You'd better tell him Wat,' he said, trying to sound serious and thoughtful as Dextus led the Castigatori towards the door.

Wat looked at Hermitage. 'Do you think so?' the weaver asked, clearly not having a clue what Hermitage was talking about. At least he was playing along.

'I do. I imagine you were keeping it for your meeting with the bishop.'

'Ah,' Wat said. 'The bishop. Yes, that's what I'd been thinking.' Seeing that Dextus's attention was on Hermitage, Wat's face turned into a very effective "what the hell is going on" mask, eyes wide and demanding.

Briston and Cwen were no better informed and they looked backwards and forwards at the nonsense being exchanged. Hermitage nodded back, hoping that his face said "it'll all be clear in a moment". He just hoped it would.

'Dextus is behaving in the most atrocious manner, I admit,' Hermitage went on. 'But he did save Cwen and the others from the night attack of the Godwins. It might be a little unfair to have him in front of the bishop before you reveal your hand.'

'Oh, I don't know,' Wat replied, without any indication that he knew what his hand actually was.

'What's this then?' Dextus said. 'Some desperately hopeless idea to get yourselves out of this? Let's have it. Get it out of the way.' He folded his arms and waited.

'Go on then,' Hermitage prompted Wat.

'I will,' Wat hissed, silently demanding that Hermitage tell him what it was he supposed to know all about.

'I know you said you wouldn't,' Hermitage said slowly and clearly. 'Not after Lady Aveline, but I think you have to.'

'Lady Aveline?' Wat let a hint of question drip into his voice as his eyes darted from side to side.

'After all, it wasn't really fair to use information like that on a lady,' Hermitage put hints on his hints, 'But Father Dextus is a different sort of drawing all together.'

'When you're ready?' Dextus encouraged.

'Ah,' Wat's eyes and voice lit up. 'Yes, lady Aveline, of course.' He transferred his gaze to Dextus. 'You see,' he explained to the priest in simple tones, 'we know the tapestry has gone.'

'Indeed it has. Gone to keep the last surviving Godwins safe, but little help to you, I'm afraid.'

'But that's not all, of course.'

'I'm waiting.'

'The sketches,' Wat said, as if everyone would know what this meant. Briston clearly did as his shoulders went back and the tide of a broad grin washed down his face.

'Sketches?'

'Of course,' Wat nodded. 'The tapestry is only the end result. It's not made up out of your head. There's a whole collection of sketches and drawings the weaver works from.'

'Is there?' Dextus's tone had darkened. He was beginning to get some ideas of his own.

'Oh yes, every character, every position, all the gory details. Have to be drawn out. Otherwise the whole thing would look a mess.'

Dextus said nothing.

'Naturally, if anyone wanted another copy of the tapestry, or the original got damaged in some way, the weaver could go back to the drawings and make another one. Exactly the same,' Wat smiled. 'Exactly.'

'And you have these drawings?' Dextus turned to Briston.

'Oh yes,' Briston joined in with some glee. 'Dozens of 'em. Got lots of the bishop, him being such a big man, if you take my drift.'

Dextus folded his arms. 'Let me guess. If I don't release you, these drawings will find their way into the hands of the Normans, who will then come down on the bishop's head like a ton of Normans.'

'Now that's a thought,' Briston said with considerable enthusiasm.

'But if I have you locked in the bishop's deepest dungeon, or God forbid,' he crossed himself, 'actually, say, dead? Then the drawings won't know to appear, will they?'

'Of course that *would* be true, if only...' Wat laid it on heavily.

'If only what?'

'If only we hadn't left them with Lord Gilbert. The Norman? With the nice daughter and the big chap with the sword?'

'You left them with Gilbert?' Dextus clearly didn't believe this. Or rather he didn't know whether to believe it or not.

'Not that he knows what they are of course. We left Briston's pack and said we'd be back for it. If we don't get back, we told him he could have it. Imagine his shock when he finds all those naughty drawings. I bet he'll go straight to the king. And then what? Straight to a sword or an axe, do you think?'

Hermitage was horrified at this blatant lie, but he saw it was a good one.

'Perhaps I could just go to this Lord Gilbert and get them back,' Dextus proposed.

'Yes, of course you could,' Wat encouraged. 'But after Hermitage here had found his daughter for him, he was only too keen to give us as much help as he could. And when we told him all about our troubles, Virgil, you, the Castigatori, he said if there was anything he could ever do...'

'Did he?'

'Oh yes, lend us Ricard, that sort of thing.'

Dextus said nothing but his thoughts were clearly burrowing away inside his head.

'And he really seems to hate Saxons,' Wat added, 'and priests. You know the sort: rough soldier, sort of man you'd want right by your side during a battle, and as far away as possible during peace?'

'I have a mind not to believe any of this,' Dextus said, but it wasn't said with any real conviction.

'Entirely up to you, of course.' Wat was bright and encouraging.

'And, of course, Hamard Godwin now seems to be a good friend of Brother Hermitage here.' Briston spoke up now. His tone was intelligent and scheming. 'If you do cart us off to the bishop, which of course you are perfectly entitled to do, Brother Hermitage might seek refuge with the Godwins, and perhaps ask them a favour or two. Very, what can you say? Lively? Very lively, the Godwins, when they put their mind to it.'

All eyes turned to Hermitage. Of course he might go to Hamard if Wat was taken away. He might do any one of a number of things. He wondered if what was going on was some negotiation. He'd heard all about it, and been told on several occasions that he was no good at it. He'd been lambasted by several priors in his time for going to market and coming back with less than was asked for and giving everything left over to the poor. Apparently that wasn't the sort of thing a monk was supposed to do. It was nice to see some professionals at work. Something seemed to be expected of him, so he simply nodded very slightly. So slightly that he might be able to deny it had been a nod at all if he was asked later.

'The bishop will not be happy.'

Hermitage noticed that word, *will*. Did this mean that Dextus had given up on his plans for Wat and Briston?

'Ah well,' Wat explained. 'When the Normans intervene, what's a humble priest to do?'

Wat seemed to be offering an explanation to Dextus, which the priest could then use with the bishop. Hermitage watched the interplay. This really was fascinating.

Dextus simply frowned.

'I mean,' Wat went on. 'The poor Castigatori incapacitated by Virgil. The Godwins turning up. The Norman Lord Gilbert. The sort of situation when you'd probably need to take the bishop's advice. Who's to know what that great man's own plans are? Particularly where the Normans are concerned.'

Hermitage had a thought. He was quite proud of it as it seemed both relevant and helpful. An unusual combination for him. He put his hand up.

'Yes, Hermitage?' Wat asked while Dextus frowned on.

'And the King's Investigator,' Hermitage offered.

'Ah yes,' Wat latched on. 'The King's Investigator. King William's own personal investigator. Sent here by the king. On king's business. You weren't to know he would turn up. What can you do when the king's very own men are on the scene? Nothing, I expect. I'm sure the bishop wouldn't want you upsetting King William over a couple of silly weavers. Much less talking about such an explicit tapestry in front of a king's man.'

'Alright!' Dextus couldn't take any more and held his hands up in surrender.

In response to a nod of the priest's head, the Castigatori untied the weavers, showing not the slightest concern that the people they'd spent all this time unconscious for were being let go.

'But I'm warning you,' Dextus now pointed the finger of defeat. 'Mend your ways, weavers.'

'Hear hear,' Hermitage muttered under his breath.

'I do not want to hear from either of you again. If there is any hint, even the slightest whiff of a rumour of a suggestion that these drawings are available, or that the tapestry even exists, let alone is being remade, well, only the King of Heaven will save your wretched skin.'

'Absolutely!' Wat and Briston nodded smiling agreement.

'And just to be on the safe side, just to make sure we understand one another, we'll take these with us.' Dextus pointed his Castigatori to Briston's box, which was still on the floor. 'You never know when the bishop might take it into his head to share the contents with the Normans. And we know how funny they are about this sort of thing. I bet they get positively furious with the people who make them.'

Wat nodded acknowledgement.

As Dextus and the Castigatori left with the box between them, the priest turned to point one more warning finger at Wat and Briston.

Caput XXX

Back to Business

ight, Briston,' Wat called for the attention of his old colleague.

The large weaver had his large grin back and was bubbling with joy. 'We saw them off, eh Watty?' He rubbed his hands in glee.

Wat reached for his belt and pulled out his death note. He opened the parchment up and presented it to Briston's eyes. Holding the thing at the top, he grasped the skin either side of a small tear in one side and pulled it apart.

Hermitage winced at such a nice piece of parchment coming to an end like this. Still, he could probably save the remainder and have two bits of smaller parchment.

'We are finished, Briston. You nearly got us all killed through your thoughtless and selfish stupidity and I want nothing more to do with you. If death threatens you, if the grim reaper comes knocking on your door, he can have you. I might come to your burial, if I'm not busy.'

Briston's face fell, but it looked like it had been pushed. It was a picture of mock fear and shame. The sort the child who has killed the chickens uses while he's planning the next massacre.

'Please yourself,' Briston said as the face sprang back up. 'We'll be on our way. Shame Dextus took the box,' he shrugged. 'Still, we can always make some more, eh?' He winked at Cwen.

'We?' Cwen asked. 'What's this we?'

Now Briston did look worried.

Hermitage welcomed the girl's stand. Perhaps there was hope for her if she was rejecting the works of Briston. He could see that the weaver wasn't happy. If Cwen had produced the Tapestry of Death, she really was very good. Briston wouldn't be happy losing her.

'Cwen,' Briston did shock again but it was a bit more genuine this time.'After all I've done for you?'

'You're right,' Cwen said.'You have done a lot for me. Taught me the craft when no one else would.'

Wat tutted at this.

'You showed me the trade and let me develop my skill.'

Briston nodded in recognition of his good works.

'All of it to your own advantage,' Cwen was now fierce.'And all of it as a weasel in a wolf pack compared to this last stunt. Letting me think you were dead and running off? How could you?'

'And he wouldn't come back to save you either,' Wat put in.

'Don't you start,' Cwen turned on Wat. 'Mister "girls can't weave,""Women can't make tapestry!" If I were you I'd keep my mouth shut.'

Wat's mouth dropped open but no words came out.

'What do you think you're going to do then?' Briston's voice was spiteful now.'Just turn up at a workshop somewhere? I don't think you'll find any masters prepared to take you in, even if you do look like a boy. and behave like one,' he added.

'Oh, I shall find plenty of work,' Cwen insisted. 'And it'll show up the rubbish you make.'

'Where?'

Cwen moved over to Wat's side and took his arm. 'Wat's going to set me up.'

'Is he?' Wat said, momentarily interested in who was going to take Cwen in.'Oh,' he added as recognition of the name came to him.

'It'll be good for him,' she went on, 'and he'll get a quality weaver at very decent rates.'

'Now just a minute,' Wat began.

'What a good idea,' Hermitage spoke up.

'And of course it's me who's got all the preliminary sketches.' Cwen tapped the side of her head. 'In here, along with a list of all Briston's clients, the works he's sold and for how much.'

'What?' Briston was horrified.

'I do pay attention, you know,' Cwen scoffed at him. 'So, if you don't want me going to them all and offering new works direct from the maker, you'd better clear off.'

Wat was grinning. 'I think she's got you, Briston,' he snorted.

'I'll have you next,' Cwen snapped.

Wat stopped grinning.

'Are we clear?' Cwen demanded. 'Briston,' she instructed, 'you clear off and never come back. Do what you like as long as it's nowhere near me. If it is, I'll remember who your clients are and tell them you've confessed all to the Normans.'

'You wouldn't,' Briston protested but it was more plea than protest.

He sent his plea round the room. There wasn't much point really. Stott and Parsimon were still asleep by the fire and Wat was no friend any more.

Hermitage gave him a look he hoped said something about shame, and just desserts, and the wages of sin.

Briston frowned as if wondering why the monk was squinting at him.

'Go!' Cwen barked, making Briston jump slightly.

He wandered slowly towards the door as if expecting to be called back at any moment. When he reached the threshold, he looked at them all once more. Cwen stood with arms folded. Eyes glaring. Briston left.

Hermitage turned and smiled at Cwen and Wat. Events seemed to have come to a conclusion and they were all still alive. Well, Virgil wasn't obviously, but no one seemed to be concerned about that.

But, Cwen and Wat weren't smiling.

'What's this about me taking you in?' Wat was incredulous.

'It makes perfect sense,' Cwen answered.

'To you maybe.'

'You were the one who went after Briston and brought him back just to save me,' she smiled.

'That was only right and proper,' Wat protested. 'You know my views on women weavers.'

'Another good reason for you to take me in. You need some education. Wouldn't you agree, Brother?'

Hermitage became the centre of attention. With remarkably rapid insight, he realised this was a dangerous debate to be anywhere near.

'I think it's probably best if you work this out for yourself,' he nodded. 'Perhaps of more immediate import is what we do now. Wat and I can hardly go back to Castle Grosmal. Not that we'd want to. Cwen, you have no home now Briston has gone. Even Lolby's hovel has been destroyed. I doubt if Master Stott is feeling hospitable after all he's been through.'

As if to confirm this, Stott grumbled and mumbled in his sleep by the fire.

'That's alright,' Cwen said. 'We'll go to Wat's place.'

'Derby?' Hermitage didn't like the sound of such a long journey. At least he assumed it was long from what Wat had said.

'Oh, that's where it is, eh?' Cwen nodded.

'Thanks, Hermitage.' Wat sounded like a broken man, but a man who didn't actually mind being broken very much.

'Not far then,' Cwen went on. 'Once we're there, we can settle down and sort out what's what.'

'Not far, eh?' Hermitage frowned at Wat. 'I suppose I could go back to De'Ath's Dingle,' he muttered without enthusiasm.

'You're coming with us,' Wat ordered. 'I'm not going there on my own,' he cast a sideways glance to Cwen, 'I think I'm going to need help.'

'I don't suppose if you're returning to tapestry, I might persuade you to review your subject matter.' Hermitage saw that accompanying the two to Derby would be a chance to achieve some good in the world. 'And I have been discharged from De'Ath's Dingle.' His mind was bright at the idea. Then it darkened again. 'But I'm supposed to be King's Investigator.'

'You are,' Wat acknowledged. 'Which, it turns out, comes in handy now and then. Of course, you could go and ask the king if he's got any more investigating he wants done.'

Hermitage accepted that this probably was his duty.

'If you can find him, of course,' Wat added, 'because he won't be at Castle Grosmal anymore.'

'And the people there are probably sworn to keep the king's whereabouts a secret,' Cwen added.

'Why?' Hermitage thought this was an odd thing for a king to do.

'Not exactly popular at the moment?' Cwen suggested. 'The invasion? The killing of a lot of Saxons? Best not to be in the country of your new enemies and then tell them exactly where you're going to be.'

'I suppose not.' Hermitage was learning more and more about the real world all the time. And he thought the monastery of De'Ath's Dingle was bad.

'I'm sure if he wants you he'll find you.' Wat was reassuring.

'You could be right. And I must say, I think the goings on outside of the monastery wall warrant some serious attention.'

'Really?' Cwen asked, clearly not seeing anything in particular.

'The fact that tapestries are made of the most appalling subject matter?' Hermitage offered as his first example. 'That priests and bishops of the church are mired in this sin? That criminal elements try to take over the business for their own gain? The list goes on. Even resolving matters involved lying and threatening people, including young women, that distasteful pictures would be released if they didn't cooperate.' Now Hermitage catalogued the details, his level of being appalled rose further. He wasn't sure he had the capacity to be this appalled.

He found he did have some more room when he noticed Cwen had stopped listening and had gone over to Stott and Parsimon. 'Well really,' he huffed.

Cwen was gently prodding Parsimon who was dead to the world. It had been a long and troublesome night.

The man woke, alarmed and disorientated.

'It's alright,' Cwen soothed. 'Just wanted to let you know we're off.'

'Off?' Parsimon's dozy state wouldn't let him take this in.

'Off?' Stott woke as well. 'Where are you off to?' The old man was quite used to waking up suddenly and carrying on a conversation as if he'd never left.

'We're leaving,' Cwen explained. 'Everyone else has gone,' she spread her arms to take in the empty hall.

'What about my door?' Stott asked, nodding towards the wrecked woodwork as he rose from his seat.

'I'm sure it can be fixed,' Cwen soothed.

'Yes, but who by?' Stott demanded. 'I don't see why I should pay for it.'

'Well, I suppose it was the Godwins who damaged it in the first place, and that Norman Ricard who finished it off. Perhaps you could ask them?' Cwen asked sweetly but with a hint of steel.

'Where's the dead one?' Stott went on, having given up on the door.

'Dead one?'

'The big feller? Rough type? Dead?'

'Oh, Virgil?'

'That's the one.'

'Erm,' Cwen was reluctant, 'in the, erm, cellar?'

'In the cellar? Well, he's no good there, is he? Don't want dead fellers in the cellar. Stink the place out. He'll have to be moved.'

'I'm sure your staff could move him,' Cwen suggested.

'I don't think so,' Stott argued. 'Old Parsimon's not up to that sort of thing. And the maid? I hardly think moving dead bodies is in her line of work. And the size of him? Have you thought about that? He's not a small chicken. you know!'

Cwen started to edge back towards the door.

'It'll take several strong men,' Stott was insistent. 'Or some equipment. Pulleys, rope, that sort of thing. Then there's the grave to dig.' Stott's worries were piling up.

'I'm sure you'll think of something,' Cwen offered.

'It's all very well you young people killing one another like this, but you never think it through. No thought for the practicalities.'

'We really must be off.'

'You can jolly well shift him first,' Stott was not giving up. 'That weaver fellow and the monk, they can do it. And him!' Stott pointed a shaking hand to the door.

Cwen turned and saw the figure of Eadric backing in through the remains of the door.

'Get away from me,' he was calling in a high pitched voice which had just a touch of the deranged about it. 'Get away. You're not real. You can't touch me!' With this, he turned on his heels and ran to the back of the room, where he crouched on the floor and hid behind a pile of pewter, mumbling and pointing.

There was a rustle of leaves from the door. Cwen, Wat, and Hermitage looked to see what on earth had frightened Eadric. What, in fact, had made him come back at all.

'Ha, ha!' A degenerate figure leaped into the room like a rotting jester – a jester who had jested in his youth, perhaps to some success, but who had seriously let himself go. He was all beard and rags but still pranced on the spot. His metaphorical bells had lost their clappers and his bladder leaked. Behind him he dragged a huge sword. The manner of his dragging said that he had carried it for a while but soon found it too much. Any thought of care for its cutting edge had been abandoned when the thing simply got too heavy.

> *If greeted by The Hoofhorn be*
> *Then straight obedience he must see.*
> *All gathered there, be friend or foe*
> *No one is allowed to go,*

The Hoofhorn cackled.

There was a stunned silence in the room as they all surveyed the thing in front of them.

Cwen giggled.

'By the power of the Hoofhorn. By the authority of the great guild of weavers!' The Hoofhorn's voice rose to a scream. He dropped the sword, which landed with a clang. He raised one tattooed and wrinkled arm and pointed a bony finger at each of them in turn. 'Where is the tapestry?' he demanded.

They all looked at The Hoofhorn and then at one another.

Wat replied calmly. 'The Godwins have it.'

The Hoofhorn's wild eyes and wild appearance stiffened as if he would never relax again.

'Oh bugger,' he said.

FINIS

The Heretics of De'Ath

Howard of Warwick

The works of Howard of Warwick are alarmingly numerous and several are available in paperback:

Once upon a time there were some Heretics of De'Ath.

The Chronicles of Brother Hermitage, Book 1

England 1066: During an utterly pointless debate at the austere monastery of De'Ath's Dingle, a monk dies in mysterious circumstances. Standing accused is Brother Hermitage, who needs to work out who did it before he's executed. More medieval than detective, he finds a companion in Wat the Weaver, producer of tapestry to make Beowulf blush. Naive and blindly deferential, Hermitage is helped through events by Wat, coming to a conclusion as startling to him as anyone. With monks, nobles and even a King, *The Heretics of De'Ath* does for the medieval crime genre.

ISBN: 978-0-9929393-0-4 £7.99

The Garderobe of Death

Howard of Warwick

And then Brother Hermitage fell into a Garderobe:

The Garderobe of Death

The Chronicles of Brother Hermitage, Book 2

England 1067: Henri de Turold, King William's favourite hunting companion has been murdered. How anyone actually did it, given the remarkably personal nature of the fatal wound, is a bit of a mystery. Lord Robert Grosmal, of disordered mind, disordered castle and Henri's host at the time, knows that King William gets very tetchy when his friends are murdered. He sends to the nearby monastery of De'Ath's Dingle for a monk to investigate. Medieval monks are usually good at this sort of thing. Brother Hermitage is a medieval monk but he's not very good at this sort of thing. Motivated by the point of a sword he and his companion Wat the weaver set off to solve the crime. Oh, by the way King William is arriving that night so they better get a move on.

ISBN: 978-0-9929393-1-1 £7.99

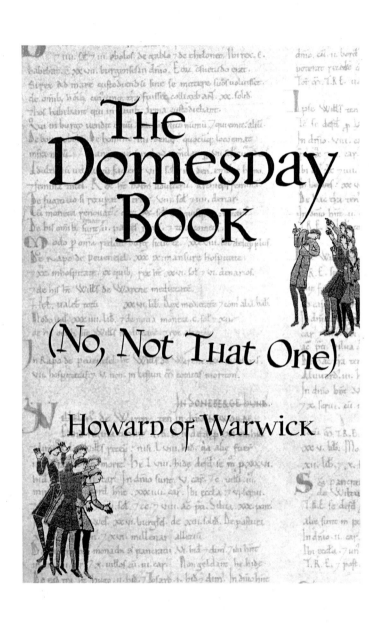

THE DOMESDAY BOOK

(No, Not That One)

Howard of Warwick

Also available: Howard of Warwick's History as it might have happened – but probably didn't.

The Domesday Book (No, Not That One)

A book so epic it has a map.

William of Normandy has just won the battle of Hastings, but has lost something precious; so precious no one must even know it is missing. Reluctantly assembling a team of incompetents, he sends them on a mission of recovery. But his secret is out and another band is after the treasure. In a race across a savage land, through a population of confused misfits, against the clock and against one another, two forces hurtle towards a finale of cataclysmic proportions; all in 29 concise and entertaining chapters.

ISBN: 978-0-9929393-2-8   £7.99

The Magna Carta

(Or is it?)

Oops!

Howard of Warwick

The Magna Carta, (Or Is It?)

Read the full text of Magna Carta in Latin and English here! But don't take the tale of its production too seriously—or seriously at all...

To mark the 800th anniversary, Howard of Warwick has forced his attentions on the most famous charter in history. Here is a Runnymede full of real people; confused, squabbling, ill-informed and largely incompetent. Never mind 800 years, it's a miracle the charter survived to the end of its first week.... if it did! In *The Magna Carta (Or Is It?)* we discover that King John entrusted the copying of the original charter to one Aelward Dunktish, a man not normally reliable enough to pour water. The King must be up to something. And so must the nobles who want Dunktish for their own purposes. And then there are the King's notorious mercenaries, the men of Touraine, who have ideas of their own, all of them involving death and horses. They're all up to no good, and Dunktish IS no good. It's the sort of tale that will end in disaster - except in the hands of Aelward Dunktish, it all starts with one.

ISBN 978-0-9929393-3-5 £7.99